THE ASPERN PAPERS

HENRY JAMES

THE ASPERN PAPERS
AND OTHER STORIES

KÖNEMANN

❧ Notes (on pp. 399 to 407)
are keyed thus in the margin

© 1998 for this edition
Könemann Verlagsgesellschaft mbH
Bonner Straße 126, D–50968 Köln

Series editor: Michael Hulse
Volume editor: Richard Aczel
Cover design: Peter Feierabend
Layout and typesetting: Birgit Beyer
Printed in Hungary
ISBN 3-8290-0893-7
10 9 8 7 6 5 4 3 2 1

CONTENTS

THE ASPERN PAPERS

THE ASPERN PAPERS

I

I had taken Mrs. Prest into my confidence; without her in truth I should have made but little advance, for the fruitful idea in the whole business dropped from her friendly lips. It was she who found the short cut and loosed the Gordian knot. It is not supposed easy for women to rise to the large free view of anything, anything to be done; but they sometimes throw off a bold conception—such as a man wouldn't have risen to—with singular serenity. "Simply make them take you in on the footing of a lodger"—I don't think that unaided I should have risen to that. I was beating about the bush, trying to be ingenious, wondering by what combination of arts I might become an acquaintance, when she offered this happy suggestion that the way to become an acquaintance was first to become an intimate. Her actual knowledge of the Misses Bordereau was scarcely larger than mine, and indeed I had brought with me from England some definite facts that were new to her. Their name had been mixed up ages before with one of the greatest names of the century, and they now lived obscurely in Venice, lived on very small means, unvisited, unapproachable, in a sequestered and dilapidated old palace: this was the substance of my friend's impression of them. She herself had been established in Venice some fifteen years and had done a great deal of good there; but the circle of her benevolence had never embraced the two shy, mysterious and, as was somehow supposed, scarcely respectable Americans— they were believed to have lost in their long exile all national quality, besides being as their name implied of some remoter French affiliation—who asked no favours and desired no attention. In the early years of her residence she had made an attempt to see them, but this had been successful only as regards the little one, as Mrs. Prest called the niece; though in fact I afterwards found her the bigger of the two in inches. She had heard Miss Bordereau was ill and had a suspicion she was in want, and had gone to the house to offer aid, so that if there were suffering, American suffering in particular, she shouldn't have it on her conscience. The "little one" had received her in the great cold tarnished Venetian *sala*, the central hall of the house, paved with marble and roofed with dim cross-beams, and hadn't even asked her to sit down. This was not encouraging for me, who wished to sit so fast, and I remarked as much to Mrs. Prest. She replied however with profundity "Ah, but there's all the difference: I went to confer a favour and you'll go to ask one. If they're proud you'll be on the right side." And she offered to show me their house to begin with—to row me thither in her gondola. I let her know I had already been to look at it half a dozen times; but I accepted her invitation, for it charmed me to hover about the place. I had made my way to it the day after my arrival in Venice—it had been described to me in advance by the friend in England to whom I owed definite information as to their possession of the papers—laying siege to it with my eyes while I considered my plan of campaign. Jeffrey Aspern had never been in it that I knew of, but some note of his voice seemed to abide there by a roundabout implication and in a "dying fall."

Mrs. Prest knew nothing about the papers, but was interested in my curiosity, as always in the joys and sorrows of her friends. As we went, however, in her gondola, gliding there under the sociable hood with the bright Venetian picture framed on either side by the moveable window, I saw how my eagerness amused her and that she found my interest in my possible spoil a fine case of monomania. "One would think you expected from it the answer to the riddle of the universe," she said; and I denied the impeachment only by replying that if I had to choose between that precious solution and a bundle of Jeffrey Aspern's letters I knew indeed which would appear to me the greater boon. She pretended to make light of his genius and I took no pains to defend him. One doesn't defend one's god: one's god is in himself a defence. Besides, today, after his long comparative obscurity, he hangs high in the heaven of our literature for all the world to see; he's a part of the light by which we walk. The most I said was that he was no doubt not a woman's poet; to which she rejoined aptly enough that he had been at least Miss Bordereau's. The strange thing had been for me to discover in England that she was still alive: it was as if I had been told Mrs. Siddons was, or Queen Caroline, or the famous Lady Hamilton, for it seemed to me that she belonged to a generation as extinct. "Why she must be tremendously old—at least a hundred," I had said; but on coming to consider dates I saw it not strictly involved that she should have far exceeded the common span. None the less she was of venerable age and her relations with Jeffrey Aspern had occurred in her early womanhood. "That's her excuse," said Mrs. Prest half-sententiously and yet also somewhat as if she were ashamed of making a speech so little in the real tone of Venice. As if a woman needed an excuse for having loved the divine poet! He had been not only one of the most brilliant minds of his day—and in those years, when the century was young, there were, as everyone knows, many—but one of the most genial men and one of the handsomest.

The niece, according to Mrs. Prest, was of minor antiquity, and the conjecture was risked that she was only a grand-niece. This was possible; I had nothing but my share in the very limited knowledge of my English fellow worshipper John Cumnor, who had never seen the couple. The world, as I say, had recognised Jeffrey Aspern, but Cumnor and I had recognised him most. The multitude today flocked to his temple, but of that temple he and I regarded ourselves as the appointed ministers. We held, justly, as I think, that we had done more for his memory than anyone else, and had done it simply by opening lights into his life. He had nothing to fear from us because he had nothing to fear from the truth, which alone at such a distance of time we could be interested in establishing. His early death had been the only dark spot, as it were, on his fame, unless the papers in Miss Bordereau's hands should perversely bring out others. There had been an impression about 1825 that he had "treated her badly," just as there had been an impression that he had "served," as the London populace says, several other ladies in the same masterful way. Each of these cases Cumnor and I had been able to investigate, and we had never failed to acquit him conscientiously of any grossness. I judged him perhaps more indulgently than my friend; certainly, at any rate, it appeared to me that no man could have walked straighter in the given circumstances. These had been almost always difficult and dangerous. Half the women of his time, to speak liberally, had flung themselves at his head, and while the fury raged—the more that it was very catching—accidents, some of them grave, had not failed to occur. He was not a woman's poet, as I had said to Mrs. Prest, in the modern phase of his reputation; but the situation had been different when the man's own voice was mingled with his song. That voice, by every testimony, was one of the most charming ever heard. "Orpheus and the Mænads!" had been of course my foreseen judgement when first I turned over his correspondence. Almost all the Mænads were unreasonable and many of them unbearable; it struck me that he had been kinder and more considerate than in his place—if I could imagine myself in any such box—I should have found the trick of.

It was certainly strange beyond all strangeness, and I shall not take up space with attempting to explain it, that whereas among all these other relations and in these other directions of research we had to deal with phantoms and dust, the mere echoes of echoes, the one living source of information that had lingered on into our time had been unheeded by us. Every one of Aspern's contemporaries had, according to our belief, passed away; we had not been able to look into a single pair of eyes into which his had looked or to feel a transmitted contact in any aged hand that his had touched. Most dead of all did poor Miss Bordereau appear, and yet she alone had survived. We exhausted in the course of months our wonder that we had not found her out sooner, and the substance of our explanation was that she had kept so quiet. The poor lady on the whole had had reason for doing so. But it was a revelation to us that self-effacement on such a scale had been possible in the latter half of the nineteenth century—the age of newspapers and telegrams and photographs and interviewers. She had taken no great trouble for it either—hadn't hidden herself away in an undiscoverable hole, had boldly settled down in a city of exhibition. The one apparent secret of her safety had been that Venice contained so many much greater curiosities. And then accident had somehow favoured her, as was shown for example in the fact that Mrs. Prest had never happened to name her to me, though I had spent three weeks in Venice—under her nose, as it were—five years before. My friend indeed had not named her much to anyone; she appeared almost to have forgotten the fact of her continuance. Of course Mrs. Prest hadn't the nerves of an editor. It was meanwhile no explanation of the old woman's having eluded us to say that she lived abroad, for our researches had again and again taken us—not only by correspondence but by personal enquiry—to France, to Germany, to Italy, in which countries, not counting his important stay in England, so many of the too few years of Aspern's career had been spent. We were glad to think at least that in all our promulgations—some people now consider I believe that we have overdone them—we had only touched in passing and in the most discreet manner on Miss Bordereau's connexion. Oddly enough, even if we had had the material—and we had often wondered what could have become of it—this would have been the most difficult episode to handle.

The gondola stopped, the old palace was there; it was a house of the class which in Venice carries even in extreme dilapidation the dignified name. "How charming! It's grey and pink!" my companion exclaimed; and that is the most comprehensive description of it. It was not particularly old, only two or three centuries; and it had an air not so much of decay as of quiet discouragement, as if it had rather missed its career. But its wide front, with a stone balcony from end to end of the *piano nobile* or most important floor, was architectural enough, with the aid of various pilasters and arches; and the stucco with which in the intervals it had long ago been endued was rosy in the April afternoon. It overlooked a clean melancholy rather lonely canal, which had a narrow *riva* or convenient footway on either side. "I don't know why—there are no brick gables," said Mrs. Prest, "but this corner has seemed to me before more Dutch than Italian, more like Amsterdam than like Venice. It's eccentrically neat, for reasons of its own; and though you may pass on foot scarcely anyone ever thinks of doing so. It's as negative—considering *where* it is—as a Protestant Sunday. Perhaps the people are afraid of the Misses Bordereau. I dare say they have the reputation of witches."

I forget what answer I made to this—I was given up to two other reflexions. The first of these was that if the old lady lived in such a big and imposing house she couldn't be in any sort of misery and therefore wouldn't be tempted by a chance to let a couple of rooms. I expressed this fear to Mrs. Prest, who gave me a very straight answer. "If she didn't live in a big house how could it be a question of her having rooms to spare? If she were not amply lodged you'd lack ground to approach her. Besides, a big house here, and especially in this *quartier perdu*, proves nothing at all: it's perfectly consistent with a state of penury. Dilapidated old palazzi, if you'll go out of the way for them, are to be had for five shillings a year. And as for the people who live in them—no, until you've explored Venice socially as much as I have, you can form no idea of their domestic desolation. They live on nothing, for they've nothing to live on." The other idea that had come into my head was connected with a high blank wall which appeared to confine an expanse of ground on one side of the house. Blank I call it, but it was figured over with the patches that please a painter, repaired breaches, crumblings of plaster, extrusions of brick that had turned pink with time; while a few thin trees, with the poles of certain rickety trellises, were visible over the top. The place was a garden and apparently attached to the house. I suddenly felt that so attached it gave me my pretext.

I sat looking out on all this with Mrs. Prest (it was covered with the golden glow of Venice) from the shade of our *felze*, and she asked me if I would go in then, while she waited for me, or come back another time. At first I couldn't decide—it was doubtless very weak of me. I wanted still to think I *might* get a footing, and was afraid to meet failure, for it would leave me, as I remarked to my companion, without another arrow for my bow. "Why not another?" she enquired as I sat there hesitating and thinking it over; and she wished to know why even now and before taking the trouble of becoming an inmate—which might be wretchedly uncomfortable after all, even if it succeeded—I hadn't the resource of simply offering them a sum of money down. In that way I might get what I wanted without bad nights.

"Dearest lady," I exclaimed, "excuse the impatience of my tone when I suggest that you must have forgotten the very fact—surely I communicated it to you—which threw me on your ingenuity. The old woman won't have her relics and tokens so much as spoken of; they're personal, delicate, intimate, and she hasn't the feelings of the day, God bless her! If I should sound that note first I should certainly spoil the game. I can arrive at my spoils only by putting her off her guard, and I can put her off her guard only by ingratiating diplomatic arts. Hypocrisy, duplicity are my only chance. I'm sorry for it, but there's no baseness I wouldn't commit for Jeffrey Aspern's sake. First I must take tea with her—then tackle the main job." And I told over what had happened to John Cumnor on his respectfully writing to her. No notice whatever had been taken of his first letter, and the second had been answered very sharply, in six lines, by the niece. "Miss Bordereau requested her to say that she couldn't imagine what he meant by troubling them. They had none of Mr. Aspern's 'literary remains,' and if they *had* had wouldn't have dreamed of showing them to anyone on any account whatever. She couldn't imagine what he was talking about and begged he would let her alone." I certainly didn't want to be met that way.

"Well," said Mrs. Prest after a moment and all provokingly, "perhaps they really haven't anything. If they deny it flat how are you sure?"

"John Cumnor's sure, and it would take me long to tell you how his conviction, or his very strong presumption—strong enough to stand against the old lady's not unnatural fib—has built itself up. Besides, he makes much of the internal evidence of the niece's letter."

"The internal evidence?"

"Her calling him 'Mr. Aspern.' "

"I don't see what that proves."

"It proves familiarity, and familiarity implies the possession of mementoes, of tangible objects. I can't tell you how that 'Mr.' affects me—how it bridges over the gulf of time and brings our hero near to me—nor what an edge it gives to my desire to see Juliana. You don't say 'Mr.' Shakespeare."

"Would I, any more, if I had a box full of his letters?"

"Yes, if he had been your lover and someone wanted them." And I added that John Cumnor was so convinced, and so all the more convinced by Miss Bordereau's tone, that he would have come himself to Venice on the undertaking were it not for the obstacle of his having, for any confidence, to disprove his identity with the person who had written to them, which the old ladies would be sure to suspect in spite of dissimulation and a change of name. If they were to ask him point-blank if he were not their snubbed correspondent it would be too awkward for him to lie; whereas I was fortunately not tied in that way. I was a fresh hand—I could protest without lying.

"But you'll have to take a false name," said Mrs. Prest. "Juliana lives out of the world as much as it is possible to live, but she has none the less probably heard of Mr. Aspern's editors. She perhaps possesses what you've published."

"I've thought of that," I returned; and I drew out of my

pocket-book a visiting-card neatly engraved with a well-chosen *nom de guerre.*

"You're very extravagant—it adds to your immorality. You might have done it in pencil or ink," said my companion.

"This looks more genuine."

"Certainly you've the courage of your curiosity. But it will be awkward about your letters; they won't come to you in that mask."

"My banker will take them in and I shall go every day to get them. It will give me a little walk."

"Shall you depend all on that?" asked Mrs. Prest. "Aren't you coming to see me?"

"Oh you'll have left Venice for the hot months long before there are any results. I'm prepared to roast all summer—as well as through the long here-after perhaps you'll say! Meanwhile John Cumnor will bombard me with letters addressed, in my feigned name, to the care of the padrona."

"She'll recognise his hand," my companion suggested.

"On the envelope he can disguise it."

"Well, you're a precious pair! Doesn't it occur to you that even if you're able to say you're not Mr. Cumnor in person they may still suspect you of being his emissary?"

"Certainly, and I see only one way to parry that."

"And what may that be?"

I hesitated a moment. "To make love to the niece."

"Ah," cried my friend, "wait till you see her!"

II

"I must work the garden—I must work the garden," I said to myself five minutes later and while I waited, upstairs, in the long, dusky sala, where the bare scagliola floor gleamed vaguely in a chink of the closed shutters. The place was impressive, yet looked somehow cold and cautious. Mrs. Prest had floated away, giving me a rendezvous at the end of half an hour by some neighbouring water-steps; and I had been let into the house, after pulling the rusty bell-wire, by a small red-headed and white-faced maidservant, who was very young and not ugly and wore clicking pattens and a shawl in the fashion of a hood. She had not contented herself with opening the door from above by the usual arrangement of a creaking pulley, though she had looked down at me first from an upper window, dropping the cautious challenge which in Italy precedes the act of admission. I was irritated as a general thing by this survival of mediæval manners, though as so fond, if yet so special, an antiquarian I suppose I ought to have liked it; but, with my resolve to be genial from the threshold at any price, I took my false card out of my pocket and held it up to her, smiling as if it were a magic token. It had the effect of one indeed, for it brought her, as I say, all the way down. I begged her to hand it to her mistress, having first written on it in Italian the words: "Could you very kindly see a gentleman, a travelling American, for a moment?" The little maid wasn't hostile—even that was perhaps something gained. She coloured, she smiled and looked both frightened and pleased. I could see that my arrival was a great affair, that visits in such a house were rare and that she was a person who would have liked a bustling place. When she pushed forward the heavy door behind me I felt my foot in the citadel and promised myself ever so firmly to keep it there. She pattered across the damp stony lower hall and I followed her up the high staircase—stonier still, as it seemed—without an invitation. I think she had meant I should wait for her below, but such was not my idea, and I took up my station in the sala. She flitted, at the far end of it, into impenetrable regions, and I looked at the place with my heart beating as I had known it to do in dentists' parlours. It had a gloomy grandeur, but owed its character almost all to its noble shape and to the fine architectural doors, as high as those of grand frontages, which, leading into the various rooms, repeated themselves on either side at intervals. They were surmounted with old faded painted escutcheons, and here and there in the spaces between them hung brown pictures, which

I noted as speciously bad, in battered and tarnished frames that were yet more desirable than the canvases themselves. With the exception of several straw-bottomed chairs that kept their backs to the wall the grand obscure vista contained little else to minister to effect. It was evidently never used save as a passage, and scantly even as that. I may add that by the time the door through which the maid-servant had escaped opened again my eyes had grown used to the want of light.

I hadn't meanwhile meant by my private ejaculation that I must myself cultivate the soil of the tangled enclosure which lay beneath the windows, but the lady who came toward me from the distance over the hard shining floor might have supposed as much from the way in which, as I went rapidly to meet her, I exclaimed, taking care to speak Italian: "The garden, the garden—do me the pleasure to tell me if it's yours!"

She stopped short, looking at me with wonder; and then, "Nothing here is mine," she answered in English, coldly and sadly.

"Oh you're English; how delightful!" I ingenuously cried. "But surely the garden belongs to the house?"

"Yes, but the house doesn't belong to me." She was a long lean pale person, habited apparently in a dull-coloured dressing-gown, and she spoke very simply and mildly. She didn't ask me to sit down, any more than years before—if she were the niece—she had asked Mrs. Prest, and we stood face to face in the empty pompous hall.

"Well then, would you kindly tell me to whom I must address myself? I'm afraid you'll think me horribly intrusive, but you know I *must* have a garden—upon my honour I must!"

Her face was not young, but it was candid; it was not fresh, but it was clear. She had large eyes which were not bright, and a great deal of hair which was not "dressed," and long fine hands which were—possibly—not clean. She clasped these members almost convulsively as, with a confused alarmed look, she broke out: "Oh don't take it away from us; we like it ourselves!"

"You have the use of it then?"

"Oh yes. If it wasn't for that—!" And she gave a wan vague smile.

"Isn't it a luxury, precisely? That's why, intending to be in Venice some weeks, possibly all summer, and having some literary work, some reading and writing to do, so that I must be quiet and yet if possible a great deal in the open air—that's why I've felt a garden to be really indispensable. I appeal to your own experience," I went on with as sociable a smile as I could risk. "Now can't I look at yours?"

"I don't know, I don't understand," the poor woman murmured, planted there and letting her weak wonder deal—helplessly enough, as I felt—with my strangeness.

"I mean only from one of those windows—such grand ones as you have here—if you'll let me open the shutters." And I walked toward the back of the house. When I had advanced halfway I stopped and waited as in the belief she would accompany me. I had been of necessity quite abrupt, but I strove at the same time to give her the impression of extreme courtesy. "I've looked at furnished rooms all over the place, and it seems impossible to find any with a garden attached. Naturally in a place like Venice gardens are rare. It's absurd if you like, for a man, but I can't live without flowers."

"There are none to speak of down there." She came nearer, as if, though she mistrusted me, I had drawn her by an invisible thread. I went on again, and she continued as she followed me: "We've a few, but they're very common. It costs too much to cultivate them; one has to have a man."

"Why shouldn't I be the man?" I asked. "I'll work without wages; or rather I'll put in a gardener. You shall have the sweetest flowers in Venice."

She protested against this with a small quaver of sound that might have been at the same time a gush of rapture for my free sketch. Then she gasped: "We don't know you—we don't know you."

"You know me as much as I know you; or rather much more,

because you know my name. And if you're English I'm almost a countryman."

"We're not English," said my companion, watching me in practical submission while I threw open the shutters of one of the divisions of the wide high window.

"You speak the language so beautifully: might I ask what you are?" Seen from above the garden was in truth shabby, yet I felt at a glance that it had great capabilities. She made no rejoinder, she was so lost in her blankness and gentleness, and I exclaimed: "You don't mean to say you're also by chance American?"

"I don't know. We used to be."

"Used to be? Surely you haven't changed?"

"It's so many years ago. We don't seem to be anything now."

"So many years that you've been living here? Well, I don't wonder at that; it's a grand old house. I suppose you all use the garden," I went on, "but I assure you I shouldn't be in your way. I'd be very quiet and stay quite in one corner."

"We all use it?" she repeated after me vaguely, not coming close to the window but looking at my shoes. She appeared to think me capable of throwing her out.

"I mean all your family—as many as you are."

"There's only one other than me. She's very old. She never goes down."

I feel again my thrill at this close identification of Juliana; in spite of which, however, I kept my head. "Only one other in all this great house!" I feigned to be not only amazed but almost scandalised. "Dear lady, you must have space then to spare!"

"To spare?" she repeated—almost as for the rich unwonted joy to her of spoken words.

"Why you surely don't live (two quiet women—I see *you* are quiet, at any rate) in fifty rooms!" Then with a burst of hope and cheer I put the question straight. "Couldn't you for a good rent *let* me two or three? That would set me up!"

I had now struck the note that translated my purpose, and I needn't reproduce the whole of the tune I played. I ended by making my entertainer believe me an undesigning person, though of course I didn't even attempt to persuade her I was not an eccentric one. I repeated that I had studies to pursue; that I wanted quiet; that I delighted in a garden and had vainly sought one up and down the city: that I would undertake that before another month was over the dear old house should be smothered in flowers. I think it was the flowers that won my suit, for I afterwards found that Miss Tina—for such the name of this high tremulous spinster proved somewhat incongruously to be—had an insatiable appetite for them. When I speak of my suit as won I mean that before I left her she had promised me she would refer the question to her aunt. I invited information as to who her aunt might be and she answered "Why Miss Bordereau!" with an air of surprise, as if I might have been expected to know. There were contradictions like this in Miss Tina which, as I observed later, contributed to make her rather pleasingly incalculable and interesting. It was the study of the two ladies to live so that the world shouldn't talk of them or touch them, and yet they had never altogether accepted the idea that it didn't hear of them. In Miss Tina at any rate a grateful susceptibility to human contact had not died out, and contact of a limited order there would be if I should come to live in the house.

"We've never done anything of the sort; we've never had a lodger or any kind of inmate." So much as this she made a point of saying to me. "We're very poor, we live very badly— almost on nothing. The rooms are very bare—those you might take; they've nothing at all in them. I don't know how you'd sleep, how you'd eat."

"With your permission I could easily put in a bed and a few tables and chairs. *C'est la moindre des choses* and the affair of an hour or two. I know a little man from whom I can hire for a trifle what I should so briefly want, what I should use; my gondolier can bring the things round in his boat. Of course in this great house you must have a second kitchen, and my servant, who's a wonderfully handy fellow"—this personage was an evocation of the moment—"can easily cook me a chop there. My tastes and habits are of the simplest: I live on flowers!" And then I ventured to add that if they were very poor it was all the more reason they should let their rooms. They were bad economists—I had never heard of such a waste of material.

I saw in a moment my good lady had never before been spoken to in any such fashion—with a humorous firmness that didn't exclude sympathy, that was quite founded on it. She might easily have told me that my sympathy was impertinent, but this by good fortune didn't occur to her. I left her with the understanding that she would submit the question to her aunt and that I might come back the next day for their decision.

"The aunt will refuse; she'll think the whole proceeding very *louche*!" Mrs. Prest declared shortly after this, when I had resumed my place in her gondola. She had put the idea into my head and now—so little are women to be counted on—she appeared to take a despondent view of it. Her pessimism provoked me and I pretended to have the best hopes; I went so far as to boast of a distinct prevision of success. Upon this Mrs. Prest broke out: "Oh I see what's in your head! You fancy you've made such an impression in five minutes that she's dying for you to come and can be depended on to bring the old one round. If you do get in you'll count it as a triumph."

I did count it as a triumph, but only for the commentator—in the last analysis—not for the man, who had not the tradition of personal conquest. When I went back on the morrow the little maid-servant conducted me straight through the long sala—it opened there as before in large perspective and was lighter now, which I thought a good omen—into the apartment from which the recipient of my former visit had emerged on that occasion. It was a spacious shabby parlour with a fine old painted ceiling under which a strange figure sat alone at one of the windows. They come back to me now almost with the palpitation they caused, the successive states marking my consciousness that as the door of the room closed behind me

I was really face to face with the Juliana of some of Aspern's most exquisite and most renowned lyrics. I grew used to her afterwards, though never completely; but as she sat there before me my heart beat as fast as if the miracle of resurrection had taken place for my benefit. Her presence seemed somehow to contain and express his own, and I felt nearer to him at that first moment of seeing her than I ever had been before or ever have been since. Yes, I remember my emotions in their order, even including a curious little tremor that took me when I saw the niece not to be there. With her, the day before, I had become sufficiently familiar, but it almost exceeded my courage—much as I had longed for the event—to be left alone with so terrible a relic as the aunt. She was too strange, too literally resurgent. Then came a check from the perception that we weren't really face to face, inasmuch as she had over her eyes a horrible green shade which served for her almost as a mask. I believed for the instant that she had put it on expressly, so that from underneath it she might take me all in without my getting at herself. At the same time it created a presumption of some ghastly death's-head lurking behind it. The divine Juliana as a grinning skull—the vision hung there until it passed. Then it came to me that she *was* tremendously old—so old that death might take her at any moment, before I should have time to compass my end. The next thought was a correction to that; it lighted up the situation. She would die next week, she would die tomorrow—then I could pounce on her possessions and ransack her drawers. Meanwhile she sat there neither moving nor speaking. She was very small and shrunken, bent forward with her hands in her lap. She was dressed in black and her head was wrapped in a piece of old black lace which showed no hair.

My emotion keeping me silent she spoke first, and the remark she made was exactly the most unexpected.

III

"Our house is very far from the centre, but the little canal is very *comme il faut*."

"It's the sweetest corner of Venice and I can imagine nothing more charming," I hastened to reply. The old lady's voice was very thin and weak, but it had an agreeable, cultivated murmur and there was wonder in the thought that that individual note had been in Jeffrey Aspern's ear.

"Please to sit down there. I hear very well," she said quietly, as if perhaps I had been shouting; and the chair she pointed to was at a certain distance. I took possession of it, assuring her I was perfectly aware of my intrusion and of my not having been properly introduced, and that I could but throw myself on her indulgence. Perhaps the other lady, the one I had had the honour of seeing the day before, would have explained to her about the garden. That was literally what had given me courage to take a step so unconventional. I had fallen in love at sight with the whole place—she herself was probably so used to it that she didn't know the impression it was capable of making on a stranger—and I had felt it really a case to risk something. Was her own kindness in receiving me a sign that I was not wholly out in my calculation? It would make me extremely happy to think so. I could give her my word of honour that I was a most respectable inoffensive person and that as a co-tenant of the palace, so to speak, they would be barely conscious of my existence. I would conform to any regulations, any restrictions, if they would only let me enjoy the garden. Moreover I should be delighted to give her references, guarantees; they would be of the very best, both in Venice and in England, as well as in America.

She listened to me in perfect stillness and I felt her look at me with great penetration, though I could see only the lower part of her bleached and shrivelled face. Independently of the refining process of old age it had a delicacy which once must have been great. She had been very fair, she had had a wonderful complexion. She was silent a little after I had ceased speaking; then she began: "If you're so fond of a garden why don't you go to *terra firma*, where there are so many far better than this?"

"Oh it's the combination!" I answered, smiling; and then with rather a flight of fancy: "It's the idea of a garden in the middle of the sea."

"This isn't the middle of the sea; you can't so much as see the water."

I stared a moment, wondering if she wished to convict me of fraud. "Can't see the water? Why, dear madam, I can come up to the very gate in my boat."

She appeared inconsequent, for she said vaguely in reply to this: "Yes, if you've got a boat. I haven't any; it's many years since I've been in one of the *gondole*." She uttered these words as if they designed a curious far-away craft known to her only by hearsay.

"Let me assure you of the pleasure with which I would put mine at your service!" I returned. I had scarcely said this however before I became aware that the speech was in questionable taste and might also do me the injury of making me appear too eager, too possessed of a hidden motive. But the old woman remained impenetrable and her attitude worried me by suggesting that she had a fuller vision of me than I had of her. She gave me no thanks for my somewhat extravagant offer, but remarked that the lady I had seen the day before was her niece; she would presently come in. She had asked her to stay away a little on purpose—had had her reasons for seeing me first alone. She relapsed into silence and I turned over the fact of these unmentioned reasons and the question of what might come yet; also that of whether I might venture on some judicious remark in praise of her companion. I went so far as to say I should be delighted to see our absent friend again: she had been so very patient with me, considering how odd she must have thought me—a declaration which drew from Miss Bordereau another of her whimsical speeches.

"She has very good manners; I bred her up myself!" I was on the point of saying that that accounted for the easy grace of the niece, but I arrested myself in time, and the next moment the old woman went on: "I don't care who you may be—I don't want to know: it signifies very little today." This had all the air of being a formula of dismissal, as if her next words would be that I might take myself off now that she had had the amusement of looking on the face of such a monster of indiscretion. Therefore I was all the more surprised when she added in her soft venerable quaver: "You may have as many rooms as you like—if you'll pay me a good deal of money."

I hesitated but an instant, long enough to measure what she meant in particular by this condition. First it struck me that she must have really a large sum in her mind; then I reasoned quickly that her idea of a large sum would probably not correspond to my own. My deliberation, I think, was not so visible as to diminish the promptitude with which I replied: "I will pay with pleasure and of course in advance whatever you may think it proper to ask me."

"Well then, a thousand francs a month," she said instantly, while her baffling green shade continued to cover her attitude.

The figure, as they say, was startling and my logic had been at fault. The sum she had mentioned was, by the Venetian measure of such matters, exceedingly large; there was many an old palace in an out-of-the-way corner that I might on such terms have enjoyed the whole of by the year. But so far as my resources allowed I was prepared to spend money, and my decision was quickly taken. I would pay her with a smiling face what she asked, but in that case I would make it up by getting hold of my "spoils" for nothing. Moreover if she had asked five times as much I should have risen to the occasion, so odious would it have seemed to me to stand chaffering with Aspern's Juliana. It was queer enough to have a question of money with her at all. I assured her that her views perfectly met my own and that on the morrow I should have the pleasure of putting three months' rent into her hand. She received this announcement with apparent complacency and with no discoverable sense that after all it would become her to say that I ought to see the rooms first. This didn't occur to her, and indeed her serenity was mainly what I wanted. Our little agreement was just concluded when the door opened and the younger lady appeared on the threshold. As soon as Miss Bordereau saw her niece she cried out almost gaily: "He'll give three thousand—three thousand tomorrow!"

Miss Tina stood still, her patient eyes turning from one of us to the other; then she brought out, scarcely above her breath: "Do you mean francs?"

"Did you mean francs or dollars?" the old woman asked of me at this.

"I think francs were what you said," I sturdily smiled.

"That's very good," said Miss Tina, as if she had felt how overreaching her own question might have looked.

"What do *you* know? You're ignorant," Miss Bordereau remarked; not with acerbity but with a strange soft coldness.

"Yes, of money—certainly of money!" Miss Tina hastened to concede.

"I'm sure you've your own fine branches of knowledge," I took the liberty of saying genially. There was something painful to me, somehow, in the turn the conversation had taken, in the discussion of dollars and francs.

"She had a very good education when she was young. I looked into that myself," said Miss Bordereau. Then she added: "But she has learned nothing since."

"I've always been with *you*," Miss Tina rejoined very mildly, and of a certainty with no intention of an epigram.

"Yes, but for that—!" her aunt declared with more satirical force. She evidently meant that but for this her niece would never have got on at all; the point of the observation however being lost on Miss Tina, though she blushed at hearing her history revealed to a stranger. Miss Bordereau went on, addressing herself to me: "And what time will you come tomorrow with the money?"

"The sooner the better. If it suits you I'll come at noon."

"I'm always here, but I have my hours," said the old woman as if her convenience were not to be taken for granted.

"You mean the times when you receive?"

"I never receive. But I'll see you at noon, when you come with the money."

"Very good, I shall be punctual." To which I added: "May I shake hands with you on our contract?" I thought there ought to be some little form; it would make me really feel easier, for I was sure there would be no other. Besides, though Miss Bordereau couldn't today be called personally attractive and there was something even in her wasted antiquity that bade one stand at one's distance, I felt an irresistible desire to hold in my own for a moment the hand Jeffrey Aspern had pressed.

For a minute she made no answer, and I saw that my proposal failed to meet with her approbation. She indulged in no movement of withdrawal, which I half-expected; she only said coldly: "I belong to a time when that was not the custom."

I felt rather snubbed but I exclaimed good-humouredly to Miss Tina "Oh you'll do as well!" I shook hands with her while she assented with a small flutter. "Yes, yes, to show it's all arranged!"

"Shall you bring the money in gold?" Miss Bordereau demanded as I was turning to the door.

I looked at her a moment. "Aren't you a little afraid, after all, of keeping such a sum as that in the house?" It was not that I was annoyed at her avidity, but was truly struck with the disparity between such a treasure and such scanty means of guarding it.

"Whom should I be afraid of if I'm not afraid of you?" she asked with her shrunken grimness.

"Ah well," I laughed, "I shall be in point of fact a protector and I'll bring gold if you prefer."

"Thank you," the old woman returned with dignity and with an inclination of her head which evidently signified my dismissal. I passed out of the room, thinking how hard it would be to circumvent her. As I stood in the sala again I saw that Miss Tina had followed me, and I supposed that as her aunt had neglected to suggest I should take a look at my quarters it was her purpose to repair the omission. But she made no such overture; she only stood there with a dim, though not a languid smile, and with an effect of irresponsible incompetent youth almost comically at variance with the faded facts of her person. She was not infirm, like her aunt, but she struck me as more deeply futile, because her inefficiency was inward, which was not the case with Miss Bordereau's. I waited to see if she would offer to show me the rest of the house, but I didn't precipitate the question, inasmuch as my plan was from this moment to spend as much of my time as possible in her society. A minute indeed elapsed before I committed myself.

"I've had better fortune than I hoped. It was very kind of her to see me. Perhaps you said a good word for me."

"It was the idea of the money," said Miss Tina.

"And did you suggest that?"

"I told her you'd perhaps pay largely."

"What made you think that?"

"I told her I thought you were rich."

"And what put that into your head?"

"I don't know; the way you talked."

"Dear me, I must talk differently now," I returned. "I'm sorry to say it's not the case."

"Well," said Miss Tina, "I think that in Venice the *forestieri* in general often give a great deal for something that after all isn't much." She appeared to make this remark with a comforting intention, to wish to remind me that if I had been extravagant I wasn't foolishly singular. We walked together along the sala, and as I took its magnificent measure I observed that I was afraid it wouldn't form a part of my *quartiere*. Were my rooms by chance to be among those that opened into it? "Not if you go above—to the second floor," she answered as if she had rather taken for granted I would know my proper place.

"And I infer that that's where your aunt would like me to be."

"She said your apartments ought to be very distinct."

"That certainly would be best." And I listened with respect while she told me that above I should be free to take whatever I might like; that there was another staircase, but only from the floor on which we stood, and that to pass from it to the garden-level or to come up to my lodging I should have in effect to cross the great hall. This was an immense point gained; I foresaw that it would constitute my whole leverage in my relations with the two ladies. When I asked Miss Tina how I was to manage at present to find my way up she replied with an access of that sociable shyness which constantly marked her manner:

"Perhaps you can't. I don't see—unless I should go with you." She evidently hadn't thought of this before.

We ascended to the upper floor and visited a long succession of empty rooms. The best of them looked over the garden; some of the others had above the opposite rough-tiled house-tops a view of the blue lagoon. They were all dusty and even a little disfigured with long neglect, but I saw that by spending a few hundred francs I should be able to make three or four of them habitable enough. My experiment was turning out costly, yet now that I had all but taken possession I ceased to allow this to trouble me. I mentioned to my companion a few of the things I should put in, but she replied rather more precipitately than usual that I might do exactly what I liked: she seemed to wish to notify me that the Misses Bordereau would take none but the most veiled interest in my proceedings. I guessed that her aunt had instructed her to adopt this tone, and I may as well say now that I came afterwards to distinguish perfectly (as I believed) between the speeches she made on her own responsibility and those the old woman imposed upon her. She took no notice of the unswept condition of the rooms and indulged neither in explanations nor in apologies. I said to myself that this was a sign Juliana and her niece—disenchanting idea!—were untidy persons with a low Italian standard; but I afterwards recognised that a lodger who had forced an entrance had no *locus standi* as a critic. We looked out of a good many windows, for there was nothing within the rooms to look at, and still I wanted to linger. I asked her what several different objects in the prospect might be, but in no case did she appear to know. She was evidently not familiar with the view—it was as if she had not looked at it for years—and I presently saw that she was too preoccupied with something else to pretend to care for it. Suddenly she said—the remark was not suggested:

"I don't know whether it will make any difference to you, but the money is for me."

"The money—?"

"The money you're going to bring."

"Why you'll make me wish to stay here two or three years!" I spoke as benevolently as possible, though it had begun to act on my nerves that these women so associated with Aspern should so constantly bring the pecuniary question back.

"That would be very good for me," she answered almost gaily.

"You put me on my honour!"

She looked as if she failed to understand this, but went on: "She wants me to have more. She thinks she's going to die."

"Ah not soon I hope!" I cried with genuine feeling. I had perfectly considered the possibility of her destroying her documents on the day she should feel her end at hand. I believed that she would cling to them till then, and I was as convinced of her reading Aspern's letters over every night or at least pressing them to her withered lips. I would have given a good deal for some view of those solemnities. I asked Miss Tina if her venerable relative were seriously ill, and she replied that she was only very tired—she had lived so extraordinarily long. That was what she said herself—she wanted to die for a change. Besides, all her friends had been dead for ages; either they ought to have remained or she ought to have gone. That was another thing her aunt often said: she was not at all resigned—resigned, that is, to life.

"But people don't die when they like, do they?" Miss Tina enquired. I took the liberty of asking why, if there was actually enough money to maintain both of them, there would not be more than enough in case of her being left alone. She considered this difficult problem a moment and then said: "Oh well, you know, she takes care of me. She thinks that when I'm alone I shall be a great fool and shan't know how to manage."

"I should have supposed rather that you took care of *her*. I'm afraid she's very proud."

"Why, have you discovered that already?" Miss Tina cried with a dimness of glad surprise.

"I was shut up with her there for a considerable time and she struck me, she interested me extremely. It didn't take me long to make my discovery. She won't have much to say to me while I'm here."

"No, I don't think she will," my companion averred.

"Do you suppose she has some suspicion of me?"

Miss Tina's honest eyes gave me no sign I had touched a mark. "I shouldn't think so—letting you in after all so easily."

"You call it easily? She has covered her risk," I said. "But where is it one could take an advantage of her?"

"I oughtn't to tell you if I knew, ought I?" And Miss Tina added, before I had time to reply to this, smiling dolefully: "Do you think we've any weak points?"

"That's exactly what I'm asking. You'd only have to mention them for me to respect them religiously."

She looked at me hereupon with that air of timid but candid and even gratified curiosity with which she had confronted me from the first; after which she said: "There's nothing to tell. We're terribly quiet. I don't know how the days pass. We've no life."

"I wish I might think I should bring you a little."

"Oh we know what we want," she went on. "It's all right."

There were twenty things I desired to ask her: how in the world they did live; whether they had any friends or visitors, any relations in America or in other countries. But I judged such probings premature; I must leave it to a later chance. "Well, don't *you* be proud," I contented myself with saying. "Don't hide from me altogether."

"Oh I must stay with my aunt," she returned without looking at me. And at the same moment, abruptly, without any ceremony of parting, she quitted me and disappeared, leaving me to make my own way downstairs. I stayed a while longer, wandering about the bright desert—the sun was pouring in—of the old house, thinking the situation over on the spot. Not even the pattering little *serva* came to look after me, and I reflected that after all this treatment showed confidence.

IV

Perhaps it did, but all the same, six weeks later, towards the middle of June, the moment when Mrs. Prest undertook her annual migration, I had made no measurable advance. I was obliged to confess to her that I had no results to speak of. My first step had been unexpectedly rapid, but there was no appearance it would be followed by a second. I was a thousand miles from taking tea with my hostesses—that privilege of which, as I reminded my good friend, we both had had a vision. She reproached me with lacking boldness and I answered that even to be bold you must have an opportunity: you may push on through a breach, but you can't batter down a dead wall. She returned that the breach I had already made was big enough to admit an army and accused me of wasting precious hours in whimpering in her salon when I ought to have been carrying on the struggle in the field. It is true that I went to see her very often—all on the theory that it would console me (I freely expressed my discouragement) for my want of success on my own premises. But I began to feel that it didn't console me to be perpetually chaffed for my scruples, especially since I was really so vigilant; and I was rather glad when my ironic friend closed her house for the summer. She had expected to draw amusement from the drama of my intercourse with the Misses Bordereau, and was disappointed that the intercourse, and consequently the drama, had not come off. "They'll lead you on to your ruin," she said before she left Venice. "They'll get all your money without showing you a scrap." I think I settled down to my business with more concentration after her departure.

It was a fact that up to that time I had not, save on a single brief occasion, had even a moment's contact with my queer hostesses. The exception had occurred when I carried them according to my promise the terrible three thousand francs. Then I found Miss Tina awaiting me in the hall, and she took the money from my hand with a promptitude that prevented my seeing her aunt. The old lady had promised to receive me, yet apparently thought nothing of breaking that vow. The money was contained in a bag of chamois leather, of respectable dimensions, which my banker had given me, and Miss Tina had to make a big fist to receive it. This she did with extreme solemnity, though I tried to treat the affair a little as a joke. It was in no jocular strain, yet it was with a clearness akin to a brightness that she enquired, weighing the money in her two palms: "Don't you think it's too much?" To which I replied that this would depend on the amount of pleasure I should get for it. Hereupon she turned away from me quickly, as she had done the day before, murmuring in a tone different from any she had used hitherto: "Oh pleasure, pleasure—there's no pleasure in this house!"

After that, for a long time, I never saw her, and I wondered the common chances of the day shouldn't have helped us to meet. It could only be evident that she was immensely on her guard against them; and in addition to this the house was so big that for each other we were lost in it. I used to look out for her hopefully as I crossed the sala in my comings and goings, but I was not rewarded with a glimpse of the tail of her dress. It was as if she never peeped out of her aunt's apartment. I used to wonder what she did there week after week and year after year. I had never met so stiff a policy of seclusion; it was more than keeping quiet—it was like hunted creatures feigning death. The two ladies appeared to have no visitors whatever and no sort of contact with the world. I judged at least that people couldn't have come to the house and that Miss Tina couldn't have gone out without my catching some view of it. I did what I disliked myself for doing—considering it but as once in a way: I questioned my servant about their habits and let him infer that I should be interested in any information he might glean. But he gleaned amazingly little for a knowing Venetian: it must be added that where there is a perpetual fast there are very few crumbs on the floor. His ability in other ways was sufficient, if not quite all I had attributed to him on the occasion of my first interview with Miss Tina. He had helped my gondolier to bring me round a boat-load of furniture; and when these articles had been carried to the top of the palace and distributed according to our associated wisdom he organised my household with such dignity as answered to its being composed exclusively of himself. He made me in short as comfortable as I could be with my indifferent prospects. I should have been glad if he had fallen in love with Miss Bordereau's maid or, failing this, had taken her in aversion: either event might have brought about some catastrophe, and a catastrophe might have led to some parley. It was my idea that she would have been sociable, and I myself on various occasions saw her flit to and fro on domestic errands, so that I was sure she was accessible. But I tasted of no gossip from that fountain, and I afterwards learned that Pasquale's affections were fixed upon an object that made him heedless of other women. This was a young lady with a powdered face, a yellow cotton gown and much leisure, who used often to come to see him. She practised, at her convenience, the art of a stringer of beads—these ornaments are made in Venice to profusion; she had her pocket full of them and I used to find them on the floor of my apartment—and kept an eye on the possible rival in the house. It was not for me of course to make the domestics tattle, and I never said a word to Miss Bordereau's cook.

It struck me as a proof of the old woman's resolve to have nothing to do with me that she should never have sent me a receipt for my three months' rent. For some days I looked out for it and then, when I had given it up, wasted a good deal of time in wondering what her reason had been for neglecting so indispensable and familiar a form. At first I was tempted to send her a reminder; after which I put by the idea—against my judgement as to what was right in the particular case—on the general ground of wishing to keep quiet. If Miss Bordereau suspected me of ulterior aims she would suspect me less if I should be businesslike, and yet I consented not to be. It was possible she intended her omission as an impertinence, a visible irony, to show how she could overreach people who attempted to overreach her. On that hypothesis it was well to let her see that one didn't notice her little tricks. The real reading of the matter, I afterwards gathered, was simply the poor lady's desire to emphasise the fact that I was in the enjoyment of a favour as rigidly limited as it had been liberally bestowed. She had given me part of her house, but she wouldn't add to that so much as a morsel of paper with her name on it. Let me say that even at first this didn't make me too miserable, for the whole situation had the charm of its oddity. I foresaw that I should have a summer after my own literary heart, and the sense of playing with my opportunity was much greater after all than any sense of being played with. There could be no Venetian business without patience, and since I adored the place I was much more in the spirit of it for having laid in a large provision. That spirit kept me perpetual company and seemed to look out at me from the revived immortal face—in which all his genius shone—of the great poet who was my prompter. I had invoked him and he had come; he hovered before me half the time; it was as if his bright ghost had returned to earth to assure me he regarded the affair as his own no less than as mine and that we should see it fraternally and fondly to a conclusion. It was as if he had said: "Poor dear, be easy with her; she has some natural prejudices; only give her time. Strange as it may appear to you she was very attractive in 1820. Meanwhile aren't we in Venice together, and what better place is there for the meeting of dear friends? See how it glows with the advancing summer; how the sky and the sea and the rosy air and the marble of the palaces all shimmer and melt together." My eccentric private errand became a part of the general romance and the general glory—I felt even a mystic companionship, a moral fraternity with all those who in the past had been in the service of art. They had worked for beauty, for a devotion; and what else was I doing? That element was in everything that Jeffrey Aspern had written, and I was only bringing it to light.

I lingered in the sala when I went to and fro; I used to watch—as long as I thought decent—the door that led to Miss Bordereau's part of the house. A person observing me might have supposed I was trying to cast a spell on it or attempting some odd experiment in hypnotism. But I was only praying it might open or thinking what treasure probably lurked behind it. I hold it singular, as I look back, that I should never have doubted for a moment that the sacred relics were there; never have failed to know the joy of being beneath the same roof with them. After all they were under my hand—they had not escaped me yet; and they made my life continuous, in a fashion, with the illustrious life they had touched at the other end. I lost myself in this satisfaction to the point of assuming—in my quiet extravagance—that poor Miss Tina also went back, and still went back, as I used to phrase it. She did indeed, the gentle spinster, but not quite so far as Jeffrey Aspern, who was simple hearsay to her quite as he was to me. Only she had lived for years with Juliana, she had seen and handled all mementoes and—even though she was stupid—some esoteric knowledge had rubbed off on her. That was what the old woman represented—esoteric knowledge; and this was the idea with which my critical heart used to thrill. It literally beat faster often, of an evening when I had been out, as I stopped with my candle in the re-echoing hall on my way up to bed. It was as if at such a moment as that, in the stillness and after the long contradiction of the day, Miss Bordereau's secrets were in the air, the wonder of her survival more vivid. These were the acute impressions. I had them in another form, with more of a certain shade of reciprocity, during the hours I sat in the garden looking up over the top of my book at the closed windows of my hostess. In these windows no sign of life ever appeared; it was as if, for fear of my catching a glimpse of them, the two ladies passed their days in the dark. But this only emphasised their having matters to conceal; which was what I had wished to prove. Their motionless shutters became as expressive as eyes consciously closed, and I took comfort in the probability that, though invisible themselves, they kept me in view between the lashes.

I made a point of spending as much time as possible in the garden, to justify the picture I had originally given of my horticultural passion. And I not only spent time, but (hang it! as I said) spent precious money. As soon as I had got my rooms arranged and could give the question proper thought I surveyed the place with a clever expert and made terms for having it put in order. I was sorry to do this, for personally I liked it better as it was, with its weeds and its wild rich tangle, its sweet characteristic Venetian shabbiness. I had to be consistent, to keep my promise that I would smother the house in flowers. Moreover I clung to the fond fancy that by flowers I should make my way—I should succeed by big nosegays. I would batter the old women with lilies—I would bombard their citadel with roses. Their door would have to yield to the pressure when a mound of fragrance should be heaped against it. The place in truth had been brutally neglected. The Venetian capacity for dawdling is of the largest, and for a good many days unlimited litter was all my gardener had to show for his ministrations. There was a great digging of holes and carting about of earth, and after a while I grew so impatient that I had thoughts of sending for my "results" to the nearest stand. But I felt sure my friends would see through the chinks of their shutters where such tribute *couldn't* have been gathered, and might so make up their minds against my veracity. I possessed my soul and finally, though the delay was long, perceived some appearances of bloom. This encouraged me and I waited serenely enough till they multiplied. Meanwhile the real summer days arrived and began to pass, and as I look back upon them they seem to me almost the happiest of my life. I took more and more care to be in the garden whenever it was not too hot. I had an arbour arranged and a low table and an armchair put into it; and I carried out books and portfolios—I had always some business of writing in hand—and worked and waited and mused and hoped, while the golden hours elapsed and the plants drank in the light and the inscrutable old palace turned pale and then, as the day waned, began to recover and flush and my papers rustled in the wandering breeze of the Adriatic.

Considering how little satisfaction I got from it at first it is wonderful I shouldn't have grown more tired of trying to guess what mystic rites of ennui the Misses Bordereau celebrated in their darkened rooms; whether this had always been the tenor of their life and how in previous years they had escaped elbowing their neighbours. It was supposable they had then had other habits, forms and resources; that they must once have been young or at least middle-aged. There was no end to the questions it was possible to ask about them and no end to the answers it was not possible to frame. I had known many of my country-people in Europe and was familiar with the strange ways they were liable to take up there; but the Misses Bordereau formed altogether a new type of the American absentee. Indeed it was clear the American name had ceased to have any application to them—I had seen this in the ten minutes I spent in the old woman's room. You could never have said whence they came from the appearance of either of them; wherever it was they had long ago shed and unlearned all native marks and notes. There was nothing in them one recognised or fitted, and, putting the question of speech aside, they might have been Norwegians or Spaniards. Miss Bordereau, after all, had been in Europe nearly three quarters of a century; it appeared by some verses addressed to her by Aspern on the occasion of his own second absence from America—verses of which Cumnor and I had after infinite conjecture established solidly enough the date—that she was even then, as a girl of twenty, on the foreign side of the sea. There was a profession in the poem—I hope not just for the phrase—that he had come back for her sake. We had no real light on her circumstances at that moment, any more than we had upon her origin, which we believed to be of the sort usually spoken of as modest. Cumnor had a theory that she had been a governess in some family in which the poet visited and that, in consequence of her position, there was from the first something unavowed, or rather something quite clandestine, in their relations. I on the other hand had hatched a little romance according to which she was the daughter of an artist, a painter or a sculptor, who had left the Western world, when the century was fresh, to study in the ancient schools. It was essential to my hypothesis that this amiable man should have lost his wife, should have been poor and unsuccessful and should have had a second daughter of a disposition quite different from Juliana's. It was also indispensable that he should have been accompanied to Europe by these young ladies and should have established himself there for the remainder of a struggling saddened life. There was a further implication that Miss Bordereau had had in her youth a perverse and reckless, albeit a generous and fascinating character, and that she had braved some wondrous chances. By what passions had she been ravaged, by what adventures and sufferings had she been blanched, what store of memories had she laid away for the monotonous future?

I asked myself these things as I sat spinning theories about her in my arbour and the bees droned in the flowers. It was incontestable that, whether for right or for wrong, most readers of certain of Aspern's poems (poems not as

41

ambiguous as the sonnets—scarcely more divine, I think—of Shakespeare) had taken for granted that Juliana had not always adhered to the steep footway of renunciation. There hovered about her name a perfume of impenitent passion, an intimation that she had not been exactly as the respectable young person in general. Was this a sign that her singer had betrayed her, had given her away, as we say nowadays, to posterity? Certain it is that it would have been difficult to put one's finger on the passage in which her fair fame suffered injury. Moreover was not any fame fair enough that was so sure of duration and was associated with works immortal through their beauty? It was a part of my idea that the young lady had had a foreign lover—and say an unedifying tragical rupture—before her meeting with Jeffrey Aspern. She had lived with her father and sister in a queer old-fashioned expatriated artistic Bohemia of the days when the æsthetic was only the academic and the painters who knew the best models for *contadina* and *pifferaro* wore peaked hats and long hair. It was a society less awake than the coteries of today-in its ignorance of the wonderful chances, the opportunities of the early bird, with which its path was strewn—to tatters of old stuff and fragments of old crockery; so that Miss Bordereau appeared not to have picked up or have inherited many objects of importance. There was no enviable *bric-à-brac*, with its provoking legend of cheapness, in the room in which I had seen her. Such a fact as that suggested bareness, but none the less it worked happily into the sentimental interest I had always taken in the early movements of my countrymen as visitors to Europe. When Americans went abroad in 1820 there was something romantic, almost heroic in it, as compared with the perpetual ferryings of the present hour, the hour at which photography and other conveniences have annihilated surprise. Miss Bordereau had sailed with her family on a tossing brig in the days of long voyages and sharp differences; she had had her emotions on the top of yellow diligences, passed the night at inns where she dreamed of travellers' tales, and was most struck, on reaching the Eternal City, with the elegance of Roman pearls and scarfs and mosaic brooches. There was something touching to me in all that, and my imagination frequently went back to the period. If Miss Bordereau carried it there of course Jeffrey Aspern had at other times done so with greater force. It was a much more important fact, if one was looking at his genius critically, that he had lived in the days before the general transfusion. It had happened to me to regret that he had known Europe at all; I should have liked to see what he would have written without that experience, by which he had incontestably been enriched. But as his fate had ruled otherwise I went with him—I tried to judge how the general old order would have struck him. It was not only there, however, I watched him; the relations he had entertained with the special new had even a livelier interest. His own country after all had had most of his life, and his muse, as they said at that time, was essentially American. That was originally what I had prized him for: that at a period when our native land was nude and crude and provincial, when the famous "atmosphere" it is supposed to lack was not even missed, when literature was lonely there and art and form almost impossible, he had found means to live and write like one of the first; to be free and general and not at all afraid; to feel, understand and express everything.

V

I was seldom at home in the evening, for when I attempted to occupy myself in my apartments the lamplight brought in a swarm of noxious insects, and it was too hot for closed windows. Accordingly I spent the late hours either on the water—the moonlights of Venice are famous—or in the splendid square which serves as a vast forecourt to the strange old church of Saint Mark. I sat in front of Florian's café eating ices, listening to music, talking with acquaintances: the traveller will remember how the immense cluster of tables and little chairs stretches like a promontory into the smooth lake of the Piazza. The whole place, of a summer's evening, under the stars and with all the lamps, all the voices and light footsteps on marble—the only sounds of the immense arcade that encloses it—is an open-air saloon dedicated to cooling drinks and to a still finer degustation, that of the splendid impressions received during the day. When I didn't prefer to keep mine to myself there was always a stray tourist, disencumbered of his Bädeker, to discuss them with, or some domesticated painter rejoicing in the return of the season of strong effects. The great basilica, with its low domes and bristling embroideries, the mystery of its mosaic and sculpture, looked ghostly in the tempered gloom, and the sea-breeze passed between the twin columns of the Piazzetta, the lintels of a door no longer guarded, as gently as if a rich curtain swayed there. I used sometimes on these occasions to think of the Misses Bordereau and of the pity of their being shut up in apartments which in the Venetian July even Venetian vastness couldn't relieve of some stuffiness. Their life seemed miles away from the life of the Piazza, and no doubt it was really too late to make the austere Juliana change her habits. But poor Miss Tina would have enjoyed one of Florian's ices, I was sure; sometimes I even had thoughts of carrying one home to her. Fortunately my patience bore fruit and I was not obliged to do anything so ridiculous.

One evening about the middle of July I came in earlier than usual—I forget what chance had led to this—and instead of going up to my quarters made my way into the garden. The temperature was very high; it was such a night as one would gladly have spent in the open air, and I was in no hurry to go to bed. I had floated home in my gondola, listening to the slow splash of the oar in the dark narrow canals, and now the only thought that occupied me was that it would be good to recline at one's length in the fragrant darkness on a garden-bench. The odour of the canal was doubtless at the bottom of that aspiration, and the breath of the garden, as I entered it, gave consistency to my purpose. It was delicious—just such an air as must have trembled with Romeo's vows when he stood among the thick flowers and raised his arms to his mistress's balcony. I looked at the windows of the palace to see if by chance the example of Verona—Verona being not far off—had been followed; but everything was dim, as usual, and everything was still. Juliana might on the summer nights of her youth have murmured down from open windows at Jeffrey Aspern, but Miss Tina was not a poet's mistress any more than I was a poet. This however didn't prevent my gratification from being great as I became aware on reaching the end of the garden that my younger padrona was seated in one of the bowers. At first I made out but an indistinct figure, not in the least counting on such an overture from one of my hostesses; it even occurred to me that some enamoured maidservant had stolen in to keep a tryst with her sweetheart. I was going to turn away, not to frighten her, when the figure rose to its height and I recognised Miss Bordereau's niece. I must do myself the justice that I didn't wish to frighten her either, and much as I had longed for some such accident I should have been capable of retreating. It was as if I had laid a trap for her by coming home earlier than usual and by adding to that oddity my invasion of the garden. As she rose she spoke to me, and then I guessed that perhaps, secure in my almost inveterate absence, it was her nightly practice to take a lonely airing. There was no trap in truth, because I had had no suspicion. At first I took the words she uttered for an impatience of my arrival; but as she repeated them—I hadn't caught them clearly—I had the surprise of hearing her say: "Oh dear, I'm so glad you've come!" She and her aunt had in common the property of unexpected speeches. She came out of the arbour almost as if to throw herself in my arms.

I hasten to add that I escaped this ordeal and that she didn't even then shake hands with me. It was an ease to her to see me and presently she told me why—because she was nervous when out-of-doors at night alone. The plants and shrubs looked so strange in the dark, and there were all sorts of queer sounds—she couldn't tell what they were—like the noises of animals. She stood close to me, looking about her with an air of greater security but without any demonstration of interest in me as an individual. Then I felt how little nocturnal prowlings could have been her habit, and I was also reminded—I had been afflicted by the same in talking with her before I took possession—that it was impossible to allow too much for her simplicity.

"You speak as if you were lost in the backwoods," I cheeringly laughed. "How you manage to keep out of this charming place when you've only three steps to take to get into it is more than I've yet been able to discover. You hide away amazingly so long as I'm on the premises, I know; but I had a hope you peeped out a little at other times. You and your poor aunt are worse off than Carmelite nuns in their cells. Should you mind telling me how you exist without air, without exercise, without any sort of human contact? I don't see how you carry on the common business of life."

She looked at me as if I had spoken a strange tongue, and her answer was so little of one that I felt it make for irritation. "We go to bed very early—earlier than you'd believe." I was on the point of saying that this only deepened the mystery, but she gave me some relief by adding: "Before you came we weren't so private. But I've never been out at night."

"Never in these fragrant alleys, blooming here under your nose?"

"Ah," said Miss Tina, "they were never nice till now!" There was a finer sense in this and a flattering comparison, so that it seemed to me I had gained some advantage. As I might follow that further by establishing a good grievance I asked her why, since she thought my garden nice, she had never thanked me in any way for the flowers I had been sending up in such quantities for the previous three weeks. I had not been discouraged—there had been, as she would have observed, a daily armful; but I had been brought up in the common forms and a word of recognition now and then would have touched me in the right place.

"Why I didn't know they were for me!"

"They were for both of you. Why should I make a difference?"

Miss Tina reflected as if she might be thinking of a reason for that, but she failed to produce one. Instead of this she asked abruptly: "Why in the world do you want so much to know us?"

"I ought after all to make a difference," I replied. "That question's your aunt's; it isn't yours. You wouldn't ask it if you hadn't been put up to it."

"She didn't tell me to ask you," Miss Tina replied without confusion. She was indeed the oddest mixture of shyness and straightness.

"Well, she has often wondered about it herself and expressed her wonder to you. She has insisted on it, so that she has put the idea into your head that I'm insufferably pushing. Upon my word I think I've been very discreet. And how completely your aunt must have lost every tradition of sociability, to see anything out of the way in the idea that respectable intelligent people, living as we do under the same roof, should occasionally exchange a remark! What could be more natural? We're of the same country and have at least some of the same tastes, since, like you, I'm intensely fond of Venice."

My friend seemed incapable of grasping more than one clause in any proposition, and she now spoke quickly, eagerly, as if she were answering my whole speech. "I'm not in the least fond of Venice. I should like to go far away!"

"Has she always kept you back so?" I went on, to show her I could be as irrelevant as herself.

"She told me to come out tonight; she has told me very often," said Miss Tina. "It is I who wouldn't come. I don't like to leave her."

"Is she too weak, is she really failing?" I demanded, with more emotion, I think, than I meant to betray. I measured this by the way her eyes rested on me in the darkness. It embarrassed me a little, and to turn the matter off I continued genially: "Do let us sit down together comfortably somewhere—while you tell me all about her."

Miss Tina made no resistance to this. We found a bench less secluded, less confidential, as it were, than the one in the arbour; and we were still sitting there when I heard midnight ring out from those clear bells of Venice which vibrate with a solemnity of their own over the lagoon and hold the air so much more than the chimes of other places. We were together more than an hour, and our interview gave, as it struck me, a great life to my undertaking. Miss Tina accepted the situation without a protest; she had avoided me for three months, yet now she treated me almost as if these three months had made me an old friend. If I had chosen I might have gathered from this that though she had avoided me she had given a good deal of consideration to doing so. She paid no attention to the flight of time—never worried at my keeping her so long away from her aunt. She talked freely, answering questions and asking them and not even taking advantage of certain longish pauses by which they were naturally broken to say she thought she had better go in. It was almost as if she were waiting for something—something I might say to her—and intended to give me my opportunity. I was the more struck by this as she told me how much less well her aunt had been for a good many days, and in a way that was rather new. She was markedly weaker; at moments she showed no strength at all; yet more than ever before she wished to be left alone. That was why she had told her to come out—not even to remain in her own room, which was alongside; she pronounced poor Miss Tina "a worry, a bore and a source of aggravation." She sat still for hours together, as if for long sleep; she had always done that, musing and dozing; but at such times formerly she gave, in breaks, some small sign of life, of interest, liking her companion to be near her with her work. This sad personage confided to me that at present her aunt was so motionless as to create the fear she was dead; moreover she scarce ate or drank—one couldn't see what she lived on. The great thing was that she still on most days got up; the serious job was to dress her, to wheel her out of her bedroom. She clung to as many of her old habits as possible and had always, little company as they had received for years, made a point of sitting in the great parlour.

I scarce knew what to think of all this—of Miss Tina's sudden conversion to sociability and of the strange fact that the more the old woman appeared to decline to her end the less she should desire to be looked after. The story hung indifferently together, and I even asked myself if it mightn't be a trap laid for me, the result of a design to make me show my hand. I couldn't have told why my companions (as they could only by courtesy be called) should have this purpose—why they should try to trip up so lucrative a lodger. But at any hazard I kept on my guard, so that Miss Tina shouldn't have occasion again to ask me what I might really be "up to." Poor woman, before we parted for the night my mind was at rest as to what *she* might be. She was up to nothing at all.

She told me more about their affairs than I had hoped; there was no need to be prying, for it evidently drew her out simply to feel me listen and care. She ceased wondering why I *should*, and at last, while describing the brilliant life they had led years before, she almost chattered. It was Miss Tina who judged it brilliant; she said that when they first came to live in Venice, years and years back—I found her essentially vague about dates and the order in which events had occurred—there was never a week they hadn't some visitor or didn't make some pleasant *passeggio* in the town. They had seen all the curiosities; they had even been to the Lido in a boat—she spoke as if I might think there was a way on foot; they had had a collation there, brought in three baskets and spread out on the grass. I asked her what people they had known and she said Oh very nice ones—the Cavaliere Bombicci and the Contessa Altemura, with whom they had had a great friendship! Also English people— the Churtons and the Goldies and Mrs. Stock-Stock, whom they had loved dearly; she was dead and gone, poor dear. That was the case with most of their kind circle—this expression was Miss Tina's own; though a few were left, which was a wonder considering how they had neglected them. She mentioned the names of two or three Venetian old women; of a certain doctor, very clever, who was so attentive—he came as a friend, he had really given up practice; of the *avvocato* Pochintesta, who wrote beautiful poems and had addressed one to her aunt. These people came to see them without fail every year, usually at the *capo d'anno*, and of old her aunt used to make them some little present—her aunt and she together: small things that she, Miss Tina, turned out with her own hand, paper lamp-shades, or mats for the decanters of wine at dinner, or those woollen things that in cold weather are worn on the wrists. The last few years there hadn't been many presents; she couldn't think what to make and her aunt had lost interest and never suggested. But the people came all the same; if the good Venetians liked you once they liked you for ever.

There was affecting matter enough in the good faith of this sketch of former social glories; the picnic at the Lido had remained vivid through the ages and poor Miss Tina evidently was of the impression that she had had a dashing youth. She had in fact had a glimpse of the Venetian world in its gossiping home-keeping parsimonious professional walks; for I noted for the first time how nearly she had acquired by contact the trick of the familiar soft-sounding almost infantile prattle of the place. I judged her to have imbibed this invertebrate dialect from the natural way the names of things and people—mostly purely local—rose to her lips. If she knew little of what they represented she knew still less of anything else. Her aunt had drawn in—the failure of interest in the table-mats and lamp-shades was a sign of that—and she hadn't been able to mingle in society or to entertain it alone; so that her range of reminiscence struck one as an old world altogether. Her tone, hadn't it been so decent, would have seemed to carry one back to the queer rococo Venice of Goldoni and Casanova. I found myself mistakenly think of her too as one of Jeffrey Aspern's contemporaries; this came from her having so little in common with my own. It was possible, I indeed reasoned, that she hadn't even heard of him; it might very well be that Juliana had forborne to lift for innocent eyes the veil that covered the temple of her glory. In this case she perhaps wouldn't know of the existence of the papers, and I welcomed that presumption—it made me feel more safe with her—till I remembered we had believed the letter of disavowal received by Cumnor to be in the handwriting of the niece. If it had been dictated to her she had of course to know what it was about; though the effect of it withal was to repudiate the idea of any connexion with the poet. I held it probable at all events that Miss Tina hadn't read a word of his poetry. Moreover if, with her companion, she had always escaped invasion and research, there was little occasion for her having got it into her head that people were "after" the letters. People had not been after them, for people hadn't heard of them. Cumnor's fruitless feeler would have been a solitary accident.

When midnight sounded Miss Tina got up; but she stopped at the door of the house only after she had wandered two or three times with me round the garden. "When shall I see you again?" I asked before she went in; to which she replied with promptness that she should like to come out the next night. She added however that she shouldn't come—she was so far from doing everything she liked.

"You might do a few things *I* like," I quite sincerely sighed.

"Oh you—I don't believe you!" she murmured at this, facing me with her simple solemnity.

"Why don't you believe me?"

"Because I don't understand you."

"That's just the sort of occasion to have faith." I couldn't say more, though I should have liked to, as I saw I only mystified her; for I had no wish to have it on my conscience that I might pass for having made love to her. Nothing less should I have seemed to do had I continued to beg a lady to "believe in me" in an Italian garden on a midsummer night. There was some merit in my scruples, for Miss Tina lingered and lingered: I made out in her the conviction that she shouldn't really soon come down again and the wish therefore to protract the present. She insisted too on making the talk between us personal to ourselves; and altogether her behaviour was such as would have been possible only to a perfectly artless and a considerably witless woman.

"I shall like the flowers better now that I know them also meant for me."

"How could you have doubted it? If you'll tell me the kind you like best I'll send a double lot."

"Oh I like them all best!" Then she went on familiarly: "Shall you study—shall you read and write—when you go up to your rooms?"

"I don't do that at night—at this season. The lamplight brings in the animals."

"You might have known that when you came."

"I did know it!"

"And in winter do you work at night?"

"I read a good deal, but I don't often write." She listened as if these details had a rare interest, and suddenly a temptation quite at odds with all the prudence I had been teaching myself glimmered at me in her plain mild face. Ah yes, she was safe and I could make her safer! It seemed to me from one moment to another that I couldn't wait longer—that I really must take a sounding. So I went on: "In general before I go to sleep (very often in bed; it's a bad habit, but I confess to it) I read some great poet. In nine cases out of ten it's a volume of Jeffrey Aspern."

I watched her well as I pronounced that name, but I saw nothing wonderful. Why should I indeed? Wasn't Jeffrey Aspern the property of the human race?

"Oh *we* read him—we *have* read him," she quietly replied.

"He's my poet of poets—I know him almost by heart."

For an instant Miss Tina hesitated; then her sociability was too much for her. "Oh by heart—that's nothing;" and, though dimly, she quite lighted. "My aunt used to know him, to know him"—she paused an instant and I wondered what she was going to say—"to know him as a visitor."

"As a visitor?" I guarded my tone.

"He used to call on her and take her out."

I continued to stare. "My dear lady, he died a hundred years ago!"

"Well," she said amusingly, "my aunt's a hundred and fifty."

"Mercy on us!" I cried; "why didn't you tell me before? I should like so to ask her about him."

"She wouldn't care for that—she wouldn't tell you," Miss Tina returned.

"I don't care what she cares for ! She *must* tell me—it's not a chance to be lost."

"Oh you should have come twenty years ago. Then she still talked about him."

"And what did she say?" I eagerly asked.

"I don't know—that he liked her immensely."

"And she—didn't she like *him?*"

"She said he was a god." Miss Tina gave me this information flatly, without expression; her tone might have made it a piece of trivial gossip. But it stirred me deeply as she dropped the words into the summer night; their sound might have been the light rustle of an old unfolded love-letter.

"Fancy, fancy!" I murmured. And then: "Tell me this, please— has she got a portrait of him? They're distressingly rare."

"A portrait? I don't know," said Miss Tina; and now there was discomfiture in her face. "Well, good-night!" she added; and she turned into the house.

I accompanied her into the wide dusky stone-paved passage that corresponded on the ground floor with our great sala. It opened at one end into the garden, at the other upon the canal, and was lighted now only by the small lamp always left for me to take up as I went to bed. An extinguished candle which Miss Tina apparently had brought down with her stood on the same table with it. "Good-night, good-night!" I replied, keeping beside her as she went to get her light. "Surely you'd know, shouldn't you, if she had one?"

"If she had what?" the poor lady asked, looking at me queerly over the flame of her candle.

"A portrait of the god. I don't know what I wouldn't give to see it."

"I don't know what she has got. She keeps her things locked up." And Miss Tina went away toward the staircase with the sense evidently of having said too much.

I let her go—I wished not to frighten her—and I contented myself with remarking that Miss Bordereau wouldn't have locked up such a glorious possession as that: a thing a person would be proud of and hang up in a prominent place on the parlour-wall. Therefore of course she hadn't any portrait. Miss Tina made no direct answer to this and, candle in hand, with her back to me, mounted two or three degrees. Then she stopped short and turned round, looking at me across the dusky space.

"Do you write—do you write?" There was a shake in her voice—she could scarcely bring it out.

"Do I write? Oh don't speak of my writing on the same day with Aspern's!"

"Do you write about *him*—do you pry into his life?"

"Ah that's your aunt's question; it can't be yours!" I said in a tone of slightly wounded sensibility.

"All the more reason then that you should answer it. Do you, please?"

I thought I had allowed for the falsehoods I should have to tell, but I found that in fact when it came to the point I hadn't. Besides, now that I had an opening there was a kind of relief in being frank. Lastly—it was perhaps fanciful, even fatuous—I guessed that Miss Tina personally wouldn't in the last resort be less my friend. So after a moment's hesitation I answered: "Yes, I've written about him and I'm looking for more material. In heaven's name have you got any?"

"*Santo Dio!*" she exclaimed without heeding my question; and she hurried upstairs and out of sight. I might count upon her in the last resort, but for the present she was visibly alarmed. The proof of it was that she began to hide again, so that for a fortnight I kept missing her. I found my patience ebbing and after four or five days of this I told the gardener to stop the "floral tributes."

VI

One afternoon, at last, however, as I came down from my quarters to go out, I found her in the sala: it was our first encounter on that ground since I had come to the house. She put on no air of being there by accident; there was an ignorance of such arts in her honest angular diffidence. That I might be quite sure she was waiting for me she mentioned it at once, but telling me with it that Miss Bordereau wished to see me: she would take me into the room at that moment if I had time. If I had been late for a love-tryst I would have stayed for this, and I quickly signified that I should be delighted to wait on my benefactress. "She wants to talk with you—to know you," Miss Tina said, smiling as if she herself appreciated that idea; and she led me to the door of her aunt's apartment. I stopped her a moment before she had opened it, looking at her with some curiosity. I told her that this was a great satisfaction to me and a great honour; but all the same I should like to ask what had made Miss Bordereau so markedly and suddenly change. It had been only the other day that she wouldn't suffer me near her. Miss Tina was not embarrassed by my question; she had as many little unexpected serenities, plausibilities almost, as if she told fibs, but the odd part of them was that they had on the contrary their source in her truthfulness. "Oh my aunt varies," she answered; "it's so terribly dull—I suppose she's tired."

"But you told me she wanted more and more to be alone."

Poor Miss Tina coloured as if she found me too pushing.

"Well, if you don't believe she wants to see you, I haven't invented it! I think people often are capricious when they're very old."

"That's perfectly true. I only wanted to be clear as to whether you've repeated to her what I told you the other night."

"What you told me?"

"About Jeffrey Aspern—that I'm looking for materials."

"If I had told her do you think she'd have sent for you?"

"That's exactly what I want to know. If she wants to keep him to herself she might have sent for me to tell me so."

"She won't speak of him," said Miss Tina. Then as she opened the door she added in a lower tone: "I told her nothing."

The old woman was sitting in the same place in which I had seen her last, in the same position, with the same mystifying bandage over her eyes. Her welcome was to turn her almost invisible face to me and show me that while she sat silent she saw me clearly. I made no motion to shake hands with her; I now felt too well that this was out of place for ever. It had been sufficiently enjoined on me that she was too sacred for trivial modernisms—too venerable to touch. There was something so grim in her aspect—it was partly the accident of her green shade—as I stood there to be measured, that I ceased on the spot to doubt her suspecting me, though I didn't in the least myself suspect that Miss Tina hadn't just spoken the truth. She hadn't betrayed me, but the old woman's brooding instinct had served her; she had turned me over and over in the long still hours and had guessed. The worst of it was that she looked terribly like an old woman who at a pinch would, even like Sardanapalus, burn her treasure. Miss Tina pushed a chair forward, saying to me "This will be a good place for you to sit." As I took possession of it I asked after Miss Bordereau's health; expressed the hope that in spite of the very hot weather it was satisfactory. She answered that it was good enough—good enough; that it was a great thing to be alive.

"Oh as to that, it depends upon what you compare it with!" I returned with a laugh.

"I don't compare—I don't compare. If I did that I should have given everything up long ago."

I liked to take this for a subtle allusion to the rapture she had known in the society of Jeffrey Aspern—though it was true that such an allusion would have accorded ill with the wish I imputed to her to keep him buried in her soul. What it accorded with was my constant conviction that no human being had ever had a happier social gift than his, and what it seemed to convey was that nothing in the world was worth speaking of if one pretended to speak of that. But one didn't pretend! Miss Tina sat down beside her aunt, looking as if she had reason to believe some wonderful talk would come off between us.

"It's about the beautiful flowers," said the old lady; "you sent us so many—I ought to have thanked you for them before. But I don't write letters and I receive company but at long intervals."

She hadn't thanked me while the flowers continued to come, but she departed from her custom so far as to send for me as soon as she began to fear they wouldn't come any more. I noted this; I remembered what an acquisitive propensity she had shown when it was a question of extracting gold from me, and I privately rejoiced at the happy thought I had had in suspending my tribute. She had missed it and was willing to make a concession to bring it back. At the first sign of this concession I could only go to meet her. "I'm afraid you haven't had many, of late, but they shall begin again immediately—to-morrow, tonight."

"Oh do send us some tonight!" Miss Tina cried as if it were a great affair.

"What else should you do with them? It isn't a manly taste to make a bower of your room," the old woman remarked.

"I don't make a bower of my room, but I'm exceedingly fond of growing flowers, of watching their ways. There's nothing unmanly in that; it has been the amusement of philosophers, of statesmen in retirement; even I think of great captains."

"I suppose you know you can sell them—those you don't use," Miss Bordereau went on. "I dare say they wouldn't give you much for them; still, you could make a bargain."

"Oh I've never in my life made a bargain, as you ought pretty well to have gathered. My gardener disposes of them and I ask no questions."

"I'd ask a few, I can promise you!" said Miss Bordereau; and it was so I first heard the strange sound of her laugh, which was as if the faint "walking" ghost of her old-time tone had suddenly cut a caper. I couldn't get used to the idea that this vision of pecuniary profit was most what drew out the divine Juliana.

"Come into the garden yourself and pick them; come as often as you like; come every day. The flowers are all for you," I pursued, addressing Miss Tina and carrying off this veracious statement by treating it as an innocent joke. "I can't imagine why she doesn't come down," I added for Miss Bordereau's benefit.

"You must make her come; you must come up and fetch her," the old woman said to my stupefaction. "That odd thing you've made in the corner will do very well for her to sit in."

The allusion to the most elaborate of my shady coverts, a sketchy "summer-house," was irreverent; it confirmed the impression I had already received that there was a flicker of impertinence in Miss Bordereau's talk, a vague echo of the boldness or the archness of her adventurous youth and which had somehow automatically outlived passions and faculties. None the less I asked: "Wouldn't it be possible for you to come down there yourself? Wouldn't it do you good to sit there in the shade and the sweet air?"

"Oh sir, when I move out of this it won't be to sit in the air, and I'm afraid that any that may be stirring around me won't be particularly sweet! It will be a very dark shade indeed. But that won't be just yet," Miss Bordereau continued cannily, as if to correct any hopes this free glance at the last receptacle of her mortality might lead me to entertain. "I've sat here many a day and have had enough of arbours in my time. But I'm not afraid to wait till I'm called."

Miss Tina had expected, as I felt, rare conversation, but perhaps she found it less gracious on her aunt's side—considering I had been sent for with a civil intention—than she had hoped. As to give the position a turn that would put our companion in a light more favourable she said to me: "Didn't I tell you the other night that she had sent me out? You see I can do what I like!"

"Do you pity her—do you teach her to pity herself?" Miss Bordereau demanded, before I had time to answer this appeal. "She has a much easier life than I had at her age."

"You must remember it has been quite open to me," I said, "to think you rather inhuman."

"Inhuman? That's what the poets used to call the women a hundred years ago. Don't try that; you won't do as well as they!" Juliana went on. "There's no more poetry in the world—that *I* know of at least. But I won't bandy words with you," she said, and I well remember the old-fashioned artificial sound she gave the speech. "You make me talk, talk, talk! It isn't good for me at all." I got up at this and told her I would take no more of her time; but she detained me to put a question. "Do you remember, the day I saw you about the rooms, that you offered us the use of your gondola?" And when I assented promptly, struck again with her disposition to make a "good thing" of my being there and wondering what she now had in her eye, she produced: "Why don't you take that girl out in it and show her the place?"

"Oh dear aunt, what do you want to do with me?" cried the "girl" with a piteous quaver. "I know all about the place!"

"Well then go with him and explain!" said Miss Bordereau, who gave an effect of cruelty to her implacable power of retort. This showed her as a sarcastic profane cynical old woman. "Haven't we heard that there have been all sorts of changes in all these years? You ought to see them, and at your age—I don't mean because you're so young—you ought to take the chances that come. You're old enough, my dear, and this gentleman won't hurt you. He'll show you the famous sunsets, if they still go on—*do* they go on? The sun set for me so long ago. But that's not a reason. Besides, I shall never miss you; you think you're too important. Take her to the Piazza; it used to be very pretty," Miss Bordereau continued, addressing herself to me. "What have they done with the funny old church? I hope it hasn't tumbled down. Let her look at the shops; she may take some money, she may buy what she likes."

Poor Miss Tina had got up, discountenanced and helpless, and as we stood there before her aunt it would certainly have struck a spectator of the scene that our venerable friend was making rare sport of us. Miss Tina protested in a confusion of exclamations and murmurs; but I lost no time in saying that if she would do me the honour to accept the hospitality of my boat I would engage she really shouldn't be bored. Or if she didn't want so much of my company the boat itself, with the gondolier, was at her service; he was a capital oar and she might have every confidence. Miss Tina, without definitely answering this speech, looked away from me and out of the window, quite as if about to weep, and I remarked that once we had Miss Bordereau's approval we could easily come to an understanding. We would take an hour, whichever she liked, one of the very next days. As I made my obeisance to the old lady I asked her if she would kindly permit me to see her again.

For a moment she kept me; then she said: "Is it very necessary to your happiness?"

"It diverts me more than I can say."

"You're wonderfully civil. Don't you know it almost kills *me*?"

"How can I believe that when I see you more animated, more brilliant than when I came in?"

"That's very true, aunt," said Miss Tina. "I think it does you good."

"Isn't it touching, the solicitude we each have that the other shall enjoy herself?" sneered Miss Bordereau. "If you think me brilliant today you don't know what you're talking about;

you've never seen an agreeable woman. What do you people know about good society?" she cried; but before I could tell her, "Don't try to pay me a compliment; I've been spoiled," she went on. "My door's shut, but you may sometimes knock."

With this she dismissed me and I left the room. The latch closed behind me, but Miss Tina, contrary to my hope, had remained within. I passed slowly across the hall and before taking my way downstairs waited a little. My hope was answered; after a minute my conductress followed me. "That's a delightful idea about the Piazza," I said. "When will you go—tonight, tomorrow?"

She had been disconcerted, as I have mentioned, but I had already perceived, and I was to observe again, that when Miss Tina was embarrassed she didn't—as most women would have in like case—turn away, floundering and hedging, but came closer, as it were, with a deprecating, a clinging appeal to be spared, to be protected. Her attitude was a constant prayer for aid and explanation, and yet no woman in the world could have been less of a comedian. From the moment you were kind to her she depended on you absolutely; her self-consciousness dropped and she took the greatest intimacy, the innocent intimacy that was all she could conceive, for granted. She didn't know, she now declared, what possessed her aunt, who had changed so quickly, who had got some idea. I replied that she must catch the idea and let me have it: we would go and take an ice together at Florian's and she should report while we listened to the band.

"Oh it will take me a long time to be able to 'report'!" she said rather ruefully; and she could promise me this satisfaction neither for that night nor for the next. I was patient now, however, for I felt I had only to wait; and in fact at the end of the week, one lovely evening after dinner, she stepped into my gondola, to which in honour of the occasion I had attached a second oar.

We swept in the course of five minutes into the Grand Canal; whereupon she uttered a murmur of ecstasy as fresh as if she had been a tourist just arrived. She had forgotten the splendour of the great water-way on a clear summer evening, and how the sense of floating between marble palaces and reflected lights disposed the mind to freedom and ease. We floated long and far, and though my friend gave no high-pitched voice to her glee I was sure of her full surrender. She was more than pleased, she was transported; the whole thing was an immense liberation. The gondola moved with slow strokes, to give her time to enjoy it, and she listened to the plash of the oars, which grew louder and more musically liquid as we passed into narrow canals, as if it were a revelation of Venice. When I asked her how long it was since she had thus floated she answered: "Oh I don't know; a long time—not since my aunt began to be ill." This was not the only show of her extreme vagueness about the previous years and the line marking off the period of Miss Bordereau's eminence. I was not at liberty to keep her out long, but we took a considerable *giro* before going to the Piazza. I asked her no questions, holding off by design from her life at home and the things I wanted to know; I poured, rather, treasures of information about the objects before and around us into her ears, describing also Florence and Rome, discoursing on the charms and advantages of travel. She reclined, receptive, on the deep leather cushions, turned her eyes conscientiously to everything I noted and never mentioned to me till some time afterwards that she might be supposed to know Florence better than I, as she had lived there for years with her kins-woman. At last she said with the shy impatience of a child: "Are we not really going to the Piazza? That's what I want to see!" I immediately gave the order that we should go straight, after which we sat silent with the expectation of arrival. As some time still passed, however, she broke out of her own movement: "I've found out what's the matter with my aunt: she's afraid you'll go!"

I quite gasped. "What has put that into her head?"

"She has had an idea you've not been happy. That's why she's different now."

"You mean she wants to make me happier?"

"Well, she wants you not to go. She wants you to stay."

"I suppose you mean on account of the rent," I remarked candidly.

Miss Tina's candour but profited. "Yes, you know; so that I shall have more."

"How much does she want you to have?" I asked with all the gaiety I now felt. "She ought to fix the sum, so that I may stay till it's made up."

"Oh that wouldn't please me," said Miss Tina. "It would be unheard of, your taking that trouble."

"But suppose I should have my own reasons for staying in Venice?"

"Then it would be better for you to stay in some other house."

"And what would your aunt say to that?"

"She wouldn't like it at all. But I should think you'd do well to give up your reasons and go away altogether."

"Dear Miss Tina," I said, "it's not so easy to give up my reasons!"

She made no immediate answer to this, but after a moment broke out afresh: "I think I know what your reasons are!"

"I dare say, because the other night I almost told you how I wished you'd help me to make them good."

"I can't do that without being false to my aunt."

"What do you mean by being false to her?"

"Why she would never consent to what you want. She has been asked, she has been written to. It makes her fearfully angry."

"Then she *has* papers of value?" I precipitately cried.

"Oh she has everything!" sighed Miss Tina with a curious weariness, a sudden lapse into gloom.

These words caused all my pulses to throb, for I regarded them as precious evidence. I felt them too deeply to speak, and in the interval the gondola approached the Piazzetta. After we had disembarked I asked my companion if she would rather walk round the square or go and sit before the great café; to which she replied that she would do whichever I liked best—I must only remember again how little time she had. I assured her there was plenty to do both, and we made the circuit of the long arcades. Her spirits revived at the sight of the bright shop-windows, and she lingered and stopped, admiring or disapproving of their contents, asking me what I thought of things, theorising about prices. My attention wandered from her; her words of a while before "Oh she has everything!" echoed so in my consciousness. We sat down at last in the crowded circle at Florian's, finding an unoccupied table among those that were ranged in the square. It was a splendid night and all the world out-of-doors; Miss Tina couldn't have wished the elements more auspicious for her return to society. I saw she felt it all even more than she told, but her impressions were well-nigh too many for her. She had forgotten the attraction of the world and was learning that she had for the best years of her life been rather mercilessly cheated of it. This didn't make her angry; but as she took in the charming scene her face had, in spite of its smile of appreciation, the flush of a wounded surprise. She didn't speak, sunk in the sense of opportunities, for ever lost, that ought to have been easy; and this gave me a chance to say to her: "Did you mean a while ago that your aunt has a plan of keeping me on by admitting me occasionally to her presence?"

"She thinks it will make a difference with you if you sometimes see her. She wants you so much to stay that she's willing to make that concession."

"And what good does she consider I think it will do me to see her?"

"I don't know; it must be interesting," said Miss Tina simply. "You told her you found it so."

"So I did; but everyone doesn't think that."

"No, of course not, or more people would try."

"Well, if she's capable of making that reflexion she's capable also of making this further one," I went on: "that I must have a particular reason for not doing as others do, in spite of the interest she offers—for not leaving her alone." Miss Tina looked as if she failed to grasp this rather complicated proposition; so I continued: "If you've not told her what I said to you the other night may she not at least have guessed it?"

"I don't know—she's very suspicious."

"But she hasn't been made so by indiscreet curiosity, by persecution?"

"No, no; it isn't that," said Miss Tina, turning on me a troubled face. "I don't know how to say it: it's on account of something—ages ago, before I was born—in her life."

"Something? What sort of thing?"—and I asked it as if I could have no idea.

"Oh she has never told me." And I was sure my friend spoke the truth.

Her extreme limpidity was almost provoking, and I felt for the moment that she would have been more satisfactory if she had been less ingenuous. "Do you suppose it's something to which Jeffrey Aspern's letters and papers—I mean the things in her possession—have reference?"

"I dare say it is!" my companion exclaimed as if this were a very happy suggestion. "I've never looked at any of those things."

"None of them? Then how do you know what they are?"

"I don't," said Miss Tina placidly. "I've never had them in my hands. But I've seen them when she has had them out."

"Does she have them out often?"

"Not now, but she used to. She's very fond of them."

"In spite of their being compromising?"

"Compromising?" Miss Tina repeated as if vague as to what that meant. I felt almost as one who corrupts the innocence of youth.

"I allude to their containing painful memories."

"Oh I don't think anything's painful."

"You mean there's nothing to affect her reputation?"

An odder look even than usual came at this into the face of Miss Bordereau's niece—a confession, it seemed, of helplessness, an appeal to me to deal fairly, generously with her. I had brought her to the Piazza, placed her among charming influences, paid her an attention she appreciated, and now I appeared to show it all as a bribe—a bribe to make her turn in some way against her aunt. She was of a yielding nature and capable of doing almost anything to please a person markedly kind to her; but the greatest kindness of all would be not to presume too much on this. It was strange enough, as I afterwards thought, that she had not the least air of resenting my want of consideration for her aunt's character, which would have been in the worst possible taste if anything less vital—from my point of view—had been at stake. I don't think she really measured it. "Do you mean she ever did something bad?" she asked in a moment.

"Heaven forbid I should say so, and it's none of my business. Besides, if she did," I agreeably put it, "that was in other ages, in another world. But why shouldn't she destroy her papers?"

"Oh she loves them too much."

"Even now, when she may be near her end?"

"Perhaps when she's sure of that she will."

"Well, Miss Tina," I said, "that's just what I should like you to prevent."

"How can I prevent it?"

"Couldn't you get them away from her?"

"And give them to you?"

This put the case, superficially, with sharp irony, but I was sure of her not intending that. "Oh I mean that you might let me see them and look them over. It isn't for myself, or that I should want them at any cost to anyone else. It's simply that they would be of such immense interest to the public, such immeasurable importance as a contribution to Jeffrey Aspern's history."

She listened to me in her usual way, as if I abounded in matters she had never heard of, and I felt almost as base as the reporter of a newspaper who forces his way into a house of mourning. This was marked when she presently said: "There was a gentleman who some time ago wrote to her in very much those words. He also wanted her papers."

"And did she answer him?" I asked, rather ashamed of not having my friend's rectitude.

"Only when he had written two or three times. He made her very angry."

"And what did she say?"

"She said he was a devil," Miss Tina replied categorically.

"She used that expression in her letter?"

"Oh no; she said it to me. She made me write to him."

"And what did you say?"

"I told him there were no papers at all."

"Ah poor gentleman!" I groaned.

"I knew there were, but I wrote what she bade me."

"Of course you had to do that. But I hope I shan't pass for a devil."

"It will depend upon what you ask me to do for you," my companion smiled.

"Oh if there's a chance of *your* thinking so my affair's in a bad way! I shan't ask you to steal for me, nor even to fib—for you *can't* fib, unless on paper. But the principal thing is this—to prevent her destroying the papers."

"Why I've no control of her," said Miss Tina. "It's she who controls me."

"But she doesn't control her own arms and legs, does she? The way she would naturally destroy her letters would be to burn them. Now she can't burn them without fire, and she can't get fire unless you give it her."

"I've always done everything she has asked," my poor friend pleaded. "Besides, there's Olimpia."

I was on the point of saying that Olimpia was probably corruptible, but I thought it best not to sound that note. So I simply put it that this frail creature might perhaps be managed.

"Everyone can be managed by my aunt," said Miss Tina. And then she remembered that her holiday was over; she must go home.

I laid my hand on her arm, across the table, to stay her a moment. "What I want of you is a general promise to help me."

"Oh how *can* I, how *can* I?" she asked, wondering and troubled. She was half-surprised, half-frightened at my attaching that importance to her, at my calling on her for action.

"This is the main thing: to watch our friend carefully and warn me in time, before she commits that dreadful sacrilege."

"I can't watch her when she makes me go out."

"That's very true."

"And when you do too."

"Mercy on us—do you think she'll have done anything to-night?"

"I don't know. She's very cunning."

"Are you trying to frighten me?" I asked.

I felt this question sufficiently answered when my companion murmured in a musing, almost envious way: "Oh but she loves them—she loves them!"

This reflexion, repeated with such emphasis, gave me great comfort; but to obtain more of that balm I said: "If she shouldn't intend to destroy the objects we speak of before her death she'll probably have made some disposition by will."

"By will?"

"Hasn't she made a will for your benefit?"

"Ah she has so little to leave. That's why she likes money," said Miss Tina.

"Might I ask, since we're really talking things over, what you and she live on?"

"On some money that comes from America, from a gentleman—I think a lawyer—in New York. He sends it every quarter. It isn't much!"

"And won't she have disposed of that?"

My companion hesitated—I saw she was blushing. "I believe it's mine," she said; and the look and tone which accompanied these words betrayed so the absence of the habit of thinking of herself that I almost thought her charming. The next instant she added: "But she had in an *avvocato* here once, ever so long ago. And some people came and signed something."

"They were probably witnesses. And you weren't asked to sign? Well then," I argued, rapidly and hopefully, "it's because you're the legatee. She must have left all her documents to you!"

"If she has it's with very strict conditions," Miss Tina responded, rising quickly, while the movement gave the words a small character of decision. They seemed to imply that the bequest would be accompanied with a proviso that the articles bequeathed should remain concealed from every inquisitive eye, and that I was very much mistaken if I thought her the person to depart from an injunction so absolute.

"Oh of course you'll have to abide by the terms," I said; and she uttered nothing to mitigate the rigour of this conclusion. None the less, later on, just before we disembarked at her own door after a return which had taken place almost in silence, she said to me abruptly: "I'll do what I can to help you." I was grateful for this—it was very well so far as it went; but it didn't keep me from remembering that night in a worried waking hour that I now had her word for it to re-enforce my own impression that the old woman was full of craft.

VII

The fear of what this side of her character might have led her to do made me nervous for days afterwards. I waited for an intimation from Miss Tina; I almost read it as her duty to keep me informed, to let me know definitely whether or no Miss Bordereau had sacrificed her treasures. But as she gave no sign I lost patience and determined to put the case to the very touch of my own senses. I sent late one afternoon to ask if I might pay the ladies a visit, and my servant came back with surprising news. Miss Bordereau could be approached without the least difficulty; she had been moved out into the sala and was sitting by the window that overlooked the garden.

I descended and found this picture correct; the old lady had been wheeled forth into the world and had a certain air, which came mainly perhaps from some brighter element in her dress, of being prepared again to have converse with it. It had not yet, however, begun to flock about her; she was perfectly alone and, though the door leading to her own quarters stood open, I had at first no glimpse of Miss Tina. The window at which she sat had the afternoon shade and, one of the shutters having been pushed back, she could see the pleasant garden, where the summer sun had by this time dried up too many of the plants—she could see the yellow light and the long shadows.

"Have you come to tell me you'll take the rooms for six months more?" she asked as I approached her, startling me by something coarse in her cupidity almost as much as if she hadn't already given me a specimen of it. Juliana's desire to make our acquaintance lucrative had been, as I have sufficiently indicated, a false note in my image of the woman who had inspired a great poet with immortal lines; but I may say here definitely that I after all recognised large allowance to be made for her. It was I who had kindled the unholy flame; it was I who had put into her head that she had the means of making money. She appeared never to have thought of that; she had been living wastefully for years, in a house five times too big for her, on a footing that I could explain only by the presumption that, excessive as it was, the space she enjoyed cost her next to nothing and that, small as were her revenues, they left her, for Venice, an appreciable margin. I had descended on her one day and taught her to calculate, and my almost extravagant comedy on the subject of the garden had presented me irresistibly in the light of a victim. Like all persons who achieve the miracle of changing their point of view late in life, she had been intensely converted: she had seized my hint with a desperate tremulous clutch.

I invited myself to go and get one of the chairs that stood, at a distance, against the wall—she had given herself no concern as to whether I should sit or stand; and while I placed it near her I began gaily: "Oh dear madam, what an imagination you have, what an intellectual sweep! I'm a poor devil of a man of letters who lives from day to day. How can I take palaces by the year? My existence is precarious. I don't know whether six months hence I shall have bread to put in my mouth. I've treated myself for once; it has been an immense luxury. But when it come to going on—!"

"Are your rooms too dear? if they are you can have more for the same money," Juliana responded. "We can arrange, we can *combinare*, as they say here."

"Well yes, since you ask me, they're too dear, much too dear," I said. "Evidently you suppose me richer than I am."

She looked at me as from the mouth of her cave. "If you write books don't you sell them?"

"Do you mean don't people buy them? A little, a very little—not so much as I could wish. Writing books, unless one be a great genius—and even then!—is the last road to fortune. I think there's no more money to be made by good letters."

"Perhaps you don't choose nice subjects. What do you write about?" Miss Bordereau implacably pursued.

"About the books of other people. I'm a critic, a commentator, an historian, in a small way." I wondered what she was coming to.

"And what other people now?"

"Oh better ones than myself: the great writers mainly—the great philosophers and poets of the past; those who are dead and gone and can't, poor darlings, speak for themselves."

"And what do you say about them?"

"I say they sometimes attached themselves to very clever women!" I replied as for pleasantness. I had measured, as I thought, my risk, but as my words fell upon the air they were to strike me as imprudent. However, I had launched them and I wasn't sorry, for perhaps after all the old woman would be willing to treat. It seemed tolerably obvious that she knew my secret: why therefore drag the process out? But she didn't take what I had said as a confession; she only asked:

"Do you think it's right to rake up the past?"

"I don't feel that I know what you mean by raking it up. How can we get at it unless we dig a little? The present has such a rough way of treading it down."

"Oh I like the past, but I don't like critics," my hostess declared with her hard complacency.

"Neither do I, but I like their discoveries."

"Aren't they mostly lies?"

"The lies are what they sometimes discover," I said, smiling at the quiet impertinence of this. "They often lay bare the truth."

"The truth is God's, it isn't man's: we had better leave it alone. Who can judge of it?—who can say?"

"We're terribly in the dark, I know," I admitted; "but if we give up trying what becomes of all the fine things? What becomes of the work I just mentioned, that of the great philosophers and poets? It's all vain words if there's nothing to measure it by."

"You talk as if you were a tailor," said Miss Bordereau whimsically; and then she added quickly and in a different manner: "This house is very fine; the proportions are magnificent. Today I wanted to look at this part again. I made them bring me out here. When your man came just now to learn if I would see you I was on the point of sending for you to ask if you didn't mean to go on. I wanted to judge what I'm letting you have. This sala is very grand," she pursued like an auctioneer, moving a little, as I guessed, her invisible eyes. "I don't believe you often have lived in such a house, eh?"

"I can't often afford to!" I said.

"Well then how much will you give me for six months?"

I was on the point of exclaiming—and the air of excruciation in my face would have denoted a moral face—"Don't, Juliana; for *his* sake, don't!" But I controlled myself and asked less passionately: "Why should I remain so long as that?"

"I thought you liked it," said Miss Bordereau with her shrivelled dignity.

"So I thought I should."

For a moment she said nothing more, and I left my own words to suggest to her what they might. I half-expected her to say, coldly enough, that if I had been disappointed we needn't continue the discussion, and this in spite of the fact that I believed her now to have in her mind—however it had come there—what would have told her that my disappointment was natural. But to my extreme surprise she ended by observing: "If you don't think we've treated you well enough perhaps we can discover some way of treating you better." This speech was somehow so incongruous that it made me laugh again, and I excused myself by saying that she talked as if I were a sulky boy pouting in the corner and having to be "brought round." I hadn't a grain of complaint to make; and could anything have exceeded Miss Tina's graciousness in accompanying me a few nights before to the Piazza? At this the old woman went on: "Well, you brought it on yourself!" And then in a different tone: "She's a very fine girl." I assented cordially to this proposition, and she expressed the hope that I did so not merely to be obliging, but that I really liked her. Meanwhile I wondered still more what Miss Bordereau was coming to. "Except for me, to-day," she said, "she hasn't a relation in the world." Did she by describing her niece as amiable and unencumbered wish to represent her as a *parti*?

It was perfectly true that I couldn't afford to go on with my rooms at a fancy price and that I had already devoted to my undertaking almost all the hard cash I had set apart for it. My patience and my time were by no means exhausted, but I should be able to draw upon them only on a more usual Venetian basis. I was willing to pay the precious personage with whom my pecuniary dealings were such a discord twice as much as any other *padrona di casa* would have asked, but I wasn't willing to pay her twenty times as much. I told her so plainly, and my plainness appeared to have some success, for she exclaimed: "Very good; you've done what I asked—you've made an offer!"

"Yes, but not for half a year. Only by the month."

"Oh I must think of that then." She seemed disappointed that I wouldn't tie myself to a period, and I guessed that she wished both to secure me and to discourage me; to say severely: "Do you dream that you can get off with less than six months? Do you dream that even by the end of that time you'll be appreciably nearer your victory?" What was most in my mind was that she had a fancy to play me the trick of making me engage myself when in fact she had sacrificed her treasure. There was a moment when my suspense on this point was so acute that I all but broke out with the question, and what kept it back was but an instinctive recoil—lest it should be a mistake—from the last violence of self-exposure. She was such a subtle old witch that one could never tell where one stood with her. You may imagine whether it cleared up the puzzle when, just after she had said she would think of my proposal and without any formal transition, she drew out of her pocket with an embarrassed hand a small object wrapped in crumpled white paper. She held it there a moment and then resumed: "Do you know much about curiosities?"

"About curiosities?"

"About antiquities, the old gimcracks that people pay so much for today. Do you know the kind of price they bring?"

I thought I saw what was coming, but I said ingenuously: "Do you want to buy something?"

"No, I want to sell. What would an amateur give me for that?" She unfolded the white paper and made a motion for me to take from her a small oval portrait. I possessed myself of it with fingers of which I could only hope that they didn't betray the intensity of their clutch, and she added: "I would part with it only for a good price."

At the first glance I recognised Jeffrey Aspern, and was well aware that I flushed with the act. As she was watching me however I had the consistency to exclaim: "What a striking face! Do tell me who he is."

"He's an old friend of mine, a very distinguished man in his day. He gave it me himself, but I'm afraid to mention his name, lest you never should have heard of him, critic and historian as you are. I know the world goes fast and one generation forgets another. He was all the fashion when I was young."

She was perhaps amazed at my assurance, but I was surprised at hers; at her having the energy, in her state of health and at her time of life, to wish to sport with me to that tune simply for her private entertainment—the humour to test me and practise on me and befool me. This at least was the interpretation that I put upon her production of the relic, for I couldn't believe she really desired to sell it or cared for any information I might give her. What she wished was to dangle it before my eyes and put a prohibitive price on it. "The face comes back to me, it torments me," I said, turning the object this way and that and looking at it very critically. It was a careful but not a supreme work of art, larger than the ordinary miniature and representing a young man with a remarkably handsome face, in a high-collared green coat and a buff waistcoat. I felt in the little work a virtue of likeness and judged it to have been painted when the model was about twenty-five. There are, as all the world knows, three other portraits of the poet in existence, but none of so early a date as this elegant image. "I've never seen the original, clearly a man of a past age, but I've seen other reproductions of this face," I went on. "You expressed doubt of this generation's having heard of the gentleman, but he strikes me for all the world as a celebrity. Now who is he? I can't put my finger on him—I can't give him a label. Wasn't he a writer? Surely he's a poet." I was determined that it should be she, not I, who should first pronounce Jeffrey Aspern's name.

My resolution was taken in ignorance of Miss Bordereau's extremely resolute character, and her lips never formed in my hearing the syllables that meant so much for her. She neglected to answer my question, but raised her hand to take back the picture, using a gesture which though impotent was in a high degree peremptory. "It's only a person who should know for himself that would give me my price," she said with a certain dryness.

"Oh then you have a price?" I didn't restore the charming thing; not from any vindictive purpose, but because I instinctively clung to it. We looked at each other hard while I retained it.

"I know the least I would take. What it occurred to me to ask you about is the most I shall be able to get."

She made a movement, drawing herself together as if, in a spasm of dread at having lost her prize, she had been impelled to the immense effort of rising to snatch it from me. I instantly placed it in her hand again, saying as I did so: "I should like to have it myself, but with your ideas it would be quite beyond my mark."

She turned the small oval plate over in her lap, with its face down, and I heard her catch her breath as after a strain or an escape. This however did not prevent her saying in a moment: "You'd buy a likeness of a person you don't know by an artist who has no reputation?"

"The artist may have no reputation, but that thing's wonderfully well painted," I replied, to give myself a reason.

"It's lucky you thought of saying that, because the painter was my father."

"That makes the picture indeed precious!" I returned with gaiety; and I may add that a part of my cheer came from this proof I had been right in my theory of Miss Bordereau's origin. Aspern had of course met the young lady on his going to her father's studio as a sitter. I observed to Miss Bordereau that if she would entrust me with her property for twenty-four hours I should be happy to take advice on it; but she made no other reply than to slip it in silence into her pocket. This convinced my still more that she had no sincere intention of selling it during her lifetime, though she may have desired to satisfy herself as to the sum her niece, should she leave it to her, might expect eventually to obtain for it. "Well, at any rate, I hope you won't offer it without giving me notice," I said as she remained irresponsive. "Remember me as a possible purchaser."

"I should want your money first!" she returned with un-expected rudeness; and then, as if she bethought herself that I might well complain of such a tone and wished to turn the matter off, asked abruptly what I talked about with her niece when I went out with her that way of an evening.

"You speak as if we had set up the habit," I replied. "Certainly I should be very glad if it were to become our pleasant custom. But in that case I should feel a still greater scruple at betraying a lady's confidence."

"Her confidence? Has my niece confidence?"

"Here she is—she can tell you herself," I said; for Miss Tina now appeared on the threshold of the old woman's parlour. "Have you confidence, Miss Tina? Your aunt wants very much to know."

"Not in her, not in her!" the younger lady declared, shaking her head with a dolefulness that was neither jocular nor affected. "I don't know what to do with her; she has fits of horrid imprudence. She's so easily tired—and yet she has begun to roam, to drag herself about the house." And she looked down at her yoke-fellow of long years with a vacancy of wonder, as if all their contact and custom hadn't made her perversities, on occasion, any more easy to follow.

"I know what I'm about. I'm not losing my mind. I dare say you'd like to think so," said Miss Bordereau with a crudity of cynicism.

"I don't suppose you came out here yourself. Miss Tina must have had to lend you a hand," I interposed for conciliation.

"Oh she insisted we should push her; and when she insists!" said Miss Tina, in the same tone of apprehension: as if there were no knowing what service she disapproved of her aunt might force her next to render.

"I've always got most things done I wanted, thank God! The people I've lived with have humoured me," the old woman continued, speaking out of the white ashes of her vanity.

I took it pleasantly up. "I suppose you mean they've obeyed you."

"Well, whatever it is—when they like one."

"It's just because I like you that I want to resist," said Miss Tina with a nervous laugh.

"Oh I suspect you'll bring Miss Bordereau upstairs next to pay me a visit," I went on; to which the old lady replied:

"Oh no; I can keep an eye on you from here!"

"You're very tired; you'll certainly be ill tonight!" cried Miss Tina.

"Nonsense, dear; I feel better at this moment than I've done for a month. Tomorrow I shall come out again. I want to be where I can see this clever gentleman."

"Shouldn't you perhaps see me better in your sitting-room?" I asked.

"Don't you mean shouldn't you have a better chance at *me*?" she returned, fixing me a moment with her green shade.

"Ah I haven't that anywhere! I look at you but don't see you."

"You agitate her dreadfully—and that's not good," said Miss Tina, giving me a reproachful deterrent headshake.

"I want to watch you—I want to watch you!" Miss Bordereau went on.

"Well then let us spend as much of our time together as possible—I don't care where. That will give you every facility."

"Oh I've seen you enough for today. I'm satisfied. Now I'll go home," Juliana said. Miss Tina laid her hands on the back of the wheeled chair and began to push, but I begged her to let me take her place. "Oh yes, you may move me this way—you shan't in any other!" the old woman cried as she felt herself propelled firmly and easily over the smooth hard floor. Before we reached the door of her own apartment she bade me stop, and she took a long last look up and down the noble sala. "Oh it's a prodigious house!" she murmured; after which I pushed her forward. When we had entered the parlour Miss Tina let me know she should now be able to manage, and at the same moment the little red-haired *donna* came to meet her mistress. Miss Tina's idea was evidently to get her aunt immediately back to bed. I confess that in spite of this urgency I was guilty of the indiscretion of lingering; it held me there to feel myself so close to the objects I coveted—which would be probably put away somewhere in the faded unsociable room. The place had indeed a bareness that suggested no hidden values; there were neither dusky nooks nor curtained corners, neither massive cabinets nor chests with iron bands. Moreover it was possible, it was perhaps even likely, that the old lady had consigned her relics to her bedroom, to some battered box that was shoved under the bed, to the drawer of some lame dressing-table, where they would be in the range of vision by the dim night-lamp. None the less I turned an eye on every article of furniture, on every conceivable cover for a hoard, and noticed that there were half a dozen things with drawers, and in particular a tall old secretary with brass ornaments of the style of the Empire—a receptacle somewhat infirm but still capable of keeping rare secrets. I don't know why this article so engaged me, small purpose as I had of breaking into it; but I stared at it so hard that Miss Tina noticed me and changed colour. Her doing this made me think I was right and that, wherever they might have been before, the Aspern papers at that moment languished behind the peevish little lock of the secretary. It was hard to turn my attention from the dull mahogany front when I reflected that a plain panel divided me from the goal of my hopes; but I gathered up my slightly scattered prudence and with an effort took leave of my hostess. To make the effort graceful I said to her that I should certainly bring her an opinion about the little picture.

"The little picture?" Miss Tina asked in surprise.

"What do *you* know about it, my dear?" the old woman demanded. "You needn't mind. I've fixed my price."

"And what may that be"

"A thousand pounds."

"Oh Lord!" cried poor Miss Tina irrepressibly.

"Is that what she talks to you about?" said Miss Bordereau.

"Imagine your aunt's wanting to know!" I had to separate from my younger friend with only those words, though I should have liked immensely to add: "For heaven's sake meet me tonight in the garden!"

VIII

As it turned out the precaution had not been needed, for three hours later, just as I had finished my dinner, Miss Tina appeared, unannounced, in the open doorway of the room in which my simple repasts were served. I remember well that I felt no surprise at seeing her; which is not a proof of my not believing in her timidity. It was immense, but in a case in which there was a particular reason for boldness it never would have prevented her from running up to my floor. I saw that she was now quite full of a particular reason; it threw her forward—made her seize me, as I rose to meet her, by the arm.

"My aunt's very ill; I think she's dying!"

"Never in the world," I answered bitterly. "Don't you be afraid!"

"Do go for a doctor—do, do! Olimpia's gone for the one we always have, but she doesn't come back; I don't know what has happened to her. I told her that if he wasn't at home she was to follow him where he had gone; but apparently she's following him all over Venice. I don't know what to do—she looks so as if she were sinking."

"May I see her, may I judge?" I asked. "Of course I shall be delighted to bring someone; but hadn't we better send my man instead, so that I may stay with you?"

Miss Tina assented to this and I dispatched my servant for the best doctor in the neighbourhood. I hurried downstairs with her, and on the way she told me that an hour after I quitted them in the afternoon Miss Bordereau had had an attack of "oppression," a terrible difficulty in breathing. This had subsided, but had left her so exhausted that she didn't come up; she seemed all spent and gone. I repeated that she wasn't gone, that she wouldn't go yet; whereupon Miss Tina gave me a sharper sidelong glance than she had ever favoured me withal and said: "Really, what do you mean? I suppose you don't accuse her of making-believe!" I forget what reply I made to this, but I fear that in my heart I thought the old woman capable of any weird manœuvre. Miss Tina wanted to know what I had done to her; her aunt had told her I had made her so angry. I declared I had done nothing whatever—I had been exceedingly careful; to which my companion rejoined that our friend had assured her she had had a scene with me—a scene that had upset her. I answered with some resentment that the scene had been of *her* making—that I couldn't think what she was angry with me for unless for not seeing my way to give a thousand pounds for the portrait of Jeffrey Aspern. "And did she show you that? Oh gracious—oh deary me?" groaned Miss Tina, who seemed to feel the situation pass out of her control and the elements of her fate thicken round her. I answered her I'd give anything to possess it, yet that I had no thousand pounds; but I stopped when we came to the door of Miss Bordereau's room. I had an immense curiosity to pass it, but I thought it my duty to represent to Miss Tina that if I made the invalid angry she ought perhaps to be spared the sight of me. "The sight of you? Do you think she can *see?*" my companion demanded almost with indignation. I did think so but forbore to say it, and I softly followed my conductress.

I remember that what I said to her as I stood for a moment beside the old woman's bed was: "Does she never show you her eyes then? Have you never seen them?" Miss Bordereau had been divested of her green shade, but—it was not my fortune to behold Juliana in her nightcap—the upper half of her face was covered by the fall of a piece of dingy lacelike muslin, a sort of extemporised hood which, wound round her head, descended to the end of her nose, leaving nothing visible but her white withered cheeks and puckered mouth, closed tightly and, as it were, consciously. Miss Tina gave me a glance of surprise, evidently not seeing a reason for my impatience. "You mean she always wears something? She does it to preserve them."

"Because they're so fine?"

"Oh today, today!" And Miss Tina shook her head speaking very low. "But they used to be magnificent!"

"Yes indeed,—we've Aspern's word for that." And as I looked again at the old woman's wrappings I could imagine her not having wished to allow any supposition that the great poet had overdone it. But I didn't waste my time in considering Juliana, in whom the appearance of respiration was so slight as to suggest that no human attention could ever help her more. I turned my eyes once more all over the room, rummaging with them the closets, the chests of drawers, the tables. Miss Tina at once noted their direction and read, I think, what was in them; but she didn't answer it, turning away restlessly, anxiously, so that I felt rebuked, with reason, for an appetite well-nigh indecent in the presence of our dying companion. All the same I took another view, endeavouring to pick out mentally the receptacle to try first, for a person who should wish to put his hand on Miss Bordereau's papers directly after her death. The place was a dire confusion; it looked like the dressing-room of an old actress. There were clothes hanging over chairs, odd-looking shabby bundles here and there, and various pasteboard boxes piled together, battered, bulging and discoloured, which might have been fifty years old. Miss Tina after a moment noticed the direction of my eyes again, and, as if she guessed how I judged such appearances—forgetting I had no business to judge them at all—said, perhaps to defend herself from the imputation of complicity in the disorder:

"She likes it this way; we can't move things. There are old bandboxes she has had most of her life." Then she added, half-taking pity on my real thought: "Those things were *there*." And she pointed to a small low trunk which stood under a sofa that just allowed room for it. I struck me as a queer superannuated coffer, of painted wood, with elaborate handles and shrivelled straps and with the colour—it had last been endued with a coat of light green—much rubbed off. It evidently had travelled with

Juliana in the olden time—in the days of her adventures, which it had shared. It would have made a strange figure arriving at a modern hotel.

"*Were* there—they aren't now?" I asked, startled by Miss Tina's implication.

She was going to answer, but at that moment the doctor came in—the doctor whom the little maid had been sent to fetch and whom she had at last overtaken. My servant, going on his own errand, had met her with her companion in tow, and in the sociable Venetian spirit, retracing his steps with them, had also come up to the threshold of the padrona's room, where I saw him peep over the doctor's shoulder. I motioned him away the more instantly that the sight of his prying face reminded me how little I myself had to do there— an admonition confirmed by the sharp way the little doctor eyed me, his air of taking me for a rival who had the field before him. He was a short fat brisk gentleman who wore the tall hat of his profession and seemed to look at everything but his patient. He kept me still in range, as if it struck him I too should be better for a dose, so that I bowed to him and left him with the women, going down to smoke a cigar in the garden. I was nervous; I couldn't go further; I couldn't leave the place. I don't know exactly what I thought might happen, but I felt it important to be there. I wandered about the alleys—the warm night had come on—smoking cigar after cigar and studying the light in Miss Bordereau's windows. They were open now, I could see; the situation was different. Sometimes the light moved, but not quickly; it didn't suggest the hurry of a crisis. Was the old woman dying or was she already dead? Had the doctor said that there was nothing to be done at her tremendous age but to let her quietly pass away? or had he simply announced with a look a little more conventional that the end of the end had come? Were the other two women just going and coming over the offices that follow in such a case? It made me uneasy not to be nearer, as if I thought the doctor himself might carry away the papers with him. I bit my cigar hard while it assailed me again that perhaps there were now no papers to carry!

I wandered about an hour and more. I looked out for Miss Tina at one of the windows, having a vague idea that she might come there to give me some sign. Wouldn't she see the red tip of my cigar in the dark and feel sure I was hanging on to know what the doctor had said? I'm afraid it's a proof of the grossness of my anxieties that I should have taken in some degree for granted at such an hour, in the midst of the greatest change that could fall on her, poor Miss Tina's having also a free mind for them. My servant came down and spoke to me; he knew nothing save that the doctor had gone after a visit of half an hour. If he had stayed half an hour then Miss Bordereau was still alive: it couldn't have taken so long to attest her decease. I sent the man out of the house; there were moments when the sense of his curiosity annoyed me, and this was one of them. *He* had been watching my cigar-tip from an upper window, if Miss Tina hadn't; he couldn't know what I was after and I couldn't tell him, though I suspected in him fantastic private theories about me which he thought fine and which, had I more exactly known them, I should have thought offensive.

I went upstairs at last, but I mounted no higher than the sala. The door of Miss Bordereau's apartment was open, showing from the parlour the dimness of a poor candle. I went toward it with a light tread, and at the same moment Miss Tina appeared and stood looking at me as I approached. "She's better, she's better," she said even before I had asked. "The doctor has given her something; she woke up, came back to life while he was there. He says there's no immediate danger."

"No immediate danger? Surely he thinks her condition serious."

"Yes, because she had been excited. That affects her dreadfully."

"It will do so again then, because she works herself up. She did so this afternoon."

"Yes, she mustn't come out any more," said Miss Tina with

one of her lapses into a deeper detachment.

"What's the use of making such a remark as that," I permitted myself to ask, "if you begin to rattle her about again the first time she bids you?"

"I won't—I won't do it any more."

"You must learn to resist her," I went on.

"Oh yes, I shall; I shall do so better if you tell me it's right."

"You mustn't do it for me—you must do it for yourself. It all comes back to you, if you're scared and upset."

"Well, I'm not upset now," said Miss Tina placidly enough. "She's very quiet."

"Is she conscious again—does she speak?"

"No, she doesn't speak, but she takes my hand. She holds it fast."

"Yes," I returned, "I can see what force she still has by the way she grabbed that picture this afternoon. But if she holds you fast how comes it that you're here?"

Miss Tina waited a little; though her face was in deep shadow—she had her back to the light in the parlour and I had put down my own candle far off, near the door of the sala—I thought I saw her smile ingenuously. "I came on purpose—I had heard your step."

"Why I came on tiptoe, as soundlessly as possible."

"Well, I had heard you," said Miss Tina.

"And is your aunt alone now?"

"Oh no—Olimpia sits there."

On my side I debated. "Shall we then pass in there?" And I nodded at the parlour; I wanted more and more to be on the spot.

"We can't talk there—she'll hear us."

I was on the point of replying that in that case we'd sit silent, but I felt too much this wouldn't do, there was something I desired so immensely to ask her. Thus I hinted we might walk a little in the sala, keeping more at the other end, where we shouldn't disturb our friend. Miss Tina assented uncon-ditionally; the doctor was coming again, she said, and she would be there to meet him at the door. We strolled through the fine superfluous hall, where on the marble floor—particularly as at first we said nothing—our footsteps were more audible than I had expected. When we reached the other end—the wide window, inveterately closed, connecting with the balcony that overhung the canal—I submitted that we had best remain there, as she would see the doctor arrive the sooner. I opened the window and we passed out on the balcony. The air of the canal seemed even heavier, hotter than that of the sala. The place was hushed and void; the quiet neighbourhood had gone to sleep. A lamp, here and there, over the narrow black water, glimmered in double; the voice of a man going homeward singing, his jacket on his shoulder and his hat on his ear, came to us from a distance. This didn't prevent the scene from being very *comme il faut*, as Miss Bordereau had called it the first time I saw her. Presently a gondola passed along the canal with its slow rhythmical plash, and as we listened we watched it in silence. It didn't stop, it didn't carry the doctor; and after it had gone on I said to Miss Tina:

"And where are they now—the things that were in the trunk?"

"In the trunk?"

"That green box you pointed out to me in her room. You said her papers had been there; you seemed to mean she had transferred them."

"Oh yes; they're not in the trunk," said Miss Tina.

"May I ask if you've looked?"

"Yes, I've looked—for you."

"How for me, dear Miss Tina? Do you mean you'd have given them to me if you had found them?"—and I fairly trembled with the question.

She delayed to reply and I waited. Suddenly she broke out: "I don't know what I'd do—what I wouldn't!"

"Would you look again—somewhere else?"

She had spoken with a strange unexpected emotion, and she went on in the same tone: "I can't—I can't—while she lies there.

It isn't decent."

"No, it isn't decent," I replied gravely. "Let the poor lady rest in peace." And the words, on my lips, were not hypocritical, for I felt reprimanded and shamed.

Miss Tina added in a moment, as if she had guessed this and were sorry for me, but at the same time wished to explain that I did push her, or at least harp on the chord, too much: "I can't deceive her that way. I can't deceive her—perhaps on her deathbed."

"Heaven forbid I should ask you, though I've been guilty myself!"

"You've been guilty?"

"I've sailed under false colours." I felt now I must make a clean breast of it, must tell her I had given her an invented name on account of my fear her aunt would have heard of me and so refuse to take me in. I explained this as well as that I had really been a party to the letter addressed them by John Cumnor months before.

She listened with great attention, almost in fact gaping for wonder, and when I had made my confession she said: "Then your real name—what is it?" She repeated it over twice when I had told her, accompanying it with the exclamation "Gracious, gracious!" Then she added: "I like your own best."

"So do I"—and I felt my laugh rueful. "Ouf! it's a relief to get rid of the other."

"So it was a regular plot—a kind of conspiracy?"

"Oh a conspiracy—we were only two," I replied, leaving out of course Mrs. Prest.

She considered; I thought she was perhaps going to pronounce us very base. But this was not her way, and she remarked after a moment, as in candid impartial contemplation: "How much you must want them!"

"Oh I do, passionately!" I grinned, I fear, to admit. And this chance made me go on, forgetting my compunction of a moment before. "How can she possibly have changed their place herself? How can she walk? How can she arrive at that sort of muscular exertion? How can she lift and carry things?"

"Oh when one wants and when one has so much will!" said Miss Tina as if she had thought over my question already herself and had simply had no choice but that answer—the idea that in the dead of night, or at some moment when the coast was clear, the old woman had been capable of a miraculous effort.

"Have you questioned Olimpia? Hasn't she helped her—hasn't she done it for her?" I asked; to which my friend replied promptly and positively that their servant had had nothing to do with the matter, though without admitting definitely that she had spoken to her. I was as if she were a little shy, a little ashamed now, of letting me see how much she had entered into my uneasiness and had me on her mind. Suddenly she said to me without any immediate relevance:

"I rather feel you a new person, you know, now that you've a new name."

"It isn't a new one; it's a very good old one, thank fortune!"

She looked at me a moment. "Well, I do like it better."

"Oh if you didn't I would almost go on with the other!"

"Would you really?"

I laughed again, but I returned for all answer: "Of course if she can rummage about that way she can perfectly have burnt them."

"You must wait—you must wait," Miss Tina mournfully moralised; and her tone ministered little to my patience, for it seemed after all to accept that wretched possibility. I would teach myself to wait, I declared nevertheless; because in the first place I couldn't do otherwise and in the second I had her promise, given me the other night, that she would help me.

"Of course if the papers are gone that's no use," she said; not as if she wished to recede, but only to be conscientious.

"Naturally. But if you could only find out!" I groaned, quivering again.

"I thought you promised you'd wait."

"Oh you mean wait even for that?"

"For what then?"

"Ah nothing," I answered rather foolishly, being ashamed to tell her what had been implied in my acceptance of delay—the idea that she would perhaps do more for me than merely find out.

I know not if she guessed this; at all events she seemed to bethink herself of some propriety of showing me more rigour. "I didn't promise to deceive, did I? I don't think I did."

"It doesn't much matter whether you did or not, for you couldn't!"

Nothing is more possible than that she wouldn't have contested this even hadn't she been diverted by our seeing the doctor's gondola shoot into the little canal and approach the house. I noted that he came as fast as if he believed our proprietress still in danger. We looked down at him while he disembarked and then went back into the sala to meet him. When he came up, however, I naturally left Miss Tina to go off with him alone, only asking her leave to come back later for news.

I went out of the house and walked far, as far as the Piazza, where my restlessness declined to quit me. I was unable to sit down; it was very late now though there were people still at the little tables in front of the cafés: I could but uneasily revolve, and I did so half a dozen times. The only comfort, none the less, was in my having told Miss Tina who I really was. At last I took my way home again, getting gradually and all but inextricably lost, as I did whenever I went out in Venice: so that it was considerably past midnight when I reached my door. The sala, upstairs, was as dark as usual and my lamp as I crossed it found nothing satisfactory to show me. I was disappointed, for I had notified Miss Tina that I would come back for a report, and I thought she might have left a light there as a sign. The door of the ladies' apartment was closed; which seemed a hint that my faltering friend had gone to bed in impatience of waiting for me. I stood in the middle of the place, considering, hoping she would hear me and perhaps peep out, saying to myself too that she would never go to bed with her aunt in a state so critical; she would sit up and watch— she would be in a chair, in her dressing-gown. I went nearer the door; I stopped there and listened. I heard nothing at all and at last I tapped gently. No answer came and after another minute I turned the handle. There was no light in the room; this ought to have prevented my entrance, but it had no such effect. If I have frankly stated the importunities, the indelicacies, of which my desire to possess myself of Jeffrey Aspern's papers had made me capable I needn't shrink, it seems to me, from confessing this last indiscretion. I regard it as the worst thing I did, yet there were extenuating circumstances. I was deeply though doubtless not disinterestedly anxious for more news of Juliana, and Miss Tina had accepted from me, as it were, a rendezvous which it might have been a point of honour with me to keep. It may be objected that her leaving the place dark was a positive sign that she released me, and to this I can only reply that I wished not to be released.

The door of Miss Bordereau's room was open and I could see beyond it the faintness of a taper. There was no sound—my footstep caused no one to stir. I came further into the room; I lingered there lamp in hand. I wanted to give Miss Tina a chance to come to me if, as I couldn't doubt, she were still with her aunt. I made no noise to call her; I only waited to see if she wouldn't notice my light. She didn't, and I explained this—I found afterwards I was right—by the idea that she had fallen asleep. If she had fallen asleep her aunt was not on her mind, and my explanation ought to have led me to go out as I had come. I must repeat again that it didn't, for I found myself at the same moment given up to something else. I had no definite purpose, no bad intention, but felt myself held to the spot by an acute, though absurd, sense of opportunity. Opportunity for what I couldn't have said, inasmuch as it wasn't in my mind that I might proceed to thievery. Even had this tempted me I was confronted with the evident fact that Miss Bordereau didn't leave her secretary, her cupboard and the drawers of her tables gaping. I had no keys, no tools and no ambition to smash her furniture. None the less it came to me that I was now, perhaps alone, unmolested, at the hour of freedom and safety, nearer to the source of my hopes than I had ever been. I held up my lamp, let the light play on the different objects as if it could tell me something. Still there came no movement from the other room. If Miss Tina was sleeping she was sleeping sound. Was she doing so—generous creature—on purpose to leave me the field? Did she know I was there and was she just keeping quiet to see what I would do—what I *could* do? Yet might I, when it came to that? She herself knew even better than I how little.

I stopped in front of the secretary, gaping at it vainly and no doubt grotesquely; for what had it to say to me after all? In the first place it was locked, and in the second it almost surely contained nothing in which I was interested. Ten to one the papers had been destroyed, and even if they hadn't the keen old woman wouldn't have put them in such a place as that after removing them from the green trunk—wouldn't have transferred them, with the idea of their safety on her brain, from the better hiding-place to the worse. The secretary was more conspicuous, more exposed in a room in which she could no longer mount guard. It opened with a key, but there was a small brass handle, like a button, as well: I saw this as I played my lamp over it. I did something more, for the climax of my crisis; I caught a glimpse of the possibility that Miss Tina wished me really to understand. If she didn't so wish me, if she wished me to keep away, why hadn't she locked the door of communication between the sitting-room and the sala? That would have been a definite sign that I was to leave them alone. If I didn't leave them alone she meant me to come for a purpose—a purpose now represented by the super-subtle inference that to oblige me she had unlocked the secretary. She hadn't left the key, but the lid would probably move if I touched the button. This possibility pressed me hard and I bent very close to judge. I didn't propose to do anything, not even—not in the least—to let down the lid; I only wanted to test my theory, to see if the cover *would* move. I touched the button with my hand—a mere touch would tell me; and as I did so—it is embarrassing for me to relate it—I looked over my shoulder. It was a chance, an instinct, for I had really heard nothing. I almost let my luminary drop and certainly I stepped back, straightening myself up at what I saw. Juliana stood there in her night-dress, by the doorway of her room, watching me; her hands were raised, she had lifted the everlasting curtain that covered half her face, and for the first, the last, the only time I beheld her extraordinary eyes. They glared at me; they were like the sudden drench, for a caught burglar, of a flood of gaslight; they made me horribly ashamed. I never shall forget her strange little bent white tottering figure, with its lifted head, her attitude, her expression; neither shall I forget the tone in which as I turned, looking at her, she hissed out passionately, furiously:

"Ah you publishing scoundrel!"

I can't now say what I stammered to excuse myself, to explain; but I went toward her to tell her I meant no harm. She waved me off with her old hands, retreating before me in horror; and the next thing I knew she had fallen back with a quick spasm, as if death had descended on her, into Miss Tina's arms.

IX

I left Venice the next morning, directly on learning that my hostess had not succumbed, as I feared at the moment, to the shock I had given her—the shock I may also say she had given me. How in the world could I have supposed her capable of getting out of bed by herself? I failed to see Miss Tina before going; I only saw the *donna*, whom I entrusted with a note for her younger mistress. In this note I mentioned that I should be absent but a few days. I went to Treviso, to Bassano, to Castelfranco; I took walks and drives and looked at musty old churches with ill-lighted pictures; I spent hours seated smoking at the doors of cafés, where there were flies and yellow curtains, on the shady side of sleepy little squares. In spite of these pastimes, which were mechanical and perfunctory, I scantly enjoyed my travels: I had had to gulp down a bitter draught and couldn't get rid of the taste. It had been devilish awkward, as the young men say, to be found by Juliana in the dead of night examining the attachment of her bureau; and it had not been less so to have to believe for a good many hours after that it was highly probable I had killed her. My humiliation galled me, but I had to make the best of it, had, in writing to Miss Tina, to minimise it, as well as account for the posture in which I had been discovered. As she gave me no word of answer I couldn't know what impression I made on her. It rankled for me that I had been called a publishing scoundrel, since certainly I did publish and no less certainly hadn't been very delicate. There was a moment when I stood convinced that the only way to purge my dishonour was to take myself straight away on the instant; to sacrifice my hopes and relieve the two poor women for ever of the oppression of my intercourse. Then I reflected that I had better try a short absence first, for I must already have had a sense (unexpressed and dim) that in disappearing completely it wouldn't be merely my own hopes I should condemn to extinction. It would perhaps answer if I kept dark long enough to give the elder lady time to believe herself rid of me. That she would wish to be rid of me after this—if I wasn't rid of her—was now not to be doubted: that midnight monstrosity would have cured her of the disposition to put up with my company for the sake of my dollars. I said to myself that after all I couldn't abandon Miss Tina, and I continued to say this even while I noted that she quite ignored my earnest request—I had given her two or three addresses, at little towns, *poste restante*—for some sign of her actual state. I would have made my servant write me news but that he was unable to manage a pen. Couldn't I measure the scorn of Miss Tina's silence—little disdainful as she had ever been? Really the soreness pressed; yet if I had scruples about going back I had others about not doing so, and I wanted to put myself on a better footing. The end of it was that I did return to Venice on the twelfth day; and as my gondola gently bumped against our palace steps a fine palpitation of suspense showed me the violence my absence had done me.

I had faced about so abruptly that I hadn't even telegraphed to my servant. He was therefore not at the station to meet me, but he poked out his head from an upper window when I reached the house. "They have put her into earth, *quella vecchia*," he said to me in the lower hall while he shouldered my valise; and he grinned and almost winked as if he knew I should be pleased with his news.

"She's dead!" I cried, giving him a very different look.

"So it appears, since they've buried her."

"It's all over then? When was the funeral?"

"The other yesterday. But a funeral you could scarcely call it, signore: *roba da niente—un piccolo passeggio brutto* of two gondolas. Poveretta!" the man continued, referring apparently to Miss Tina. His conception of funerals was that they were mainly to amuse the living.

I wanted to know about Miss Tina, how she might be and generally where; but I asked him no more questions till we had got upstairs. Now that the fact had met me I took a bad view of it, especially of the idea that poor Miss Tina had had to manage by herself after the end. What did she know about arrangements, about the steps to take in such a case? Poveretta indeed! I could only hope the doctor had given her support and that she hadn't been neglected by the old friends of whom she had told me, the little band of the faithful whose fidelity consisted in coming to the house once a year. I elicited from my servant that two old ladies and an old gentleman had in fact rallied round Miss Tina and had supported her—they had come for her in a gondola of their own—during the journey to the cemetery, the little red-walled island of tombs which lies to the north of the town and on the way to Murano. It appeared from these signs that the Misses Bordereau were Catholics, a discovery I had never made, as the old woman couldn't go to church and her niece, so far as I perceived, either didn't, or went only to early mass in the parish before I was stirring. Certainly even the priests respected their seclusion; I had never caught the whisk of the curato's skirt. That evening, an hour later, I sent my servant down with five words on a card to ask if Miss Tina would see me a few moments. She was not in the house, where he had sought her, he told me when he came back, but in the garden walking about to refresh herself and picking the flowers quite as if they belonged to her. He had found her there and she would be happy to see me.

I went down and passed half an hour with poor Miss Tina. She had always had a look of musty mourning, as if she were wearing out old robes of sorrow that wouldn't come to an end; and in this particular she made no different show. But she clearly had been crying, crying a great deal—simply, satisfyingly, refreshingly, with a primitive retarded sense of solitude and violence. But she had none of the airs or graces of grief, and I was almost surprised to see her stand there in the first dusk with her hands full of admirable roses and smile at me with reddened eyes. Her white face, in the frame of her mantilla, looked longer, leaner than usual. I hadn't doubted her being irreconcileably disgusted with me, her considering I ought to have been on the spot to advise her, to help her; and, though I believed there was no rancour in her composition and no great conviction of the importance of her affairs, I had prepared myself for a change in her manner, for some air of injury and estrangement, which should say to my conscience: "Well, you're a nice person to have professed things!" But historic truth compels me to declare that this poor lady's dull face ceased to be dull, almost ceased to be plain, as she turned it gladly to her late aunt's lodger. That touched him extremely and he thought it simplified his situation until he found it didn't. I was as kind to her that evening as I knew how to be, and I walked about the garden with her as long as seemed good. There was no explanation of any sort between us; I didn't ask her why she hadn't answered my letter. Still less did I repeat what I had said to her in that communication; if she chose to let me suppose she had forgotten the position in which Miss Bordereau had surprised me and the effect of the discovery on the old woman, I was quite willing to take it that way: I was grateful to her for not treating me as if I had killed her aunt.

We strolled and strolled, though really not much passed between us save the recognition of her bereavement, conveyed in my manner and in the expression she had of depending on me now, since I let her see I still took an interest in her. Miss Tina's was no breast for the pride or the pretence of independence; she didn't in the least suggest that she knew at present what would become of her. I forbore to press on that question, however, for I certainly was not prepared to say that I would take charge of her. I was cautious; not ignobly, I think, for I felt her knowledge of life to be so small that in her unsophisticated vision there would be no reason why—since I seemed to pity her—I shouldn't somehow look after her. She told me how her aunt had died, very peacefully at the last, and how everything had been done afterwards by the care of her good friends—fortunately, thanks to me, she said, smiling, there was money in the house. She repeated that when once the "nice" Italians like you they are your friends for life, and when we had gone into this she asked me about my *giro*, my impressions, my adventures, the places I had seen. I told her what I could, making it up partly, I'm afraid, as in my disconcerted state I had taken little in; and after she had heard me she exclaimed, quite as if she had forgotten her aunt and her sorrow, "Dear, dear, how much I should like to do such things—to take an amusing little journey!" It came over me for the moment that I ought to propose some enterprise, say I would accompany her anywhere she liked; and I remarked at any rate that a pleasant excursion—to give her a change—might be managed: we would think of it, talk it over. I spoke never a word of the Aspern documents, asked no question as to what she had ascertained or what had otherwise happened with regard to them before Juliana's death. It wasn't that I wasn't on pins and needles to know, but that I thought it more decent not to show greed again so soon after the catastrophe. I hoped she herself would say something, but she never glanced that way, and I thought this natural at the time. Later on, however, that night, it occurred to me that her silence was matter for suspicion; since if she had talked of my movements, of anything so detached as the Giorgione at Castelfranco, she might have alluded to what she could easily remember was in my mind. It was not to be supposed the emotion produced by her aunt's death had blotted out the recollection that I was interested in that lady's relics, and I fidgeted afterwards as it came to me that her reticence might very possibly just mean that no relics survived. We separated in the garden—it was she who said she must go in; now that she was alone on the *piano nobile* I felt that (judged at any rate by Venetian ideas) I was on rather a different footing in regard to the invasion of it. As I shook hands with her for good-night I asked if she had some general plan, had thought over what she had best do. "Oh yes, oh yes, but I haven't settled anything yet," she replied quite cheerfully. Was her cheerfulness explained by the impression that I would settle for her?

I was glad the next morning that we had neglected practical questions, as this gave me a pretext for seeing her again immediately. There was a practical enough question now to be touched on. I owed it to her to let her know formally that of course I didn't expect her to keep me on as a lodger, as also to show some interest in her own tenure, what she might have on her hands in the way of a lease. But I was not destined, as befell, to converse with her for more than an instant on either of these points. I sent her no message; I simply went down to the sala and walked to and fro there. I knew she would come out; she would promptly see me accessible. Somehow I preferred not to be shut up with her; gardens and big halls seemed better places to talk. It was a splendid morning, with something in the air that told of the waning of the long Venetian summer; a freshness from the sea that stirred the flowers in the garden and made a pleasant draught in the house, less shuttered and darkened now than when the old woman was alive. It was the beginning of autumn, of the end of the golden months. With this it was the end of my experiment—or would be in the course of half an hour, when I should really have learned that my dream had been reduced to ashes. After that there would be nothing left for me but to go to the station; for seriously—and as it struck me in the morning light—I couldn't linger there to act as guardian to a piece of middle-aged female helplessness. If she hadn't saved the papers wherein should I be indebted to her? I think I winced a little as I asked myself how much, if she *had* saved them, I should have to recognise and, as it were, reward such a courtesy. Mightn't that service after all saddle me with a guardianship? If this idea didn't make me more uncomfortable as I walked up and down it was because I was convinced I had nothing to look to. If the old woman hadn't destroyed everything before she pounced on me in the parlour she had done so the next day.

It took Miss Tina rather longer than I had expected to act on my calculation; but when at last she came out she looked at me without surprise. I mentioned I had been waiting for her and she asked why I hadn't let her know. I was glad a few hours later on that I had checked myself before remarking that a friendly intuition might have told her: it turned to comfort for me that I hadn't played even to that mild extent on her sensibility. What I did say was virtually the truth—that I was too nervous, since I expected her now to settle my fate.

"Your fate?" said Miss Tina, giving me a queer look; and as she spoke I noticed a rare change in her. Yes, she was other than she had been the evening before—less natural and less easy. She had been crying the day before and was not crying now, yet she struck me as less confident. It was as if something had happened to her during the night, or at least as if she had thought of something that troubled her—something in particular that affected her relations with me, made them more embarrassing and more complicated. Had she simply begun to feel that her aunt's not being there now altered my position?

"I mean about our papers. *Are* there any? You must know now."

"Yes, there are a great many; more than I supposed." I was struck with the way her voice trembled as she told me this.

"Do you mean you've got them in there—and that I may see them?"

"I don't think you can see them," said Miss Tina with an extraordinary expression of entreaty in her eyes, as if the dearest hope she had in the world now was that I wouldn't take them from her. But how could she expect me to make such a sacrifice as that after all that had passed between us? What had I come back to Venice for but to see them, to take them? My joy at learning they were still in existence was such that if the poor woman had gone down on her knees to beseech me never to mention them again I would have treated the proceeding as a bad joke. "I've got them but I can't show them," she lamentably added.

"Not even to me? Ah Miss Tina!" I broke into a tone of infinite remonstrance and reproach.

She coloured and the tears came back to her eyes; I measured the anguish it cost her to take such a stand, which a dreadful sense of duty had imposed on her. It made me quite sick to find myself confronted with that particular obstacle; all the more that it seemed to me I had been distinctly encouraged to leave it out of account. I quite held Miss Tina to have assured me that if she had no greater hindrance than that—! "You don't mean to say you made her a deathbed promise? It was precisely against your doing anything of that sort that I thought I was safe. Oh I would rather she had burnt the papers outright than have to reckon with such a treachery as that."

"No, it isn't a promise," said Miss Tina.

"Pray what is it then?"

She hung fire, but finally said: "She tried to burn them, but I prevented it. She had hid them in her bed."

"In her bed—?"

"Between the mattresses. That's where she put them when she took them out of the trunk. I can't understand how she did it, because Olimpia didn't help her. She tells me so and I believe her. My aunt only told her afterwards, so that she shouldn't undo the bed—anything but the sheets. So it was very badly made," added Miss Tina simply.

"I should think so! And how did she try to burn them?"

"She didn't try much; she was too weak those last days. But she told me—she charged me. Oh it was terrible! She couldn't speak after that night. She could only make signs."

"And what did you do?"

"I took them away. I locked them up."

"In the secretary?"

"Yes, in the secretary," said Miss Tina, reddening again.

"Did you tell her you'd burn them?"

"No, I didn't—on purpose."

"On purpose to gratify me?"

"Yes, only for that."

"And what good will you have done me if after all you won't show them?"

"Oh none. I know that—I know that," she dismally sounded.

"And did she believe you had destroyed them?"

"I don't know what she believed at the last. I couldn't tell—she was too far gone."

"Then if there was no promise and no assurance I can't see what ties you."

"Oh she hated it so—she hated it so! She was so jealous. But here's the portrait—you may have that," the poor woman announced, taking the little picture, wrapped up in the same manner in which her aunt had wrapped it, out of her pocket.

"I may have it—do you mean you give it to me?" I gasped as it passed into my hand.

"Oh yes."

"But it's worth money—a large sum."

"Well!" said Miss Tina, still with her strange look.

I didn't know what to make of it, for it could scarcely mean that she wanted to bargain like her aunt. She spoke as for making me a present. "I can't take it from you as a gift," I said, "and yet I can't afford to pay you for it according to the idea Miss Bordereau had of its value. She rated it at a thousand pounds."

"Couldn't we sell it?" my friend threw off.

"God forbid! I prefer the picture to the money."

"Well then keep it."

"You're very generous."

"So are you."

"I don't know why you should think so," I returned; and this was true enough, for the good creature appeared to have in her mind some rich reference that I didn't in the least seize.

"Well, you've made a great difference for me," she said.

I looked at Jeffrey Aspern's face in the little picture, partly in order not to look at that of my companion, which had begun to trouble me, even to frighten me a little—it had taken so very odd, so strained and unnatural a cast. I made no answer to this last declaration; I but privately consulted Jeffrey Aspern's delightful eyes with my own—they were so young and brilliant and yet so wise and so deep: I asked him what on earth was the matter with Miss Tina. He seemed to smile at me with mild mockery; he might have been amused at my case. I had got into a pickle for him—as if he needed it! He was unsatisfactory for the only moment since I had known him. Nevertheless, now that I held the little picture in my hand I felt it would be a precious possession. "Is this a bribe to make me give up the papers?" I presently and all perversely asked. "Much as I value this, you know, if I were to be obliged to choose the papers are what I should prefer. Ah but ever so much!"

"How can you choose—how can you choose?" Miss Tina returned slowly and woefully.

"I see! Of course there's nothing to be said if you regard the interdiction that rests on you as quite insurmountable. In this case it must seem to you that to part with them would be an impiety of the worst kind, a simple sacrilege!"

She shook her head, only lost in the queerness of her case. "You'd understand if you had known her. I'm afraid," she quavered suddenly—"I'm afraid! She was terrible when she was angry."

"Yes, I saw something of that, that night. She was terrible. Then I saw her eyes. Lord, they were fine!"

"I see them—they stare at me in the dark!" said Miss Tina.

"You've grown nervous with all you've been through."

"Oh yes, very—very!"

"You mustn't mind; that will pass away," I said kindly. Then I added resignedly, for it really seemed to me that I must accept the situation: "Well, so it is, and it can't be helped. I must renounce." My friend, at this, with her eyes on me, gave a low soft moan, and I went on: "I only wish to goodness she had destroyed them: then there would be nothing more to say. And I can't understand why, with her ideas, she didn't."

"Oh she lived on them!" said Miss Tina.

"You can imagine whether that makes me want less to see them," I returned not quite so desperately. "But don't let me stand here as if I had it in my soul to tempt you to anything base. Naturally, you understand, I give up my rooms. I leave Venice immediately." And I took up my hat, which I had placed on a chair. We were still rather awkwardly on our feet in the middle of the sala. She had left the door of the apartments open behind her, but had not led me that way.

A strange spasm came into her face as she saw me take my hat. "Immediately—do you mean today?" The tone of the words was tragic—they were a cry of desolation.

"Oh no; not so long as I can be of the least service to you."

"Well, just a day or two more—just two or three days," she panted. Then controlling herself she added in another manner: "She wanted to say something to me—the last day—something very particular. But she couldn't."

"Something very particular?"

"Something more about the papers."

"And did you guess—have you any idea?"

"No, I've tried to think—but I don't know. I've thought all kinds of things."

"As for instance?"

"Well, that if you were a relation it would be different."

I wondered. "If I were a relation—?"

"If you weren't a stranger. Then it would be the same for you as for me. Anything that's mine would be yours, and you could do what you like. I shouldn't be able to prevent you—and you'd have no responsibility."

She brought out this droll explanation with a nervous rush and as if speaking words got by heart. They gave me the impression of a subtlety which at first I failed to follow. But after a moment her face helped me to see further, and then the queerest of lights came to me. It was embarrassing, and I bent my head over Jeffrey Aspern's portrait. What an odd expression was in his face! "Get out of it as you can, my dear fellow!" I put the picture into the pocket of my coat and said to Miss Tina: "Yes, I'll sell it for you. I shan't get a thousand pounds by any means, but I shall get something good."

She looked at me through pitiful tears, but seemed to try to smile as she returned: "We can divide the money."

"No, no, it shall be all yours." Then I went on: "I think I know what your poor aunt wanted to say. She wanted to give directions that her papers should be buried with her."

Miss Tina appeared to weigh this suggestion; after which she answered with striking decision, "Oh no, she wouldn't have thought that safe!"

"It seems to me nothing could be safer."

"She had an idea that when people want to publish they're capable—!" And she paused, very red.

"Of violating a tomb? Mercy on us, what must she have thought of me!"

"She wasn't just, she wasn't generous!" my companion cried

103

with sudden passion.

The light that had come into my mind a moment before spread further. "Ah don't say that, for we *are* a dreadful race." Then I pursued: "If she left a will, that may give you some idea."

"I've found nothing of the sort—she destroyed it. She was very fond of me," Miss Tina added with an effect of extreme inconsequence. "She wanted me to be happy. And if any person should be kind to me—she wanted to speak of that."

I was almost awestricken by the astuteness with which the good lady found herself inspired, transparent astuteness as it was and stitching, as the phrase is, with white thread. "Depend upon it she didn't want to make any provision that would be agreeable to *me*."

"No, not to you, but quite to me. She knew I should like it if you could carry out your idea. Not because she cared for you, but because she did think of me," Miss Tina went on with her unexpected persuasive volubility. "You could see the things— you could use them." She stopped, seeing I grasped the sense of her conditional—stopped long enough for me to give some sign that I didn't give. She must have been conscious, however, that though my face showed the greatest embarrassment ever painted on a human countenance it was not set as a stone, it was also full of compassion. It was a comfort to me a long time afterwards to consider that she couldn't have seen in me the smallest symptom of disrespect. "I don't know what to do; I'm too tormented, I'm too ashamed!" she continued with vehemence. Then turning away from me and burying her face in her hands she burst into a flood of tears. If she didn't know what to do it may be imagined whether I knew better. I stood there dumb, watching her while her sobs resounded in the great empty hall. In a moment she was up at me again with her streaming eyes. "I'd give you everything, and she'd understand, where she is—she'd forgive me!"

"Ah Miss Tina—ah Miss Tina," I stammered for all reply. I didn't know what to do, as I say, but at a venture I made a wild vague movement in consequence of which I found myself at the door. I remember standing there and saying "It wouldn't do, it wouldn't do!"—saying it pensively, awkwardly, grotesquely, while I looked away to the opposite end of the sala as at something very interesting. The next thing I remember is that I was downstairs and out of the house. My gondola was there and my gondolier, reclining on the cushions, sprang up as soon as he saw me. I jumped in and to his usual "*Dove commanda?*" replied, in a tone that made him stare: "Anywhere, anywhere; out into the lagoon!"

He rowed me away and I sat there prostrate, groaning softly to myself, my hat pulled over my brow. What in the name of the preposterous did she mean if she didn't mean to offer me her hand? That was the price—that was the price! And did she think I wanted it, poor deluded infatuated extravagant lady? My gondolier, behind me, must have seen my ears red as I wondered, motionless there under the fluttering *tenda* with my hidden face, noticing nothing as we passed—wondered whether her delusion, her infatuation had been my own reckless work. Did she think I had made love to her even to get the papers? I hadn't, I hadn't; I repeated that over to myself for an hour, for two hours, till I was wearied if not convinced. I don't know where, on the lagoon, my gondolier took me; we floated aimlessly and with slow rare strokes. At last I became conscious that we were near the Lido, far up, on the right hand, as you turn your back to Venice, and I made him put me ashore. I wanted to walk, to move, to shed some of my bewilderment. I crossed the narrow strip and got to the sea-beach—I took my way toward Malamocco. But presently I flung myself down again on the warm sand, in the breeze, on the coarse dry grass. It took it out of me to think I had been so much at fault, that I had unwittingly but none the less deplorably trifled. But I hadn't given her cause—distinctly I hadn't. I had said to Mrs. Prest that I would make love to her; but it had been a joke without consequences and I had never said it to my victim. I had been as kind as possible because I really liked her; but since when had that become a crime where a woman of such an age and such an appearance was concerned? I am far from remembering clearly the succession of events and feelings during this long day of confusion, which I spent entirely in wandering about, without going home, until late at night: it only comes back to me that there were moments when I pacified my conscience and others when I lashed it into pain. I didn't laugh all day—that I do recollect; the case, however it might have struck others, seemed to me so little amusing. I should have been better employed perhaps in taking in the comic side of it. At any rate, whether I had given cause or not, there was no doubt whatever that I couldn't pay the price. I couldn't accept the proposal. I couldn't, for a bundle of tattered papers, marry a ridiculous pathetic provincial old woman. It was a proof of how little she supposed the idea would come to me that she should have decided to suggest it herself in that practical argumentative heroic way—with the timidity, however, so much more striking than the boldness, that her reasons appeared to come first and her feelings afterward.

As the day went on I grew to wish I had never heard of Aspern's relics, and I cursed the extravagant curiosity that had put John Cumnor on the scent of them. We had more than enough material without them, and my predicament was the just punishment of that most fatal of human follies, our not having known when to stop. It was very well to say it was no predicament, that the way out was simple, that I had only to leave Venice by the first train in the morning, after addressing Miss Tina a note which should be placed in her hand as soon as I got clear of the house; for it was strong proof of my quandary that when I tried to make up the note to my taste in advance—I would put it on paper as soon as I got home, before going to bed—I couldn't think of anything but "How can I thank you for the rare confidence you've placed in me?" That would never do; it sounded exactly as if an acceptance were to follow. Of course I might get off without writing at all, but that would be brutal, and my idea was still to exclude brutal solutions. As my confusion cooled I lost myself in wonder at the importance I had attached to Juliana's crumpled scraps; the thought of them became odious to me and I was as vexed with the old witch for the superstition that had prevented her from destroying them as I was with myself for having already spent more money than I could afford in attempting to control their fate. I forget what I did, where I went after leaving the Lido and at what hour or with what recovery of composure I made my way back to my boat. I only know that in the afternoon, when the air was aglow with the sunset, I was standing before the church of Saints John and Paul and looking up at the small square-jawed face of Bartolommeo Colleoni, the terrible *condottiere* who sits so sturdily astride of his huge bronze horse on the high pedestal on which Venetian gratitude maintains him. The statue is incomparable, the finest of all mounted figures, unless that of Marcus Aurelius, who rides benignant before the Roman Capitol, be finer: but I was not thinking of that; I only found myself staring at the triumphant captain as if he had had an oracle on his lips. The western light shines into all his grimness at that hour and makes it wonderfully personal. But he continued to look far over my head, at the red immersion of another day—he had seen so many go down into the lagoon through the centuries—and if he were thinking of battles and stratagems they were of a different quality from any I had to tell him of. He couldn't direct me what to do, gaze up at him as I might. Was it before this or after that I wandered about for an hour in the small canals, to the continued stupefaction of my gondolier, who had never seen me so restless and yet so void of a purpose and could extract from me no order but "Go anywhere—everywhere—all over the place"? He reminded me that I had not lunched and expressed therefore respectfully the hope that I would dine earlier. He had had long periods of leisure during the day, when I had left the boat and rambled, so that I was not obliged to consider him, and I told him that till the morrow, for reasons, I should touch no meat. It was an effect of

107

poor Miss Tina's proposal, not altogether auspicious, that I had quite lost my appetite. I don't know why it happened that on this occasion I was more than ever struck with that queer air of sociability, of cousinship and family life, which makes up half the expression of Venice. Without streets and vehicles, the uproar of wheels, the brutality of horses, and with its little winding ways where people crowd together, where voices sound as in the corridors of a house, where the human step circulates as if it skirted the angles of furniture and shoes never wear out, the place has the character of an immense collective apartment, in which Piazza San Marco is the most ornamented corner and palaces and churches, for the rest, play the part of great divans of repose, tables of entertainment, expanses of decoration. And somehow the splendid common domicile, familiar domestic and resonant, also resembles a theatre with its actors clicking over bridges and, in straggling processions, tripping along fondamentas. As you sit in your gondola the footways that in certain parts edge the canals assume to the eye the importance of a stage, meeting it at the same angle, and the Venetian figures, moving to and fro against the battered scenery of their little houses of comedy, strike you as members of an endless dramatic troupe.

I went to bed that night very tired and without being able to compose an address to Miss Tina. Was this failure the reason why I became conscious the next morning as soon as I awoke of a determination to see the poor lady again the first moment she would receive me? That had something to do with it, but what had still more was the fact that during my sleep the oddest revulsion had taken place in my spirit. I found myself aware of this almost as soon as I opened my eyes: it made me jump out of my bed with the movement of a man who remembers that he has left the house-door ajar or a candle burning under a shelf. Was I still in time to save my goods? That question was in my heart; for what had now come to pass was that in the unconscious cerebration of sleep I had swung back to a passionate appreciation of Juliana's treasure. The pieces composing it were now more precious than ever and a positive ferocity had come into my need to acquire them. The condition Miss Tina had attached to that act no longer appeared an obstacle worth thinking of, and for an hour this morning my repentant imagination brushed it aside. It was absurd I should be able to invent nothing; absurd to renounce so easily and turn away helpless from the idea that the only way to become possessed was to unite myself to her for life. I mightn't unite myself, yet I might still have what she had. I must add that by the time I sent down to ask if she would see me I had invented no alternative, though in fact I drew out my dressing in the interest of my wit. This failure was humiliating, yet what could the alternative be? Miss Tina sent back word I might come; and as I descended the stairs and crossed the sala to her door—this time she received me in her aunt's forlorn parlour—I hoped she wouldn't think my announcement was to be "favourable." She certainly would have understood my recoil of the day before.

As soon as I came into the room I saw that she had done so, but I also saw something which had not been in my forecast. Poor Miss Tina's sense of her failure had produced a rare alteration in her, but I had been too full of stratagems and spoils to think of that. Now I took it in; I can scarcely tell how it startled me. She stood in the middle of the room with a face of mildness bent upon me, and her look of forgiveness, of absolution, made her angelic. It beautified her; she was younger; she was not a ridiculous old woman. This trick of her expression, this magic of her spirit, transfigured her, and while I still noted it I heard a whisper somewhere in the depths of my conscience: "Why not, after all—why not?" It seemed to me I *could* pay the price. Still more distinctly however than the whisper I heard Miss Tina's own voice. I was so struck with the different effect she made on me that at first I wasn't clearly aware of what she was saying; then I recognised she had bade me good-bye—she said something about hoping I should be very happy.

"Good-bye—good-bye?" I repeated with an inflexion interrogative and probably foolish.

I saw she didn't feel the interrogation, she only heard the words: she had strung herself up to accepting our separation and they fell upon her ear as a proof. "Are you going today?" she asked. "But it doesn't matter, for whenever you go I shall not see you again. I don't want to." And she smiled strangely, with an infinite gentleness. She had never doubted my having left her the day before in horror. How *could* she, since I hadn't come back before night to contradict, even as a simple form, even as an act of common humanity, such an idea? And now she had the force of soul—Miss Tina with force of soul was a new conception—to smile at me in her abjection.

"What shall you do—where shall you go?" I asked.

"Oh I don't know. I've done the great thing. I've destroyed the papers."

"Destroyed them?" I wailed.

"Yes; what was I to keep them for? I burnt them last night, one by one, in the kitchen."

"One by one?" I coldly echoed it.

"It took a long time—there were so many." The room seemed to go round me as she said this and a real darkness for a moment descended on my eyes. When it passed Miss Tina was there still, but the transfiguration was over and she had changed back to a plain dingy elderly person. It was in this character she spoke as she said "I can't stay with you longer, I can't"; and it was in this character she turned her back upon me, as I had turned mine upon her twenty-four hours before, and moved to the door of her room. Here she did what I hadn't done when I quitted her—she paused long enough to give me one look. I have never forgotten it and I sometimes still suffer from it, though it was not resentful. No, there was no resentment, nothing hard or vindictive in poor Miss Tina; for when, later, I sent her, as the price of the portrait of Jeffrey Aspern, a larger sum of money than I had hoped to be able to gather for her, writing to her that I had sold the picture, she kept it with thanks; she never sent it back. I wrote her that I had sold the picture, but I admitted to Mrs. Prest at the time—I met this other friend in London that autumn—that it hangs above my writing-table. When I look at it I can scarcely bear my loss— I mean of the precious papers.

THE LIAR

THE LIAR

I

The train was half an hour late and the drive from the station longer than he had supposed, so that when he reached the house its inmates had dispersed to dress for dinner and he was conducted straight to his room. The curtains were drawn in this asylum, the candles lighted, the fire bright, and when the servant had quickly put out his clothes the comfortable little place might have been one of the minor instruments in a big orchestra—seemed to promise a pleasant house, a various party, talk, acquaintances, affinities, to say nothing of very good cheer. He was too occupied with his profession often to pay country visits, but he had heard people who had more time for them speak of establishments where "they do you very well." He foresaw that the proprietors of Stayes would do him very well. In his bedroom on such occasions he always looked first at the books on the shelf and the prints on the walls; these things would give in a sort the social, the conversational value of his hosts. Though he had but little time to devote to them on this occasion a cursory inspection assured him that if the literature, as usual, was mainly American and humorous the art consisted neither of the water-colour studies of the children nor of "goody" engravings. The walls were adorned with old-fashioned lithographs, mostly portraits of country gentlemen with high collars and riding-gloves: this suggested—and it was encouraging—that the tradition of portraiture was held in esteem. There was the customary novel of Mr. Le Fanu for the bedside, the ideal reading in a country house for the hours after midnight. Oliver Lyon could scarcely forbear beginning it while he buttoned his shirt.

Perhaps that is why he not only found everyone assembled in the hall when he went down, but saw from the way the move to dinner was instantly made that they had been waiting for him. There was no delay to introduce him to a lady, for he went out unimportant and in a group of unmated men. The men, straggling behind, sidled and edged as usual at the door of the dining-room, and the *dénouement* of this little comedy was that he came to his place last of all. This made him suppose himself in a sufficiently distinguished company, for if he had been humiliated—which he was not—he couldn't have consoled himself with the reflexion that such a fate was natural to an obscure and struggling young artist. He could no longer think of himself as notably young, alas, and if his position wasn't so brilliant as it ought to be he could no longer justify it by calling it a struggle. He was appreciably "known" and was now apparently in a society of the known if not of the knowing. This idea added to the curiosity with which he looked up and down the long table as he settled himself in his place.

It was a numerous party—five-and-twenty people; rather an odd occasion to have proposed to him, as he thought. He wouldn't be surrounded by the quiet that ministers to good work; however, it had never interfered with his work to feel the human scene enclose it as a ring. And though he didn't know this, it was never quiet at Stayes. When he was working well he found himself in that happy state—the happiest of all for an artist—in which things in general interweave with his particular web and make it thicker and stronger and more many-coloured. Moreover there was an exhilaration (he had felt it before) in the rapid change of scene—the jump, in the dusk of the afternoon, from foggy London and his familiar studio to a centre of festivity in the middle of Hertfordshire and a drama half-acted, a drama of pretty women and noted men and wonderful orchids in silver jars. He observed as a not unimportant fact that one of the pretty women was beside him: a gentleman sat on his other hand. But he appraised his neighbours little as yet: he was busy with the question of Sir David, whom he had never seen and about whom he naturally was curious.

Evidently, however, Sir David was not at dinner, a circumstance sufficiently explained by the other circumstance forming our friend's principal knowledge of him—his being ninety years of age. Oliver Lyon had looked forward with pleasure to painting a picked nonagenarian, so that though the old man's absence from table was something of a disappointment—it was an opportunity the less to observe him before going to work—it seemed a sign that he was rather a sacred and perhaps therefore an impressive relic. Lyon looked at his son with the greater interest—wondered if the glazed bloom of such a cheek had been transmitted from Sir David. That would be jolly to paint in the old man—the withered ruddiness of a winter apple, especially if the eye should be still alive and the white hair carry out the frosty look. Arthur Ashmore's hair had a midsummer glow, but Lyon was glad his call had been for the great rather than the small bearer of the name, in spite of his never having seen the one and of the other's being seated there before him now in the very highest relief of impersonal hospitality.

Arthur Ashmore was a fresh-coloured thick-necked English gentleman, but he was just not a subject; he might have been a farmer and he might have been a banker; you could scarcely paint him in character. His wife didn't make up the amount; she was a large bright negative woman who had the same air as her husband of being somehow tremendously new; an appearance as of fresh varnish—Lyon could scarcely tell whether it came from her complexion or from her clothes—so that one felt she ought to sit in a gilt frame and be dealt with by reference to a catalogue or a price-list. It was as if she were already rather a bad though expensive portrait, knocked off by an eminent hand, and Lyon had no wish to copy that work. The pretty woman on his right was engaged with her neighbour, while the gentleman on his other side looked detached and desperate, so that he had time to lose himself in his favourite diversion of watching face after face. This amusement gave him the greatest pleasure he knew, and he often thought it a mercy the human mask did interest him and that it had such a need, frequently even in spite of itself, to testify, since he was to make his living by reproducing it. Even if Arthur Ashmore wouldn't be inspiring to paint (a certain anxiety rose in him lest, should he make a hit with her father-in-law, Mrs. Arthur should take it into her head that he had now proved himself worthy to handle her husband); even if he had looked a little less like a page—fine as to print and margin—without punctuation, he would still be a refreshing iridescent surface. But the gentleman four persons off—what was he? Would he be a subject, or was his face only the legible door-plate of his identity, burnished with punctual washing and shaving—the least thing that was decent you might know him by?

This face arrested Oliver Lyon, striking him at first as very handsome. The gentleman might still be called young, and his features were regular: he had a plentiful fair moustache that curled up at the ends, a brilliant gallant almost adventurous air, together with a big shining breastpin in the middle of his shirt. He appeared a fine satisfied soul, and Lyon perceived that wherever he rested his friendly eye there fell an influence as pleasant as the September sun—as if he could make grapes and pears or even human affection ripen by looking at them. What was odd in him was a certain mixture of the correct and the extravagant: as if he were an adventurer imitating a gentleman with rare perfection, or a gentleman who had taken a fancy to go about with hidden arms. He might have been a dethroned prince or the war-correspondent of a newspaper: he re-presented both enterprise and tradition, good manners and bad taste. Lyon at length fell into conversation with the lady beside him—they dispensed, as he had had to dispense at dinner-parties before, with an introduction—by asking who this personage might be.

"Oh Colonel Capadose, don't you know?" Lyon didn't know and asked for further information. His neighbour had a sociable manner and evidently was accustomed to quick transitions; she turned from her other interlocutor with the promptness of a good cook who lifts the cover of the next saucepan. "He has been a great deal in India—isn't he rather celebrated?" she put it. Lyon confessed he had never heard of him, and she went on: "Well, perhaps he isn't; but he says he is, and if you think it that's just the same, isn't it?"

"If *you* think it?"

"I mean if he thinks it—that's just as good, I suppose."

"Do you mean if he thinks he has done things he hasn't?"

"Oh dear no; because I never really know the difference between what people say—! He's exceedingly clever and amusing—quite the cleverest person in the house, unless indeed you're more so. But that I can't tell yet, can I? I only know about the people I know; I think that's celebrity enough!"

"Enough for them?"

"Oh I see you're clever. Enough for me! But I've heard of you," the lady went on. "I know your pictures; I admire them. But I don't think you look like them."

"They're mostly portraits," Lyon said; "and what I usually try for is not my own resemblance."

"I see what you mean. But they've much more colour. Don't you suppose Vandyke's things tell a lot about him? And now you're going to do someone here?"

"I've been invited to do Sir David. I'm rather disappointed at not seeing him this evening."

"Oh he goes to bed at some unnatural hour—eight o'clock, after porridge and milk. You know he's rather an old mummy."

"An old mummy?" Oliver Lyon repeated.

"I mean he wears half a dozen waistcoats and sits by the fire. He's always cold."

"I've never seen him and never seen any portrait or photograph of him," Lyon said. "I'm surprised at his never having had anything done—at their waiting all these years."

"Ah that's because he was afraid, you know; it was his pet superstition. He was sure that if anything were done he would die directly afterwards. He has only consented today."

"He's ready to die then?"

"Oh now he's so old he doesn't care."

"Well, I hope I shan't kill him," said Lyon. "It was rather unnatural of his son to send for me."

"Oh they've nothing to gain—everything is theirs already!" his companion rejoined, as if she took this speech quite literally. Her talkativeness was systematic—she fraternised as seriously as she might have played whist. "They do as they like—they fill the house with people—they have *carte blanche*."

"I see—but there's still the 'title.'"

"Yes, but what's the tuppenny title?"

Our artist broke into laughter at this, whereat his companion stared. Before he had recovered himself she was scouring the plain with her other neighbour. The gentleman on his left at last risked an observation as if it had been a move at chess, exciting in Lyon however a comparative wantonness. This personage played his part with difficulty: he uttered a remark as a lady fires a pistol, looking the other way. To catch the ball Lyon had to bend his ear, and this movement led to his observing a handsome creature who was seated on the same side, beyond his interlocutor. Her profile was presented to him and at first he was only struck with its beauty; then it produced an impression still more agreeable—a sense of undimmed remembrance and intimate association. He had not recognised her on the instant only because he had so little expected to see her there; he had not seen her anywhere for so long, and no news of her now ever came to him. She was often in his thoughts, but she had passed out of his life. He thought of her twice a week; that may be called often, even for fidelity, when it has been kept up a dozen years. The moment after he recognised her he felt how true it was that only she could carry that head, the most charming head in the world and of which there could never be a replica. She was leaning forward a little; she remained in profile, slightly turned to some further neighbour. She was listening, but her eyes moved, and after a moment Lyon followed their direction. They rested on the gentleman who had been described to him as Colonel Capadose—rested, he made out, as with an habitual visible complacency. This was not strange, for the Colonel was unmistakeably formed to attract the sympathetic gaze of woman; but Lyon felt it as the source of an ache that she could let *him* look at her so long without giving him a glance. There was nothing between them today and he had no rights, but she must have known he was coming—it was of course no such tremendous event, but she couldn't have been staying in the house without some echo of it—and it wasn't natural this should absolutely fail to affect her.

She was looking at Colonel Capadose as if she had been in love with him—an odd business for the proudest, most reserved of women. But doubtless it was all right if her husband was satisfied: he had heard indefinitely, years before, that she was married, and he took for granted—as he had not heard—the presence of the happy man on whom she had conferred what she had refused to a poor art-student at Munich. Colonel Capadose seemed aware of nothing, and this fact, incongruously enough, rather annoyed Lyon than pleased him. Suddenly the lady moved her head, showing her full face to our hero. He was so prepared with a greeting that he instantly smiled, as a shaken jug overflows; but she made no response, turned away again and sank back in her chair. All her face said in that instant was "You see I'm as handsome as ever." To which he mentally subjoined: "Yes, and as much good as ever it does me!" He asked the young man beside him if he knew who that beautiful being was—the fourth person beyond him. The young man leaned forward, considered and then said: "I think she's Mrs. Capadose."

"Do you mean his wife—that fellow's?" And Lyon indicated the subject of the information given him by his other neighbour.

"Oh is *he* Mr. Capadose?" said the young man, to whom it appeared to mean little. He admitted his ignorance of these values and explained it by saying that there were so many people and he had come but the day before. What was definite to our friend was that Mrs. Capadose was in love with her husband—so that he wished more than ever he might have married her.

"She's very fond and true," he found himself saying three minutes later, with a small ironic ring, to the lady on his right. He added that he meant Mrs. Capadose.

"Ah you know her then?"

"I knew her once upon a time—when I was living abroad."

"Why then were you asking me about her husband?"

"Precisely for that reason." Lyon was clear. "She married after that—I didn't even know her present name."

"How then do you know it now?"

"This gentleman has just told me—he appears to know."

"I didn't know he knew anything," said the lady with a crook that took him in.

"I don't think he knows anything but that."

"Then you've found out for yourself that she's—what do you call it?—tender and true? What do you mean by that?"

"Ah you mustn't question me—I want to put things to *you*," Lyon said. "How do you all like her here?"

"You ask too much! I can only speak for myself. I think she's hard."

"That's only because she's honest and straight-forward."

"Do you mean I like people in proportion as they deceive?"

"I think we all do, so long as we don't find them out," Lyon said. "And then there's something in her face—a sort of nobleness of the Roman type, in spite of her having such English eyes. In fact she's English down to the ground; but her complexion, her low forehead and that beautiful close little wave in her dark hair make her look like a transfigured Trasteverina."

"Yes, and she always sticks pins and daggers into her head, to bring out that effect. I must say I like her husband better: he *gives* so much."

"Well, when I knew her there was no comparison that could injure her," Lyon richly sighed. "She was altogether the most delightful thing in Munich."

"In Munich?"

"Her people lived there; they weren't rich—in pursuit of

economy in fact, and Munich was very cheap. Her father was the younger son of some noble house; he had married a second time and had a lot of little mouths to feed. She was the child of the first wife and didn't like her stepmother, but she was charming to her little brothers and sisters. I once made a sketch of her as Werther's Charlotte cutting bread and butter while the children clustered round her. All the artists in the place were in love with her, but she wouldn't look at 'the likes' of us. She was too proud—I grant you that, but not stuck up nor young-ladyish, only perfectly simple and frank about it. She used to remind me of Thackeray's Ethel Newcome. She told me she must marry well: it was the one thing she could do for her family. I suppose you'd say she *has* married well."

"She told *you?*" smiled Lyon's neighbour.

"Oh of course I proposed to her too. But she evidently thinks so herself!" he added. "I mean that it's no mistake."

When the ladies left the table the host as usual bade the gentlemen draw together, so that Lyon found himself opposite to Colonel Capadose. The conversation was mainly about the "run," for it had apparently been a great day in the hunting-field. Most of the men had a comment or an anecdote, several had many; but the Colonel's pleasant voice was the most audible in the chorus. It was a bright and fresh but masculine organ, just such a voice as, to Lyon's sense, such a "fine man" ought to have had. It appeared from his allusions that he was a very straight rider, which was also very much what Lyon would have expected. Not that he swaggered, for his points were all quietly and casually made; but they had all to do with some dangerous experiment or close shave. Lyon noted after a little that the attention paid by the company to the Colonel's remarks was not in direct proportion to the interest they seemed to offer; the result of which was that the speaker, who noticed that *he* at least was listening, began to treat him as his particular auditor and to fix his eyes on him as he talked. Lyon had nothing to do but to look sympathetic and assent—the narrator building on the tribute so rendered. A neighbouring squire had had an accident; he had come a cropper in an awkward place—just at the finish—with consequences that looked grave. He had struck his head; he remained insensible up to the last accounts: there had evidently been concussion of the brain. There was some exchange of views as to his recovery, how soon it would take place or whether it would take place at all; which led the Colonel to confide to our artist across the table that *he* shouldn't despair of a fellow even if he didn't come round for weeks—for weeks and weeks and weeks—for months, almost for years. He leaned forward (Lyon leaned forward to listen) and mentioned that he knew from personal experience how little limit there really was to the time a fellah might lie like a stone without being the worse for it. It had happened to him in Ireland years before; he had been pitched out of a dogcart, had turned a sheer somersault and landed on his head. They had thought he was dead, but he wasn't; they had carried him first to the nearest cabin, where he lay for some days with the pigs, and then to an inn in a neighbouring town—it was a near thing they hadn't put him underground. He had been completely insensible—without a ray of recognition of any human thing—for three whole months; hadn't had a glimmer of consciousness of any blessed thing. It had been touch and go to that degree that they couldn't come near him, couldn't feed him, could scarcely look at him. Then one day he had opened his eyes—as fit as a flea!

"I give you my honour it had done me good—it rested my brain." He conveyed, though without excessive emphasis, that with an intelligence so active as his these periods of repose were providential. Lyon was struck by his story, but wanted to ask if he hadn't shammed a little; not in relating it, only in keeping so quiet. He hesitated however, in time, to betray a doubt—he was so impressed with the tone in which Colonel Capadose pronounced it the turn of a hair that they hadn't buried him alive. That had happened to a friend of his in India—a fellow who was supposed to have died of jungle-fever and whom they clapped into a coffin. He was going on to recite the further fate of this unfortunate gentleman when Mr. Ashmore said a word and everyone rose for the move to the drawing-room. Lyon noticed that by this time no one was heeding his new friend's prodigies. These two came round on either side of the table and met while their companions hung back for each other.

"And do you mean your comrade was literally buried alive?" asked Lyon in some suspense.

The Colonel looked at him as with the thread of the conversation already lost. Then his face brightened—and when it brightened it was doubly handsome. "Upon my soul he was shoved into the ground!"

"And left there?"

"Left there till I came and hauled him out."

"*You* came?"

"I dreamed about him—it's the most extraordinary story: I heard him calling to me in the night. I took on myself to dig him up. You know there are people in India—a kind of beastly race, the ghouls—who violate graves. I had a sort of presentiment that they would get at him first. I rode straight, I can tell you; and, by Jove, a couple of them had just broken ground! Crack—crack from a couple of barrels, and they showed me their heels as you may believe. Would you credit that I took him out myself? The air brought him round and he was none the worse. He has got his pension—he came home the other day. He'd do anything for me," the narrator added.

"He called to you in the night?" said Lyon, much thrilled.

"That's the interesting point. Now *what was it?* It wasn't his ghost, because he wasn't dead. It wasn't himself, because he couldn't. It was some confounded brain-wave or other! You see India's a strange country—there's an element of the mysterious: the air's full of things you can't explain."

They passed out of the dining-room, and this master of anecdote, who went among the first, was separated from his newest victim; but a minute later, before they reached the drawing-room, he had come back. "Ashmore tells me who you are. Of course I've often heard of you. I'm very glad to make your acquaintance. My wife used to know you."

"I'm glad she remembers me. I recognised her at dinner and was afraid she didn't."

"Ah I dare say she was ashamed," said the Colonel with genial ease.

"Ashamed of me?" Lyon replied in the same key.

"Wasn't there something about a picture? Yes; you painted her portrait."

"Many times," Lyon said; "and she may very well have been ashamed of what I made of her."

"Well, *I* wasn't, my dear sir; it was the sight of that picture, which you were so good as to present to her, that made me first fall in love with her."

Our friend lived over again for a few seconds a lost felicity. "Do you mean one with the children—cutting bread and butter?"

"Bread and butter? Bless me, no—vine-leaves and a leopard-skin. A regular Bacchante."

"Ah yes," said Lyon; "I remember. It was the first decent portrait I painted. I should be curious to see it today."

"Don't ask her to show it to you—she'll feel it awkward," the Colonel went on.

"Awkward?"—our artist wondered.

"We parted with it—in the most disinterested manner," the other laughed. "An old friend of my wife's—her family had known him intimately when they lived in Germany—took the most extraordinary fancy to it: the Grand Duke of Silberstadt-Schreckenstein, don't you know? He came out to Bombay while we were there and he spotted your picture (you know he's one of the greatest collectors in Europe) and made such eyes at it that, upon my word—it happened to be his birthday—she told him he might have it to get rid of him. He was perfectly enchanted—but we miss the picture."

"It's very good of you," Lyon said. "If it's in a great collection—a work of my incompetent youth—I'm infinitely honoured."

"Oh he keeps it in one of his castles; I don't know which—you know he has so many. He sent us, before he left India—to return the compliment—a magnificent old vase."

"That was more than the thing was worth," Lyon modestly urged.

Colonel Capadose gave no heed to this observation; his thoughts now seemed elsewhere. After a moment, however, he said: "If you'll come and see us in town she'll show you the vase." And as they passed into the drawing-room he gave his fellow visitor a friendly propulsion. "Go and speak to her; there she is. She'll be delighted."

Oliver Lyon took but a few steps into the wide saloon; he stood there a moment looking at the bright composition of the lamplit group of fair women, the single figures, the great setting of white and gold, the panels of old damask, in the centre of each of which was a single celebrated picture. There was a subdued lustre in the scene and an air as of the shining trains of dresses tumbled over the carpet. At the furthest end of the room sat Mrs. Capadose, rather isolated; she was on a small sofa with an empty place beside her. Lyon couldn't flatter himself she had been keeping it for him; her failure to take up his shy signal at table contradicted this, but his desire to join her was too strong. Moreover he had her husband's sanction; so he crossed the room, stepping over the tails of gowns, and stood before her with his appeal. "I hope you don't mean to repudiate me."

She looked up at him with frank delight. "I'm so glad to see you. I was charmed when I heard you were coming."

"I tried to get a smile from you at dinner—but I couldn't," Lyon returned.

"I didn't see—I didn't understand. Besides, I hate smirking and telegraphing. Also I'm very shy—you won't have forgotten that. Now we can communicate comfortably." And she made a better place for him on her sofa. He sat down and they had a talk that smote old chords in him; the sense of what he had loved her for came back to him, as well as not a little of the actual effect of that cause. She was still the least spoiled beauty he had ever seen, with an absence of the "wanton" or of any insinuating art that resembled an omitted faculty: she affected him at moments as some fine creature from an asylum—a surprising deaf-mute or one of the operative blind. Her noble pagan head gave her privileges that she neglected, and when people were admiring her brow she was wondering if there were a good fire in her bedroom, or at the very most in theirs. She was simple, kind and good; inexpressive but not inhuman, not stupid. Now and again she dropped something, some small fruit of discrimination, that might have come from a mind, have been an impression at first hand. She had no imagination and only the simpler feelings, but several of these had grown up to full size. Lyon talked of the old days in Munich, reminded her of incidents, pleasures and pains, asked her about her father and the others; and she spoke in return of her being so impressed with his own fame, his brilliant position in the world, that she hadn't felt sure he would notice her or that his mute appeal at table was meant for her. This was plainly a perfectly truthful speech—she was incapable of any other—and he was affected by such humility on the part of a woman whose grand line was unique. Her father was dead; one of her brothers was in the navy and the other on a ranch in America; two of her sisters were married and the youngest just coming out and very pretty. She didn't mention her stepmother. She questioned him on his own story, and he described it mainly as his not having married.

"Oh you ought to," she answered. "It's the best thing."

"I like that—from you!"

"Why not from me? I'm very happy."

"That's just why I can't be," he returned. "It's cruel of you to praise your state. But I've had the pleasure of making the acquaintance of your husband. We had a good bit of talk in the other room."

"You must know him better—you must know him really well," said Mrs. Capadose.

"I'm sure that the further you go the more you find. But he makes a fine show too."

She rested her good grey eyes on this recovered "backer." "Don't you think he's handsome?"

"Handsome and clever and entertaining. You see I'm generous."

"Yes; you must know him well," Mrs. Capadose repeated.

"He has seen a great deal of life," said her companion.

"Ah we've been in so many situations. You must see my little girl. She's nine years old—she's too beautiful."

Lyon rose fully to the occasion. "You must bring her to my studio some day—I should like to paint her."

"Oh don't speak of that," said Mrs. Capadose. "It reminds me of something so distressing."

"I hope you don't mean of when *you* used to sit to me—though that may well have bored you."

"It's not what you did—it's what we've done. It's a confession I must make—it's a weight on my mind! I mean on the subject of the lovely picture you gave me—it used to be so much admired. When you come to see me in London—and I count on your doing that very soon—I shall see you looking all round. I can't tell you I keep it in my own room because I love it so, for the simple reason—" It fairly pulled her up.

"Because you can't tell wicked lies," said Lyon.

"No, I can't. So before you ask for it—"

"Oh I know you parted with it—the blow has already fallen," Lyon interrupted.

"Ah then you've heard? I was sure you would! But do you know what we got for it? Two hundred pounds."

"You might have got much more," the artist smiled.

"That seemed a great deal at the time. We were in want of the money—it was a good while ago, when we first married. Our means were very small then, but fortunately that has changed rather for the better. We had the chance; it really seemed a big sum, and I'm afraid we jumped at it. My husband had expectations which have partly come into effect, so that now we do well enough. But meanwhile the picture went."

"Fortunately the original remained. But do you mean that two hundred was the value of the vase?" Lyon asked.

"Of the vase?"

"The beautiful old Indian vase—the Grand Duke's offering."

"The Grand Duke?"

"What's his name?—Silberstadt-Schreckenstein. Your husband mentioned the transaction."

"Oh my husband!" said Mrs. Capadose; and Lyon now saw her change colour.

Not to add to her embarrassment, but to clear up the ambiguity, which he perceived the next moment he had better have left alone, he went on: "He tells me it's now in his collection."

"In the Grand Duke's? Ah you know its reputation? I believe it contains treasures." She was bewildered, but she recovered herself, and Lyon made the mental reflexion that for some reason which would seem good when he knew it the husband and the wife had prepared different versions of the same incident. It was true that he didn't exactly see Everina Brant preparing a version; that wasn't her line of old, and indeed there was no such subterfuge in her eyes today. At any rate they both had the matter too much on their conscience. He changed the subject—said Mrs. Capadose must really bring the little girl. He sat with her some time longer and imagined—perhaps too freely—her equilibrium slightly impaired, as if she were annoyed at their having been even for a moment at cross-purposes. This didn't prevent his saying to her at the last, just as the ladies began to gather themselves for bed: "You seem much impressed, from what you say, with my renown and my prosperity, and you are so good as greatly to exaggerate them. Would you have married me if you had known I was destined to success?"

"I did know it."

"*I* didn't, then!"

"You were too modest."

"You didn't think so when I proposed to you."

"Well, if I had married you I couldn't have married *him*—and he's so awfully nice," Mrs. Capadose said. Lyon knew this was her faith—he had learned that at dinner—but it vexed him a little to hear her proclaim it. The gentleman designated by the pronoun came up, amid the prolonged handshaking for good-night, and Mrs. Capadose remarked to her husband as she turned away, "He wants to paint Amy."

"Ah she's a charming child, a most interesting little creature," the Colonel said to Lyon. "She does the most remarkable things."

Mrs. Capadose stopped in the rustling procession that followed the hostess out of the room. "Don't tell him, please don't," she said.

"Don't tell him what?"

"Why, what she does. Let him find out for himself." And she passed on.

"She thinks I swagger about the child—that I bore people," said the Colonel. "I hope you smoke." He appeared ten minutes later in the smoking-room, brilliantly equipped in a suit of crimson foulard covered with little white spots. He gratified Lyon's eye, made him feel that the modern age has its splendour too and its opportunities for costume. If his wife was an antique he was a fine specimen of the period of colour: he might have passed for a Venetian of the sixteenth century. They were a remarkable couple, Lyon thought, and as he looked at the Colonel standing in bright erectness before the chimney-piece and emitting great smoke-puffs he didn't wonder Everina couldn't regret she hadn't married *him*. All the men collected at Stayes were not smokers and some of them had gone to bed. Colonel Capadose remarked that there probably would be a smallish muster, they had had such a hard day's work. That was the worst of a hunting-house—the men were so sleepy after dinner; it was a great sell for the ladies, even for those who hunted themselves, women being so tough that they never showed it. But most fellows revived under the stimulating influences of the smoking-room, and some of them, in this confidence, would turn up yet. Some of the grounds of their confidence—not all—might have been seen in a cluster of glasses and bottles on a table near the fire, which made the great salver and its contents twinkle sociably. The others lurked as yet in various improper corners of the minds of the most loquacious. Lyon was alone with Colonel Capadose for some moments before their companions, in varied eccentricities of uniform, straggled in, and he felt how little loss of vital tissue this wonderful man had to repair.

They talked about the house, Lyon having noticed an oddity of construction in the smoking-room; and the Colonel explained that it consisted of two distinct parts, one of very great antiquity. They were two complete houses in short, the old and the new, each of great extent and each very fine in its way. The two formed together an enormous structure—Lyon must make a point of going all over it. The modern piece had been erected by the old man when he bought the property; oh yes, he had bought it forty years before—it hadn't been in the family: there hadn't been any particular family for it to be in. He had had the good taste not to spoil the original house—he had not touched it beyond what was just necessary for joining it on. It was very curious indeed—a most irregular rambling mysterious pile, where they now and then discovered a walled-up room or a secret staircase. To his mind it was deadly depressing, however; even the modern additions, splendid as they were, failed to make it cheerful. There was some story of how a skeleton had been found years before, during some repairs, under a stone slab of the floor of one of the passages; but the family were rather shy of its being talked about. The place they were in was of course in the old part, which contained after all some of the best rooms: he had an idea it had been the primitive kitchen, half-modernised at some intermediate period.

"My room is in the old part too then—I'm very glad," Lyon said. "It's very comfortable and contains all the latest conveniences, but I observed the depth of the recess of the door and the evident antiquity of the corridor and staircase—the first short one—after I came out. That panelled corridor is admirable; it looks as if it stretched away, in its brown dimness (the lamps didn't seem to me to make much impression on it) for half a mile."

"Oh don't go to the end of it!" the Colonel warningly smiled.

"Does it lead to the haunted room?" Lyon asked.

His companion looked at him a moment. "Ah you know about that?"

"No, I don't speak from knowledge, only from hope. I've never had any luck—I've never stayed in a spooky house. The places I go to are always as safe as Charing Cross. I want to see—whatever there is, the regular thing. *Is* there a ghost here?"

"Of course there is—a rattling good one."

"And have you seen him?"

"Oh don't ask me what *I've* seen—I should tax your credulity. I don't like to talk of these things. But there are two or three as bad—that is, as good!—rooms as you'll find anywhere."

"Do you mean in my corridor?" Lyon asked.

"I believe the worst is at the far end. But you'd be ill-advised to sleep there."

"Ill-advised?"

"Until you've finished your job. You'll get letters of importance the next morning and take the 10.20."

"Do you mean I shall invent a pretext for running away?"

"Unless you're braver than almost anyone has ever been. They don't often put people to sleep there, but sometimes the house is so crowded that they have to. The same thing always happens—ill-concealed agitation at the breakfast-table and letters of the greatest importance. Of course it's a bachelor's room, and my wife and I are at the other end of the house. But we saw the comedy three days ago—the day after we got here. A young fellow had been put there—I forget his name—the house was so full; and the usual consequence followed. Letters at breakfast—an awfully queer face—an urgent call to town—so sorry his visit was cut short. Ashmore and his wife looked at each other and off the poor devil went."

"Ah that wouldn't suit me; I must do my job," said Lyon. "But do they mind your speaking of it? Some people who've a good ghost are very proud of it, you know."

What answer Colonel Capadose was on the point of making to this query our hero was not to learn, for at that moment their host had walked into the room accompanied by three or four of their fellow guests. Lyon was conscious that he was partly answered by the Colonel's not going on with the subject. This on the other hand was rendered natural by the fact that one of the gentlemen appealed to him for an opinion on a point under discussion, something to do with the everlasting history of the day's run. To Lyon himself Mr. Ashmore began to talk, expressing his regret for the delay of this pleasure. The topic that suggested itself was naturally that most closely connected with the motive of the artist's visit. The latter observed that it was a great disadvantage to him not to have had some preliminary acquaintance with Sir David—in most cases he found this so important. But the present sitter was so far advanced in life that there was doubtless no time to lose. "Oh I can tell you all about him," said Mr. Ashmore; and for half an hour he told him a good deal. It was very interesting as well as a little extravagant, and Lyon felt sure he was a fine old boy to have endeared himself so to a son who was evidently not a gusher. At last he got up—he said he must go to bed if he wished to be fresh for his work in the morning. To which his host replied "Then you must take your candle; the lights are out; past this hour I don't keep my servants up."

In a moment Lyon had his glimmering taper in hand, and as he was leaving the room—he didn't disturb the others with a good-night, they were absorbed in the lemon-squeezer and the soda-water cork—he remembered other occasions on which he had made his way to bed alone through a darkened country-house: such occasions had not been rare, for he was almost always the first to leave the smoking-room. If he hadn't stayed at places of markedly evil repute he had, none the less—having too much imagination—sometimes found the great black halls and staircases rather "creepy": there had been often a sinister effect for his nerves in the sound of his tread through the long passages or the way the winter moon peeped into tall windows on landings. It occurred to him that if houses without supernatural pretensions could look so wicked at night the old corridors of Stayes would certainly give him a sensation. He didn't know whether the proprietors were sensitive; very often, as he had said to Colonel Capadose, people enjoyed the impeachment. What determined him to speak despite the risk was a need that had suddenly come to him to measure the Colonel's accuracy. As he had his hand on the door he said to his host: "I hope I shan't meet any ghosts."

"Any ghosts?"

"You ought to have some—in this fine old part."

"We do our best, but they're difficult to raise," said Mr. Ashmore. "I don't think they like the hot-water pipes."

"They remind them too much of their own climate? But haven't you a haunted room—at the end of my passage?"

"Oh there are stories—we try to keep them up."

"I should like very much to sleep there," Lyon said.

"Well, you can move there tomorrow if you like."

"Perhaps I had better wait," Lyon smiled, "till I've done my work." But he was to have presently the slightly humiliated sense of having been "arch" about nothing.

"Very good; but you won't work there, you know. My father will sit to you in his own apartments."

"Oh it isn't that; it's the fear of running away—like that gentleman three days ago."

"Three days ago? What gentleman?" Mr. Ashmore asked.

"The one who got urgent letters at breakfast and fled by the 10.20. Did he stand more than one night?"

"I don't know what you're talking about"—the son of Stayes was sturdy and blank. "There was no such gentleman—three days ago."

"Ah so much the better," said Lyon, nodding good-night and departing. He took his course, as he remembered it, with his wavering candle, and, though he encountered a great many gruesome objects, safely reached the passage out of which his room opened. In the complete darkness it seemed to stretch away still further, but he followed it, for the curiosity of the thing, to the end. He passed several doors with the name of the room painted up, but found nothing else. He was tempted to try the last door, to look into the room his friend had incriminated; but he felt this would be indiscreet, that gentleman's warrant was somehow a document of too many flourishes. There might be apparitions or other uncanny things and there mightn't; but there was surely nothing in the house so odd as Colonel Capadose.

II

Lyon found Sir David Ashmore a beautiful subject as well as the serenest and blandest of sitters. Moreover he was a very informing old man, tremendously puckered but not in the least dim; and he wore exactly the furred dressing-gown his portrayer would have chosen. He was proud of his age but ashamed of his infirmities, which however he greatly exaggerated and which didn't prevent his submitting to the brush as bravely as he might have to the salutary surgical knife. He sat there with the firm eyes and set smile of "Well, do your worst!" He demolished the legend of his having feared the operation would be fatal, giving an explanation which pleased our friend much better. He held that a gentleman should be painted but once in his life—that it was eager and fatuous to be hung up all over the place. That was good for women, who made a pretty wall-pattern; but the male face didn't lend itself to decorative repetition. The proper time for the likeness was at the last, when the whole man was there, when you got the sum of his experience. Lyon couldn't reply, as he would have done in many a case, that this was not a real synthesis—you had to allow so for leakage; since there had been no crack in Sir David's crystallisation. He spoke of his portrait as a plain map of the country, to be consulted by his children in a case of uncertainty. A proper map could be drawn up only when the country had been travelled. He gave Lyon his mornings, till luncheon, and they talked of many things, not neglecting, as a stimulus to gossip, the company at Stayes. Now that he didn't "go out," as he said, he saw much less of the people in his house—processions that came and went, that he knew nothing about and that he liked to hear Lyon describe. The artist sketched with a fine point and didn't caricature, and it usually befell that when Sir David didn't know the sons and daughters he had known the fathers and mothers. He was one of those terrible old persons who keep the book of antecedents. But in the case of the Capadose family, at whom they arrived by an easy stage, his knowledge embraced two, or even three, generations. General Capadose was an old crony, and he remembered his father before him. The General was rather a smart soldier, but in private life of too speculative a turn—always sneaking into the City to put his money into some rotten thing. He had married a girl who brought him something—and with it half a dozen children. He scarcely knew what had become of the rest of them, except that one was in the Church and had found preferment—wasn't he Dean of Rockingham? Clement, the fellow who was at Stayes, had apparently some gift for arms; he had served in the East and married a pretty girl. He had been at Eton with Arthur and used then to come to Stayes in his holidays. Lately, back in England, he had turned up with his wife again; that was before he—the old man—had been put to grass. He was a taking dog but had a monstrous foible.

"A monstrous foible?" Lyon echoed.

"He pulls the long bow—the longest that ever was."

Lyon's brush stopped short, while he repeated, for somehow the words both startled him and brought light: "'The longest that ever was'?"

"You're very lucky not to have had to catch him."

Lyon debated. "Well, I think I *have* rather caught him. He revels in the miraculous."

"Oh it isn't always the miraculous. He'll lie about the time of day, about the name of his hatter. It's quite disinterested."

"Well, it's very base," Lyon declared, feeling rather sick for what Everina Brant had done with herself.

"Oh it's an extraordinary trouble to take," said the old man, "but this fellow isn't in himself at all base. There's no harm in him and no bad intention; he doesn't steal nor cheat nor gamble nor drink; he's very kind—he sticks to his wife, is fond of his children. He simply can't give you a straight answer."

"Then everything he told me last night, I now see, was tarred with that brush: he delivered himself of a series of the steepest statements. They stuck when I tried to swallow them, yet I never thought of so simple an explanation."

"No doubt he was in the vein," Sir David went on. "It's a natural peculiarity—as you might limp or stutter or be left-handed. I believe it comes and goes with changes of the wind. My son tells me that his friends quite allow for it and don't pin him down—for the sake of his wife, whom everyone likes."

"Oh his wife—his wife!" Lyon murmured, painting fast.

"I dare say she's used to it."

"Never in the world, Sir David. How can she be used to it?"

"Why, my dear sir, when a woman's fond—! And don't they mostly rather handle that instrument themselves? They're connoisseurs in the business," Sir David cackled with a harmless old-time cynicism. "They've a sympathy for a fellow performer."

Lyon wondered; he had no ground for denying that Mrs. Capadose was attached to her husband. But after a little he rejoined: "Oh not this one! I knew her years ago—before her marriage; knew her well and admired her. She was as clear as a bell."

"I like her very much," Sir David said, "but I've seen her back him up."

Lyon considered his host a moment not in the light of a sitter. "Are you very sure?"

The old man grinned and brought out: "My dear sir, you're in love with her."

"Very likely. God knows I used to be!"

"She must help him out—she can't expose him."

"She can hold her tongue," Lyon returned.

"Well, before you probably she will."

"That's what I'm curious to see." And he added privately: "Mercy on us, what he must have made of her!" He kept this reflexion to himself, for he considered that he had sufficiently betrayed his state of mind with regard to Mrs. Capadose. None the less it occupied him now immensely, the question of how such a woman would arrange herself in such a position. He watched her with an interest deeply quickened when he mingled with the company; he had had his own troubles in life, but had rarely been so anxious about anything as about this question of what the loyalty of a wife and the infection of an example would have made of a perfectly candid mind. Oh he would answer for it that whatever other women might be prone to do she, of old, had struck to the truth as a bather who can't swim sticks to shallow water. Even if she hadn't been too simple for deviations she would have been too proud, and if she hadn't had too much conscience would have had too little eagerness. The lie was the last thing she would have endured or condoned—the particular thing she wouldn't have forgiven. Did she sit in torment while her husband gave the rein, or was she now too so perverse that she thought it a fine thing to be striking at the expense—Lyon would have been ready to say—of one's decency? It would have taken a wondrous alchemy—working backwards, as it were—to produce this latter result. Besides these alternatives—that she suffered misery in silence and that she was so much in love that her husband's exorbitance seemed to her but an added richness, a proof of life and talent—there was still the possibility that she hadn't found him out, that she took his false coinage at his own valuation. A little reflexion rendered this hypothesis untenable; it was too evident that the account he gave of things must repeatedly have contradicted her own knowledge. Within an hour or two of his meeting them Lyon had seen her confronted with that perfectly gratuitous invention about the profit they had made of his early picture. Even then indeed she had not, so far as he could see, smarted, and—but for the present he could only stare at the mystery!

Even if it hadn't been interfused, through his uneradicated interest in Mrs. Capadose, with an element of suspense, the question would still have been attaching and worrying; since, truly, he hadn't painted portraits so many years without becoming curious of queer cases. His attention was limited for the moment to the opportunity the following three days might yield, as the Colonel and his wife were going on to another house. It fixed itself largely of course upon the Colonel too— the fellow was *so* queer a case. Moreover it had to go on very quickly. Lyon was at once too discreet and too fond of his own intimate inductions to ask other people how they answered his conundrum—too afraid also of exposing the woman he once had loved. It was probable indeed that light would come to him from the talk of their companions; the Colonel's idiosyncrasy, both as it affected his own situation and as it affected his wife, would be a familiar theme in any house in which he was in the habit of staying. Lyon hadn't observed in the circles in which he visited any marked abstention from comment on the singularities of their members. It interfered with his progress that the Colonel hunted all day, while he plied his brushes and chatted with Sir David; but a Sunday intervened and that partly made it up. Mrs. Capadose fortunately didn't hunt and, his work done, was not in-accessible. He took a couple of good walks with her—she was fond of good walks—and beguiled her at tea into a friendly nook in the hall. Regard her as he might he couldn't make out to himself that she was consumed by a hidden shame; the sense of being married to a man whose word had no worth was not, in her spirit, so far as he could guess, the canker within the rose. Her mind appeared to have nothing on it but its own placid frankness, and when he sounded her eyes—with the long plummet he occasionally permitted himself to use—they had no uncomfortable consciousness. He talked to her again and still again of the dear old days—reminded her of things he hadn't had (before this reunion) any sense of himself remembering. Then he spoke to her of her husband, praised his appearance, his talent for conversation, professed to have felt a quick friendship for him and asked, with an amount of "cheek" for which he almost blushed, what manner of man he was. "What manner?" she echoed. "Dear me, how can one describe one's husband? I like him very much."

"Ah you've insisted on that to me already!" Lyon growled to exaggeration.

"Then why do you ask me again?" She added in a moment, as if she were so happy that she could afford to take pity on him: "He's everything that's good and true and kind. He's a soldier and a gentleman and a dear! He hasn't a fault. And he has great, great ability."

"Yes, he strikes one as having great, great ability. But of course I can't think him a dear."

"I don't care what you think him!" Everina laughed, looking still handsomer in the act than he had ever seen her. She was either utterly brazen or of a contrition quite impenetrable, and he had little prospect of extorting from her what he somehow so longed for—some avowal that she had after all better have married a man who was not a by-word for the most contemptible, the least heroic of vices. Hadn't she seen, hadn't she felt, the smile, the cold faded smile of complete de-preciation, go round when her husband perjured himself to some particularly characteristic blackness? How could a woman of her quality live with that day after day, year after year, except by her quality's altering? But he would believe in the alteration only when he should have heard *her* lie. He was held by his riddle and yet impatient of it, he asked himself all kinds of questions. Didn't she lie, after all, when she let *his* lies pass without turning a hair? Wasn't her life a perpetual complicity, and didn't she aid and abet him by the simple fact that she wasn't disgusted with him? Then again perhaps she *was* disgusted and it was the mere desperation of her pride that had given her an inscrutable mask. Perhaps she protested in private, passionately; perhaps every night, in their own apartments, after the day's low exhibition, she had things out with him in a manner known only to the pair themselves. But if such scenes were of no avail and he took no more trouble to cure himself, how could she regard him, and after so many years of marriage too, with the perfectly artless complacency that Lyon had surprised in her in the course of the first day's dinner? If our friend hadn't been in love with her he would surely have taken the Colonel's delinquencies less to heart. As the case stood they fairly turned to the tragical for him, even while he was sharply aware of how merely "his funny way" they were to others—and of how funny his, Oliver Lyon's, own way of regarding them would have seemed to everyone.

The observation of these three days showed him that if Capadose was an abundant he was not a malignant liar and that his fine faculty exercised itself mainly on subjects of small direct importance. "He's the liar platonic," he said to himself; "he's disinterested, as Sir David said, he doesn't operate with a hope of gain or with a desire to injure. It's art for art—he's prompted by some love of beauty. He has an inner vision of what might have been, of what ought to be, and he helps on the good cause by the simple substitution of a shade. He lays on colour, as it were, and what less do I do myself?" His disorder had a wide range, but a family likeness ran through all its forms, which consisted mainly of their singular futility. It was this that made them an affliction; they encumbered the field of conversation, took up valuable space, turned it into the desert of a perpetual shimmering mirage. For the falsehood uttered under stress a convenient place can usually be found, as for a person who presents himself with an author's order at the first night of a play. But the mere luxurious lie is the gentleman without a voucher or a ticket who accommodates himself with a stool in the passage.

Of one possible charge Lyon acquitted his successful rival; it had puzzled him that, irrepressible as he was, he had never got into a mess in the Service. But it was to be made out that he drew the line at the Service—over that august institution he never flapped his wings. Moreover, for all the personal pretension in his talk it rarely came, oddly enough, to swagger about his military exploits. He had a passion for the chase, he had followed it in far countries, and some of his finest flowers were reminiscences of what he had prodigiously done and miraculously escaped when off by himself. The more by himself he had been of course the bigger the commemorative nosegay bloomed. A new acquaintance always received from him, in honour of their meeting, one of the most striking of these tributes—that generalisation Lyon very promptly made. And the extraordinary man had inconsistencies and un-expected lapses—lapses into the very commonplace of the credible. Lyon recognised what Sir David had told him, that he flourished and drooped by an incalculable law and would sometimes keep the truce of God for a month at a time. The muse of improvisation breathed on him at her pleasure and appeared sometimes quite to avert her face. He would neglect the finest openings and then set sail with everything against him. As a general thing he affirmed the impossible rather than denied the certain, though this too had lively exceptions. Very often, when it was loud enough—for he liked a noise about him—he joined in the reprobation that cast him out, he allowed he was trying it on and that one didn't know what had happened to one till one *had* tried. Still, he never completely retracted nor retreated—he dived and came up in another place. Lyon guessed him capable on occasion of defending his position with violence, though only when it was very bad. Then he might easily be dangerous—then he would hit out and not care whom he touched. Such moments as those would test his wife's philosophy—Lyon would have liked to see her there. In the smoking-room and elsewhere the company, so far as it was composed of his familiars, had an hilarious protest always at hand; but among the men who had known him long his big brush was an old story, so old that they had ceased to talk about it, and Lyon didn't care, as I have said, to bring to a point those impatiences that might have resembled his own.

The oddest thing of all was that neither surprise nor familiarity prevented the Colonel's being liked; his largest appeals even to proved satiety passed for an overflow of life and high spirits—almost of simple good looks. If he was fond of treating his gallantry with a flourish he was none the less unmistakeably gallant. He was a first-rate rider and shot, in spite of his fund of anecdote illustrating these accomplishments: in short he was very nearly as clever and brave, and his adventures and observations had been very nearly as numerous and wonderful, as the list he unrolled. His best quality however remained that indiscriminate sociability which took interest and favour for granted and about which he bragged least. It made him cheap, it made him even in a manner vulgar; but it was so contagious that his listener was more or less on his side as against the probabilities. It was a private reflexion of Oliver Lyon's that he not only was mendacious but made any charmed converser feel as much so by the very action of the charm—of a certain guilty submission of which no intention of ridicule could yet purge you. In the evening, at dinner and afterwards, our friend, better placed for observation than the first night, watched his wife's face to see if some faint shade or spasm never passed over it. But she continued to show nothing, and the wonder was that when he spoke she almost always listened. That was her pride: she wished not to be even suspected of not facing the music. Lyon had none the less an importunate vision of a veiled figure coming the next day in the dusk to certain places to repair the Colonel's ravages, as the relatives of kleptomaniacs punctually call at the shops that have suffered from their depredations.

"I must apologise; of course it wasn't true; I hope no harm is done; it's only his incorrigible—" oh to hear that woman's voice in that deep abasement! Lyon had no harsh design, no conscious wish to practise on her sensibility or her loyalty; but he did say to himself that he should have liked to bring her round, liked to see her *show* him that a vision of the dignity of not being married to a mountebank sometimes haunted her dreams. He even imagined the hour when, with a burning face, she might ask *him* not to take the question up. Then he should be almost consoled—he would be magnanimous.

He finished his picture and took his departure, after having worked in a glow of interest which made him believe in his success, until he found he had pleased everyone, especially Mr. and Mrs. Ashmore, when he began to be sceptical. The party at any rate changed: Colonel and Mrs. Capadose went their way. He was able to say to himself however that his parting with Everina wasn't so much an end as a beginning, and he called on her soon after his return to town. She had told him the hours she was at home—she seemed to like him. If she liked him why hadn't she married him, or at any rate why wasn't she sorry she hadn't? If she was sorry she concealed it too well. The point he made of some visible contrition in her on this head may strike the reader as extravagant, but something must be allowed so disappointed a man. He didn't ask much after all; not that she should love him today or that she should allow him to tell her that he loved her, but only that she should give him some sign she didn't feel her choice as *all* gain. Instead of this, for the present, she contented herself with exhibiting her small daughter to him. The child was beautiful and had the prettiest eyes of innocence he had ever seen: which didn't prevent his wondering if she told horrid fibs. This idea much occupied and rather darkly amused him—the picture of the anxiety with which her mother would watch as she grew older for symptoms of the paternal strain. That was a pleasant care for such a woman as Everina Brant! Did she lie to the child herself about her father—was that necessary when she pressed her daughter to her bosom to cover up his tracks? Did he control himself before the little girl—so that she mightn't hear him say things she knew to be other than his account of them? Lyon scarcely thought that probable: his genius would be ever too strong for him, and the only guard for Amy would be in her being too simple for criticism. One couldn't judge yet—she was too young to show. If she should grow up clever she would be sure to tread in his steps—a delightful improvement in her mother's situation! Her little face was not shifty, but neither was her father's big one; so that proved nothing.

Lyon reminded his friends more than once of their promise that Amy should sit to him, and it was now only a question of his own leisure. The desire grew in him to paint the Colonel also—an operation from which he promised himself a rich private satisfaction. He would draw him out, he would set him up in that totality about which he had talked with Sir David, and none but the initiated would know. They, however, would rank the picture high, and it would be indeed six rows deep—a masterpiece of fine characterisation, of legitimate treachery. He had dreamed for years of some work that should show the master of the deeper vision as well as the mere reporter of the items, and here at last was his subject. It was a pity it wasn't better, but that wasn't *his* fault. It was his impression that already no one "drew" the Colonel in the social sense more effectively than he, and he did this not only by instinct but on a plan. There were moments when he almost winced at the success of his plan—the poor gentleman went so terribly far. He would pull up some day, look at his critic between the eyes and guess he was being played upon—which would lead to his wife's guessing it also. Not that Lyon cared much for that however, so long as she failed to suppose—and she couldn't divine it—that *she* was a part of his joke. He formed such a habit now of going to see her of a Sunday afternoon that he was angry when she went out of town. This occurred often, as the couple were great visitors and the Colonel was always looking for sport, which he liked best when it could be had at the expense of others. Lyon would have supposed the general gregarious life, the constant presence of a gaping "gallery," particularly little to her taste, for it was naturally in country-houses that her husband came out strongest. To let him go off without her, not to see him expose himself—that ought properly to have been her relief and her nearest approach to a luxury. She mentioned to her friend in fact that she preferred staying at home, but she didn't say it was because in other people's houses she was on the rack: the reason she gave was that she liked so to be with the child. It wasn't perhaps criminal to deal in such "whoppers," but it was damned vulgar: poor Lyon was delighted when he arrived at that formula. Certainly some day too he would cross the line—he would practise the fraud to which his talked "rot" had the same relation as the experiments of the forger have to the signed cheque. And in the mean time, yes, he was vulgar, in spite of his facility, his impunity, his so remarkably fine person. Twice, by exception, toward the end of the winter, when he left town for a few days' hunting, his wife remained at home. Lyon hadn't yet reached the point of asking himself if the wish not to miss two of his visits might have had something to do with this course. That enquiry would perhaps have been more in place later, when he began to paint her daughter and she made a rule of coming with her. But it wasn't in her to give the wrong name, to affect motives, and Lyon could see she had the maternal passion in spite of the bad blood in the little girl's veins.

She came inveterately, though Lyon multiplied the sittings: Amy was never entrusted to the governess or the maid. He had knocked off poor old Sir David in ten days, but the simple face of the child held him and worried him and gave him endless work. He asked for sitting after sitting, and it might have struck a solicitous spectator that he was wearing the little girl out. He knew better, however, and Mrs. Capadose also knew: they were present together at the long intermissions he gave her, when she left her pose and roamed about the great studio, amusing herself with its curiosities, playing with the old draperies and costumes, having unlimited leave to handle. Then her mother and their so patient friend—much more patient than her piano-mistress—sat and talked; he laid aside his brushes and leaned back in his chair; he always gave her tea. What Mrs. Capadose couldn't suspect was the rate at which, during these weeks, he neglected other orders: women have no faculty of imagination with regard to a man's work beyond a vague idea that it doesn't matter. Lyon in fact put off everything and made high celebrities wait. There were half-hours of silence, when he plied his brushes, during which he was mainly conscious that Everina was sitting there. She easily fell into that if he didn't insist on talking, and she wasn't embarrassed nor bored by any lapse of communication. Sometimes she took up a book—there were plenty of them about; sometimes, a little way off in her chair, she watched his progress—though without in the least advising or correcting—as if she cared for every stroke that was to contribute to his result. These strokes were occasionally a little wild; he was thinking so much more of his heart than of his hand. He wasn't more embarrassed than she, but he was more agitated: it was as if in the sittings (for the child too was admirably quiet) something had beautifully settled itself between them or had already grown—a tacit confidence, an inexpressible secret. He at least felt it that way, but he after all couldn't be sure she did. What he wanted her to do for him was very little; it wasn't even to allow that she was unhappy. She would satisfy him by letting him know even by some quite silent sign that she could imagine her happiness with him—well, more unqualified. Perhaps indeed—his presumption went so far—that was what she did mean by contentedly sitting there.

III

At last he broached the question of painting the Colonel: it was now very late in the season—there would be little time before the common dispersal. He said they must make the most of it; the great thing was to begin; then in the autumn, with the resumption of their London life, they could go forward. Mrs. Capadose objected to this that she really couldn't consent to accept another present of such value. Lyon had sacrificed to her the portrait of herself of old—he knew what they had had the indelicacy to do with it. Now he had offered her this wondrous memorial of the child—wondrous it would evidently be when he should be able to bring it to a finish; a precious possession that, this time, they would cherish for ever. But his generosity and their indiscretion must stop there—they couldn't be so tremendously "beholden" to him. They couldn't order the picture, which of course he would understand without her explaining: it was a luxury beyond their reach, since they knew the great prices he received. Besides, what had they ever done—what above all had *she* ever done, that he should overload them with benefits? No, he was too dreadfully good; it was really impossible that Clement should sit. Lyon listened to her without protest, without interruption, while he bent forward at his work; and at last returned: "Well, if you won't take it why not let him sit just for my own pleasure and profit? Let it be a favour, a service I ask of him. All the generosity and charity will so be on your side. It will do me a lot of good to paint him and the picture will remain in my hands."

"How will it do you a lot of good?" Mrs. Capadose asked.

"Why he's such a rare model—such an interesting subject. He has such an expressive face. It will teach me no end of things."

"Expressive of what?" said Mrs. Capadose.

"Why of his inner man."

"And you want to paint his inner man?"

"Of course I do. That's what a great portrait gives you, and with a splendid comment on it thrown in for the money. I shall make the Colonel's a great one. It will put me up high. So you see my request is eminently interested."

"How can you be higher than you are?"

"Oh I'm an insatiable climber. So don't stand in my way," said Lyon.

"Well, everything in him is very noble," Mrs. Capadose gravely contended.

"Ah trust me to bring everything out!" Lyon returned, feeling a little ashamed of himself.

Mrs. Capadose, before she went, humoured him to the point of saying that her husband would probably comply with his invitation; but she added: "Nothing would induce me to let you pry into *me* that way!"

"Oh you," her friend laughed—"I could do you in the dark!"

The Colonel shortly afterwards placed his leisure at the painter's disposal and by the end of July had paid him several visits. Lyon was disappointed neither in the quality of his sitter nor in the degree to which he himself rose to the occasion; he felt really confident of producing what he had conceived. He was in the spirit of it, charmed with his motive and deeply interested in his problem. The only point that troubled him was the idea that when he should send his picture to the Academy he shouldn't be able to inscribe it in the catalogue under the simple rubric to which all propriety pointed. He couldn't in short send in the title as "The Liar"— more was the pity. However, this little mattered, for he had now determined to stamp that sense on it as legibly—and to the meanest intelligence—as it was stamped for his own vision on the living face. As he saw nothing else in the Colonel today, so he gave himself up to the joy of "rendering" nothing else. How he did it he couldn't have told you, but he felt a miracle of method freshly revealed to him every time he sat down to work. It was in the eyes and it was in the mouth, it was in every line of the face and every fact of the attitude, in the indentation of the chin, in the way the hair was planted, the moustache was twisted, the smile came and went, the breath rose and fell. It was in the way he looked out at a bamboozled world in short—the way he would look out for ever. There were half a dozen portraits in Europe that Lyon rated as supreme; he thought of them always as immortal things, for they were as perfectly preserved as they were consummately painted. It was to this small exemplary group that he aspired to attach the canvas on which he was now engaged. One of the productions that helped to compose it was the magnificent Moroni of the National Gallery—the young tailor in the white jacket at his board with his shears. The Colonel was not a tailor, nor was Moroni's model, unlike many tailors, a liar; the very man, body and soul, should bloom into life under his hand with just that assurance of no loss of a drop of the liquor. The Colonel, as it turned out, liked to sit, and liked to talk while sitting: which was very fortunate, as his talk was half the inspiration of his artist. Lyon applied without mercy his own gift of provocation; he couldn't possibly have been in a better relation to him for the purpose. He encouraged, beguiled, excited him, manifested an unfathomable credulity, and his own sole lapses were when the Colonel failed, as he called it, to "act." He had his intermissions, his hours of sterility, and then Lyon knew that the picture also drooped. The higher his companion soared, the more he circled and sang in the blue, the better he felt himself paint; he only couldn't make the flights and the evolutions last. He lashed his victim on when he flagged; his one difficulty was his fear again that his game might be suspected. The Colonel, however, was easily beguiled; he basked and expanded in the fine steady light of the painter's attention. In this way the picture grew very fast, astonishingly faster, in spite of its so much greater "importance," than the simple-faced little girl's. By the fifth of August it was pretty well finished: that was the date of the last sitting the Colonel was for the present able to give—he was leaving town the next day with his wife. Lyon was amply content—he saw his way so clear: he should be able to do at leisure the little that remained, in respect to which his friend's attendance would be a minor matter. As there was no hurry, in any case, he would let the thing stand over till his own return to London, in November, when he should come back to it with a fresh eye. On the Colonel's asking him if Everina

might have a sight of it next day, should she find a minute—
this being so greatly her desire—Lyon begged as a special
favour that she would wait: what he had yet to do was small
in amount, but it would make all the difference. This was the
repetition of a proposal Mrs. Capadose had made on the
occasion of his last visit to her, and he had then
recommended her not coming till he should be himself
better pleased. He had really never been, at a corresponding
stage, better pleased; and he blushed a little for his subtlety.

By the fifth of August the weather was very warm, and on
that day, while the Colonel sat at his usual free practice Lyon
opened for the sake of ventilation a little subsidiary door
which led directly from his studio into the garden and
sometimes served as an entrance and an exit for models and
for visitors of the humbler sort, and as a passage for canvases,
frames, packing-boxes and other professional gear. The main
entrance was through the house and his own apartments,
and this approach had the charming effect of admitting you
first to a high gallery, from which a winding staircase, happily
disposed, dropped to the wide decorated encumbered room.
The view of this room beneath them, with all its artistic
ingenuities and the objects of value that Lyon had collected,
never failed to elicit exclamations of delight from persons
stepping into the gallery. The way from the garden was
plainer and at once more practicable and more private.
Lyon's domain, in Saint John's Wood, was not vast, but when
the door stood open of a summer's day it offered a glimpse
of flowers and trees, there was a sweetness in the air and you
heard the birds. On this particular morning the side-door had
been found convenient by an unannounced visitor, a
youngish woman who stood in the room before the Colonel
was aware of her, but whom he was then the first to see. She
was very quiet—she looked from one of the men to the other.
"Oh dear, here's another!" Lyon exclaimed as soon as his eyes
rested on her. She belonged in fact to the somewhat
importunate class of the model in search of employment, and

she explained that she had ventured to come straight in, that way, because very often when she went to call upon gentlemen the servants played her tricks, turned her off and wouldn't take in her name.

"But how did you get into the garden?" Lyon asked.

"The gate was open, sir—the servants' gate. The butcher's cart was there."

"The butcher ought to have closed it," said Lyon.

"Then you don't require me, sir?" the lady continued.

Lyon continued to paint; he had given her a sharp look at first, but now his eyes were only for his work. The Colonel, however, examined her with interest. She was a person of whom you could scarcely say whether being young she looked old or old looked young; she had at any rate clearly rounded several of the corners of life; she had a face that was rosy, yet that failed to suggest freshness. She was nevertheless rather pretty and even looked as if at one time she might have sat for the complexion. She wore a hat with many feathers, a dress with many bugles, long black gloves encircled with silver bracelets, and very bad shoes. There was something about her not exactly of the governess out of place nor completely of the actress seeking an engagement, but that savoured of a precarious profession, perhaps even of a blighted career. She was perceptibly soiled and tarnished, and after she had been in the room a few moments the air, or at any rate the nostril, became acquainted with a vague alcoholic waft. She was unpractised in the *h*, and when Lyon at last thanked her and said he didn't want her—he was doing nothing for which she could be useful—she replied in rather a wounded manner: "Well, you know you '*ave* 'ad me!"

"I don't remember you," Lyon protested.

"Well, I dare say the people who saw your pictures do! I haven't much time, but I thought I'd look in."

"I'm much obliged to you."

"If ever you should require me and just send me a postcard—"

"I never send postcards," said Lyon.

"Oh well, I should value a private letter! Anything to Miss Geraldine, Mortimer Terrace Mews, Notting 'ill—"

"Very good; I'll remember," said Lyon.

Miss Geraldine lingered. "I thought I'd just stop on the chance."

"I'm afraid I can't hold out hopes, I'm so busy with portraits," Lyon continued.

"Yes; I see you are. I wish I was in the gentleman's place."

"I'm afraid in that case it wouldn't look like the gentleman," the Colonel sociably laughed.

"Oh of course it couldn't compare—it wouldn't be so 'andsome! But I do hate them portraits!" Miss Geraldine declared. "It's so much bread out of our mouths."

"Well, there are many who can't paint them," Lyon suggested for comfort.

"Oh I've sat to the very first—and only to the first! There's many that couldn't do anything without me."

"I'm glad you're in such demand." Lyon's amusement had turned to impatience and he added that he wouldn't detain her—he would send for her in case of need.

"Very well; remember it's the Mews—more's the pity! You don't sit so well as *us!*" Miss Geraldine pursued, looking at the Colonel. "If *you* should require me, sir—"

"You put him out; you embarrass him," said Lyon.

"Embarrass him, oh gracious!" the visitor cried with a laugh that diffused a fragrance. "Perhaps *you* send postcards, eh?" she went on to the Colonel; but she retreated with a wavering step. She passed out into the garden as she had come.

"How very dreadful—she's drunk!" said Lyon. He was painting hard, but looked up, checking himself: Miss Geraldine, in the open doorway, had thrust in her head again.

"Yes, I do hate it—that sort of thing!" she cried with an explosion of mirth which confirmed Lyon's charge. On which she disappeared.

"What sort of thing—what does she mean?" the Colonel asked.

"Oh my painting you when I might be painting her."

"And have you ever painted her?"

"Never in the world; I've never seen her. She's quite mistaken."

The Colonel just waited; then he remarked: "She was very pretty—ten years ago."

"I dare say, but she's quite ruined. For me the least 'drop too much' spoils them; I shouldn't care for her at all."

"My dear fellow, she's not a model," the Colonel laughed.

"Today, no doubt, she's not worthy of the name; but she has done her time."

"*Jamais de la vie!* That's all a pretext."

"A pretext?" Lyon pricked up his ears—he wondered what now would come.

"She didn't want you—she wanted *me*."

"I noticed she paid you some attention. What then does she want of you?"

"Oh to do me an ill turn. She hates me—lots of women do. She's watching me—she follows me."

Lyon leaned back in his chair—without a single grain of faith. He was all the more delighted with what he heard and with the Colonel's bright and candid manner. The story had shot up and bloomed, from the dropped seed, on the spot. "My dear Colonel!" he murmured with friendly interest and commiseration.

"I was vexed when she came in—but I wasn't upset," his sitter continued.

"You concealed it very well if you were."

"Ah when one has been through what I have! Today, however, I confess I was half-prepared. I've noticed her hanging about—she knows my movements. She was near my house this morning—she must have followed me."

"But who is she then—with such charming 'cheek'?"

"Yes, she has plenty of cheek," said the Colonel; "but as you observe she was primed. Still, she carried it off as a cool hand. Oh she's a bad 'un! She isn't a model and never was; no doubt she has known some of those women and picked up their form. She had hold of a friend of mine ten years ago—a young jackanapes who might have been left to be plucked but whom I was obliged to take an interest in for family reasons. It's a long story—I had really forgotten all about it. She's thirty-seven if she's a day. I was able to make a diversion and let him get off— after which I sent her about her business. She knew it was me she had to thank. She has never forgiven me—I think she's off her head. Her name isn't Geraldine at all and I doubt very much if that's her address."

"Ah what *is* her name?" Lyon was all participation. He had always noted that when once his friend was launched there was no danger in asking; the more you asked the more abundantly you were served.

"It's Pearson—Harriet Pearson; but she used to call herself Grenadine—wasn't that a rum notion? Grenadine—Geraldine— the jump was easy." Lyon was charmed with this flow of facility, and his interlocutor went on: "I hadn't thought of her for years—I had quite lost sight of her. I don't know what her idea is, but practically she's harmless. As I came in I thought I saw her a little way up the road. She must have found out I come here and have arrived before me. I dare say—or rather I'm sure—she's waiting for me there now."

"Hadn't you better have protection?" Lyon asked with amusement.

"The best protection 's five shillings—I'm willing to go that length. Unless indeed she has a bottle of vitriol. But they only throw vitriol on the fellows who have 'undone' them, and I never undid her—I told her the first time I saw her that it wouldn't do. Oh if she's there we'll walk a little way together and talk it over, and, as I say, I'll go as far as five shillings."

"Well," said Lyon, "I'll contribute another five." He felt this little to pay for what he was getting.

That entertainment was interrupted, however, for the time, by the Colonel's departure. Lyon hoped for some sequel to match—a report, by note, of the next scene in the drama as his friend had met it, but this genius apparently didn't operate with the pen. At any rate he left town without writing—they had taken a tryst for three months later. Oliver Lyon always passed the holidays in the same way; during the first weeks he paid a visit to his elder brother, the happy possessor, in the south of England, of a rambling old house with formal gardens, in which he delighted, and then he went abroad— usually to Italy or Spain. This year he carried out his custom after taking a last look at his all but finished work and feeling as nearly pleased with it as decency permitted, the translation of the idea by the hand appearing always to him at the best a pitiful compromise. One yellow afternoon in the country, as he smoked his pipe on one of the old terraces, he was taken with a fancy for another look at what he had lately done, and with that in particular of doing two or three things more to it: he had been much haunted with this unrest while he lounged there. The provocation was not to be resisted, and though he was at any rate so soon to be back in London he was unable to brook delay. Five minutes with his view of the Colonel would be enough—it would clear up questions that hummed in his brain; so that the next morning, to give himself this luxury, he took the train for town. He sent no word in advance; he would lunch at his club and probably return into Sussex by the 5.45.

In Saint John's Wood the tide of human life flows at no time very fast, and in the first days of September Lyon found mere desolation in the straight sunny roads where the little plastered garden-walls, with their incommunicative doors, looked feebly Oriental. There was definite stillness in his own house, to which he admitted himself by his pass-key, it being a matter of conscience with him sometimes to take his servants unawares. The good woman set in authority over them and who cumulated the functions of cook and housekeeper was, however, quickly summoned by his step, and—as he cultivated frankness of intercourse with his domestics—received him without the confusion of surprise.

He reassured her as to any other effect of unpreparedness—
he had come up but for a few hours and should be busy in
the studio. She announced that he was just in time to see a
lady and a gentleman who were there at the moment—they
had arrived five minutes before. She had told them he was
absent but they said it was all right; they only wanted to look
at a picture and would be very careful of everything. "I hope
it's all right, sir," this informant concluded. "The gentleman
says he's a sitter and he gave me his name—rather an odd
name; I think it's military. The lady's a very fine lady, sir; at
any rate there they are."

"Oh it's all right"—Lyon read the identity of his visitors. The
good woman couldn't know, having when he was at home so
little to do with the comings and goings; his man, who showed
people in and out, had accompanied him to the country. He
was a good deal surprised at the advent of Mrs. Capadose, who
knew how little he wished her to see the portrait unfinished,
but it was a familiar truth to him that she was a woman of a
high spirit. Besides, perhaps the lady wasn't Everina; the
Colonel might well have brought some inquisitive friend, a
person who perhaps wanted a portrait of *her* husband. What
were they doing in town, in any case, at that moment? Lyon
made his way to the studio with a certain curiosity; he
wondered vaguely what his friends were "up to." He laid his
hand upon the curtain draping the door of communication,
the door opening upon the gallery constructed for relief at the
time the studio was added to the house; but with his motion to
slide the tapestry on its rings arrested in the act. A singular
startling sound reached him from the room beneath; it had the
appearance of a passionate wail, or perhaps rather a
smothered shriek, accompanied by a violent burst of tears.
Oliver Lyon listened intently and then passed in to the balcony,
which was covered with an old thick Moorish rug. His step was
noiseless without his trying to keep it so, and after that first
instant he found himself profiting irresistibly by the accident
of his not having attracted the attention of the two persons in

the studio, who were some twenty feet below him. They were in truth so deeply and strangely engaged that their unconsciousness of observation was explained. The scene that took place before Lyon's eyes was more extraordinary than any he had ever felt free to overlook. Delicacy and the failure to understand kept him at first from interfering—what he saw was a woman who had thrown herself in a flood of tears on her companion's bosom; after which surprise and discretion gave way to a force that made him step back behind the curtain. This same force, further—the force of a *need* to know—caused him to avail himself for better observation of a crevice formed by his gathering together the two halves of his swinging tapestry. He was perfectly aware of what he was about—he was for the moment an eavesdropper and a spy; but he was also aware that something irregular, as to which his confidence had been trifled with, was on foot, and that he was as much concerned with the reasons of it as he might be little concerned with the taken form. His observation, his reflexions, accomplished themselves in a flash.

His visitors were in the middle of the room; Mrs. Capadose clung to her husband, weeping; she sobbed as if her heart would break. Her distress was horrible to Oliver Lyon, but his astonishment was greater than his horror when he heard the Colonel respond to it by the vehement imprecation "Damn him, damn him, damn him!" What in the world had happened? why was she sobbing and whom was he damning? What had happened, Lyon saw the next instant, was that the Colonel had finally rummaged out the canvas before which he had been sitting—he knew the corner where the artist usually placed it, out of the way and its face to the wall—and had set it up for his wife on an empty easel. She had looked at it a few moments and then—apparently—what she saw in it had produced an explosion of dismay and resentment. She was too overcome, and the Colonel too busy holding her and re-expressing his wrath, to look round or look up. The scene was so unexpected to Lyon that all impulse failed in him on the spot for a proof of the triumph of his hand—of a tremendous hit: he could only wonder what on earth was the matter. The idea of the triumph was yet to come. He could see his projected figure, however, from where he stood; he was startled with its look of life—he hadn't supposed the force of the thing could so prevail. Mrs. Capadose flung herself away from her husband—she dropped into the nearest chair, leaned against a table, buried her face in her arms. The sound of her woe diminished, but she shuddered there as if overwhelmed with anguish and shame. Her husband stood a moment glaring at the picture, then went to her, bent over her, took hold of her again, soothed her. "What is it, darling—what the devil is it?"

Lyon fairly drank in her answer. "It's cruel—oh it's too cruel!"

"Damn him, damn him, damn him!" the Colonel repeated.

"It's all there—it's all there!" Mrs. Capadose went on.

"Hang it, what's all there?"

"Everything there oughtn't to be—everything he has seen. It's too dreadful!"

"Everything he has seen? Why, ain't I a good-looking fellow? I'll be bound to say he has made me handsome."

Mrs. Capadose had sprung up again; she had darted another glance at the painted betrayal. "Handsome? Hideous, hideous! Not that—never, never!"

"Not *what*, in heaven's name?" the Colonel almost shouted. Lyon could see his flushed bewildered face.

"What he has made of you—what you know! *He* knows—he has seen. Everyone will, everyone know and see. Fancy that thing in the Academy!"

"You're going wild, darling; but if you hate it so it needn't go," the poor branded man declared.

"Ah he'll send it—it's so good! Come away—come away!" Mrs. Capadose wailed, seizing her husband.

"It's so good?" the victim cried.

"Come away—come away," she only repeated, and she turned toward the staircase that ascended to the gallery.

"Not that way—not through the house in the state you're in,"

Lyon heard her companion object. "This way—we can pass," he added; and he drew his wife to the small door that opened into the garden. It was bolted, but he pushed the bolt and opened the door. She passed out quickly, but he stood there looking back into the room. "Wait for me a moment!" he cried out to her; and with an excited stride he reentered the studio. He came up to the picture again—again he covered it with his baffled glare. "Damn him—damn him—damn him!" he broke out once more. Yet it wasn't clear to Lyon whether this malediction had for object the guilty original or the guilty painter. The Colonel turned away and moved about as if looking for something; Lyon for the moment wondered at his intention; saying to himself the next, however, below his breath: "He's going to do it a harm!" His first impulse was to raise a preventive cry, but he paused with the sound of Everina Brant's sobs still in his ears. The Colonel found what he was looking for—found it among some odds and ends on a small table and strode back with it to the easel. At one and the same moment Lyon recognised the object seized as a small Eastern dagger and saw that he had plunged it into the canvas. Animated as with a sudden fury and exercising a rare vigour of hand, he dragged the instrument down—Lyon knew it to have no very fine edge—making a long and abominable gash. Then he plucked it out and dashed it again several times into the face of the likeness, exactly as if he were stabbing a human victim: it had the most portentous effect—that of some act of prefigured or rehearsed suicide. In a few seconds more the Colonel had tossed the dagger away—he looked at it in this motion as for the sight of blood—and hurried out of the place with a bang of the door.

The strangest part of all was—as will doubtless appear—that Oliver Lyon lifted neither voice nor hand to save his picture. The point is that he didn't feel as if he were losing it or didn't care if he were, so much more was he conscious of gaining a certitude. His old friend *was* ashamed of her husband, and he had made her so, and he had scored a great success, even at the sacrifice of his precious labour. The revelation so excited him—as indeed the whole scene did—that when he came down the steps after the Colonel had gone he trembled with his happy agitation; he was dizzy and had to sit down a moment. The portrait had a dozen jagged wounds—the Colonel literally had hacked himself to death. Lyon left it there where it grimaced, never touched it, scarcely looked at it; he only walked up and down his studio with a sense of such achieved success as nothing finished and framed, varnished and delivered and paid for had ever given him. At the end of this time his good woman came to offer him luncheon; there was a passage under the staircase from the offices.

"Ah the lady and gentleman have gone, sir? I didn't hear them."

"Yes; they went by the garden."

But she had stopped, staring at the picture on the easel. "Gracious, how you 'ave served it, sir!"

Lyon imitated the Colonel. "Yes, I cut it up—in a fit of disgust."

"Mercy, after all your trouble! Because they weren't pleased, sir?"

"Yes; they weren't pleased."

"Well, they must be very grand! Blest if I would!"

"Have it chopped up; it will do to light fires," Lyon magnificently said.

He returned to the country by the 3.30 and a few days later passed over to France. There was something he found himself looking for during these two months on the Continent; he had an expectation—he could hardly have said of what; of some characteristic sign or other on the Colonel's part. Wouldn't he write, wouldn't he explain, wouldn't he take for granted Lyon had discovered the way he had indeed been "served" and hold it only decent to show some form of pity for his mystification? Would he plead guilty or would he repudiate suspicion? The latter course would be difficult, would really put his genius to the test, in view of the ready and responsible witness who had admitted the visitors the day of the ravage and would establish the connexion between their presence and that perpetration. Would the Colonel proffer some apology or some amends, or would any word from him be only a further expression of that exasperated wonder which our friend had seen his wife so suddenly and so fatally communicate? He would have either to take oath that he hadn't touched the picture or to admit that he had, and in either case would be at costs for a difficult version. Lyon was impatient for this probably remarkable story, and as no letter came was disappointed at the failure of the exhibition. His impatience however was much greater in respect to Mrs. Capadose's inevitable share in the report, if report there was to be; for certainly that would be the real test, would show how far she would go for her husband on the one side or for himself on the other. He could scarcely wait to see what line she would take—whether she would simply adopt the Colonel's, whatever it might be. It would have met his impatience most to draw her out without waiting, to get an idea in advance. He wrote to her, to this end, from Venice, in the tone of their established friendship, asking for news, telling her of his movements, hoping for their reunion in London and not saying a word about the picture. Day followed day, after the time, and he received no answer; on which he reflected that she couldn't trust herself to write—was still too deeply ruffled, too disconcerted, by his "betrayal." Her husband had espoused her resentment and she had espoused the action he had taken in consequence of it; the rupture was therefore complete and everything at an end. Lyon was frankly rueful over this prospect, at the same time that he thought it deplorable such charming people should have put themselves so grossly in the wrong. He was at last cheered, though little further enlightened, by the arrival of a letter, brief but breathing good humour and hinting neither at a grievance nor at a bad conscience. The most interesting part of it to him was the postscript, which ran as follows: "I have a confession to make to you. We were in town for a couple of days, early in September, and I took the occasion to defy your authority: this was very bad of me but I couldn't help it. I made Clement take me to your studio— I wanted so dreadfully to see what you had done with him, your wishes to the contrary notwithstanding. We made your servants let us in and I took a good look at the picture. It is really wonderful!" "Wonderful" was non-committal, but at least with this letter there was no rupture.

The third day after his return was a Sunday, so that he could go and ask Mrs. Capadose for luncheon. She had given him in the spring a general invitation to do so and he had several times profited by it. These had been the occasions, before his sittings, when he saw the Colonel most familiarly. Directly after the meal his host disappeared (went out, as he said, to call on *his* women) and the second half-hour was the best, even when there were other people. Now, in the first days of December, Lyon had the luck to find the pair alone, without even Amy, who appeared but little in public. They were in the drawing-room, waiting for the repast to be announced, and as soon as he came in the Colonel broke out: "My dear fellow, I'm delighted to see you! I'm so keen to begin again."

"Oh do go on; it's so beautiful," Mrs. Capadose said as she gave him her hand.

Lyon looked from one to the other; he didn't know what he had expected, but he hadn't expected this. "Ah then you think I've got something?"

"You've got everything." And Mrs. Capadose smiled from her golden-brown eyes.

"She wrote you of our little crime?" her husband asked. "She dragged me there—I had to go." Lyon wondered for a moment whether he meant by their little crime the assault on the canvas; but his friend's next words made this impossible. "You know I like to sit—you want me animated, and it leaves me so to wag my tongue. And just now I've time."

"You must remember how near I had got to the end," Lyon returned.

"So you had. More's the pity. I should like you to begin again."

"My dear fellow, I shall have to begin again!" laughed the painter with his eyes on Mrs. Capadose. She didn't meet them—she had got up to ring for luncheon. "The picture has been smashed," Lyon continued.

"Smashed? Ah what did you do that for?" cried Everina, standing there before him in all her clear rich beauty. Now that she did look at him she was impenetrable.

"I didn't—I found it so—with a dozen holes punched in it!"

"I say!" cried the Colonel—"what a jolly shame!"

Lyon took him in with a wide smile. "I hope *you* didn't go for it?"

"Is it done for?" the Colonel earnestly asked. He was as brightly true as his wife and he looked simply as if Lyon's question couldn't be serious. "For the love of sitting to you? My dear fellow, if I had thought of it I would!"

"Nor you either?" the painter demanded of Mrs. Capadose.

Before she had time to reply her husband had seized her arm as if a lurid light had come to him. "I say, my dear, that woman—that woman!"

"That woman?" Mrs. Capadose repeated; and Lyon too wondered what woman he meant.

"Don't you remember when we came out, she was at the door—or a little way from it? I spoke to you of her—I told you about her. Geraldine—Grenadine—the one who burst in that day," he explained to Lyon. "We saw her hanging about—I called Everina's attention to her."

"Do you mean she got at my picture?"

"Ah yes, I remember," said Mrs. Capadose with a vague recovery.

"She burst in again—she had learned the way—she was waiting for her chance," the Colonel continued. "Ah the horrid little brute!"

Lyon looked down; he felt himself colouring. This was what he had been waiting for—the day the Colonel should wantonly sacrifice some innocent person. And could his wife be a party to that final atrocity? He had reminded himself repeatedly during the previous weeks that when her husband perpetrated his misdeed she had already quitted the room; but he had argued none the less—it was a virtual certainty—that he had on rejoining her at once mentioned his misdeed. He was in the flush of performance; and even if he hadn't reported what he had done she would have guessed it. Lyon didn't for an instant believe poor Miss Geraldine to have been hovering about his door, nor had the account given by the Colonel the summer before of his relations with this lady affected him as in the least convincing. Lyon had never seen her till the day she planted herself in his studio, but he knew her and classified her as if he had made her. He was acquainted with the London model in all her feminine varieties—in every phase of her development and every step of her decay. When he entered his house that September morning just after the arrival of his two friends there had been no symptoms whatever, up and down the road, of Miss Geraldine's reappearance. That fact had been fixed in his mind by his recollecting the vacancy of the prospect when his cook told him that a lady and a gentleman were in his studio: he had wondered there was neither carriage nor cab at his door. Then he had reflected that they would have come by the underground railway; he was near the Marlborough Road station and he knew the Colonel, repeating his pilgrimage so often, habitually made use of that convenience. "How in the world did she get in?" He addressed the question to his companions indifferently.

"Let us go down to luncheon," said Mrs. Capadose, passing out of the room.

"We went by the garden—without troubling your servant—I wanted to show my wife." Lyon followed his hostess with her husband, and the Colonel stopped him at the top of the stairs.

"My dear fellow, I *can't* have been guilty of the folly of not fastening the door?"

"I'm sure I don't know, Colonel," Lyon said as they went down. "It was a very determined hand that did the deed—in the spirit of a perfect wild-cat."

"Well, she *is* a wild-cat—confound her! That's why I wanted to get him away from her."

"But I don't understand her motive."

"Well, she's practically off her head—and she hates me. That was her motive."

"But she doesn't hate me, my dear fellow!" Lyon amusedly urged.

"She hated the picture—don't you remember she said so? The more portraits, the less employment for such as her."

"Yes; but if she's not really the model she pretends to be, how can that hurt her?" Lyon asked.

The question baffled the Colonel an instant—but only an instant. "Ah she's so bad she goes it blind. She doesn't know where she is."

They passed into the dining-room, where Mrs. Capadose was taking her place. "It's too low, it's too horrid!" she said. "You see the fates are against you. Providence won't let you be so disinterested—throwing off masterpieces for nothing."

"Did *you* see the woman?' Lyon put to her with something like a sternness he couldn't mitigate.

She seemed not to feel it, or not to heed it if she did. "There was a person, not far from your door, whom Clement called my attention to. He told me something about her, but we were going the other way."

"And do you think she did it?"

"How can I tell? If she did she was mad, poor wretch."

"I should like very much to get hold of her," said Lyon. This was a false plea for the truth: he had no desire for any further conversation with Miss Geraldine. He had exposed his friends to his own view, but without wish to expose them to others, and least of all to themselves.

"Oh depend upon it she'll never show again. You're all right *now!*" the Colonel guaranteed.

"But I remember her address—Mortimer Terrace Mews, Notting Hill."

"Oh that's pure humbug. There isn't any such place."

"Lord, what a practised deceiver!" said Lyon.

"Is there anyone else you suspect?" his host went on.

"Not a creature."

"And what do your servants say?"

"They say it wasn't *them*, and I reply that I never said it was. That's about the substance of our interviews."

"And when did they discover the havoc?"

"They never discovered it at all. I noticed it first—when I came back."

"Well, she could easily have stepped in," said the subject of Miss Geraldine's pursuit. "Don't you remember how she turned up that day like the clown in the ring?"

"Yes, yes; she could have done the job in three seconds, except that the picture wasn't out."

"Ah my dear fellow," the Colonel groaned, "don't utterly curse me!—but of course I dragged it out."

"You didn't put it *back?*" Lyon tragically cried.

"Ah Clement, Clement, didn't I tell you to?" Mrs. Capadose reproachfully wailed.

The Colonel almost howled for compunction; he covered his face with his hands. His wife's words were for Lyon the finishing touch; they made his whole vision crumble—his theory that she had secretly kept herself true. Even to her old lover she wouldn't be so! He was sick; he couldn't eat; he knew how strange he must have looked. He attempted some platitude about spilled milk and the folly of crying over it—he tried to turn the talk to other things. But it was a horrid effort and he wondered how it pressed upon *them*. He wondered all sorts of things: whether they guessed he disbelieved them—that he had seen them of course they would never guess; whether they had arranged their story in advance or it was only an inspiration of the moment; whether she had resisted, protested, when the Colonel proposed it to her, and then had been borne down by him; whether in short she didn't loathe herself as she sat there. The cruelty, the cowardice of fastening their unholy act upon the wretched woman struck him as monstrous—no less monstrous indeed than the levity that could make them run the risk of her giving them, in her righteous indignation, the lie. Of course that risk could only exculpate her and not inculpate them—the probabilities protected them so perfectly; and what the Colonel counted on—what he would have counted upon the day he delivered himself, after first seeing her, at the studio, if he had thought about the matter then at all and not spoken from the pure spontaneity of his genius—was simply that Miss Geraldine must have vanished for ever into her native unknown. Lyon wanted so much to cut loose, in his disgust, that when after a little Mrs. Capadose said to him "But can nothing be done, can't the picture be repaired? You know they do such wonders in that way now," he only made answer: "I don't know, I don't care, it's all over, *n'en parlons plus!*" Her hypocrisy revolted him. And yet by way of plucking off the last veil of her shame he broke out to her again, shortly afterwards: "And you *did* like it, really?" To which she returned, looking him straight in his face, without a blush, a pallor, an evasion: "Oh *cher grand maître*, I loved it!" Truly her husband had trained her well. After that Lyon said no more, and his companions forbore temporarily to insist, like people of tact and sympathy aware that the odious accident had made him sore.

When they quitted the table the Colonel went away without coming upstairs; but Lyon returned to the drawing-room with his hostess, remarking to her however on the way that he could remain but a moment. He spent that moment—it prolonged itself a little—standing with her before the chimney-piece. She neither sat down nor asked him to; her manner betrayed some purpose of going out. Yes, her husband had trained her well; yet Lyon dreamed for a moment that now he was alone with her she would perhaps break down, retract, apologise, confide, say to him: "My dear old friend, forgive this hideous comedy—you understand!" And then how he would have loved her and pitied her, guarded her, helped her always! If she weren't ready to do something of that sort why had she treated him so as a dear old friend; why had she let him for months suppose certain things—or almost; why had she come to his studio day after day to sit near him on the pretext of her child's portrait, as if she liked to think what might have been? Why had she come so near a tacit confession if she wasn't willing to go an inch further? And she wasn't willing—she wasn't; he could see that as he lingered there. She moved about the room a little, rearranging two or three objects on the tables, but she did nothing more. Suddenly he said to her: "Which way was she going when you came out?"

"She—the woman we saw?"

"Yes, your husband's strange friend. It's a clue worth following." He didn't want to scare or to shake her; he only wanted to communicate the impulse that would make her say: "Ah spare me—and spare *him!* There was no such person."

Instead of this Everina replied: "She was going away from us—she crossed the road. We were coming toward the station."

"And did she appear to recognise the Colonel—did she look round?"

"Yes; she looked round, but I didn't notice much. A hansom came along and we got into it. It wasn't till then that Clement told me who she was: I remember he said that she was there for no good. I suppose we ought to have gone back."

"Yes; you'd have saved the picture."

For a moment she said nothing; then she smiled. "For you, *cher maître*, I'm very sorry. But you must remember I possess the original!"

At this he turned away. "Well, I must go," he said; and he left her without any other farewell and made his way out of the house. As he went slowly up the street the sense came back to him of that first glimpse of her he had had at Stayes—of how he had seen her gaze across the table at her husband. He stopped at the corner, looking vaguely up and down. He would never go back—he couldn't. Nor should he ever sound her abyss. He believed in her absolute straightness where she and her affairs alone might be concerned, but she was still in love with the man of her choice, and since she couldn't redeem him she would adopt and protect him. So he had trained her.

THE LESSON
OF THE MASTER

THE LESSON OF THE MASTER

I

He had been told the ladies were at church, but this was corrected by what he saw from the top of the steps—they descended from a great height in two arms, with a circular sweep of the most charming effect—at the threshold of the door which, from the long bright gallery, overlooked the immense lawn. Three gentlemen, on the grass, at a distance, sat under the great trees, while the fourth figure showed a crimson dress that told as a "bit of colour" amid the fresh rich green. The servant had so far accompanied Paul Overt as to introduce him to this view, after asking him if he wished first to go to his room. The young man declined that privilege, conscious of no disrepair from so short and easy a journey and always liking to take at once a general perceptive possession of a new scene. He stood there a little with his eyes on the group and on the admirable picture, the wide grounds of an old country-house near London—that only made it better—on a splendid Sunday in June. "But that lady, who's *she*?" he said to the servant before the man left him.

"I think she's Mrs. St. George, sir."

"Mrs. St. George the wife of the distinguished—" Then Paul Overt checked himself, doubting if a footman would know.

"Yes, sir—probably, sir," said his guide, who appeared to wish to intimate that a person staying at Summersoft would naturally be, if only by alliance, distinguished. His tone, however, made poor Overt himself feel for the moment scantly so.

"And the gentlemen?" Overt went on.

"Well, sir, one of them's General Fancourt."

"Ah yes, I know; thank you." General Fancourt was distinguished, there was no doubt of that, for something he had done, or perhaps even hadn't done—the young man couldn't remember which—some years before in India. The

175

servant went away, leaving the glass doors open into the gallery, and Paul Overt remained at the head of the wide double staircase, saying to himself that the place was sweet and promised a pleasant visit, while he leaned on the balustrade of fine old ironwork which, like all the other details, was of the same period as the house. It all went together and spoke in one voice—a rich English voice of the early part of the eighteenth century. It might have been church-time on a summer's day in the reign of Queen Anne: the stillness was too perfect to be modern, the nearness counted so as distance, and there was something so fresh and sound in the originality of the large smooth house, the expanse of beautiful brickwork that showed for pink rather than red and that had been kept clear of messy creepers by the law under which a woman with a rare complexion disdains a veil. When Paul Overt became aware that the people under the trees had noticed him he turned back through the open doors into the great gallery which was the pride of the place. It marched across from end to end and seemed—with its bright colours, its high panelled windows, its faded flowered chintzes, its quickly-recognised portraits and pictures, the blue-and-white china of its cabinets and the attenuated festoons and rosettes of its ceiling—a cheeerful upholstered avenue into the other century.

Our friend was slightly nervous; that went with his character as a student of fine prose, went with the artist's general disposition to vibrate; and there was a particular thrill in the idea that Henry St. George might be a member of the party. For the young aspirant he had remained a high literary figure, in spite of the lower range of production to which he had fallen after his three first great successes, the comparative absence of quality in his later work. There had been moments when Paul Overt almost shed tears for this; but now that he was near him—he had never met him—he was conscious only of the fine original source and of his own immense debt. After he had taken a turn or two up and down the gallery he came out again and descended the steps. He was but slenderly supplied with a certain social boldness—it was really a weakness in him—so that, conscious of a want of acquaintance with the four persons in the distance, he gave way to motions recommended by their not committing him to a positive approach. There was a fine English awkwardness in this—he felt that too as he sauntered vaguely and obliquely across the lawn, taking an independent line. Fortunately there was an equally fine English directness in the way one of the gentlemen presently rose and made as if to "stalk" him, though with an air of conciliation and reassurance. To this demonstration Paul Overt instantly responded, even if the gentleman were not his host. He was tall, straight and elderly and had, like the great house itself, a pink smiling face, and into the bargain a white moustache. Our young man met him halfway while he laughed and said: "Er—Lady Watermouth told us you were coming; she asked me just to look after you." Paul Overt thanked him, liking him on the spot, and turned round with him to walk toward the others. "They've all gone to church—all except us," the stranger continued as they went; "we're just sitting here—it's so jolly." Overt pronounced it jolly indeed: it was such a lovely place. He mentioned that he was having the charming impression for the first time.

"Ah, you've not been here before?" said his companion. "It's a nice little place—not much to *do*, you know." Overt wondered what he wanted to "do"—he felt that he himself was doing so much. By the time they came to where the others sat he had recognised his initiator for a military man and—such was the turn of Overt's imagination—had found him thus still more sympathetic. He would naturally have a need for action, for deeds at variance with the pacific pastoral scene. He was evidently so good-natured, however, that he accepted the inglorious hour for what it was worth. Paul Overt shard it with him and with his companions for the next twenty minutes; the latter looked at him and he looked at them without knowing much who they were, while the talk went on without much telling him even what it meant. It seemed indeed to mean nothing in particular; it wandered, with casual pointless pauses and short terrestrial flights, amid names of persons and places—names which, for our friend, had no great power of evocation. It was all sociable and slow, as was right and natural of a warm Sunday morning.

His first attention was given to the question, privately considered, of whether one of the two younger men would be Henry St. George. He knew many of his distinguished contemporaries by their photographs, but had never, as happened, seen a portrait of the great misguided novelist. One of the gentlemen was unimaginable—he was too young; and the other scarcely looked clever enough, with such mild undiscriminating eyes. If those eyes were St. George's the problem presented by the ill-matched parts of his genius would be still more difficult of solution. Besides, the deportment of their proprietor was not, as regards the lady in the red dress, such as could be natural, toward the wife of his bosom, even to a writer accused by several critics of sacrificing too much to manner. Lastly, Paul Overt had a vague sense that if the gentleman with the expressionless eyes bore the name that had set his heart beating faster (he also had contradictory conventional whiskers—the young admirer of the celebrity had never in a mental vision seen *his* face in so vulgar a frame) he would have given him a sign of recognition or of friendliness, would have heard of him a little, would know something about *Ginistrella*, would have an impression of how that fresh fiction had caught the eye of real criticism. Paul Overt had a dread of being grossly proud, but even morbid modesty might view the authorship of *Ginistrella* as constituting a degree of identity. His soldierly friend became clear enough: he was "Fancourt," but was also "the General"; and he mentioned to the new visitor in the course of a few moments that he had but lately returned from twenty years' service abroad.

"And now you remain in England?" the young man asked.

"Oh yes; I've bought a small house in London."

"And I hope you like it," said Overt, looking at Mrs. St. George.

"Well, a little house in Manchester Square—there's a limit to the enthusiasm *that* inspires."

"Oh I meant being at home again—being back in Piccadilly."

"My daughter likes Piccadilly—that's the main thing. She's very fond of art and music and literature and all that kind of thing. She missed it in India and she finds it in London, or she hopes she'll find it. Mr. St. George has promised to help her—he has been awfully kind to her. She has gone to church—she's fond of that too—but they'll all be back in a quarter of an hour. You must let me introduce you to her—she'll be so glad to know you. I daresay she has read every blest word you've written."

"I shall be delighted—I haven't written so very many," Overt pleaded, feeling, and without resentment, that the General at least was vagueness itself about that. But he wondered a little why, expressing this friendly disposition, it didn't occur to the doubtless eminent soldier to pronounce the word that would put him in relation with Mrs. St. George. If it was a question of introductions Miss Fancourt—apparently as yet unmarried—was far away, while the wife of his illustrious confrère was almost between them. This lady struck Paul Overt as altogether pretty, with a surprising juvenility and a high smartness of aspect, something that—he could scarcely have said why—served for mystification. St. George certainly had every right to a charming wife, but he himself would never have imagined the important little woman in the aggressively Parisian dress the partner for life, the *alter ego*, of a man of letters. That partner in general, he knew, that second self, was far from presenting herself in a single type: observation had taught him that she was not inveterately, not necessarily plain. But he had never before seen her look so much as if her prosperity had deeper foundations than an ink-spotted study-table littered with proof-sheets. Mrs. St. George might have been the wife of a gentleman who "kept" books rather than wrote them, who carried on great affairs in the City and made better bargains than those that poets mostly make with publishers. With this she hinted at a success more personal—a success peculiarly stamping the age in which

179

society, the world of conversation, is a great drawing-room with the City for its antechamber. Overt numbered her years at first as some thirty, and then ended by believing that she might approach her fiftieth. But she somehow in this case juggled away the excess and the difference—you only saw them in a rare glimpse, like the rabbit in the conjuror's sleeve. She was extraordinarily white, and her every element and item was pretty; her eyes, her ears, her hair, her voice, her hands, her feet—to which her relaxed attitude in her wicker chair gave a great publicity—and the numerous ribbons and trinkets with which she was bedecked. She looked as if she had put on her best clothes to go to church and then had decided they were too good for that and had stayed at home. She told a story of some length about the shabby way Lady Jane had treated the Duchess, as well as an anecdote in relation to a purchase she had made in Paris—on her way back from Cannes; made for Lady Egbert, who had never refunded the money. Paul Overt suspected her of a tendency to figure great people as larger than life, until he noticed the manner in which she handled Lady Egbert, which was so sharply mutinous that it reassured him. He felt he should have understood her better if he might have met her eye; but she scarcely so much as glanced at him. "Ah here they come—all the good ones!" she said at last; and Paul Overt admired at his distance the return of the churchgoers—several persons, in couples and threes, advancing in a flicker of sun and shade at the end of a larger green vista formed by the level grass and the overarching boughs.

"If you mean to imply that *we're* bad, I protest," said one of the gentleman—"after making one's self agreeable all the morning!"

"Ah if they've found you agreeable—!" Mrs. St. George gaily cried. "But if we're good the others are better."

"They must be angels then," said the amused General.

"Your husband was an angel, the way he went off at your bidding," the gentleman who had first spoken declared to Mrs. St. George.

"At my bidding?"

"Didn't you make him go to church?"

"I never made him do anything in my life but once—when I made him burn up a bad book. That's all!" At her "That's all!" our young friend broke into an irrepressible laugh; it lasted only a second, but it drew her eyes to him. His own met them, though not long enough to help him to understand her; unless it were a step towards this that he saw on the instant how the burnt book—the way she alluded to it!—would have been one of her husband's finest things.

"A bad book?" her interlocutor repeated.

"I didn't like it. He went to church because your daughter went," she continued to General Fancourt. "I think it my duty to call your attention to his extraordinary demonstrations to your daughter."

"Well, if you don't mind them I don't!" the General laughed.

"*Il s'attache à ses pas.* But I don't wonder—she's so charming."

"I hope she won't make him burn any books!" Paul Overt ventured to exclaim.

"If she'd make him write a few it would be more to the purpose," said Mrs. St. George. "He has been of a laziness of late—!"

Our young man stared—he was so struck with the lady's phraseology. Her "Write a few" seemed to him almost as good as her "That's all." Didn't she, as the wife of a rare artist, know what it was to produce *one* perfect work of art? How in the world did she think they were turned off? His private conviction was that, admirably as Henry St. George wrote, he had written for the last ten years, and especially for the last five, only too much, and there was an instant during which he felt inwardly solicited to make this public. But before he had spoken a diversion was effected by the return of the absentees. They strolled up dispersedly—there were eight or ten of them—and the circle under the trees rearranged itself as they took their place in it. They made it much larger, so that Paul Overt could feel—he was always feeling that sort of thing, as he said to himself—that if the company had already been interesting to watch the interest would now become intense. He shook hands with his hostess, who welcomed him without many words, in the manner of a woman able to trust him to understand and conscious that so pleasant an occasion would in every way speak for itself. She offered him no particular facility for sitting by her, and when they had all subsided again he found himself still next General Fancourt, with an unknown lady on his other flank.

"That's my daughter—that one opposite," the General said to him without loss of time. Overt saw a tall girl, with magnificent red hair, in a dress of a pretty grey-green tint and of a limp silken texture, a garment that clearly shirked every modern effect. It had therefore somehow the stamp of the latest thing, so that our beholder quickly took her for nothing if not contemporaneous.

"She's very handsome—very handsome," he repeated while he considered her. There was something noble in her head, and she appeared fresh and strong.

Her good father surveyed her with complacency, remarking soon: "She looks too hot—that's her walk. But she'll be all right presently. Then I'll make her come over and speak to you."

"I should be sorry to give you that trouble. If you were to take me over *there*—!" the young man murmured.

"My dear sir, do you suppose I put myself out that way? I don't mean for you, but for Marian," the General added.

"*I* would put myself out for her soon enough," Overt replied; after which he went on: "Will you be so good as to tell me which of those gentlemen is Henry St. George?"

"The fellow talking to my girl. By Jove, he *is* making up to her—they're going off for another walk."

"Ah is that he—really?" Our friend felt a certain surprise, for the personage before him seemed to trouble a vision which had been vague only while not confronted with the reality. As soon as the reality dawned the mental image, retiring with a sigh, became substantial enough to suffer a slight wrong. Overt, who had spent a considerable part of his short life in foreign lands, made now, but not for the first time, the reflexion that whereas in those countries he had almost always recognised the artist and the man of letters by his personal "type," the mould of his face, the character of his head, the expression of his figure, and even the indications of his dress, so in England this identification was as little as possible a matter of course, thanks to the greater conformity, the habit of sinking the profession instead of advertising it, the general diffusion of the air of the gentleman—the gentleman committed to no particular set of ideas. More than once, on returning to his own country, he had said to himself about people met in society: "One sees them in this place and that, and one even talks with them; but to find out what they *do* one would really have to be a detective." In respect to several individuals whose work he was the opposite of "drawn to"—perhaps he was wrong—he found himself adding, "No wonder they conceal it—when it's so bad!" He noted that oftener than in France and in Germany his artist looked like a gentleman—that is, like an English one—while, certainly outside a few exceptions, his gentleman didn't look like an artist. St. George was not one of the exceptions; that circumstance he definitely apprehended before the great man had turned his back to walk off with Miss Fancourt. He certainly looked better behind than any foreign man of letters—showed for beautifully correct in his tall black hat and his superior frock coat. Somehow, all the same, these very garments—he wouldn't have minded them so much on a week-day—were disconcerting to Paul Overt, who forgot for the moment that the head of the profession was not a bit better dressed than himself. He had caught a glimpse of a regular face, a fresh colour, a brown moustache and a pair of eyes surely never visited by a fine frenzy, and he promised himself to study these denotements on the first occasion. His superficial sense was that their owner might have passed for a lucky stockbroker—a gentleman driving eastward every morning from a sanitary suburb in a smart dog-cart. That carried out the impression already derived from his wife. Paul's glance, after a moment, travelled back to this lady, and he saw how her own had followed her husband as he moved off with Miss Fancourt. Overt permitted himself to wonder a little if she were jealous when another woman took him away. Then he made out that Mrs. St. George wasn't glaring at the indifferent maiden. Her eyes rested but on her husband, and with unmistakable serenity. That was the way she wanted him to be—she liked his conventional uniform. Overt longed to hear more about the book she had induced him to destroy.

II

As they all came out from luncheon General Fancourt took hold of him with an "I say, I want you to know my girl!" as if the idea had just occurred to him and he hadn't spoken of it before. With the other hand he possessed himself all paternally of the young lady. "You know all about him. I've seen you with his books. She reads everything—everything!" he went on to Paul. The girl smiled at him and then laughed at her father. The General turned away and his daughter spoke—"Isn't papa delightful?"

"He is indeed, Miss Fancourt."

"As if I read you because I read 'everything'!"

"Oh I don't mean for saying that," said Paul Overt. "I liked him from the moment he began to be kind to me. Then he promised me this privilege."

"It isn't for you he means it—it's for me. If you flatter yourself that he thinks of anything in life but me you'll find you're mistaken. He introduces everyone. He thinks me insatiable."

"You speak just like him," laughed our youth.

"Ah but sometimes I want to"—and the girl coloured. "I don't read everything—I read very little. But I *have* read you."

"Suppose we go into the gallery," said Paul Overt. She

pleased him greatly, not so much because of this last remark—though that of course was not too disconcerting—as because, seated opposite to him at luncheon, she had given him for half an hour the impression of her beautiful face. Something else had come with it—a sense of generosity, of an enthusiasm which, unlike many enthusiasms, was not all manner. That was not spoiled for him by his seeing that the repast had placed her again in familiar contact with Henry St. George. Sitting next her this celebrity was also opposite our young man, who had been able to note that he multiplied the attentions lately brought by his wife to the General's notice. Paul Overt had gathered as well that this lady was not in the least discomposed by these fond excesses and that she gave every sign of an unclouded spirit. She had Lord Masham on one side of her and on the other the accomplished Mr. Mulliner, editor of the new high-class lively evening paper which was expected to meet a want felt in circles increasingly conscious that Conservatism must be made amusing, and unconvinced when assured by those of another political colour that it was already amusing enough. At the end of an hour spent in her company Paul Overt thought her still prettier than at the first radiation, and if her profane allusions to her husband's work had not still rung in his ears he should have liked her—so far as it could be a question of that in connexion with a woman to whom he had not yet spoken and to whom probably he should never speak if it were left to her. Pretty women were a clear need to this genius, and for the hour it was Miss Fancourt who supplied the want. If Overt had promised himself a closer view the occasion was now of the best, and it brought consequences felt by the young man as important. He saw more in St. George's face, which he liked the better for its not having told its whole story in the first three minutes. That story came out as one read, in short instalments—it was excusable that one's analogies should be somewhat professional—and the text was a style considerably involved, a language not easy to translate at sight. There were shades of meaning in it and a vague perspective of history which receded as you advanced. Two facts Paul had particularly heeded. The first of these was that he liked the measured mask much better at inscrutable rest than in social agitation; its almost convulsive smile above all displeased him (as much as any impression from that source could), whereas the quiet face had a charm that grew in proportion as stillness settled again. The change to the expression of gaiety excited, he made out, very much the private protest of a person sitting gratefully in the twilight when the lamp is brought in too soon. His second reflexion was that, though generally averse to the flagrant use of ingratiating arts by a man of age "making up" to a pretty girl, he was not in this case too painfully affected: which seemed to prove either that St. George had a light hand or the air of being younger than he was, or else that Miss Fancourt's own manner somehow made everything right.

Overt walked with her into the gallery, and they strolled to the end of it, looking at the pictures, the cabinets, the charming vista, which harmonised with the prospect of the summer afternoon, resembling it by a long brightness, with great divans and old chairs that figured hours of rest. Such a place as that had the added merit of giving those who came into it plenty to talk about. Miss Fancourt sat down with her new acquaintance on a flowered sofa, the cushions of which, very numerous, were tight ancient cubes of many sizes, and presently said: "I'm so glad to have a chance to thank you."

"To thank me—?" He had to wonder.

"I liked your book so much. I think it splendid."

She sat there smiling at him, and he never asked himself which book she meant; for after all he had written three or four. That seemed a vulgar detail, and he wasn't even gratified by the idea of the pleasure she told him—her handsome bright face told him—he had given her. The feeling she appealed to, or at any rate the feeling she excited, was something larger, something that had little to do with any quickened pulsation of his own vanity. It was responsive admiration of the life she embodied, the young purity and richness of which appeared to imply that real success was to resemble *that*, to live, to bloom, to present the perfection of a fine type, not to have hammered out headachy fancies with a bent back at an ink-stained table. While her grey eyes rested on him—there was a wideish space between these, and the division of her rich-coloured hair, so thick that it ventured to be smooth, made a free arch above them—he was almost ashamed of that exercise of the pen which it was her present inclination to commend. He was conscious he should have liked better to please her in some other way. The lines of her face were those of a woman grown, but the child lingered on in her complexion and in the sweetness of her mouth. Above all she was natural—that was indubitable now; more natural than he had supposed at first, perhaps on account of her esthetic toggery, which was conventionally unconventional, suggesting what he might have called a tortuous spontaneity. He had feared that sort of thing in other cases, and his fears had been justified; for, though he was an artist to the essence, the modern reactionary nymph, with the brambles of the woodland caught in her folds and a look as if the satyrs had toyed with her hair, made him shrink, not as a man of starch and patent leather, but as a man potentially himself a poet or even a faun. The girl was really more candid than her costume, and the best proof of it was her supposing her liberal character suited by any uniform. This was a fallacy, since if she was draped as a pessimist he was sure she liked the taste of life. He thanked her for her appreciation—aware at the same time that he didn't appear to thank her enough and that she might think him ungracious. He was afraid she would ask him to explain something he had written, and he always winced at that—perhaps too timidly—for to his own ear the explanation of a work of art sounded fatuous. But he liked her so much as to feel a confidence that in the long run he should be able to show her he wasn't rudely evasive.

Moreover, she surely wasn't quick to take offence, wasn't irritable; she could be trusted to wait. So when he said to her, "Ah don't talk of anything I've done, don't talk of it *here*; there's another man in the house who's the actuality!"—when he uttered this short sincere protest it was with the sense that she would see in the words neither mock humility nor the impatience of a successful man bored with praise.

"You mean Mr. St. George—isn't he delightful?"

Paul Overt met her eyes, which had a cool morning-light that would have half-broken his heart if he hadn't been so young. "Alas I don't know him. I only admire him at a distance."

"Oh you *must* know him—he wants so to talk to you," returned Miss Fancourt, who evidently had the habit of saying the things that, by her quick calculation, would give people pleasure. Paul saw how she would always calculate on everything's being simple between others.

"I shouldn't have supposed he knew anything about me," he professed.

"He does then—everything. And if he didn't I should be able to tell him."

"To tell him everything?" our friend smiled.

"You talk just like the people in your book," she answered.

"Then they must all talk alike."

She thought a moment, not a bit disconcerted. "Well, it must be so difficult. Mr. St. George tells me it *is*—terribly. I've tried too—and I find it so. I've tried to write a novel."

"Mr. St. George oughtn't to discourage you," Paul went so far as to say.

"You do much more—when you wear that expression."

"Well, after all, why try to be an artist?" the young man pursued. "It's so poor—so poor!"

"I don't know what you mean," said Miss Fancourt, who looked grave.

"I mean as compared with being a person of action—as living your works."

"But what's art but an intense life—if it be real?" she asked. "I think it's the only one—everything else is so clumsy!" Her companion laughed, and she brought out with her charming serenity what next struck her. "It's so interesting to meet so many celebrated people."

"So I should think—but surely it isn't new to you."

"Why, I've never seen anyone—anyone: living always in Asia."

The way she talked of Asia somehow enchanted him. "But doesn't that continent swarm with great figures? Haven't you administered provinces in India and had captive rajahs and tributary princes chained to your car?"

It was as if she didn't care even *should* he amuse himself at her cost. "I was with my father, after I left school to go out there. It was delightful being with him—we're alone together in the world, he and I—but there was none of the society I like best. One never heard of a picture—never of a book, except bad ones."

"Never of a picture? Why, wasn't all life a picture?"

She looked over the delightful place where they sat. "Nothing to compare to this. I adore England!" she cried.

It fairly stirred in him the sacred chord. "Ah of course I don't deny that we must do something with her, poor old dear, yet!"

"She hasn't been touched, really," said the girl.

"Did Mr. St. George say that?"

There was a small and, as he felt, harmless spark of irony in his question; which, however, she answered very simply, not noticing the insinuation. "Yes, he says England hasn't been touched—not considering all there is," she went on eagerly. "He's so interesting about our country. To listen to him makes one want so to do something."

"It would make *me* want to," said Paul Overt, feeling strongly, on the instant, the suggestion of what she said and that of the emotion with which she said it, and well aware of what an incentive, on St. George's lips, such a speech might be.

"Oh you—as if you hadn't! I should like so to hear you talk together," she added ardently.

"That's very genial of you; but he'd have it all his own way. I'm prostrate before him."

She had an air of earnestness. "Do you think, then, he's so perfect?"

"Far from it. Some of his later books seem to me of a queerness—!"

"Yes, yes—he knows that."

Paul Overt stared. "That they seem to me of a queerness—?"

"Well yes, or at any rate that they're not what they should be. He told me he didn't esteem them. He has told me such wonderful things—he's so interesting."

There was a certain shock for Paul Overt in the knowledge that the fine genius they were talking of had been reduced to so explicit a confession and had made it, in his misery, to the first comer; for though Miss Fancourt was charming what was she after all but an immature girl encountered at a country-house? Yet precisely this was part of the sentiment he himself had just expressed: he would make way completely for the poor peccable great man, not because he didn't read him clear, but altogether because he did. His consideration was half composed of tenderness for superficialities which he was sure their perpetrator judged privately, judged more ferociously than anyone, and which represented some tragic intellectual secret. He would have his reasons for his psychology *à fleur de peau*, and these reasons could only be cruel ones, such as would make him dearer to those who already were fond of him. "You excite my envy. I have my reserves, I discriminate—but I love him," Paul said in a moment. "And seeing him for the first time this way is a great event for me."

"How momentous—how magnificent!" cried the girl. "How delicious to bring you together!"

"*Your* doing it—that makes it perfect," our friend returned.

"He's as eager as you," she went on. "But it's so odd you shouldn't have met."

"It's not really so odd as it strikes you. I've been out of England so much—made repeated absences all these last years."

She took this in with interest. "And yet you write of it as well as if you were always here."

"It's just the being away perhaps. At any rate the best bits, I suspect, are those that were done in dreary places abroad."

"And why were they dreary?"

"Because they were health-resorts—where my poor mother was dying."

"Your poor mother?"—she was all sweet wonder.

"We went from place to place to help her to get better. But she never did. To the deadly Riviera (I hate it!), to the high Alps, to Algiers, and far away—a hideous journey—to Colorado."

"And she isn't better?" Miss Fancourt went on.

"She died a year ago."

"Really?—like mine! Only that's years since. Some day you must tell me about your mother," she added.

He could at first, on this, only gaze at her. "What right things you say! If you say them to St. George I don't wonder he's in bondage."

It pulled her up for a moment. "I don't know what you mean. He doesn't make speeches and professions at all—he isn't ridiculous."

"I'm afraid you consider, then, that I am."

"No, I don't"—she spoke it rather shortly. And then she added: "He understands—understands everything."

The young man was on the point of saying jocosely: "And I don't—is that it?" But these words, in time, changed themselves to others slightly less trivial. "Do you suppose he understands his wife?"

Miss Fancourt made no direct answer, but after a moment's hesitation put it: "Isn't she charming?"

"Not in the least!"

"Here he comes. Now you must know him," she went on. A small group of visitors had gathered at the other end of the gallery and had been there overtaken by Henry St. George, who strolled in from a neighbouring room. He stood near them a moment, not falling into the talk but taking up an old miniature from a table and vaguely regarding it. At the end of a minute he became aware of Miss Fancourt and her companion in the

191

distance; whereupon, laying down his miniature, he approached them with the same procrastinating air, his hands in his pockets and his eyes turned, right and left, to the pictures. The gallery was so long that this transit took some little time, especially as there was a moment when he stopped to admire the fine Gainsborough. "He says Mrs. St. George has been the making of him," the girl continued in a voice slightly lowered.

"Ah he's often obscure!" Paul laughed.

"Obscure?" she repeated as if she heard it for the first time. Her eyes rested on her other friend, and it wasn't lost upon Paul that they appeared to send out great shafts of softness. "He's going to speak to us!" she fondly breathed. There was a sort of rapture in her voice, and our friend was startled. "Bless my soul, does she care for him like *that*?—is she in love with him?" he mentally inquired. "Didn't I tell you he was eager?" she had meanwhile asked of him.

"It's eagerness dissimulated," the young man returned as the subject of their observation lingered before his Gainsborough. "He edges toward us shyly. Does he mean that she saved him by burning that book?"

"That book? what book did she burn?" The girl quickly turned her face to him.

"Hasn't he told you, then?"

"Not a word."

"Then he doesn't tell you everything!" Paul had guessed that she pretty much supposed he did. The great man had now resumed his course and come nearer; in spite of which his more qualified admirer risked a profane observation. "St. George and the Dragon is what the anecdote suggests!"

His companion, however, didn't hear it; she smiled at the dragon's adversary. "He *is* eager—he is!" she insisted.

"Eager for you—yes."

But meanwhile she had called out: "I'm sure you want to know Mr. Overt. You'll be great friends, and it will always be delightful to me to remember I was here when you first met and that I had something to do with it."

There was a freshness of intention in the words that carried them off; nevertheless our young man was sorry for Henry St. George, as he was sorry at any time for any person publicly invited to be responsive and delightful. He would have been so touched to believe that a man he deeply admired should care a straw for him that he wouldn't play with such a presumption if it were possibly vain. In a single glance of the eye of the pardonable master he read—having the sort of divination that belonged to his talent—that this personage had ever a store of friendly patience, which was part of his rich outfit, but was versed in no printed page of a rising scribbler. There was even a relief, a simplification, in that: liking him so much already for what he had done, how could one have liked him any more for a perception which must at the best have been vague? Paul Overt got up, trying to show his compassion, but at the same instant he found himself encompassed by St. George's happy personal art—a manner of which it was the essence to conjure away false positions. It all took place in a moment. Paul was conscious that he knew him now, conscious of his handshake and of the very quality of his hand; of his face, seen nearer and consequently seen better, of a general fraternising assurance, and in particular of the circumstance that St. George didn't dislike him (as yet at least) for being imposed by a charming but too gushing girl, attractive enough without such danglers. No irritation at any rate was reflected in the voice with which he questioned Miss Fancourt as to some project of a walk—a general walk of the company round the park. He had soon said something to Paul about a talk—"We must have a tremendous lot of talk; there are so many things, aren't there?"—but our friend could see this idea wouldn't in the present case take very immediate effect. All the same he was extremely happy, even after the matter of the walk had been settled—the three presently passed back to the other part of the gallery, where it was discussed with several members of the party; even when, after they had all gone out together, he found himself for half an hour conjoined with Mrs. St. George. Her husband had taken the advance with Miss Fancourt, and this pair were quite out of sight. It was the prettiest of rambles for a summer afternoon—a grassy circuit, of immense extent, skirting the limit of the park within. The park was completely surrounded by its old mottled but perfect red wall, which, all the way on their left, constituted in itself an object of interest. Mrs. St. George mentioned to him the surprising number of acres thus enclosed, together with numerous other facts relating to the property and the family, and the family's other pro-perties: she couldn't too strongly urge on him the importance of seeing their other houses. She ran over the names of these and rang the changes on them with the facility of practice, making them appear an almost endless list. She had received Paul Overt very amiably on his breaking ground with her by the mention of his joy in having just made her husband's acquaintance, and struck him as so alert and so accommodating a little woman that he was rather ashamed of his *mot* about her to Miss Fancourt; though he reflected that a hundred other people, on a hundred occasions, would have been sure to make it. He got on with Mrs. St. George, in short, better than he expected; but this didn't prevent her suddenly becoming aware that she was faint with fatigue and must take her way back to the house by the shortest cut. She professed that she hadn't the strength of a kitten and was a miserable wreck; a character he had been too preoccupied to discern in her while he wondered in what sense she could be held to have been the making of her husband. He had arrived at a glimmering of the answer when she announced that she must leave him, though this perception was of course provisional. While he was in the very act of placing himself at her disposal for the return the situation underwent a change; Lord Masham had suddenly turned up, coming back to them, overtaking them, emerging from the shrubbery—Overt could scarcely have said how he appeared—and Mrs. St. George had protested that she wanted to be left alone and not to break up the party. A moment later she was walking off with Lord Masham. Our friend fell back and joined Lady Watermouth, to whom he presently mentioned that Mrs. St. George had been obliged to renounce the attempt to go further.

"She oughtn't to have come out at all," her ladyship rather grumpily remarked.

"Is she so very much of an invalid?"

"Very bad indeed." And his hostess added with still greater austerity: "She oughtn't really to come to one!" He wondered what was implied by this, and presently gathered that it was not a reflexion on the lady's conduct or her moral nature: it only represented that her strength was not equal to her aspirations.

III

The smoking-room at Summersoft was on the scale of the rest of the place—high light commodious and decorated with such refined old carvings and mouldings that it seemed rather a bower for ladies who should sit at work at fading crewels than a parliament of gentlemen smoking strong cigars. The gentlemen mustered there in considerable force on the Sunday evening, collecting mainly at one end, in front of one of the cool fair fireplaces of white marble, the entablature of which was adorned with a delicate little Italian "subject." There was another in the wall that faced it, and, thanks to the mild summer night, a fire in neither; but a nucleus for aggregation was furnished on one side by a table in the chimney-corner laden with bottles, decanters and tall tumblers. Paul Overt was a faithless smoker; he would puff a cigarette for reasons with which tobacco had nothing to do. This was particularly the case on the occasion of which I speak; his motive was the vision of a little direct talk with Henry St. George. The "tremendous" communion of which the great man had held out hopes to him earlier in the day had not yet come off, and this saddened him considerably, for the party was to go its several ways immediately after breakfast on the morrow. He had, however, the disappointment of finding that apparently the author of *Shadowmere* was not disposed to prolong his vigil. He wasn't among the gentlemen assembled when Paul entered, nor was he one of those who turned up, in bright habiliments, during the next ten minutes. The young man waited a little, wondering if he had only gone to put on something extraordinary; this would account for his delay as well as contribute further to Overt's impression of his tendency to do the approved superficial thing. But he didn't arrive—he must have been putting on something more extraordinary than was probable. Our hero gave him up, feeling a little injured, a little wounded, at this loss of twenty coveted words. He wasn't angry, but he puffed his cigarette sighingly, with the sense of something rare possibly missed. He wandered away with his regret and moved slowly round the room, looking at the old prints on the walls. In this attitude he presently felt a hand on his shoulder and a friendly voice in his ear: "This is good. I hoped I should find you. I came down on purpose." St. George was there without a change of dress and with a fine face—his graver one—to which our young man all in a flutter responded. He explained that it was only for the Master—the idea of a little talk—that he had sat up, and that, not finding him, he had been on the point of going to bed.

"Well, you know, I don't smoke—my wife doesn't let me," said St. George, looking for a place to sit down. "It's very good for me—very good for me. Let us take that sofa."

"Do you mean smoking's good for you?"

"No, no—her not letting me. It's a great thing to have a wife who's so sure of all the things one can do without. One might never find them out one's self. She doesn't allow me to touch a cigarette." They took possession of a sofa at a distance from the group of smokers, and St. George went on: "Have you got one yourself?"

"Do you mean a cigarette?"

196

"Dear no—a wife!"

"No; and yet I'd give up my cigarette for one."

"You'd give up a good deal more than that," St. George returned. "However, you'd get a great deal in return. There's a something to be said for wives," he added, folding his arms and crossing his outstretched legs. He declined tobacco altogether and sat there without returning fire. His companion stopped smoking, touched by his courtesy; and after all they were out of the fumes, their sofa was in a faraway corner. It would have been a mistake, St. George went on, a great mistake for them to have separated without a little chat; "for I know all about you," he said, "I know you're very remarkable. You've written a very distinguished book."

"And how do you know it?" Paul asked.

"Why, my dear fellow, it's in the air, it's in the papers, it's everywhere." St. George spoke with the immediate familiarity of a confrère—a tone that seemed to his neighbour the very rustle of the laurel. "You're on all men's lips and, what's better, on all women's. And I've just been reading your book."

"Just? You hadn't read it this afternoon," said Overt.

"How do you know that?"

"I think you should know how I know it," the young man laughed.

"I suppose Miss Fancourt told you."

"No indeed—she led me rather to suppose you had."

"Yes—that's much more what she'd do. Doesn't she shed a rosy glow over life? But you didn't believe her?" asked St. George.

"No, not when you came to us there."

"Did I pretend? did I pretend badly?" But without waiting for an answer to this St. George went on: "You ought always to believe such a girl as that—always, always. Some women are meant to be taken with allowances and reserves; but you must take *her* just as she is."

"I like her very much," said Paul Overt.

Something in his tone appeared to excite on his companion's part a momentary sense of the absurd; perhaps it was the air of deliberation attending this judgement. St. George broke into a laugh to reply. "It's the best thing you can do with her. She's a rare young lady! In point of fact, however, I confess I hadn't read you this afternoon."

"Then you see how right I was in this particular case not to believe Miss Fancourt."

"How right? how can I agree to that when I lost credit by it?"

"Do you wish to pass exactly for what she represents you? Certainly you needn't be afraid," Paul said.

"Ah, my dear young man, don't talk about passing—for the likes of me! I'm passing away—nothing else than that. She has a better use for her young imagination (isn't if fine?) than in 'representing' in any way such a weary wasted used-up animal!" The Master spoke with a sudden sadness that produced a protest on Paul's part; but before the protest could be uttered he went on, reverting to the latter's striking novel: "I had no idea you were so good—one hears of so many things. But you're surprisingly good."

"I'm going to be surprisingly better," Overt made bold to reply.

"I see that, and it's what fetches me. I don't see so much else— as one looks about—that's going to be surprisingly better. They're going to be consistently worse—most of the things. It's so much easier to be worse—heaven knows I've found it so. I'm not in a great glow, you know, about what's breaking out all over the place. But you *must* be better, you really must keep it up. I haven't of course. It's very difficult—that's the devil of the whole thing, keeping it up. But I see you'll be able to. It will be a great disgrace if you don't."

"It's very interesting to hear you speak of yourself; but I don't know what you mean by your allusions to your having fallen off," Paul Overt observed with pardonable hypocrisy. He liked his companion so much now that the fact of any decline of talent or of care had ceased for the moment to be vivid to him.

"Don't say that—don't say that," St. George returned gravely, his head resting on the top of the sofa-back and his eyes on the ceiling. "You know perfectly what I mean. I haven't read twenty pages of your book without seeing that you can't help it."

"You make me very miserable," Paul ecstatically breathed.

"I'm glad of that, for it may serve as a kind of warning. Shocking enough it must be, especially to a young fresh mind, full of faith—the spectacle of a man meant for better things sunk at my age in such dishonour." St. George, in the same contemplative attitude, spoke softly but deliberately, and without perceptible emotion. His tone indeed suggested an impersonal lucidity that was practically cruel—cruel to himself—and made his young friend lay an argumentative hand on his arm. But he went on while his eyes seemed to follow the graces of the eighteenth-century ceiling: "Look at me well, take my lesson to heart—for it *is* a lesson. Let that good come of it at least that you shudder with your pitiful impression, and that this may help to keep you straight in the future. Don't become in your old age what I have in mine— the depressing, the deplorable illustration of the worship of false gods!"

"What do you mean by your old age?" the young man asked.

"It has made me old. But I like your youth."

Paul answered nothing—they sat for a minute in silence. They heard the others going on about the governmental majority. Then "What do you mean by false gods?" he inquired.

His companion had no difficulty whatever in saying, "The idols of the market; money and luxury and 'the world'; placing one's children and dressing one's wife; everything that drives one to the short and easy way. Ah the vile things they make one do!"

"But surely one's right to want to place one's children."

"One has no business to have any children," St. George placidly declared. "I mean of course if one wants to do any-thing good."

"But aren't they an inspiration—an incentive?"

"An incentive to damnation, artistically speaking."

"You touch on very deep things—things I should like to discuss with you," Paul said. "I should like you to tell me volumes about yourself. This is a great feast for *me* !"

"Of course it is, cruel youth. But to show you I'm still not incapable, degraded as I am, of an act of faith, I'll tie my vanity to the stake for you and burn it to ashes. You must come and see me—you must come and see us," the Master quickly substituted. "Mrs. St. George is charming; I don't know whether you've had any opportunity to talk with her. She'll be delighted to see you; she likes great celebrities, whether incipient or predominant. You must come and dine—my wife will write to you. Where are you to be found?"

"This is my little address"—and Overt drew out his pocket-book and extracted a visiting-card. On second thoughts, however, he kept it back, remarking that he wouldn't trouble his friend to take charge of it but would come and see him straightway in London and leave it at his door if he should fail to obtain entrance.

"Ah you'll probably fail; my wife's always out—or when she isn't out is knocked up from having *been* out. You must come and dine—though that won't do much good either, for my wife insists on big dinners." St. George turned it over further, but then went on: "You must come down and see us in the country, that's the best way; we've plenty of room and it isn't bad."

"You've a house in the country?" Paul asked enviously.

"Ah not like this! But we have a sort of place we go to—an hour from Euston. That's one of the reasons."

"One of the reasons?"

"Why my books are so bad."

"You must tell me all the others!" Paul longingly laughed.

His friend made no direct rejoinder to this, but spoke again abruptly. "Why have I never seen you before?"

The tone of the question was singularly flattering to our hero, who felt it to imply the great man's now perceiving he had for years missed something. "Partly, I suppose, because there has been no particular reason why you should see me. I haven't lived in the world—in your world. I've spent many years out of England, in different places abroad."

"Well, please don't do it any more. You must do England—there's such a lot of it."

"Do you mean I must write about it?"—and Paul struck the note of the listening candour of a child.

"Of course you must. And tremendously well, do you mind? That takes off a little of my esteem for this thing of yours—that it goes on abroad. Hang 'abroad'! Stay at home and do things here—do subjects we can measure."

"I'll do whatever you tell me," Overt said, deeply attentive. "But pardon me if I say I don't understand how you've been reading my book," he added. "I've had you before me all the afternoon, first in that long walk, then at tea on the lawn, till we went to dress for dinner, and all the evening at dinner and in this place."

St. George turned his face about with a smile. "I gave it but a quarter of an hour."

"A quarter of an hour's immense, but I don't understand where you put it in. In the drawing-room after dinner you weren't reading—you were talking to Miss Fancourt."

"It comes to the same thing, because we talked about *Ginistrella*. She described it to me—she lent me her copy."

"Lent it to you?"

"She travels with it."

"It's incredible," Paul blushed.

"It's glorious for you, but it also turned out very well for me. When the ladies went off to bed she kindly offered to send the book down to me. Her maid brought it to me in the hall, and I went to my room with it. I hadn't thought of coming here, I do that so little. But I don't sleep early, I always have to read an hour or two. I sat down to your novel on the spot, without undressing, without taking off anything but my coat. I think that's a sign my curiosity had been strongly roused about it. I read a quarter of an hour, as I tell you, and even in a quarter of an hour I was greatly struck."

"Ah the beginning isn't very good—it's the whole thing!" said Overt, who had listened to this recital with extreme interest. "And you laid down the book and came after me?" her asked.

"That's the way it moved me. I said to myself, 'I see it's off his own bat, and he's there, by the way, and the day's over, and I haven't said twenty words to him.' It occurred to me that you'd probably be in the smoking-room and that it wouldn't be too late to repair my omission. I wanted to do something civil to you, so I put on my coat and came down. I shall read your book again when I go up."

Our friend faced round in his place—he was touched as he had scarce ever been by the picture of such a demonstration in his favour. "You're really the kindest of men. *Cela c'est passé comme ça?*—and I've been sitting here with you all this time and never apprehended it and never thanked you!"

"Thank Miss Fancourt—it was she who wound me up. She has made me feel as if I had read your novel."

"She's an angel from heaven!" Paul declared.

"She is indeed. I've never seen anyone like her. Her interest in literature's touching—something quite peculiar to herself; she takes it all so seriously. She feels the arts and she wants to feel them more. To those who practise them it's almost humiliating—her curiosity, her sympathy, her good faith. How can anything be as fine as she supposes it?"

"She's a rare organisation," the younger man sighed.

"The richest I've ever seen—an artistic intelligence really of the first order. And lodged in such a form!" St. George exclaimed.

"One would like to represent such a girl as that," Paul continued.

"Ah there it is—there's nothing like life!" said his companion. "When you're finished, squeezed dry and used up and you think the sack's empty, you're still appealed to, you still get touches and thrills, the idea springs up—out of the lap of the actual—and shows you there's always something to be done. But I shan't do it—she's not for me!"

"How do you mean, not for you?"

"Oh it's all over—she's for you, if you like."

"Ah much less!" said Paul. "She's not for a dingy little man of letters; she's for the world, the bright rich world of bribes and rewards. And the world will take hold of her—it will carry her away."

"It will try—but it's just a case in which there may be a fight. It would be worth fighting, for a man who had it in him, with youth and talent on his side."

These words rang not a little in Paul Overt's consciousness—they held him briefly silent. "It's a wonder she has remained as she is; giving herself away so—with so much to give away."

"Remaining, you mean, so ingenuous—so natural? Oh she doesn't care a straw—she gives away because she overflows. She has her own feelings, her own standards; she doesn't keep remembering that she must be proud. And then she hasn't been here long enough to be spoiled; she has picked up a fashion or two, but only the amusing ones. She's a provincial—a provincial of genius," St. George went on; "her very blunders are charming, her mistakes are interesting. She has come back from Asia with all sorts of excited curiosities and unappeased appetites. She's first-rate herself and she expends herself on the second-rate. She's life herself and she takes a rare interest in imitations. She mixes all things up, but there are none in regard to which she hasn't perceptions. She sees things in a perspective—as if from the top of the Himalayas—and she enlarges everything she touches. Above all she exaggerates—to herself, I mean. She exaggerates you and me!"

There was nothing in that description to allay the agitation caused in our younger friend by such a sketch of a fine subject. It seemed to him to show the art of St. George's admired hand, and he lost himself in gazing at the vision—this hovered there before him—of a woman's figure which should be part of the glory of novel. But at the end of a moment the thing had turned into smoke, and out of the smoke—the last puff of a big cigar—proceeded the voice of General Fancourt, who had left the others and come and planted himself before the gentlemen on the sofa. "I suppose that when you fellows get talking you sit up half the night."

"Half the night?—*jamais de la vie!* I follow a hygiene"—and St. George rose to his feet.

"I see—you're hothouse plants," laughed the General. "That's the way you produce your flowers."

"I produce mine between ten and one every morning—I bloom with a regularity!" St. George went on.

"And with a splendour!" added the polite General, while Paul noted how little the author of *Shadowmere* minded, as he phrased it to himself, when addressed as a celebrated story-teller. The young man had an idea *he* should never get used to that; it would always make him uncomfortable—from the suspicion that people would think they had to—and he would want to prevent it. Evidently his great colleague had toughened and hardened—had made himself a surface. The group of men had finished their cigars and taken up their bedroom candlesticks; but before they all passed out Lord Watermouth invited the pair of guests who had been so absorbed together to "have" something. It happened that they both declined; upon which General Fancourt said: "Is that the hygiene? You don't water the flowers?"

"Oh I should drown them!" St. George replied; but, leaving the room still at his young friend's side, he added whimsically, for the latter's benefit, in a lower tone: "My wife doesn't let me."

"Well I'm glad I'm not one of you fellows!" the General richly concluded.

The nearness of Summersoft to London had this consequence, chilling to a person who had had a vision of sociability in a railway-carriage, that most of the company, after breakfast, drove back to town, entering their own vehicles, which had come out to fetch them, while their servants returned by train with their luggage. Three or four young men, among whom was Paul Overt, also availed themselves of the common convenience; but they stood in the portico of the house and saw the others roll away. Miss Fancourt got into a victoria with her father after she had shaken hands with our hero and said, smiling in the frankest way in the world, "I *must* see you more. Mrs. St. George is so nice; she has promised to ask us both to dinner together." This lady and her husband took their places in a perfectly-appointed brougham—she required a closed carriage—and as our young man waved his hat to them in response to their nods and flourishes he reflected that, taken together, they were an honourable image of success, of the material rewards and the social credit of literature. Such things were not the full measure, but he nevertheless felt a little proud for literature.

IV

Before a week had elapsed he met Miss Fancourt in Bond Street, at a private view of the works of a young artist in "black-and-white" who had been so good as to invite him to the stuffy scene. The drawings were admirable, but the crowd in the one little room was so dense that he felt himself up to his neck in a sack of wool. A fringe of people at the outer edge endeavoured by curving forward their backs and presenting, below them, a still more convex surface of resistance to the pressure of the mass, to preserve an interval between their noses and the glazed mounts of the pictures; while the central body, in the comparative gloom projected by a wide horizontal screen hung under the skylight and allowing only a margin for the day, remained upright dense and vague, lost in the contemplation of its own ingredients. This contemplation sat especially in the sad eyes of certain female heads, surmounted with hats of strange convolution and plumage, which rose on long necks above the others. One of the heads, Paul perceived, was much the most beautiful of the collection, and his next discovery was that it belonged to Miss Fancourt. Its beauty was enhanced by the glad smile she sent him across surrounding obstructions, a smile that drew him to her as fast as he could make his way. He had seen for himself at Summersoft that the last thing her nature contained was an affectation of indifference; yet even with this circumspection he took a fresh satisfaction in her not having pretended to await his arrival with composure. She smiled as radiantly as if she wished to make him hurry, and as soon as he came within earshot she broke out in her voice of joy: "He's here—he's here; he's coming back in a moment!"

"Ah your father?" Paul returned as she offered him her hand.

"Oh dear no, this isn't in my poor father's line. I mean Mr. St. George. He has just left me to speak to someone—he's coming back. It's he who brought me—wasn't it charming?"

"Ah that gives him a pull over me—I couldn't have 'brought' you, could I?"

"If you had been so kind as to propose it—why not you as well as he?" the girl returned with a face that, expressing no cheap coquetry, simply affirmed a happy fact.

"Why he's a *père de famille*. They've privileges," Paul explained. And then quickly: "Will you go to see places with *me*?" he asked.

"Anything you like," she smiled. "I know what you mean, that girls have to have a lot of people—!" Then she broke off: "I don't know; I'm free. I've always been like that—I can go about with anyone. I'm so glad to meet you," she added with a sweet distinctness that made those near her turn round.

"Let me at least repay that speech by taking you out of this squash," her friend said. "Surely people aren't happy here!"

"No, they're awfully *mornes*, aren't they? But I'm very happy indeed and I promised Mr. St. George to remain on this spot till he comes back. He's going to take me away. They send him invitations for things of this sort—more than he wants. It was so kind of him to think of me."

"They also send me invitations of this kind—more than *I* want. And if thinking of *you* will do it—!" Paul went on.

"Oh I delight in them—everything that's life, everything that's London!"

"They don't have private views in Asia, I suppose," he laughed. "But what a pity that for this year, even in this gorged city, they're pretty well over."

"Well, next year will do, for I hope you believe we're going to be friends always. Here he comes!" Miss Fancourt continued before Paul had time to respond.

He made out St. George in the gaps of the crowd, and this perhaps led to his hurrying a little to say: "I hope that doesn't mean I'm to wait till next year to see you."

"No, no—aren't we to meet at dinner on the twenty-fifth?" she panted with an eagerness as happy as his own.

"That's almost next year. Is there no means of seeing you before?"

She started with all her brightness. "Do you mean you'd *come?*"

"Like a shot, if you'll be so good as to ask me!"

"On Sunday then—this next Sunday?"

"What have I done that you should doubt it?" the young man asked with delight.

Miss Fancourt turned instantly to St. George, who had now joined them, and announced triumphantly: "He's coming on Sunday—this next Sunday!"

"Ah my day—my day too!" said the famous novelist, laughing, to their companion.

"Yes, but not yours only. You shall meet in Manchester Square; you shall talk—you shall be wonderful!"

"We don't meet often enough," St. George allowed, shaking hands with his disciple. "Too many things—ah too many things! But we must make it up in the country in September. You won't forget you've promised me that?"

"Why, he's coming on the twenty-fifth—you'll see him then," said the girl.

"On the twenty-fifth?" St. George asked vaguely.

"We dine with you; I hope you haven't forgotten. He's dining out that day," she added gaily to Paul.

"Oh bless me, yes—that's charming! And you're coming? My wife didn't tell me," St. George said to him. "Too many things—too many things!" he repeated.

"Too many people—too many people!" Paul exclaimed, giving ground before the penetration of an elbow.

"You oughtn't to say that. They all read you."

"Me? I should like to see them! Only two or three at most," the young man returned.

"Did you ever hear anything like that? He knows, haughtily, how good he is!" St. George declared, laughing, to Miss Fancourt. "They read *me*, but that doesn't make me like them any better. Come away from them, come away!" And he led the way out of the exhibition.

"He's going to take me to the Park," Miss Fancourt observed to Overt with elation as they passed along the corridor that led to the street.

"Ah does he go there?" Paul asked, taking the fact for a somewhat unexpected illustration of St. George's *mœurs*.

"It's a beautiful day—there'll be a great crowd. We're going to look at the people, to look at types," the girl went on. "We shall sit under the trees; we shall walk by the Row."

"I go once a year—on business," said St. George, who had overheard Paul's question.

"Or with a country cousin, didn't you tell me? I'm the country cousin!" she continued over her shoulder to Paul as their friend drew her toward a hansom to which he had signalled. The young man watched them get in; he returned, as he stood there, the friendly wave of the hand with which, ensconced in the vehicle beside her, St. George took leave of him. He even lingered to see the vehicle start away and lose itself in the confusion of Bond Street. He followed it with his eyes; it put to him embarrassing things. "She's not for *me*!" the great novelist had said emphatically at Summersoft; but his manner of conducting himself toward her appeared not quite in harmony with such a conviction. How could he have behaved differently if she *had* been for him? An indefinite envy rose in Paul Overt's heart as he took his way on foot alone; a feeling addressed alike, strangely enough, to each of the occupants of the hansom. How much he should like to rattle about London with such a girl! How much he should like to go and look at "types" with St. George!

The next Sunday at four o'clock he called in Manchester Square, where his secret wish was gratified by his finding Miss Fancourt alone. She was in a large bright friendly occupied room, which was painted red all over, draped with the quaint cheap florid stuffs that are represented as coming from southern and eastern countries, where they are fabled to serve as the counterpanes of the peasantry, and bedecked with pottery of vivid hues, ranged on casual shelves, and with many water-colour drawings from the hand (as the visitor learned) of the young lady herself, commemorating with a brave breadth the sunsets, the mountains, the temples and palaces of India. He sat an hour—more than an hour, two hours—and all the while no one came in. His hostess was so good as to remark, with her liberal humanity, that it was delightful they weren't interrupted: it was so rare in London, especially at that season, that people got a good talk. But luckily now, of a fine Sunday, half the world went out of town, and that made it better for those who didn't go, when these others were in sympathy. It was the defect of London—one of two or three, the very short list of those she recognised in the teeming world-city she adored—that there were too few good chances for talk: you never had time to carry anything far.

"Too many things, too many things!" Paul said, quoting St. George's exclamation of a few days before.

"Ah yes, for him there are too many—his life's too complicated."

"Have you seen it *near*? That's what I should like to do; it might explain some mysteries," her visitor went on. She asked him what mysteries he meant, and he said: "Oh peculiarities of his work, inequalities, superficialities. For one who looks at it from the artistic point of view it contains a bottomless ambiguity."

She became at this, on the spot, all intensity. "Ah do describe that more—it's so interesting. There are no such suggestive questions. I'm so fond of them. He thinks he's a failure—fancy!" she beautifully wailed.

"That depends on what his ideal may have been. With his gifts it ought to have been high. But till one knows what he really proposed to himself—! Do *you* know by chance?" the young man broke off.

"Oh he doesn't talk to me about himself. I can't make him. It's too provoking."

Paul was on the point of asking what, then, he did talk about, but discretion checked it and he said instead: "Do you think he's unhappy at home?"

She seemed to wonder. "At home?"

"I mean in his relations with his wife. He has a mystifying little way of alluding to her."

"Not to me," said Marian Fancourt with her clear eyes. "That wouldn't be right, would it?" she asked gravely.

"Not particularly; so I'm glad he doesn't mention her to you. To praise her might bore you, and he has no business to do anything else. Yet he knows you better than me."

"Ah but he respects *you*!" the girl cried as with envy.

Her visitor stared a moment, then broke into a laugh. "Doesn't he respect you?"

"Of course, but not in the same way. He respects what you've done—he told me so the other day."

Paul drank it in, but retained his faculties. "When you went to look at types?"

"Yes—we found so many: he has such an observation of them! He talked a great deal about your book. He says it's really important."

"Important! Ah the grand creature!"—and the author of the work in question groaned for joy.

"He was wonderfully amusing, he was inexpressibly droll, while we walked about. He sees everything; he has so many comparisons and images, and they're always exactly right. *C'est d'un trouvé*, as they say!"

"Yes, with his gifts, such things as he ought to have done!" Paul sighed.

"And don't you think he *has* done them?"

Ah it was just the point. "A part of them, and of course even that part's immense. But he might have been one of the greatest. However, let us not make this an hour of qualifications. Even as they stand," our friend earnestly concluded, "his writings are a mine of gold."

To this proposition she ardently responded, and for half an hour the pair talked over the Master's principal productions. She knew them well—she knew them even better than her visitor, who was struck with her critical intelligence and with something large and bold in the movement in her mind. She said things that startled him and that evidently had come to her directly; they weren't picked-up phrases—she placed them too well. St. George had been right about her being first-rate, about her not being afraid to gush, not remembering that she must be proud. Suddenly something came back to her, and she said: "I recollect that he did speak of Mrs. St. George to me once. He said, apropos of something or other, that she didn't care for perfection."

"That's a great crime in an artist's wife," Paul returned.

"Yes, poor thing!" and the girl sighed with a suggestion of many reflexions, some of them mitigating. But she presently added: "Ah perfection, perfection—how one ought to go in for it! I wish *I* could."

"Everyone can in his way," her companion opined.

"In *his* way, yes—but not in hers. Women are so hampered—so condemned! Yet it's a kind of dishonour if you don't, when you want to *do* something, isn't it?" Miss Fancourt pursued, dropping one train in her quickness to take up another, an accident that was common with her. So these two young persons sat discussing high themes in their eclectic drawing-room, in their London "season"—discussing, with extreme seriousness, the high theme of perfection. It must be said in extenuation of this eccentricity that they were interested in the business. Their tone had truth and their emotion beauty; they weren't posturing for each other or for someone else.

The subject was so wide that they found themselves reducing it; the perfection to which for the moment they agreed to confine their speculations was that of the valid, the exemplary work of art. Our young woman's imagination, it appeared, had wandered far in that direction, and her guest had the rare delight of feeling in their conversation a full interchange. This episode will have lived for years in his memory and even in his wonder; it had the quality that fortune distils in a single drop at a time—the quality that lubricates many ensuing frictions. He still, whenever he likes, has a vision of the room, the bright red sociable talkative room with the curtains that, by a stroke of successful audacity, had the note of vivid blue. He remembers where certain things stood, the particular book open on the table and the almost intense odour of the flowers placed, at the left, somewhere behind him. These facts were the fringe, as it were, of a fine special agitation which had its birth in those two hours and of which perhaps the main sign was in its leading him inwardly and repeatedly to breathe, "I had no idea there was anyone like this—I had no idea there was anyone like this!" Her freedom amazed him and charmed him—it seemed so to simplify the practical question. She was on the footing of an independent personage—a motherless girl who had passed out of her teens and had a position and responsibilities, who wasn't held down to the limitations of a little miss. She came and went with no dragged duenna, she received people alone, and, though she was totally without hardness, the question of protection or patronage had no relevancy in regard to her. She gave such an impression of the clear and the noble combined with the easy and the natural that in spite of her eminent modern situation she suggested no sort of sisterhood with the "fast" girl. Modern she was indeed, and made Paul Overt, who loved old colour, the golden glaze of time, think with some alarm of the muddled palette of the future. He couldn't get used to her interest in the arts he cared for; it seemed too good to be real—it was so unlikely an adventure to tumble into such a well of sympathy. One might stray into the desert easily—that was on the cards and that was the law of life; but it was too rare an accident to stumble on a crystal well. Yet if her aspirations seemed at one moment too extravagant to be real they struck him at the next as too intelligent to be false. They were both high and lame, and, whims for whims, he preferred them to any he had met in a like relation. It was probable enough she would leave them behind—exchange them for politics or "smartness" or mere prolific maternity, as was the custom of scribbling daubing educated flattered girls in an age of luxury and a society of leisure. He noted that the water-colours on the walls of the room she sat in had mainly the quality of being naïves, and reflected that naïveté in art is like a zero in a number: its importance depends on the figure it is united with. Meanwhile, however, he had fallen in love with her. Before he went away, at any rate, he said to her: "I thought St. George was coming to see you today, but he doesn't turn up."

For a moment he supposed she was going to cry "*Comment donc?* Did you come here only to meet him?" But the next he became aware of how little such a speech would have fallen in with any note of flirtation he had as yet perceived in her. She only replied: "Ah yes, but I don't think he'll come. He recommended me not to expect him." Then she gaily but all gently added: "He said it wasn't fair to you. But I think I could manage two."

"So could I," Paul Overt returned, stretching the point a little to meet her. In reality his appreciation of the occasion was so completely an appreciation of the woman before him that another figure in the scene, even so esteemed a one as St. George, might for the hour have appealed to him vainly. He left the house wondering what the great man had meant by its not being fair to him; and, still more than that, whether he had actually stayed away from the force of that idea. As he took his course through the Sunday solitude of Manchester Square, swinging his stick and with a good deal of emotion fermenting in his soul, it appeared to him he was living in a world strangely magnanimous. Miss Fancourt had told him it was possible she should be away, and that her father should be, on the following Sunday, but that she had the hope of a visit from him in the other event. She promised to let him know should their absence fail, and then he might act accordingly. After he had passed into one of the streets that open from the Square he stopped, without definite intentions, looking sceptically for a cab. In a moment he saw a hansom roll through the place from the other side and come a part of the way toward him. He was on the point of hailing the driver when he noticed a "fare" within; then he waited, seeing the man prepare to deposit his passenger by pulling up at one of the houses. The house was apparently the one he himself had just quitted; at least he drew that inference as he recognised Henry St. George in the person who stepped out of the hansom. Paul turned off as quickly as if he had been caught in the act of spying. He gave up his cab—he preferred to walk; he would go nowhere else. He was glad St. George hadn't renounced his visit altogether—that would have been too absurd. Yes, the world was magnanimous, and even he himself felt so as, on looking at his watch, he noted but six o'clock, so that he could mentally congratulate his successor on having an hour still to sit in Miss Fancourt's drawing-room. He himself might use that hour for another visit, but by the time he reached the Marble Arch the idea of such a course had become incongruous to him. He passed beneath that architectural effort and walked into the Park till he had got upon the spreading grass. Here he continued to walk; he took his way across the elastic turf and came out by the Serpentine. He watched with a friendly eye the diversions of the London people, he bent a glance almost encouraging on the young ladies paddling their sweethearts about the lake and the guardsmen tickling tenderly with their bearskins the artificial flowers in the Sunday hats of their partners. He prolonged his meditative walk; he went into Kensington Gardens, he sat upon the penny chairs, he looked at the little sail-boats launched upon the round pond and was glad he had no engagement to dine. He repaired for this purpose, very late, to his club, where he found himself unable to order a repast and told the waiter to bring whatever there was. He didn't even observe what he was served with, and he spent the evening in the library of the establishment, pretending to read an article in an American magazine. He failed to discover what it was about; it appeared in a dim way to be about Marian Fancourt.

Quite late in the week she wrote to him that she was not to go into the country—it had only just been settled. Her father, she added, would never settle anything, but put it all on her. She felt her responsibility—she had to—and since she was forced this was the way she had decided. She mentioned no reasons, which gave our friend all the clearer field for bold conjecture about them. In Manchester Square on this second Sunday he esteemed his fortune less good, for she had three or four other visitors. But there were three or four compensations; perhaps the greatest of which was that, learning how her father had after all, at the last hour, gone out of town alone, the bold conjecture I just now spoke of found itself becoming a shade more bold. And then her presence was her presence, and the personal red room was there and was full of it, whatever phantoms passed and vanished, emitting incomprehensible sounds. Lastly, he had the resource of staying till everyone had come and gone and of believing this grateful to her, though she gave no particular sign. When they were alone together he came to his point. "But St. George did come— last Sunday. I saw him as I looked back."

"Yes, but it was the last time."

"The last time?"

"He said he would never come again."

Paul Overt stared. "Does he mean he wishes to cease to see you?"

"I don't know what he means," the girl bravely smiled. "He won't at any rate see me here."

"And pray why not?"

"I haven't the least idea," said Marian Fancourt, whose visitor found her more perversely sublime than ever yet as she professed this clear helplessness.

V

"Oh I say, I want you to stop a little," Henry St. George said to him at eleven o'clock the night he dined with the head of the profession. The company—none of it indeed *of* the profession—had been numerous and was taking its leave; our young man, after bidding good-night to his hostess, had put out his hand in farewell to the master of the house. Besides drawing from the latter the protest I have cited this movement provoked a further priceless word about their chance now to have a talk, their going into his room, his having still everything to say. Paul Overt was all delight at this kindness; nevertheless he mentioned in weak jocose qualification the bare fact that he had promised to go to another place which was at a considerable distance.

"Well, then, you'll break your promise, that's all. You quite awful humbug!" St. George added in a tone that confirmed our young man's ease.

"Certainly I'll break it—but it was a real promise."

"Do you mean to Miss Fancourt? You're following her?" his friend asked.

He answered by a question. "Oh is *she* going?"

"Base impostor!" his ironic host went on. "I've treated you handsomely on the article of that young lady: I won't make another concession. Wait three minutes—I'll be with you." He gave himself to his departing guests, accompanied the long-trained ladies to the door. It was a hot night, the windows were open, the sound of the quick carriages and of the linkmen's call came into the house. The affair had rather glittered; a sense of festal things was in the heavy air: not only the influence of that particular entertainment, but the suggestion of the wide hurry of pleasure which in London on summer nights fills so many of the happier quarters of the complicated town. Gradually Mrs. St. George's drawing-room emptied itself; Paul was left alone with his hostess, to whom he explained the motive of his waiting. "Ah yes, some intellectual, some *professional*, talk," she leered; "at this season doesn't one miss it? Poor dear Henry, I'm so glad!" The young man looked out of the window a moment, at the called hansoms that lurched up, at the smooth broughams that rolled away. When he turned round Mrs. St. George had disappeared; her husband's voice rose to him from below—he was laughing and talking, in the portico, with some lady who awaited her carriage. Paul had solitary possession, for some minutes, of the warm deserted rooms where the covered tinted lamplight was soft, the seats had been pushed about and the odour of flowers lingered. They were large, they were pretty, they contained objects of value; everything in the picture told of a "good house." At the end of five minutes a servant came in with a request from the Master that he would join him downstairs; upon which, descending, he followed his conductor through a long passage to an apartment thrown out, in the rear of the habitation, for the special requirements, as he guessed, of a busy man of letters.

St. George was in his shirt-sleeves in the middle of a large high room—a room without windows, but with a wide skylight at the top, that of a place of exhibition. It was furnished as a library, and the serried bookshelves rose to the ceiling, a surface of incomparable tone produced by dimly-gilt "backs" interrupted here and there by the suspension of old prints and drawings. At the end furthest from the door of admission was a tall desk, of great extent, at which the person using it could write only in the erect posture of a clerk in a counting-house; and stretched from the entrance to this structure was a wide plain band of crimson cloth, as straight as a garden-path and almost as long, where, in his mind's eye, Paul at once beheld the Master pace to and fro during vexed hours—hours, that is, of admirable composition. The servant gave him a coat, an old jacket with a hang of experience, from a cupboard in the wall, retiring afterwards with the garment he had taken off. Paul Overt welcomed the coat; it was a coat for talk, it promised confidences—having visibly received so many—and had tragic literary elbows. "Ah we're practical—we're practical!" St. George said as he saw his visitor look the place over. "Isn't it a good big cage for going round and round? My wife invented it and she locks me up here every morning."

Our young man breathed—by way of tribute—with a certain oppression. "You don't miss a window—a place to look out?"

"I did at first awfully; but her calculation was just. It saves time, it has saved me many months in these ten years. Here I stand, under the eye of day—in London of course, very often, it's rather a bleared old eye—walled in to my trade. I can't get away—so the room's a fine lesson in concentration. I've learnt the lesson, I think; look at that big bundle of proof and acknowledge it." He pointed to a fat roll of papers, on one of the tables, which had not been undone.

"Are you bringing out another—?" Paul asked in a tone the fond deficiencies of which he didn't recognise till his companion burst out laughing, and indeed scarce even then.

"You humbug, you humbug!"—St. George appeared to enjoy caressing him, as it were, with that opprobrium. "Don't I know what you think of them?" he asked, standing there with his hands in his pockets and with a new kind of smile. It was as if he were going to let his young votary see him all now.

"Upon my word in that case you know more than I do!" the latter ventured to respond, revealing a part of the torment of being able neither clearly to esteem nor distinctly to renounce him.

"My dear fellow," said the more and more interesting Master, "don't imagine I talk about my books specifically; they're not a decent subject—*il ne manquerait plus que ça!* I'm not so bad as you may apprehend. About myself, yes, a little, if you like;

though it wasn't for that I brought you down here. I want to ask you something—very much indeed; I value this chance. Therefore sit down. We're practical, but there *is* a sofa, you see—for she does humour my poor bones so far. Like all really great administrators and disciplinarians she knows when wisely to relax." Paul sank into the corner of a deep leathern couch, but his friend remained standing and explanatory. "If you don't mind, in this room, this is my habit. From the door to the desk and from the desk to the door. That shakes up my imagination gently; and don't you see what a good thing it is that there's no window for her to fly out of? The eternal standing as I write (I stop at that bureau and put it down, when anything comes, and so we go on) was rather wearisome at first, but we adopted it with an eye to the long run: you're in better order—if your legs don't break down!—and you can keep it up for more years. Oh we're practical—we're practical!" St. George repeated, going to the table and taking up all mechanically the bundle of proofs. But, pulling off the wrapper, he had a change of attention that appealed afresh to our hero. He lost himself a moment, examining the sheets of his new book, while the younger man's eyes wandered over the room again.

"Lord, what good things I should do if I had such a charming place as this to do them in!" Paul reflected. The outer world, the world of accident and ugliness, was so successfully excluded, and within the rich protecting square, beneath the patronising sky, the dream-figures, the summoned company, could hold their particular revel. It was a fond prevision of Overt's rather than an observation on actual data, for which occasions had been too few, that the Master thus more closely viewed would have the quality, the charming gift, of flashing out, all surprisingly, in personal intercourse and at moments of suspended or perhaps even of diminished expectation. A happy relation with him would be a thing proceeding by jumps, not by traceable stages.

"Do you read them—really?" he asked, laying down the

proofs on Paul's inquiring of him how soon the work would be published. And when the young man answered, "Oh yes, always," he was moved to mirth again by something he caught in his manner of saying that. "You go to see your grandmother on her birthday—and very proper it is, especially as she won't last for ever. She has lost every faculty and every sense; she neither sees, nor hears, nor speaks; but all customary pieties and kindly habits are respectable. Only you're strong if you *do* read 'em! *I* couldn't, my dear fellow. You *are* strong, I know; and that's just a part of what I wanted to say to you. You're very strong indeed. I've been going into your other things—they've interested me immensely. Someone ought to have told me about them before—someone I could believe. But whom can one believe? You're wonderfully on the right road—it's awfully decent work. Now do you mean to keep it up?—that's what I want to ask you."

"Do I mean to do others?" Paul asked, looking up from his sofa at his erect inquisitor and feeling partly like a happy little boy when the schoolmaster is gay, and partly like some pilgrim of old who might have consulted a world-famous oracle. St. George's own performance had been infirm, but as an adviser he would be infallible.

"Others—others? Ah the number won't matter; one other would do, if it were really a further step—a throb of the same effort. What I mean is have you it in your heart to go in for some sort of decent perfection?"

"Ah decency, ah perfection—!" the young man sincerely sighed. "I talked of them the other Sunday with Miss Fancourt."

It produced on the Master's part a laugh of odd acrimony. "Yes, they'll 'talk' of them as much as you like! But they'll do little to help one to them. There's no obligation of course; only you strike me as capable," he went on. "You must have thought it all over. I can't believe you're without a plan. That's the sensation you give me, and it's so rare that it really stirs one up—it makes you remarkable. If you haven't a plan, if you *don't* mean to keep it up, surely you're within your rights; it's nobody's business, no one can force you, and not more than two or three people will notice you don't go straight. The others—*all* the rest, every blest soul in England, will think you do—will think you *are* keeping it up: upon my honour they will! I shall be one of the two or three who know better. Now the question is whether you can do it for two or three. Is that the stuff you're made of?"

It locked his guest a minute as in closed throbbing arms. "I could do it for one, if you were the one."

"Don't say that; I don't deserve it; it scorches me," he protested with eyes suddenly grave and glowing. "The 'one' is of course one's self, one's conscience, one's idea, the singleness of one's aim. I think of that pure spirit as a man thinks of a woman he has in some detested hour of his youth loved and forsaken. She haunts him with reproachful eyes, she lives for ever before him. As an artist, you know, I've married for money." Paul stared and even blushed a little, confounded by this avowal; whereupon his host, observing the expression of his face, dropped a quick laugh and pursued: "You don't follow my figure. I'm not speaking of my dear wife, who had a small fortune—which, however, was not my bribe. I fell in love with her, as many other people have done. I refer to the mercenary muse whom I led to the altar of literature. Don't, my boy, put your nose into *that* yoke. The awful jade will lead you a life!"

Our hero watched him, wondering and deeply touched. "Haven't you been happy!"

"Happy? It's a kind of hell."

"There are things I should like to ask you," Paul said after a pause.

"Ask me anything in all the world. I'd turn myself inside out to save you."

"To 'save' me?" he quavered.

"To make you stick to it—to make you see it through. As I said to you the other night at Summersoft, let my example be vivid to you."

"Why, your books are not so bad as that," said Paul, fairly laughing and feeling that if ever a fellow had breathed the air of art—!

"So bad as what?"

"Your talent's so great that it's in everything you do, in what's less good as well as in what's best. You've some forty volumes to show for it—forty volumes of wonderful life, of rare observation, of magnificent ability."

"I'm very clever, of course I know that"—but it was a thing, in fine, this author made nothing of. "Lord, what rot they'd all be if I hadn't been! I'm a successful charlatan," he went on—"I've been able to pass off my system. But do you know what it is? It's *carton-pierre*."

"*Carton-pierre?*" Paul was struck, and gaped.

"Lincrusta-Walton!"

"Ah don't say such things—you make me bleed!" the younger man protested. "I see you in a beautiful fortunate home, living in comfort and honour."

"Do you call it honour?"—his host took him up with an intonation that often comes back to him. "That's what I want *you* to go in for. I mean the real thing. This is brummagem."

"Brummagem?" Paul ejaculated while his eyes wandered, by a movement natural at the moment, over the luxurious room.

"Ah they make it so well today—it's wonderfully deceptive!"

Our friend thrilled with the interest and perhaps even more with the pity of it. Yet he wasn't afraid to seem to patronise when he could still so far envy. "Is it deceptive that I find you living with every appearance of domestic felicity—blest with a devoted, accomplished wife, with children whose acquaintance I haven't yet had the pleasure of making, but who *must* be delightful young people, from what I know of their parents?"

St. George smiled as for the candour of his question. "It's all excellent, my dear fellow—heaven forbid I should deny it. I've made a great deal of money; my wife has known how to take care of it, to use it without wasting it, to put a good bit of it by, to make it fructify. I've got a loaf on the shelf; I've got everything in fact but the great thing."

"The great thing?" Paul kept echoing.

"The sense of having done the best—the sense which is the real life of the artist and the absence of which is his death, of having drawn from his intellectual instrument the finest music that nature had hidden in it, of having played it as it should be played. He either does that or he doesn't—and if he doesn't he isn't worth speaking of. Therefore, precisely, those who really know *don't* speak of him. He may still hear a great chatter, but what he hears most is the incorruptible silence of Fame. I've squared her, you may say, for my little hour—but what's my little hour? Don't imagine for a moment," the Master pursued, "that I'm such a cad as to have brought you down here to abuse or to complain of my wife to you. She's a woman of distinguished qualities, to whom my obligations are immense; so that, if you please, we'll say nothing about her. My boys—my children are all boys—are straight and strong, thank God, and have no poverty of growth about them, no penury of needs. I receive periodically the most satisfactory attestation from Harrow, from Oxford, from Sandhurst—oh we've done the best for them!—of their eminence as living thriving consuming organisms."

"It must be delightful to feel that the son of one's loins is at Sandhurst," Paul remarked enthusiastically.

"It is—it's charming. Oh I'm a patriot!"

The young man then could but have the greater tribute of questions to pay. "Then what did you mean—the other night at Summersoft—by saying that children are a curse?"

"My dear youth, on what basis are we talking?" and St. George dropped upon the sofa at a short distance from him. Sitting a little sideways he leaned back against the opposite arm with his hands raised and interlocked behind his head. "On the supposition that a certain perfection's possible and even desirable—isn't it so? Well, all I say is that one's children interfere with perfection. One's wife interferes. Marriage interferes."

223

"You think, then, the artist shouldn't marry?"

"He does so at his peril—he does so at his cost."

"Not even when his wife's in sympathy with his work?"

"She never is—she can't be! Women haven't a conception of such things."

"Surely they on occasion work themselves," Paul objected.

"Yes, very badly indeed. Oh of course, often, they think they understand, they think they sympathise. Then it is they're most dangerous. Their idea is that you shall do a great lot and get a great lot of money. Their great nobleness and virtue, their exemplary conscientiousness as British females, is in keeping you up to that. My wife makes all my bargains with my publishers for me, and has done so for twenty years. She does it consummately well—that's why I'm really pretty well off. Aren't you the father of their innocent babes, and will you withhold from them their natural sustenance? You asked me the other night if they're not an immense incentive. Of course they are—there's no doubt of that!"

Paul turned it over: it took, from eyes he had never felt open so wide, so much looking at. "For myself I've an idea I need incentives."

"Ah well, then, *n'en parlons plus!*" his companion handsomely smiled.

"*You* are an incentive, I maintain," the young man went on. "You don't affect me in the way you'd apparently like to. Your great success is what I see—the pomp of Ennismore Gardens!"

"Success?"—St. George's eyes had a cold fine light. "Do you call it success to be spoken of as you'd speak of me if you were sitting here with another artist—a young man intelligent and sincere like yourself? Do you call it success to make you blush—as you *would* blush!—if some foreign critic (some fellow, of course I mean, who should know what he was talking about and should have shown you he did, as foreign critics like to show it) were to say to you: 'He's the one, in this country, whom they consider the most perfect, isn't he?' Is it success to be the occasion of a young Englishman's having to stammer as you would have to stammer at such a moment for old England? No, no; success is to have made people wriggle to another tune. Do try it!"

Paul continued all gravely to glow. "Try what?"

"Try to do some really good work."

"Oh I want to, heaven knows!"

"Well, you can't do it without sacrifices—don't believe that for a moment," the Master said. "I've made none. I've had everything. In other words, I've missed everything."

"You've had the full rich masculine human general life, with all the responsibilities and duties and burdens and sorrows and joys—all the domestic and social initiations and complications. They must be immensely suggestive, immensely amusing," Paul anxiously submitted.

"Amusing?"

"For a strong man—yes."

"They've given me subjects without number, if that's what you mean; but they've taken away at the same time the power to use them. I've touched a thousand things, but which one of them have I turned into gold? The artist has to do only with that—he knows nothing of any baser metal. I've led the life of the world, with my wife and my progeny; the clumsy conventional expensive materialised vulgarised brutalised life of London. We've got everything handsome, even a carriage—we're perfect Philistines and prosperous hospitable eminent people. But, my dear fellow, don't try to stultify yourself and pretend you don't know what we *haven't* got. It's bigger than all the rest. Between artists—come!" the Master wound up. "You know as well as you sit there that you'd put a pistol-ball into your brain if you had written my books!"

It struck his listener that the tremendous talk promised by him at Summersoft had indeed come off, and with a promptitude, a fulness, with which the latter's young imagination had scarcely reckoned. His impression fairly shook him and he throbbed with the excitement of such deep soundings and such strange confidences. He throbbed indeed with the conflict of his feelings—bewilderment and re-cognition and alarm, enjoyment and protest and assent, all commingled with tenderness (and a kind of shame in the participation) for the sores and bruises exhibited by so fine a creature, and with a sense of the tragic secret nursed under his trappings. The idea of *his*, Paul Overt's, becoming the occasion of such an act of humility made him flush and pant, at the same time that his consciousness was in certain directions too much alive not to swallow—and not intensely to taste—every offered spoonful of the revelation. It had been his odd fortune to blow upon the deep waters, to make them surge and break in waves of strange eloquence. But how couldn't he give out a passionate contradiction of his host's last extravagance, how couldn't he enumerate to him the parts of his work he loved, the splendid things he had found in it, beyond the compass of any other writer of the day? St. George listened a while, courteously; then he said, laying his hand on his visitor's: "That's all very well; and if your idea's to do nothing better there's no reason you shouldn't have as many good things as I—as many human and material appendages, as many sons or daughters, a wife with as many gowns, a house with as many servants, a stable with as many horses, a heart with as many aches." The Master got up when he had spoken thus—he stood a moment—near the sofa, looking down on his agitated pupil. "Are you possessed of any property?" it occurred to him to ask.

"None to speak of."

"Oh well then there's no reason why you shouldn't make a goodish income—if you set about it the right way. Study *me* for that—study me well. You may really have horses."

Paul sat there some minutes without speaking. He looked straight before him—he turned over many things. His friend had wandered away, taking up a parcel of letters from the table where the roll of proofs had lain. "What was the book Mrs. St. George made you burn—the one she didn't like?" our young man brought out.

"The book she made me burn—how did you know that?" The

Master looked up from his letters quite without the facial convulsion the pupil had feared.

"I heard her speak of it at Summersoft."

"Ah yes—she's proud of it. I don't know—it was rather good."

"What was it about?"

"Let me see." And he seemed to make an effort to remember. "Oh yes—it was about myself." Paul gave an irrepressible groan for the disappearance of such a production, and the elder man went on: "Oh but *you* should write it—*you* should do me." And he pulled up—from the restless motion that had come upon him; his fine smile a generous glare. "There's a subject, my boy: no end of stuff in it!"

Again Paul was silent, but it was all tormenting. "Are there no women who really understand—who can take part in a sacrifice?"

"How can they take part? They themselves are the sacrifice. They're the idol and the altar and the flame."

"Isn't there even *one* who sees further?" Paul continued.

For a moment St. George made no answer; after which, having torn up his letters, he came back to the point all ironic. "Of course I know the one you mean. But not even Miss Fancourt."

"I thought you admired her so much."

"It's impossible to admire her more. Are you in love with her?" St. George asked.

"Yes," Paul Overt presently said.

"Well, then, give it up."

Paul stared. "Give up my 'love'?"

"Bless me, no. Your idea." And then as our hero but still gazed: "The one you talked with her about. The idea of a decent perfection."

"She'd help it—she'd help it!" the young man cried.

"For about a year—the first year, yes. After that she'd be as a millstone round its neck."

Paul frankly wondered. "Why, she has a passion for the real thing, for good work—for everything you and I care for most."

"'You and I' is charming, my dear fellow!" his friend laughed. "She has it indeed, but she'd have a still greater passion for her children—and very proper too. She'd insist on everything's being made comfortable, advantageous, propitious for them. That isn't the artist's business."

"The artist—the artist! Isn't he a man all the same?"

St. George had a grand grimace. "I mostly think not. You know as well as I what he has to do: the concentration, the finish, the independence he must strive for from the moment he begins to wish his work really decent. Ah my young friend, his relation to women, and especially to the one he's most intimately concerned with, is at the mercy of the damning fact that whereas he can in the nature of things have but one standard, they have about fifty. That's what makes them so superior," St. George amusingly added. "Fancy an artist with a change of standards as you'd have a change of shirts or of dinner-plates. To *do* it—to do it and make it divine—is the only thing he has to think about. 'Is it done or not?' is his only question. Not 'Is it done as well as a proper solicitude for my dear little family will allow?' He has nothing to do with the relative—he has only to do with the absolute; and a dear little family may represent a dozen relatives."

"Then you don't allow him the common passions and affections of men?" Paul asked.

"Hasn't he a passion, an affection, which includes all the rest? Besides, let him have all the passions he likes—if he only keeps his independence. He must be able to be poor."

Paul slowly got up. "Why, then, did you advise me to make up to her?"

St. George laid a hand on his shoulder. "Because she'd make a splendid wife! And I hadn't read you then."

The young man had a strained smile. "I wish you had left me alone!"

"I didn't know that that wasn't good enough for you," his host returned.

"What a false position, what a condemnation of the artist, that he's a mere disfranchised monk and can produce his effect only by giving up personal happiness. What an arraignment of art!" Paul went on with a trembling voice.

"Ah you don't imagine by chance that I'm defending art? 'Arraignment'—I should think so! Happy the societies in which it hasn't made its appearance, for from the moment it comes they have a consuming ache, they have an incurable corruption, in their breast. Most assuredly is the artist in a false position! But I thought we were taking him for granted. Pardon me," St. George continued:

"*Ginistrella* made me!"

Paul stood looking at the floor—one o'clock struck, in the stillness, from a neighbouring church-tower. "Do you think she'd ever look at me?" he put to his friend at last.

"Miss Fancourt—as a suitor? Why shouldn't I think it? That's why I've tried to favour you—I've had a little chance or two of bettering your opportunity."

"Forgive my asking you, but do you mean by keeping away yourself?" Paul said with a blush.

"I'm an old idiot—my place isn't there," St. George stated gravely.

"I'm nothing yet, I've no fortune; and there must be so many others," his companion pursued.

The Master took this considerably in, but made little of it. "You're a gentleman and a man of genius. I think you might do something."

"But if I must give that up—the genius?"

"Lots of people, you know, think I've kept mine," St. George wonderfully grinned.

"You've a genius for mystification!" Paul declared, but grasping his hand gratefully in attenuation of this judgement.

"Poor dear boy, I do worry you! But try, try, all the same. I think your chances are good and you'll win a great prize."

Paul held fast the other's hand a minute; he looked into the strange deep face. "No, I *am* an artist—I can't help it!"

"Ah show it then!" St. George pleadingly broke out. "Let me see before I die the thing I most want, the thing I yearn for: a life in which the passion—ours—is really intense. If you can be rare don't fail of it! Think what it is—how it counts—how it lives!"

They had moved to the door and he had closed both his hands over his companion's. Here they paused again and our hero breathed deep. "I want to live!"

"In what sense?"

"In the greatest."

"Well, then, stick to it—see it through."

"With your sympathy—your help?"

"Count on that—you'll be a great figure to me. Count on my highest appreciation, my devotion. You'll give me satisfaction—if that has any weight with you!" After which, as Paul appeared still to waver, his host added: "Do you remember what you said to me at Summersoft?"

"Something infatuated, no doubt!"

"'I'll do anything in the world you tell me.' You said that."

"And you hold me to it?"

"Ah what am I?" the Master expressively sighed.

"Lord, what things I shall have to do!" Paul almost moaned as he departed.

VI

"It goes on too much abroad—hang abroad!" These or something like them had been the Master's remarkable words in relation to the action of *Ginistrella*; and yet, though they had made a sharp impression on the author of that work, like almost all spoken words from the same source, he a week after the conversation I have noted left England for a long absence and full of brave intentions. It is not a perversion of the truth to pronounce that encounter the direct cause of his departure. If the oral utterance of the eminent writer had the privilege of moving him deeply it was especially on his turning it over at leisure, hours and days later, that it appeared to yield him its full meaning and exhibit its extreme importance. He spent the summer in Switzerland and, having in September begun a new task, determined not to cross the Alps till he should have made a good start. To this end he returned to a quiet corner he knew well, on the edge of the Lake of Geneva and within sight of the towers of Chillon: a region and a view for which he had an affection that sprang from old associations and was capable of mysterious revivals and refreshments. Here he lingered late, till the snow was on the nearer hills, almost down to the limit to which he could climb when his stint, on the shortening afternoons, was performed. The autumn was fine, the lake was blue, and his book took form and direction. These felicities, for the time, embroidered his life, which he suffered to cover him with its mantle. At the end of six weeks he felt he had learnt St. George's lesson by heart, had tested and proved its doctrine. Nevertheless he did a very inconsistent thing: before crossing the Alps he wrote to Marian Fancourt. He was aware of the perversity of this act, and it was only as a luxury, an amusement, the reward of a strenuous autumn, that he justified it. She had asked of him no such favour when, shortly before he left London, three days after their dinner in Ennismore Gardens, he went to take leave of her. It was true she had had no ground—he hadn't named his intention of absence. He had kept his counsel for want of due assurance: it was that particular visit that was, the next thing, to settle the matter. He had paid the visit to see how much he really cared for her, and quick departure, without so much as an explicit farewell, was the sequel to this inquiry, the answer to which had created within him a deep yearning. When he wrote her from Clarens he noted that he owed her an explanation (more than three months after!) for not having told her what he was doing.

She replied now briefly but promptly, and gave him a striking piece of news: that of the death, a week before, of Mrs. St. George. This exemplary woman had succumbed, in the country, to a violent attack of inflammation of the lungs—he would remember that for a long time she had been delicate.

Miss Fancourt added that she believed her husband was overwhelmed by the blow; he would miss her too terribly—she had been everything in life to him. Paul Overt, on this, immediately wrote to St. George. He would from the day of their parting have been glad to remain in communication with him, but had hitherto lacked the right excuse for troubling so busy a man. Their long nocturnal talk came back to him in every detail, but this was no bar to an expression of proper sympathy with the head of the profession, for hadn't that very talk made it clear that the late accomplished lady was the influence that ruled his life? What catastrophe could be more cruel than the extinction of such an influence? This was to be exactly the tone taken by St. George in answering his young friend upwards of a month later. He made no allusion of course to their important discussion. He spoke of his wife as frankly and generously as if he had quite forgotten that occasion, and the feeling of deep bereavement was visible in his words. "She took everything off my hands—off my mind. She carried on our life with the greatest art, the rarest devotion, and I was free, as few men can have been, to drive my pen, to shut myself up with my trade. This was a rare service—the highest she could have rendered me. Would I could have acknowledged it more fitly!"

A certain bewilderment, for our hero, disengaged itself from these remarks: they struck him as a contradiction, a retractation, strange on the part of a man who hadn't the excuse of witlessness. He had certainly not expected his correspondent to rejoice in the death of his wife, and it was perfectly in order that the rupture of a tie of more than twenty years should have left him sore. But if she had been so clear a blessing what in the name of consistency had the dear man meant by turning *him* upside down that night—by dosing him to that degree, at the most sensitive hour of his life, with the doctrine of renunciation? If Mrs. St. George was an irreparable loss, then her husband's inspired advice had been a bad joke and renunciation was a mistake. Overt was on the point of rushing back to London to show that, for his part, he was perfectly willing to consider it so, and he went so far as to take the manuscript of the first chapters of his new book out of his table-drawer and insert it into a pocket of his portmanteau. This led to his catching a glimpse of certain pages he hadn't looked at for months, and that accident, in turn, to his being struck with the high promise they revealed—a rare result of such retrospections, which it was his habit to avoid as much as possible: they usually brought home to him that the glow of composition might be a purely subjective and misleading emotion. On this occasion a certain belief in himself disengaged itself whimsically from the serried erasures of his first draft, making him think it best after all to pursue his present trial to the end. If he could write so well under the rigour of privation it might be a mistake to change the conditions before that spell had spent itself. He would go back to London of course, but he would go back only when he should have finished his book. This was the vow he privately made, restoring his manuscript to the table-drawer. It may be added that it took him a long time to finish his book, for the subject was as difficult as it was fine, and he was literally embarrassed by the fulness of his notes. Something within him warned him he must make it supremely good—otherwise he should lack, as regards his private behaviour, a handsome excuse. He had a horror of this deficiency and found himself as firm as need be on the question of the lamp and the file. He crossed the Alps at last and spent the winter, the spring, the ensuing summer, in Italy, where still, at the end of a twelvemonth, his task was unachieved. "Stick to it—see it through": this general injunction of St. George's was good also for the particular case. He applied it to the utmost, with the result that when in its slow order the summer had come round again he felt he had given all that was in him. This time he put his papers into his portmanteau, with the address of his publisher attached, and took his way northward.

He had been absent from London for two years; two years

which, seeming to count as more, had made such a difference in his own life—through the production of a novel far stronger, he believed, than *Ginistrella*—that he turned out into Piccadilly, the morning after his arrival, with a vague expectation of changes, of finding great things had happened. But there were few transformations in Piccadilly—only three or four big red houses where there had been low black ones—and the brightness of the end of June peeped through the rusty railings of the Green Park and glittered in the varnish of the rolling carriages as he had seen it in other, more cursory Junes. It was a greeting he appreciated; it seemed friendly and pointed, added to the exhilaration of his finished book, of his having his own country and the huge oppressive amusing city that suggested everything, that contained everything, under his hand again. "Stay at home and do things here—do subjects we can measure," St. George had said; and now it struck him he should ask nothing better than to stay at home for ever. Late in the afternoon he took his way to Manchester Square, looking out for a number he hadn't forgotten. Miss Fancourt, however, was not at home, so that he turned rather dejectedly from the door. His movement brought him face to face with a gentleman just approaching it and recognised on another glance as Miss Fancourt's father. Paul saluted this personage, and the General returned the greeting with his customary good manner—a manner so good, however, that you could never tell whether it meant he placed you. The disappointed caller felt the impulse to address him; then, hesitating, became both aware of having no particular remark to make, and convinced that though the old soldier remembered him he remembered him wrong. He therefore went his way without computing the irresistible effect his own evident recognition would have on the General, who never neglected a chance to gossip. Our young man's face was expressive, and observation seldom let it pass. He hadn't taken ten steps before he heard himself called after with a friendly semi-articulate "Er—I beg your pardon!" He turned round and the General, smiling at him from the porch, said: "Won't you come in? I won't leave you the advantage of me!" Paul declined to come in, and then felt regret, for Miss Fancourt, so late in the afternoon, might return at any moment. But her father gave him no second chance; he appeared mainly to wish not to have struck him as ungracious. A further look at the visitor had recalled something, enough at least to enable him to say: "You've come back, you've come back?" Paul was on the point of replying that he had come back the night before, but he suppressed, the next instant, this strong light on the immediacy of his visit and, giving merely a general assent, alluded to the young lady he deplored not having found. He had come late in the hope she would be in. "I'll tell her—I'll tell her," said the old man; and then he added quickly, gallantly: "You'll be giving us something new? It's a long time, isn't it?" Now he remembered him right.

"Rather long. I'm very slow," Paul explained. "I met you at Summersoft a long time ago."

"Oh yes—with Henry St. George. I remember very well. Before his poor wife—" General Fancourt paused a moment, smiling a little less. "I daresay you know."

"About Mrs. St. George's death? Certainly—I heard at the time."

"Oh no, I mean—I mean he's to be married."

"Ah I've not heard that!" But just as Paul was about to add "To whom?" the General crossed his intention.

"When did you come back? I know you've been away—by my daughter. She was very sorry. You ought to give her something new."

"I came back last night," said our young man, to whom something had occurred which made his speech for the moment a little thick.

"Ah most kind of you to come so soon. Couldn't you turn up at dinner?"

"At dinner?" Paul just mechanically repeated, not liking to ask whom St. George was going to marry, but thinking only of that.

"There are several people, I believe. Certainly St. George. Or afterwards if you like better. I believe my daughter expects—" He appeared to notice something in the visitor's raised face (on his steps he stood higher) which led him to interrupt himself, and the interruption gave him a momentary sense of awkwardness, from which he sought a quick issue. "Perhaps, then, you haven't heard she's to be married."

Paul gaped again. "To be married?"

"To Mr. St. George—it has just been settled. Odd marriage, isn't it?" Our listener uttered no opinion on this point: he only continued to stare. "But I daresay it will do—she's so awfully literary!" said the General.

Paul had turned very red. "Oh it's a surprise—very interesting, very charming! I'm afraid I can't dine—so many thanks!"

"Well, you must come to the wedding!" cried the General. "Oh I remember that day at Summersoft. He's a great man, you know."

"Charming—charming!" Paul stammered for retreat. He shook hands with the General and got off. His face was red and he had the sense of its growing more and more crimson. All the evening at home—he went straight to his rooms and remained there dinnerless—his cheek burned at intervals as if it had been smitten. He didn't understand what had happened to him, what trick had been played him, what treachery practised. "None, none," he said to himself. "I've nothing to do with it. I'm out of it—it's none of my business." But that bewildered murmur was followed again and again by the incongruous ejaculation: "Was it a plan—was it a plan?" Sometimes he cried to himself, breathless, "Have I been duped, sold, swindled?" If at all, he was an absurd, an abject victim. It was as if he hadn't lost her till now. He had renounced her, yes; but that was another affair—that was a closed but not a locked door. Now he seemed to see the door quite slammed in his face. Did he expect her to wait—was she to give him his time like that: two years at a stretch? He didn't know what he had expected—he only knew what he hadn't. It wasn't this—it wasn't this. Mystification bitterness and wrath rose and boiled in him when he thought of the deference, the devotion, the credulity with which had listened to St. George. The evening wore on and the light was long; but even when it had darkened he remained without a lamp. He had flung himself on the sofa, where he lay through the hours with his eyes either closed or gazing at the gloom, in the attitude of a man teaching himself to bear something, to bear having been made a fool of. He had made it too easy—that idea passed over him like a hot wave. Suddenly, as he heard eleven o'clock strike, he jumped up, remembering what General Fancourt had said about his coming after dinner. He'd go—he'd see her at least; perhaps he should see what it meant. He felt as if some of the elements of a hard sum had been given him and the others were wanting: he couldn't do his sum till he had got all his figures.

He dressed and drove quickly, so that by half-past eleven he was at Manchester Square. There were a good many carriages at the door—a party was going on; a circumstance which at the last gave him a slight relief, for now he would rather see her in a crowd. People passed him on the staircase; they were going away, going "on" with the hunted herdlike movement of London society at night. But sundry groups remained in the drawing-room, and it was some minutes, as she didn't hear him announced, before he discovered and spoke to her. In this short interval he had seen St. George talking to a lady before the fireplace; but he at once looked away, feeling unready for an encounter, and therefore couldn't be sure the author of *Shadowmere* noticed him. At all events he didn't come over; though Miss Fancourt did as soon as she saw him—she almost rushed at him, smiling rustling radiant beautiful. He had forgotten what her head, what her face offered to the sight; she was in white, there were gold figures on her dress and her hair was a casque of gold. He saw in a single moment that she was happy, happy with an aggressive splendour. But she wouldn't speak to him of that, she would speak only of himself.

"I'm so delighted; my father told me. How kind of you to come!" She struck him as so fresh and brave, while his eyes moved over her, that he said to himself irresistibly: "Why to *him*, why not to youth, to strength, to ambition, to a future? Why, in her rich young force, to failure, to abdication, to superannuation?" In his thought at that sharp moment he blasphemed even against all that had been left of his faith in the peccable master. "I'm so sorry I missed you," she went on. "My father told me. How charming of you to have come so soon!"

"Does that surprise you?" Paul Overt asked.

"The first day? No, from you—nothing that's nice." She was interrupted by a lady who bade her good-night, and he seemed to read that it cost her nothing to speak to him in that tone; it was her old liberal lavish way, with a certain added amplitude that time had brought; and if this manner began to operate on the spot, at such a juncture in her history, perhaps in the other days too it had meant just as little or as much—a mere mechanical charity, with the difference now that she was satisfied, ready to give but in want of nothing. Oh she was satisfied—and why shouldn't she be? Why shouldn't she have been surprised at his coming the first day—for all the good she had ever got from him? As the lady continued to hold her attention Paul turned from her with a strange irritation in his complicated artistic soul and a sort of disinterested disappointment. She was so happy that it was almost stupid—a disproof of the extraordinary intelligence he had formerly found in her. Didn't she know how bad St. George could be, hadn't she recognised the awful thinness—? If she didn't she was nothing, and if she did why such an insolence of serenity? This question expired as our young man's eyes settled at last on the genius who had advised him in a great crisis. St. George was still before the chimney-piece, but now he was alone—fixed, waiting, as if he meant to stop after everyone—and he met the clouded gaze of the young friend so troubled as to the degree of his right (the right his resentment would have enjoyed) to regard himself as a victim. Somehow the ravage of the question was checked by the Master's radiance. It was as fine in its way as Marian Fancourt's, it denoted the happy human being; but also it represented to Paul Overt that the author of *Shadowmere* had now definitely ceased to count—ceased to count as a writer. As he smiled a welcome across the place he was almost *banal*, was almost smug. Paul fancied that for a moment he hesitated to make a movement, as if, for all the world, he *had* his bad conscience; then they had already met in the middle of the room and had shaken hands—expressively, cordially on St. George's part. With which they had passed back together to where the elder man had been standing, while St. George said: "I hope you're never going away again. I've been dining here; the General told me." He was handsome, he was young, he looked as if he had still a great fund of life. He bent the friendliest, most unconfessing eyes on his disciple of a couple of years before; asked him about everything, his health, his plans, his late occupations, the new book. "When will it be out—soon, soon, I hope? Splendid, eh? That's right; you're a comfort, you're a luxury! I've read you all over again these last six months." Paul waited to see if he'd tell him what the General had told him in the afternoon and what Miss Fancourt, verbally at least, of course hadn't. But as it didn't come out he at last put the question, "Is it true, the great news I hear—that you're to be married?"

"Ah you *have* heard it, then?"

"Didn't the General tell you?" Paul asked.

The Master's face was wonderful. "Tell me what?"

"That he mentioned it to me this afternoon?"

"My dear fellow, I don't remember. We've been in the midst of people. I'm sorry, in the case, that I lose the pleasure, myself, of announcing to you a fact that touches me so nearly. It *is* a fact, strange as it may appear. It has only just become one. Isn't it ridiculous?" St. George made this speech without confusion, but on the other hand, so far as our friend could judge, without latent impudence. It struck his interlocutor that, to talk so

239

comfortably and coolly, he must simply have forgotten what had passed between them. His next words, however, showed he hadn't, and they produced, as an appeal to Paul's own memory, an effect which would have been ludicrous if it hadn't been cruel. "Do you recall the talk we had at my house that night, into which Miss Fancourt's name entered? I've often thought of it since."

"Yes; no wonder you said what you did"—Paul was careful to meet his eyes.

"In the light of the present occasion? Ah but there was no light then. How could I have foreseen this hour?"

"Didn't you think it probable?"

"Upon my honour, no," said Henry St. George. "Certainly I owe you that assurance. Think how my situation has changed."

"I see—I see," our young man murmured.

His companion went on as if, now that the subject had been broached, he was, as a person of imagination and tact, quite ready to give every satisfaction—being both by his genius and his method so able to enter into everything another might feel. "But it's not only that; for honestly, at my age, I never dreamed—a widower with big boys and with so little else! It has turned out differently from anything one could have dreamed, and I'm fortunate beyond all measure. She has been so free, and yet she consents. Better than anyone else perhaps—for I remember how you liked her before you went away, and how she liked you—you can intelligently congratulate me."

"She has been so free!" Those words made a great impression on Paul Overt, and he almost writhed under that irony in them as to which it so little mattered whether it was designed or casual. Of course she had been free, and appreciably perhaps by his own act; for wasn't the Master's allusion to her having liked him a part of the irony too? "I thought that by your theory you disapproved of a writer's marrying."

"Surely—surely. But you don't call me a writer?"

"You ought to be ashamed," said Paul.

"Ashamed of marrying again?"

"I won't say that—but ashamed of your reasons."

The elder man beautifully smiled. "You must let me judge of them, my good friend."

"Yes; why not? For you judged wonderfully of mine."

The tone of these words appeared suddenly, for St. George, to suggest the unsuspected. He stared as if divining a bitterness. "Don't you think I've been straight?"

"You might have told me at the time perhaps."

"My dear fellow, when I say I couldn't pierce futurity—!"

"I mean afterwards."

The Master wondered. "After my wife's death?"

"When this idea came to you."

"Ah never, never! I wanted to save you, rare and precious as you are."

Poor Overt looked hard at him. "Are you marrying Miss Fancourt to save me?"

"Not absolutely, but it adds to the pleasure. I shall be the making of you," St. George smiled. "I was greatly struck, after our talk, with the brave devoted way you quitted the country, and still more perhaps with your force of character in remaining abroad. You're very strong—you're wonderfully strong."

Paul tried to sound his shining eyes; the strange thing was that he seemed sincere—not a mocking fiend. He turned away, and as he did so heard the Master say something about his giving them all the proof, being the joy of his old age. He faced him again, taking another look. "Do you mean to say you've stopped writing?"

"My dear fellow, of course I have. It's too late. Didn't I tell you?"

"I can't believe it!"

"Of course you can't—with your own talent! No, no; for the rest of my life I shall only read *you*."

"Does she know that—Miss Fancourt?"

"She will—she will." Did he mean this, our young man

wondered, as a covert intimation that the assistance he should derive from that young lady's fortune, moderate as it was, would make the difference of putting it in his power to cease to work ungratefully an exhausted vein? Somehow, standing there in the ripeness of his successful manhood, he didn't suggest that any of his veins were exhausted. "Don't you remember the moral I offered myself to you that night as pointing?" St. George continued. "Consider at any rate the warning I am at present."

This was too much—he *was* the mocking fiend. Paul turned from him with a mere nod for good-night and the sense in a sore heart that he might come back to him and his easy grace, his fine way of arranging things, some time in the far future, but couldn't fraternise with him now. It was necessary to his soreness to believe for the hour in the intensity of his grievance—all the more cruel for its not being a legal one. It was doubtless in the attitude of hugging this wrong that he descended the stairs without taking leave of Miss Fancourt, who hadn't been in view at the moment he quitted the room. He was glad to get out into the honest dusky unsophisticating night, to move fast, to take his way home on foot. He walked a long time, going astray, paying no attention. He was thinking of too many other things. His steps recovered their direction, however, and at the end of an hour he found himself before his door in the small inexpensive empty street. He lingered, questioning himself still before going in, with nothing around and above him but moonless blackness, a bad lamp or two and a few far-away dim stars. To these last faint features he raised his eyes; he had been saying to himself that he should have been "sold" indeed, diabolically sold, if now, on his new foundation, at the end of a year, St. George were to put forth something of his prime quality—something of the type of *Shadowmere* and finer than his finest. Greatly as he admired his talent Paul literally hoped such an incident wouldn't occur; it seemed to him just then that he shouldn't be able to bear it. His late adviser's words were still in his ears—"You're very strong, wonderfully strong." Was he really? Certainly he would have to be, and it might a little serve for revenge. *Is* he? the reader may ask in turn, if his interest has followed the perplexed young man so far. The best answer to that perhaps is that he's doing his best, but that it's too soon to say. When the new book came out in the autumn Mr. and Mrs. St. George found it really magnificent. The former still has published nothing, but Paul doesn't even yet feel safe. I may say for him, however, that if this event were to occur he would really be the very first to appreciate it: which is perhaps a proof that the Master was essentially right and that Nature had dedicated him to intellectual, not to personal passion.

THE DEATH
OF THE LION

THE DEATH OF THE LION

I

I had simply, I suppose, a change of heart, and it must have begun when I received my manuscript back from Mr. Pinhorn. Mr. Pinhorn was my "chief," as he was called in the office: he had accepted the high mission of bringing the paper up. This was a weekly periodical, and had been supposed to be almost past redemption when he took hold of it. It was Mr. Deedy who had let it down so dreadfully: he was never mentioned in the office now save in connection with that misdemeanour. Young as I was I had been in a manner taken over from Mr. Deedy, who had been owner as well as editor; forming part of a promiscuous lot, mainly plant and office-furniture, which poor Mrs. Deedy, in her bereavement and depression, parted with at a rough valuation. I could account for my continuity only on the supposition that I had been cheap. I rather resented the practice of fathering all flatness on my late protector, who was in his unhonoured grave; but as I had my way to make I found matter enough for complacency in being on a "staff." At the same time I was aware that I was exposed to suspicion as a product of the old lowering system. This made me feel that I was doubly bound to have ideas, and had doubtless been at the bottom of my proposing to Mr. Pinhorn that I should lay my lean hands on Neil Paraday. I remember that he looked at me first as if he had never heard of this celebrity, who indeed at that moment was by no means in the centre of the heavens; and even when I had knowingly explained he expressed but little confidence in the demand for any such matter. When I had reminded him that the great principle on which we were supposed to work was just to create the demand we required, he considered a moment and then rejoined: "I see; want to write him up."

"Call it that if you like."

"And what's your inducement?"

"Bless my soul—my admiration!"

Mr. Pinhorn pursed up his mouth. "Is there much to be done with him?"

"Whatever there is, we should have it all to ourselves, for he hasn't been touched."

This argument was effective, and Mr. Pinhorn responded: "Very well, touch him." Then he added: "But where can you do it?"

"Under the fifth rib!"

Mr. Pinhorn stared. "Where's that?"

"You want me to go down and see him?" I inquired when I had enjoyed his visible search for this obscure suburb.

"I don't 'want' anything—the proposal's your own. But you must remember that that's the way we do things *now*," said Mr. Pinhorn, with another dig at Mr. Deedy.

Unregenerate as I was, I could read the queer implications of this speech. The present owner's superior virtue as well as his deeper craft spoke in his reference to the late editor as one of that baser sort who deal in false representations. Mr. Deedy would as soon have sent me to call on Neil Paraday as he would have published a "holiday-number;" but such scruples presented themselves as mere ignoble thrift to his successor, whose own sincerity took the form of ringing door-bells and whose definition of genius was the art of finding people at home. It was as if Mr. Deedy had published reports without his young men's having, as Pinhorn would have said, really been there. I was unregenerate, as I have hinted, and I was not concerned to straighten out the journalistic morals of my chief, feeling them indeed to be an abyss over the edge of which it was better not to peer. Really to be there this time moreover was a vision that made the idea of writing something subtle about Neil Paraday only the more inspiring. I would be as considerate as even Mr. Deedy could have wished, and yet I should be as present as only Mr. Pinhorn could conceive. My allusion to the sequestered manner in which Mr. Paraday lived (which had formed part of my explanation, though I knew of it only by hearsay) was, I could divine, very much what had made Mr. Pinhorn nibble. It struck him as inconsistent with the success of his paper that anyone should be so sequestered as that. And then was not an immediate exposure of everything just what the public wanted? Mr. Pinhorn effectually called me to order by reminding me of the promptness with which I had met Miss Braby at Liverpool on her return from her fiasco in the States. Hadn't we published, while its freshness and flavour were unimpaired, Miss Braby's own version of that great international episode? I felt somewhat uneasy at this lumping of the actress and the author, and I confess that after having enlisted Mr. Pinhorn's sympathies I procrastinated a little. I had succeeded better than I wished, and I had, as it happened, work nearer at hand. A few days later I called on Lord Crouchley and carried off in triumph the most unintelligible statement that had yet appeared of his lordship's reasons for his change of front. I thus set in motion in the daily papers columns of virtuous verbiage. The following week I ran down to Brighton for a chat, as Mr. Pinhorn called it, with Mrs. Bounder, who gave me, on the subject of her divorce, many curious particulars that had not been articulated in court. If ever an article flowed from the primal fount it was that article on Mrs. Bounder. By this time, however, I became aware that Neil Paraday's new book was on the point of appearing and that its approach had been the ground of my original appeal to Mr. Pinhorn, who was now annoyed with me for having lost so many days. He bundled me off—we would at least not lose another. I have always thought his sudden alertness a remarkable example of the journalistic instinct. Nothing had occurred, since I first spoke to him, to create a visible urgency, and no enlightenment could possibly have reached him. It was a pure case of professional *flair*—he had smelt the coming glory as an animal smells its distant prey.

II

I may as well say at once that this little record pretends in no degree to be a picture either of my introduction to Mr. Paraday or of certain proximate steps and stages. The scheme of my narrative allows no space for these things, and in any case a prohibitory sentiment would be attached to my recollection of so rare an hour. These meagre notes are essentially private, so that if they see the light the insidious forces that, as my story itself shows, make at present for publicity will simply have overmastered my precautions. The curtain fell lately enough on the lamentable drama. My memory of the day I alighted at Mr. Paraday's door is a fresh memory of kindness, hospitality, compassion, and of the wonderful illuminating talk in which the welcome was conveyed. Some voice of the air had taught me the right moment, the moment of his life at which an act of unexpected young allegiance might most come home. He had recently recovered from a long, grave illness. I had gone to the neighbouring inn for the night, but I spent the evening in his company, and he insisted the next day on my sleeping under his roof. I had not an indefinite leave: Mr. Pinhorn supposed us to put our victims through on the gallop. It was later, in the office, that the dance was set to music. I fortified myself, however, as my training had taught me to do, by the conviction that nothing could be more advantageous for my article than to be written in the very atmosphere. I said nothing to Mr. Paraday about it, but in the morning, after my removal from the inn, while he was occupied in his study, as he had notified me that he should need to be, I committed to paper the quintessence of my impressions. Then thinking to commend myself to Mr. Pinhorn by my celerity, I walked out and posted my little packet before luncheon. Once my paper was written I was free to stay on, and if it was designed to divert attention from my frivolity in so doing I could reflect with satisfaction that I had never been so clever. I don't mean to deny of course that I was aware it was much too good for Mr. Pinhorn; but I was equally conscious that Mr. Pinhorn had the supreme shrewdness of recognising from time to time the cases in which an article was not too bad only because it was too good. There was nothing he loved so much as to print on the right occasion a thing he hated. I had begun my visit to Mr. Paraday on a Monday, and on the Wednesday his book came out. A copy of it arrived by the first post, and he let me go out into the garden with it immediately after breakfast. I read it from beginning to end that day, and in the evening he asked me to remain with him the rest of the week and over the Sunday.

That night my manuscript came back from Mr. Pinhorn, accompanied with a letter, of which the gist was the desire to know what I meant by sending him such stuff. That was the meaning of the question, if not exactly its form, and it made my mistake immense to me. Such as this mistake was I could now only look it in the face and accept it. I knew where I had failed, but it was exactly where I couldn't have succeeded. I had been sent down there to be personal, and in point of fact I hadn't been personal at all: what I had sent up to London was just a little finicking, feverish study of my author's talent. Anything less relevant to Mr. Pinhorn's purpose couldn't well be imagined, and he was visibly angry at my having (at his expense, with a second-class ticket) approached the object of our arrangement only to be so deucedly distant. For myself, I knew but too well what had happened, and how a miracle—as pretty as some old miracle of legend—had been wrought on the spot to save me. There had been a big brush of wings, the flash of an opaline robe, and then, with a great cool stir of the air, the sense of an angel's having swooped down and caught me to his bosom. He held me only till the danger was over, and it all took place in a minute. With my manuscript back on my hands I understood the phenomenon better, and the reflections I made on it are what I meant, at the beginning of this anecdote, by my change of heart. Mr. Pinhorn's note was not only a rebuke decidedly stern, but an invitation immediately to send him (it was the case to say so) the genuine article, the revealing and reverberating sketch to the promise of which—and of which alone—I owed my squandered privilege. A week or two later I recast my peccant paper, and giving it a particular application to Mr. Paraday's new book, obtained for it the hospitality of another journal, where, I must admit, Mr. Pinhorn was so far justified that it attracted not the least attention.

III

I was frankly, at the end of three days, a very prejudiced critic, so that one morning when, in the garden, Neil Paraday had offered to read me something I quite held my breath as I listened. It was the written scheme of another book—something he had put aside long ago, before his illness, and lately taken out again to reconsider. He had been turning it round when I came down upon him, and it had grown magnificently under this second hand. Loose, liberal, confident, it might have passed for a great gossiping, eloquent letter—the overflow into talk of an artist's amorous plan. The subject I thought singularly rich, quite the strongest he had yet treated; and this familiar statement of it, full too of fine maturities, was really, in summarised splendour, a mine of gold, a precious, independent work. I remember rather profanely wondering whether the ultimate production could possibly be so happy. His reading of the epistle, at any rate, made me feel as if I were, for the advantage of posterity, in close correspondence with him—were the distinguished person to whom it had been affectionately addressed. It was high distinction simply to be told such things. The idea he now communicated had all the freshness, the flushed fairness of the conception untouched and untried: it was Venus rising from the sea, before the airs had blown upon her. I had never been so throbbingly present at such an unveiling. But when he had tossed the last bright word after the others, as I had seen cashiers in banks, weighing mounds of coin, drop a final sovereign into the tray, I became conscious of a sudden prudent alarm.

"My dear master, how, after all, are you going to do it?" I asked. "It's infinitely noble, but what time it will take, what patience and independence, what assured, what perfect conditions it will demand! Oh for a lone isle in a tepid sea!"

"Isn't this practically a lone isle, and aren't you, as an encircling medium, tepid enough?" he replied, alluding with a laugh to the wonder of my young admiration and the narrow limits of his little provincial home. "Time isn't what I've lacked hitherto: the question hasn't been to find it, but to use it. Of course my illness made a great hole, but I daresay there would have been a hole at any rate. The earth we tread has more pockets than a billiard-table. The great thing is now to keep on my feet."

"That's exactly what I mean."

Neil Paraday looked at me with eyes—such pleasant eyes as he had—in which, as I now recall their expression, I seem to have seen a dim imagination of his fate. He was fifty years old, and his illness had been cruel, his convalescence slow. "It isn't as if I weren't all right."

"Oh, if you weren't all right I wouldn't look at you!" I tenderly said.

We had both got up, quickened by the full sound of it all, and he had lighted a cigarette. I had taken a fresh one, and, with an intenser smile, by way of answer to my exclamation, he touched it with the flame of his match. "If I weren't better I shouldn't have thought of *that*!" He flourished his epistle in his hand.

"I don't want to be discouraging, but that's not true," I returned. "I'm sure that during the months you lay here in pain you had visitations sublime. You thought of a thousand things. You think of more and more all the while. That's what makes you, if you will pardon my familiarity, so respectable. At a time when so many people are spent you come into your second wind. But, thank God, all the same, you're better! Thank God, too, you're not, as you were telling me yesterday, 'successful.' If

you weren't a failure, what would be the use of trying? That's
my one reserve on the subject of your recovery—that it makes
you 'score,' as the newspapers say. It looks well in the
newspapers, and almost anything that does that is horrible.
'We are happy to announce that Mr. Paraday, the celebrated
author, is again in the enjoyment of excellent health.'
Somehow I shouldn't like to see it."

"You won't see it; I'm not in the least celebrated—my
obscurity protects me. But couldn't you bear even to see I was
dying or dead?" my companion asked.

"Dead—*passe encore*; there's nothing so safe. One never
knows what a living artist may do—one has mourned so many.
However, one must make the worst of it; you must be as dead
as you can."

"Don't I meet that condition in having just published a
book?"

"Adequately, let us hope; for the book is verily a
masterpiece."

At this moment the parlour-maid appeared in the door that
opened into the garden: Paraday lived at no great cost, and the
frisk of petticoats, with a timorous "Sherry, sir?" was about his
modest mahogany. He allowed half his income to his wife,
from whom he had succeeded in separating without
redundancy of legend. I had a general faith in his having
behaved well, and I had once, in London, taken Mrs. Paraday
down to dinner. He now turned to speak to the maid, who
offered him, on a tray, some card or note, while agitated,
excited, I wandered to the end of the garden. The idea of his
security became supremely dear to me, and I asked myself if I
were the same young man who had come down a few days
before to scatter him to the four winds. When I retraced my
steps he had gone into the house, and the woman (the second
London post had come in) had placed my letters and a
newspaper on a bench. I sat down there to the letters, which
were a brief business, and then, without heeding the address,
took the paper from its envelope. It was the journal of highest

renown, *The Empire* of that morning. It regularly came to Paraday, but I remembered that neither of us had yet looked at the copy already delivered. This one had a great mark on the "editorial" page, and, uncrumpling the wrapper, I saw it to be directed to my host and stamped with the name of his publishers. I instantly divined that *The Empire* had spoken of him, and I have not forgotten the odd little shock of the circumstance. It checked all eagerness and made me drop the paper a moment. As I sat there conscious of a palpitation I think I had a vision of what was to be. I had also a vision of the letter I would presently address to Mr. Pinhorn, breaking as it were with Mr. Pinhorn. Of course, however, the next minute the voice of *The Empire* was in my ears.

The article was not, I thanked heaven, a review; it was a "leader," the last of three, presenting Neil Paraday to the human race. His new book, the fifth from his hand, had been but a day or two out, and *The Empire*, already aware of it, fired, as if on the birth of a prince, a salute of a whole column. The guns had been booming these three hours in the house without our suspecting them. The big blundering newspaper had discovered him, and now he was proclaimed and anointed and crowned. His place was assigned him as publicly as if a fat usher with a wand had pointed to the topmost chair; he was to pass up and still up, higher and higher, between the watching faces and the envious sounds— away up to the daïs and the throne. The article was a date; he had taken rank at a bound—waked up a national glory. A national glory was needed, and it was an immense convenience he was there. What all this meant rolled over me, and I fear I grew a little faint—it meant so much more than I could say "yea" to on the spot. In a flash, somehow, all was different; the tremendous wave I speak of had swept something away. It had knocked down, I suppose, my little customary altar, my twinkling tapers and my flowers, and had reared itself into the likeness of a temple vast and bare. When Neil Paraday should come out of the house he would come

out a contemporary. That was what had happened: the poor
man was to be squeezed into his horrible age. I felt as if he
had been overtaken on the crest of the hill and brought back
to the city. A little more and he would have dipped down the
short cut to posterity and escaped.

IV

When he came out it was exactly as if he had been in custody,
for beside him walked a stout man with a big black beard, who,
save that he wore spectacles, might have been a policeman,
and in whom at a second glance I recognised the highest
contemporary enterprise.

"This is Mr. Morrow," said Paraday, looking, I thought, rather
white: "he wants to publish heaven knows what about me."

I winced as I remembered that this was exactly what I myself
had wanted. "Already?" I exclaimed, with a sort of sense that my
friend had fled to me for protection.

Mr. Morrow glared, agreeably, through his glasses: they
suggested the electric headlights of some monstrous modern
ship, and I felt as if Paraday and I were tossing terrified under
his bows. I saw that his momentum was irresistible. "I was
confident that I should be the first in the field," he declared. "A
great interest is naturally felt in Mr. Paraday's surroundings."

"I hadn't the least idea of it," said Paraday, as if he had been
told he had been snoring.

"I find he has not read the article in *The Empire*," Mr. Morrow
remarked to me. "That's so very interesting—it's something to
start with," he smiled. He had begun to pull off his gloves,
which were violently new, and to look encouragingly round
the little garden. As a "surrounding" I felt that I myself had
already been taken in; I was a little fish in the stomach of a
bigger one. "I represent," our visitor continued, "a syndicate of
influential journals, no less than thirty-seven, whose public—
whose publics, I may say—are in peculiar sympathy with Mr.
Paraday's line of thought. They would greatly appreciate any

expression of his views on the subject of the art he so brilliantly practises. Besides my connection with the syndicate just mentioned, I hold a particular commission from *The Tatler*, whose most prominent department, 'Smatter and Chatter'—I daresay you've often enjoyed it—attracts such attention. I was honoured only last week, as a representative of *The Tatler*, with the confidence of Guy Walsingham, the author of 'Obsessions.' She expressed herself thoroughly pleased with my sketch of her method; she went so far as to say that I had made her genius more comprehensible even to herself."

Neil Paraday had dropped upon the garden-bench and sat there at once detached and confused; he looked hard at a bare spot in the lawn, as if with an anxiety that had suddenly made him grave. His movement had been interpreted by his visitor as an invitation to sink sympathetically into a wicker chair that stood hard by, and as Mr. Morrow so settled himself I felt that he had taken official possession and that there was no undoing it. One had heard of unfortunate people's having "a man in the house," and this was just what we had. There was a silence of a moment, during which we seemed to acknowledge in the only way that was possible the presence of universal fate; the sunny stillness took no pity, and my thought, as I was sure Paraday's was doing, performed within the minute a great distant revolution. I saw just how emphatic I should make my rejoinder to Mr. Pinhorn, and that having come, like Mr. Morrow, to betray, I must remain as long as possible to save. Not because I had brought my mind back, but because our visitor's last words were in my ear, I presently inquired with gloomy irrelevance if Guy Walsingham were a woman.

"Oh yes, a mere pseudonym; but convenient, you know, for a lady who goes in for the larger latitude. 'Obsessions, by Miss So-and-so,' would look a little odd, but men are more naturally indelicate. Have you peeped into 'Obsessions'?" Mr. Morrow continued sociably to our companion.

Paraday, still absent, remote, made no answer, as if he had not heard the question: a manifestation that appeared to suit the cheerful Mr. Morrow as well as any other. Imperturbably bland, he was a man of resources—he only needed to be on the spot. He had pocketed the whole poor place while Paraday and I were woolgathering, and I could imagine that he had already got his "heads." His system, at any rate, was justified by the inevitability with which I replied, to save my friend the trouble: "Dear, no; he hasn't read it. He doesn't read such things!" I unwarily added.

"Things that are *too* far over the fence, eh?" I was indeed a godsend to Mr. Morrow. It was the psychological moment; it determined the appearance of his notebook, which, however, he at first kept slightly behind him, even as the dentist, approaching his victim, keeps the horrible forceps. "Mr. Paraday holds with the good old proprieties—I see!" And thinking of the thirty-seven influential journals, I found myself, as I found poor Paraday, helplessly gazing at the promulgation of this ineptitude. "There's no point on which distinguished views are so acceptable as on this question—raised perhaps more strikingly than ever by Guy Walsingham—of the permissibility of the larger latitude. I have an appointment, precisely in connection with it, next week, with Dora Forbes, the author of 'The Other Way Round,' which everybody is talking about. Has Mr. Paraday glanced at 'The Other Way Round'?" Mr. Morrow now frankly appealed to me. I took upon myself to repudiate the supposition, while our companion, still silent, got up nervously and walked away. His visitor paid no heed to his withdrawal; he only opened out the notebook with a more motherly pat. "Dora Forbes, I gather, takes the ground, the same as Guy Walsingham's, that the larger latitude has simply got to come. He holds that it has got to be squarely faced. Of course his sex makes him a less prejudiced witness. But an authoritative word from Mr. Paraday—from the point of view of *his* sex, you know—would go right round the globe. He takes the line that we *haven't* got to face it?"

I was bewildered: it sounded somehow as if there were three sexes. My interlocutor's pencil was poised, my private responsibility great. I simply sat staring, however, and only found presence of mind to say: "Is this Miss Forbes a gentleman?"

Mr. Morrow hesitated an instant, smiling. "It wouldn't be 'Miss'—there's a wife!"

"I mean is she a man?"

"The wife?"—Mr. Morrow, for a moment, was as confused as myself. But when I explained that I alluded to Dora Forbes in person he informed me, with visible amusement at my being so out of it, that this was the "pen-name" of an indubitable male—he had a big red moustache. "He only assumes a feminine personality because the ladies are such popular favourites. A great deal of interest is felt in this assumption, and there's every prospect of its being widely imitated." Our host at this moment joined us again, and Mr. Morrow remarked invitingly that he should be happy to make a note of any observation the movement in question, the bid for success under a lady's name, might suggest to Mr. Paraday. But the poor man, without catching the allusion, excused himself, pleading that, though he was greatly honoured by his visitor's interest, he suddenly felt unwell and should have to take leave of him—have to go and lie down and keep quiet. His young friend might be trusted to answer for him, but he hoped Mr. Morrow didn't expect great things even of his young friend. His young friend, at this moment, looked at Neil Paraday with an anxious eye, greatly wondering if he were doomed to be ill again; but Paraday's own kind face met his question reassuringly, seemed to say in a glance intelligible enough: "Oh, I'm not ill, but I'm scared: get him out of the house as quietly as possible." Getting newspaper-men out of the house was odd business for an emissary of Mr. Pinhorn, and I was so exhilarated by the idea of it that I called after him as he left us:

"Read the article in *The Empire*, and you'll soon be all right!"

V

"Delicious my having come down to tell him of it!" Mr. Morrow ejaculated. "My cab was at the door twenty minutes after *The Empire* had been laid upon my breakfast-table. Now what have you got for me?" he continued, dropping again into his chair, from which, however, the next moment he quickly rose. "I was shown into the drawing-room, but there must be more to see— his study, his literary sanctum, the little things he has about, or other domestic objects or features. He wouldn't be lying down on his study-table? There's a great interest always felt in the scene of an author's labours. Sometimes we're favoured with very delightful peeps. Dora Forbes showed me all his table-drawers, and almost jammed my hand into one into which I made a dash! I don't ask that of you but if we could talk things over right there where he sits I feel as if I should get the keynote."

I had no wish whatever to be rude to Mr. Morrow, I was much too initiated not to prefer the safety of other ways; but I had a quick inspiration and I entertained an insurmountable, an almost superstitious objection to his crossing the threshold of my friend's little lonely, shabby, consecrated workshop. "No, no— we shan't get at his life that way," I said. "The way to get at his life is to—But wait a moment!" I broke off and went quickly into the house; then, in three minutes, I reappeared before Mr. Morrow with the two volumes of Paraday's new book. "His life's here," I went on, "and I'm so full of this admirable thing that I can't talk of anything else. The artist's life's his work, and this is the place to observe him. What he has to tell us he tells us with *this* perfection. My dear sir, the best interviewer's the best reader."

Mr. Morrow good-humouredly protested. "Do you mean to say that no other source of information should be open to us?"

"None other till this particular one—by far the most copious— has been quite exhausted. Have you exhausted it, my dear sir? Had you exhausted it when you came down here? It seems to me in our time almost wholly neglected, and something should surely be done to restore its ruined credit. It's the course to which the artist himself at every step, and with such pathetic confidence, refers us. This last book of Mr. Paraday's is full of revelations."

"Revelations?" panted Mr. Morrow, whom I had forced again into his chair.

"The only kind that count. It tells you with a perfection that seems to me quite final all the author thinks, for instance, about the advent of the 'larger latitude.'"

"Where does it do that?" asked Mr. Morrow, who had picked up the second volume and was insincerely thumbing it.

"Everywhere—in the whole treatment of his case. Extract the opinion, disengage the answer—those are the real acts of homage."

Mr. Morrow, after a minute, tossed the book away. "Ah, but you mustn't take me for a reviewer."

"Heaven forbid I should take you for anything so dreadful! You came down to perform a little act of sympathy, and so, I may confide to you, did I. Let us perform our little act together. These pages overflow with the testimony we want: let us read them and taste them and interpret them. You will of course have perceived for yourself that one scarcely does read Neil Paraday till one reads him aloud; he gives out to the ear an extraordinary quality, and it's only when you expose it confidently to that test that you really get near his style. Take up your book again and let me listen, while you pay it out, to that wonderful fifteenth chapter. If you feel that you can't do it justice, compose yourself to attention while I produce for you—I think I can!—this scarcely less admirable ninth."

Mr. Morrow gave me a straight glance which was as hard as a blow between the eyes; he had turned rather red, and a question had formed itself in his mind which reached my sense as distinctly as if he had uttered it: "What sort of a damned fool are *you*?" Then he got up, gathering together his hat and gloves, buttoning his coat, projecting hungrily all over the place the big transparency of his mask. It seemed to flare over Fleet Street and somehow made the actual spot distressingly humble: there was so little for it to feed on unless he counted the blisters of our stucco or saw his way to do something with the roses. Even the poor roses were common kinds. Presently his eyes fell upon the manuscript from which Paraday had been reading to me and which still lay on the bench. As my own followed them I saw that it looked promising, looked pregnant, as if it gently throbbed with the life the reader had given it. Mr. Morrow indulged in a nod toward it and a vague thrust of his umbrella. "What's that?"

"Oh, it's a plan—a secret."

"A secret!" There was an instant's silence, and then Mr. Morrow made another movement. I may have been mistaken, but it affected me as the translated impulse of the desire to lay hands on the manuscript, and this led me to indulge in a quick anticipatory grab which may very well have seemed ungraceful, or even impertinent, and which at any rate left Mr. Paraday's two admirers very erect, glaring at each other while one of them held a bundle of papers well behind him. An instant later Mr. Morrow quitted me abruptly, as if he had really carried something off with him. To reassure myself, watching his broad back recede, I only grasped my manuscript the tighter. He went to the back-door of the house, the one he had come out from, but on trying the handle he appeared to find it fastened. So he passed round into the front garden, and by listening intently enough I could presently hear the outer gate close behind him with a bang. I thought again of the thirty-seven influential journals and wondered what would be his revenge. I hasten to add that he was magnanimous: which was just the most dreadful thing he could have been. *The Tatler* published a charming, chatty, familiar account of Mr. Paraday's "Home-life," and on the wings of the thirty-seven influential journals it went, to use Mr. Morrow's own expression, right round the globe.

VI

A week later, early in May, my glorified friend came up to town, where, it may be veraciously recorded, he was the king of the beasts of the year. No advancement was ever more rapid, no exaltation more complete, no bewilderment more teachable. His book sold but moderately, though the article in *The Empire* had done unwonted wonders for it; but he circulated in person in a manner that the libraries might well have envied. His formula had been found—he was a "revelation." His momentary terror had been real, just as mine had been—the overclouding of his passionate desire to be left to finish his work. He was far from unsociable, but he had the finest conception of being let alone that I have ever met. For the time, however, he took his profit where it seemed most to crowd upon him, having in his pocket the portable sophistries about the nature of the artist's task. Observation too was a kind of work and experience a kind of success; London dinners were all material and London ladies were fruitful toil. "No one has the faintest conception of what I'm trying for," he said to me, "and not many have read three pages that I've written; but I must dine with them first—they'll find out why when they've time." It was rather rude justice, perhaps; but the fatigue had the merit of being a new sort, and the phantasmagoric town was probably after all less of a battlefield than the haunted study. He once told me that he had had no personal life to speak of since his fortieth year, but had had more than was good for him before. London closed the parenthesis and exhibited him in relations; one of the most inevitable of these being that in which he found himself to Mrs. Weeks Wimbush, wife of the boundless brewer and pro-prietress of the universal menagerie. In this establishment, as everybody knows, on occasions when the crush is great, the animals rub shoulders freely with the spectators and the lions sit down for whole evenings with the lambs.

It had been ominously clear to me from the first that in Neil Paraday this lady, who, as all the world agreed, was tremendous fun, considered that she had secured a prime attraction, a creature of almost heraldic oddity. Nothing could exceed her enthusiasm over her capture, and nothing could exceed the confused apprehensions it excited in me. I had an instinctive fear of her which I tried without effect to conceal from her victim, but which I let her perceive with perfect impunity. Paraday heeded it, but she never did, for her conscience was that of a romping child. She was a blind, violent force, to which I could attach no more idea of responsibility than to the creaking of a sign in the wind. It was difficult to say what she conduced to but to circulation. She was constructed of steel and leather, and all I asked of her for our tractable friend was not to do him to death. He had consented for a time to be of india-rubber, but my thoughts were fixed on the day he should resume his shape or at least get back into his box. It was evidently all right, but I should be glad when it was well over. I had a special fear—the impression was ineffaceable of the hour when, after Mr. Morrow's departure, I had found him on the sofa in his study. That pretext of indisposition had not in the least been meant as a snub to the envoy of *The Tatler*—he had gone to lie down in very truth. He had felt a pang of his old pain, the result of the agitation wrought in him by this forcing open of a new period. His old programme, his old ideal even had to be changed. Say what one would, success was a complication and recognition had to be reciprocal. The monastic life, the pious illumination of the missal in the convent cell were things of the gathered past. It didn't engender despair, but it at least required adjustment. Before I left him on that occasion we had passed a bargain, my part of which was that I should make it my business to take care of him. Let whoever would represent the interest in his presence (I had a mystical prevision of Mrs. Weeks Wimbush) I should represent the interest in his work—in other words in his absence. These two interests were in their essence opposed; and I doubt, as youth is fleeting, if I shall ever again know the intensity of joy with which I felt that in so good a cause I was willing to make myself odious.

One day, in Sloane Street, I found myself questioning Paraday's landlord, who had come to the door in answer to my knock. Two vehicles, a barouche and a smart hansom, were drawn up before the house.

"In the drawing-room, sir? Mrs. Weeks Wimbush."

"And in the dining-room?"

"A young lady, sir—waiting: I think a foreigner."

It was three o'clock, and on days when Paraday didn't lunch out he attached a value to these subjugated hours. On which days, however, didn't the dear man lunch out? Mrs. Wimbush, at such a crisis, would have rushed round immediately after her own repast. I went into the dining-room first, postponing the pleasure of seeing how, upstairs, the lady of the barouche would, on my arrival, point the moral of my sweet solicitude. No one took such an interest as herself in his doing only what was good for him, and she was always on the spot to see that he did it. She made appointments with him to discuss the best means of economising his time and protecting his privacy. She further made his health her special business, and had so much sympathy with my own zeal for it that she was the author of pleasing fictions on the subject of what my devotion had led me to give up. I gave up nothing (I don't count Mr. Pinhorn) because I had nothing, and all I had as yet achieved was to find myself also in the menagerie. I had dashed in to save my friend, but I had only got domesticated and wedged; so that I could do nothing for him but exchange with him over people's heads looks of intense but futile intelligence.

VII

The young lady in the dining-room had a brave face, black hair, blue eyes, and in her lap a big volume. "I've come for his autograph," she said when I had explained to her that I was under bonds to see people for him when he was occupied.

"I've been waiting half an hour, but I'm prepared to wait all day." I don't know whether it was this that told me she was American, for the propensity to wait all day is not in general characteristic of her race. I was enlightened probably not so much by the spirit of the utterance as by some quality of its sound. At any rate I saw she had an individual patience and a lovely frock, together with an expression that played among her pretty features like a breeze among flowers. Putting her book upon the table, she showed me a massive album, showily bound and full of autographs of price. The collection of faded notes, of still more faded "thoughts," of quotations, platitudes, signatures, represented a formidable purpose.

"Most people apply to Mr. Paraday by letter, you know," I said.

"Yes, but he doesn't answer. I've written three times."

"Very true," I reflected; "the sort of letter you mean goes straight into the fire."

"How do you know the sort I mean?" My interlocutress had blushed and smiled, and in a moment she added: "I don't believe he gets many like them!"

"I'm sure they're beautiful, but he burns without reading." I didn't add that I had told him he ought to.

"Isn't he then in danger of burning things of importance?"

"He would be, if distinguished men hadn't an infallible nose for nonsense."

She looked at me a moment—her face was sweet and gay. "Do *you* burn without reading, too?" she asked; in answer to which I assured her that if she would trust me with her repository I would see that Mr. Paraday should write his name in it.

She considered a little. "That's very well, but it wouldn't make me see him."

"Do you want very much to see him?" It seemed ungracious to catechise so charming a creature, but somehow I had never yet taken my duty to the great author so seriously.

"Enough to have come from America for the purpose."

I stared. "All alone?"

"I don't see that that's exactly your business; but if it will make me more appealing I'll confess that I'm quite by myself. I had to come alone or not come at all."

She was interesting; I could imagine that she had lost parents, natural protectors—could conceive even that she had inherited money. I was in a phase of my own fortune when keeping hansoms at doors seemed to me pure swagger. As a trick of this bold and sensitive girl, however, it became romantic—a part of the general romance of her freedom, her errand, her innocence. The confidence of young Americans was notorious, and I speedily arrived at a conviction that no impulse could have been more generous than the impulse that had operated here. I foresaw at that moment that it would make her my peculiar charge, just as circumstances had made Neil Paraday. She would be another person to look after, and one's honour would be concerned in guiding her straight. These things became clearer to me later; at the instant I had scepticism enough to observe to her, as I turned the pages of her volume, that her net had, all the same, caught many a big fish. She appeared to have had fruitful access to the great ones of the earth; there were people moreover whose signatures she had presumably secured without a personal interview. She couldn't have worried George Washington and Friedrich Schiller and Hannah More. She met this argument, to my surprise, by throwing up the album without a pang. It wasn't even her own; she was responsible for none of its treasures. It belonged to a girl-friend in America, a young lady in a western city. This young lady had insisted on her bringing it, to pick up more autographs: she thought they might like to see, in Europe, in what company they would be. The "girl-friend," the western city, the immortal names, the curious errand, the idyllic faith, all made a story as strange to me, and as beguiling, as some tale in the Arabian Nights. Thus it was that my informant had encumbered herself with the ponderous tome; but she hastened to assure me that this was the first time she had brought it out. For her visit to Mr. Paraday it had simply been a pretext. She didn't really care a straw that he should write his name; what she did want was to look straight into his face.

I demurred a little. "And why do you require to do that?"

"Because I just love him!" Before I could recover from the agitating effect of this crystal ring my companion had continued: "Hasn't there ever been any face that you've wanted to look into?"

How could I tell her so soon how much I appreciated the opportunity of looking into hers? I could only assent in general to the proposition that there were certainly for everyone such hankerings, and even such faces; and I felt that the crisis demanded all my lucidity, all my wisdom. "Oh, yes, I'm a student of physiognomy. Do you mean," I pursued, "that you've a passion for Mr. Paraday's books?"

"They've been everything to me and a little more beside—I know them by heart. They've completely taken hold of me. There's no author about whom I feel as I do about Neil Paraday."

"Permit me to remark then," I presently rejoined, "that you're one of the right sort."

"One of the enthusiasts? Of course I am!"

"Oh, there are enthusiasts who are quite of the wrong. I mean you're one of those to whom an appeal can be made."

"An appeal?" Her face lighted as if with the chance of some great sacrifice.

If she was ready for one it was only waiting for her, and in a moment I mentioned it. "Give up this crude purpose of seeing him. Go away without it. That will be far better."

She looked mystified; then she turned visibly pale. "Why, hasn't he any personal charm?" The girl was terrible and laughable in her bright directness.

"Ah, that dreadful word 'personal!'" I exclaimed; "we're dying of it, and you women bring it out with murderous effect. When you encounter a genius as fine as this idol of ours, let him off the dreary duty of being a personality as well. Know him only by what's best in him, and spare him for the same sweet sake."

My young lady continued to look at me in confusion and mistrust, and the result of her reflection on what I had just said was to make her suddenly break out: "Look here, sir—what's the matter with him?"

"The matter with him is that, if he doesn't look out, people will eat a great hole in his life."

She considered a moment. "He hasn't any disfigurement?"

"Nothing to speak of!"

"Do you mean that social engagements interfere with his occupations?"

"That but feebly expresses it."

"So that he can't give himself up to his beautiful imagination?"

"He's badgered, bothered, overwhelmed, on the pretext of being applauded. People expect him to give them his time, his golden time, who wouldn't themselves give five shillings for one of his books."

"Five? I'd give five thousand!"

"Give your sympathy—give your forbearance. Two-thirds of those who approach him only do it to advertise themselves."

"Why, it's too bad!" the girl exclaimed with the face of an angel. "It's the first time I was ever called crude!" she laughed.

I followed up my advantage. "There's a lady with him now who's a terrible complication, and who yet hasn't read, I am sure, ten pages that he ever wrote."

My visitor's wide eyes grew tenderer. "Then how does she talk—?"

"Without ceasing. I only mention her as a single case. Do you want to know how to show a superlative consideration? Simply avoid him."

"Avoid him?" she softly wailed.

"Don't force him to have to take account of you; admire him in silence, cultivate him at a distance and secretly appropriate his message. Do you want to know," I continued, warming to my idea, "how to perform an act of homage really sublime?"

Then as she hung on my words: "Succeed in never seeing him at all!"

"Never at all?" she pathetically gasped.

"The more you get into his writings the less you'll want to; and you'll be immensely sustained by the thought of the good you're doing him."

She looked at me without resentment or spite, and at the truth I had put before her with candour, credulity, pity. I was afterwards happy to remember that she must have recognised in my face the liveliness of my interest in herself. "I think I see what you mean."

"Oh, I express it badly; but I should be delighted if you would let me come to see you—to explain it better."

She made no response to this, and her thoughtful eyes fell on the big album, on which she presently laid her hands as if to take it away. "I did use to say out West that they might write a little less for autographs (to all the great poets, you know) and study the thoughts and style a little more."

"What do they care for the thoughts and style? They didn't even understand you. I'm not sure," I added, "that I do myself, and I daresay that you by no means make me out." She had got up to go, and though I wanted her to succeed in not seeing Neil Paraday I wanted her also, inconsequently, to remain in the house. I was at any rate far from desiring to hustle her off. As Mrs. Weeks Wimbush, upstairs, was still saving our friend in her own way, I asked my young lady to let me briefly relate, in illustration of my point, the little incident of my having gone down into the country for a profane purpose and been converted on the spot to holiness. Sinking again into her chair to listen, she showed a deep interest in the anecdote. Then thinking it over gravely, she exclaimed with her odd intonation:

"Yes, but you do see him!" I had to admit that this was the case; and I was not so prepared with an effective attenuation as I could have wished. She eased the situation off, however, by the charming quaintness with which she finally said: "Well, I wouldn't want him to be lonely!" This time she rose in earnest, but I persuaded her to let me keep the album to show to Mr. Paraday. I assured her I would bring it back to her myself. "Well, you'll find my address somewhere in it, on a paper!" she sighed resignedly, at the door.

VIII

I blush to confess it, but I invited Mr. Paraday that very day to transcribe into the album one of his most characteristic passages. I told him how I had got rid of the strange girl who had brought it—her ominous name was Miss Hurter, and she lived at an hotel; quite agreeing with him moreover as to the wisdom of getting rid with equal promptitude of the book itself. This was why I carried it to Albemarle Street no later than on the morrow. I failed to find her at home, but she wrote to me and I went again: she wanted so much to hear more about Neil Paraday. I returned repeatedly, I may briefly declare, to supply her with this information. She had been immensely taken, the more she thought of it, with that idea of mine about the act of homage: it had ended by filling her with a generous rapture. She positively desired to do something sublime for him, though indeed I could see that, as this particular flight was difficult, she appreciated the fact that my visits kept her up. I had it on my conscience to keep her up; I neglected nothing that would contribute to it, and her conception of our cherished author's independence became at last as fine as his own conception. "Read him, read him," I constantly repeated; while, seeking him in his works, she represented herself as convinced that, according to my assurance, this was the system that had, as she expressed it, weaned her. We read him together when I could find time, and the generous creature's sacrifice was fed by our conversation. There were twenty selfish women, about whom I told her, who stirred her with a beautiful rage. Immediately after my first visit her sister, Mrs. Milsom, came over from Paris, and the two ladies began to present, as they called it, their letters. I thanked our stars that none had been presented to Mr. Paraday. They received invitations and dined out, and some of these occasions enabled Fanny Hurter to perform, for consistency's sake, touching feats of submission. Nothing indeed would now have induced her even to look at the object of her admiration. Once, hearing his name announced at a party, she instantly left the room by another door and then straightway quitted the house. At another time, when I was at the opera with them (Mrs. Milsom had invited me to their box) I attempted to point Mr. Paraday out to her in the stalls. On this she asked her sister to change places with her, and while that lady devoured the great man through a powerful glass, presented, all the rest of the evening, her inspired back to the house. To torment her tenderly I pressed the glass upon her, telling her how wonderfully near it brought our friend's handsome head. By way of answer she simply looked at me in charged silence, letting me see that tears had gathered in her eyes. These tears, I may remark, produced an effect on me of which the end is not yet. There was a moment when I felt it my duty to mention them to Neil Paraday; but I was deterred by the reflection that there were questions more relevant to his happiness.

These questions indeed, by the end of the season, were reduced to a single one—the question of reconstituting, so far as might be possible, the conditions under which he had produced his best work. Such conditions could never all come back, for there was a new one that took up too much place; but some perhaps were not beyond recall. I wanted above all things to see him sit down to the subject of which, on my making his acquaintance, he had read me that admirable sketch. Something told me there was no security but in his doing so before the new factor, as we used to say at Mr. Pinhorn's, should render the problem incalculable. It only half reassured me that the sketch itself was so copious and so eloquent that even at the worst there would be the making of a small but complete book, a tiny volume which, for the faithful, might well become an object of adoration. There would even not be wanting critics to declare, I foresaw, that the plan was a thing to be more thankful for than the structure to have been reared on it. My impatience for the structure, none the less, grew and grew with the interruptions. He had, on coming up to town, begun to sit for his portrait to a young painter, Mr. Rumble, whose little game, as we also used to say at Mr. Pinhorn's, was to be the first to perch on the shoulders of renown. Mr. Rumble's studio was a circus in which the man of the hour, and still more the woman, leaped through the hoops of his showy frames almost as electrically as they burst into telegrams and "specials." He pranced into the exhibitions on their back; he was the reporter on canvas, the Vandyke up to date, and there was one roaring year in which Mrs. Bounder and Miss Braby, Guy Walsingham and Dora Forbes proclaimed in chorus from the same pictured walls that no one had yet got ahead of him.

Paraday had been promptly caught and saddled, accepting with characteristic good-humour his confidential hint that to figure in his show was not so much a consequence as a cause of immortality. From Mrs. Wimbush to the last "representative" who called to ascertain his twelve favourite dishes, it was the same ingenuous assumption that he would rejoice in the repercussion. There were moments when I fancied I might have had more patience with them if they had not been so fatally benevolent. I hated, at all events, Mr. Rumble's picture, and had my bottled resentment ready when, later on, I found my distracted friend had been stuffed by Mrs. Wimbush into the mouth of another cannon. A young artist in whom she was intensely interested, and who had no connection with Mr. Rumble, was to show how far he could make him go. Poor Paraday, in return, was naturally to write something somewhere about the young artist. She played her victims against each other with admirable ingenuity, and her establishment was a huge machine in which the tiniest and the biggest wheels went round to the same treadle. I had a scene with her in which I tried to express that the function of such a man was to exercise his genius—not to serve as a hoarding for pictorial posters. The people I was perhaps angriest with were the editors of magazines who had introduced what they called new features, so aware were they that the newest feature of all would be to make him grind their axes by contributing his views on vital topics and taking part in the periodical prattle about the future of fiction. I made sure that before I should have done with him there would scarcely be a current form of words left me to be sick of; but meanwhile I could make surer still of my animosity to bustling ladies for whom he drew the water that irrigated their social flower-beds.

I had a battle with Mrs. Wimbush over the artist she protected, and another over the question of a certain week, at the end of July, that Mr. Paraday appeared to have contracted to spend with her in the country. I protested against this visit; I intimated that he was too unwell for hospitality without a *nuance*, for caresses without imagination; I begged he might rather take the time in some restorative way. A sultry air of promises, of ponderous parties, hung over his August, and he would greatly profit by the interval of rest. He had not told me he was ill again—that he had had a warning; but I had not needed this, and I found his reticence his worst symptom. The only thing he said to me was that he believed a comfortable attack of something or other would set him up: it would put out of the question everything but the exemptions he prized. I am afraid I shall have presented him as a martyr in a very small cause if I fail to explain that he surrendered himself much more liberally than I surrendered him. He filled his lungs, for the most part, with the comedy of his queer fate: the tragedy was in the spectacles through which I chose to look. He was conscious of inconvenience, and above all of a great renouncement; but how could he have heard a mere dirge in the bells of his accession? The sagacity and the jealousy were mine, and his the impressions and the anecdotes. Of course, as regards Mrs. Wimbush, I was worsted in my encounters, for was not the state of his health the very reason for his coming to her at Prestidge? Wasn't it precisely at Prestidge that he was to be coddled, and wasn't the dear Princess coming to help her to coddle him? The dear Princess, now on a visit to England, was of a famous foreign house, and, in her gilded cage, with her retinue of keepers and feeders, was the most expensive specimen in the good lady's collection. I don't think her august presence had had to do with Paraday's consenting to go, but it is not impossible that he had operated as a bait to the illustrious stranger. The party had been made up for him, Mrs. Wimbush averred, and everyone was counting on it, the dear Princess most of all. If he was well enough he was to read them something absolutely fresh, and it was on that particular prospect the Princess had set her heart. She was so fond of genius, in *any* walk of life, and she was so used to it, and understood it so well; she was the greatest of Mr. Paraday's admirers, she devoured everything he wrote. And then he read like an angel. Mrs. Wimbush reminded me that he had again and again given her, Mrs. Wimbush, the privilege of listening to him.

I looked at her a moment. "What has he read to you?" I crudely inquired.

For a moment too she met my eyes, and for the fraction of a moment she hesitated and coloured. "Oh, all sorts of things!"

I wondered whether this were an imperfect recollection or only a perfect fib, and she quite understood my unuttered comment on her perception of such things. But if she could forget Neil Paraday's beauties she could of course forget my rudeness, and three days later she invited me, by telegraph, to join the party at Prestidge. This time she might indeed have had a story about what I had given up to be near the master. I addressed from that fine residence several communications to a young lady in London, a young lady whom, I confess, I quitted with reluctance and whom the reminder of what she herself could give up was required to make me quit at all. It adds to the gratitude I owe her on other grounds that she kindly allows me to transcribe from my letters a few of the passages in which that hateful sojourn is candidly commemorated.

IX

"I suppose I ought to enjoy the joke of what's going on here," I wrote, "but somehow it doesn't amuse me. Pessimism on the contrary possesses me and cynicism solicits. I positively feel my own flesh sore from the brass nails in Neil Paraday's social harness. The house is full of people who like him, as they mention, awfully, and with whom his talent for talking nonsense has prodigious success. I delight in his nonsense myself; why is it therefore that I grudge these happy fold their artless satisfaction? Mystery of the human heart—abyss of the critical spirit! Mrs. Wimbush thinks she can answer that question, and as my want of gaiety has at last worn out her patience she has given me a glimpse of her shrewd guess. I am made restless by the selfishness of the insincere friend—I want to monopolise Paraday in order that he may push me on. To be intimate with him is a feather in my cap; it gives me an importance that I couldn't naturally pretend to, and I seek to deprive him of social refreshment because I fear that meeting more disinterested people may enlighten him as to my real motive. All the disinterested people here are his particular admirers and have been carefully selected as such. There is supposed to be a copy of his last book in the house, and in the hall I come upon ladies, in attitudes, bending gracefully over the first volume. I discreetly avert my eyes, and when I next look round the precarious joy has been superseded by the book of life. There is a sociable circle or a confidential couple, and the relinquished volume lies open on its face, as if it had been dropped under extreme coercion. Somebody else presently finds it and transfers it, with its air of momentary desolation, to another piece of furniture. Everyone is asking everyone about it all day, and everyone is telling everyone where they put it last. I'm sure it's rather smudgy about the twentieth page. I have a strong impression too that the second volume is lost—has been packed in the bag of some departing guest; and yet everybody has the impression that somebody else has read to the end. You see therefore that the beautiful book plays a great part in our conversation. Why should I take the occasion of such distinguished honours to say that I begin to see deeper into Gustave Flaubert's doleful refrain about the hatred of literature? I refer you again to the perverse constitution of man.

"The Princess is a massive lady with the organisation of an athlete and the confusion of tongues of a *valet de place*. She contrives to commit herself extraordinarily little in a great many languages, and is entertained and conversed with in detachments and relays, like an institution which goes on from generation to generation or a big building contracted for under a forfeit. She can't have a personal taste any more than, when her husband succeeds, she can have a personal crown, and her opinion on any matter is rusty and heavy and plain—made, in the night of ages, to last and be transmitted. I feel as if I ought to pay someone a fee for my glimpse of it. She has been told everything in the world and has never perceived anything, and the echoes of her education respond awfully to the rash footfall—I mean the casual remark—in the cold Valhalla of her memory. Mrs. Wimbush delights in her wit and says there is nothing so charming as to hear Mr. Paraday draw it out. He is perpetually detailed for this job, and he tells me it has a peculiarly exhausting effect. Everyone is beginning—at the end of two days—to sidle obsequiously away from her, and Mrs. Wimbush pushes him again and again into the breach. None of the uses I have yet seen him put to irritate me quite so much. He looks very fagged, and has at last confessed to me that his condition makes him uneasy—has even promised me that he will go straight home instead of returning to his final engagements in town. Last night I had some talk with him about going today, cutting his visit short; so sure am I that he will be better as soon as he is shut up in his lighthouse. He told me that this is what he would like to do; reminding me, however, that the first lesson of his greatness has been precisely that he can't do what he likes. Mrs. Wimbush would never forgive him if he should leave her before the Princess has received the last hand. When I say that a violent rupture with our hostess would be the best thing in the world for him he gives me to understand that if his reason assents to the proposition his courage hangs woefully back. He makes no secret of being mortally afraid of her, and when I ask what harm she can do him that she hasn't already done he simply repeats: 'I'm afraid, I'm afraid! Don't inquire too closely,' he said last night; 'only believe that I feel a sort of terror. It's strange, when she's so kind! At any rate, I would as soon overturn that piece of priceless Sèvres as tell her that I must go before my date'. It sounds dreadfully weak, but he has some reason, and he pays for his imagination, which puts him (I should hate it) in the place of others and makes him feel, even against himself, their feelings, their appetites, their motives. It's indeed inveterately against himself that he makes his imagination act. What a pity he has such a lot of it! He's too beastly intelligent. Besides, the famous reading is still to come off, and it has been postponed a day, to allow Guy Walsingham to arrive. It appears that this eminent lady is staying at a house a few miles off, which means of course that Mrs. Wimbush has forcibly annexed her. She's to come over in a day or two—Mrs. Wimbush wants her to hear Mr. Paraday.

"Today's wet and cold, and several of the company, at the invitation of the Duke, have driven over to luncheon at Bigwood. I saw poor Paraday wedge himself, by command, into the little supplementary seat of a brougham in which the Princess and our hostess were already ensconced. If the front glass isn't open on his dear old back perhaps he'll survive. Bigwood, I believe, is very grand and frigid, all marble and precedence, and I wish him well out of the adventure. I can't tell you how much more and more *your* attitude to him, in the midst of all this, shines out by contrast. I never willingly talk to these people about him, but see what a comfort I find it to scribble to you! I appreciate it—it keeps me warm; there are no fires in the house. Mrs. Wimbush goes by the calendar, the

278

temperature goes by the weather, the weather goes by God knows what, and the Princess is easily heated. I have nothing but my acrimony to warm me, and have been out under an umbrella to restore my circulation. Coming in an hour ago, I found Lady Augusta Minch rummaging about the hall. When I asked her what she was looking for she said she had mislaid something that Mr. Paraday had lent her. I ascertained in a moment that the article in question is a manuscript, and I have a foreboding that it's the noble morsel he read me six weeks ago. When I expressed my surprise that he should have bandied about anything so precious (I happen to know it's his only copy—in the most beautiful hand in all the world) Lady Augusta confessed to me that she had not had it from himself, but from Mrs. Wimbush, who had wished to give her a glimpse of it as a salve for her not being able to stay and hear it read.

"'Is that the piece he's to read,' I asked, 'when Guy Walsingham arrives?'

"'It's not for Guy Walsingham they're waiting now, it's for Dora Forbes,' Lady Augusta said. 'She's coming, I believe, early tomorrow. Meanwhile Mrs. Wimbush has found out about *him*, and is actively wiring to him. She says he also must hear him.'

"'You bewilder me a little,' I replied; 'in the age we live in one gets lost among the genders and the pronouns. The clear thing is that Mrs. Wimbush doesn't guard such a treasure as jealously as she might.'

"'Poor dear, she has the Princess to guard! Mr. Paraday lent her the manuscript to look over.'

"'Did she speak as if it were the morning paper?'

"'Lady Augusta stared—my irony was lost upon her. 'She didn't have time, so she gave me a chance first; because unfortunately I go tomorrow to Bigwood.'

"'And your chance has only proved a chance to lose it?'

"'I haven't lost it. I remember now—it was very stupid of me to have forgotten. I told my maid to give it to Lord Dorimont—or at least to his man.'

"'And Lord Dorimont went away directly after luncheon.'

"'Of course he gave it back to my maid—or else his man did,' said Lady Augusta. 'I daresay it's all right.'

"The conscience of these people is like a summer sea. They haven't time to 'look over' a priceless composition; they've only time to kick it about the house. I suggested that the 'man,' fired with a noble emulation, had perhaps kept the work for his own perusal; and her ladyship wanted to know whether, if the thing didn't turn up again in time for the session appointed by our hostess, the author wouldn't have something else to read that would do just as well. Their questions are too delightful! I declared to Lady Augusta briefly that nothing in the world can ever do so well as the thing that does best; and at this she lookd a little confused and scared. But I added that if the manuscript had gone astray our little circle would have the less of an effort of attention to make. The piece in question was very long—it would keep them three hours.

"'Three hours! Oh, the Princess will get up!' said Lady Augusta.

"'I thought she was Mr. Paraday's greatest admirer.'

"'I daresay she is—she's so awfully clever. But what's the use of being a Princess—'

"'If you can't dissemble your love?' I asked, as Lady Augusta was vague. She said, at any rate, that she would question her maid; and I am hoping that when I go down to dinner I shall find the manuscript has been recovered."

X

"It has not been recovered," I wrote early the next day, "and I am moreover much troubled about our friend. He came back from Bigwood with a chill and, being allowed to have a fire in his room, lay down awhile before dinner. I tried to send him to bed, and indeed thought I had put him in the way of it; but after I had gone to dress Mrs. Wimbush came up to see him, with the inevitable result that when I returned I found him under arms and flushed and feverish, though decorated with the rare flower she had brought him for his button-hole. He came down to dinner, but Lady Augusta Minch was very shy of him. Today he's in great pain, and the advent of *ces dames*—I mean of Guy Walsingham and Dora Forbes—doesn't at all console me. It does Mrs. Wimbush however, for she has consented to his remaining in bed, so that he may be all right tomorrow for the listening circle. Guy Walsingham is already on the scene, and the doctor, for Paraday, also arrived early. I haven't yet seen the author of 'Obsessions,' but of course I've had a moment by myself with the doctor. I tried to get him to say that our invalid must go straight home—I mean tomorrow or next day; but he quite refuses to talk about the future. Absolute quiet and warmth and the regular administration of an important remedy are the points he mainly insists on. He returns this afternoon, and I'm to go back to see the patient at one o'clock, when he next takes his medicine. It consoles me a little that he certainly won't be able to read—an exertion he was already more than unfit for. Lady Augusta went off after breakfast, assuring me that her first care would be to follow up the lost manuscript. I can see she thinks me a shocking busybody and doesn't understand my alarm, but she will do what she can, for she's a good-natured woman. 'So are they all honourable men.' That was precisely what made her give the thing to Lord Dorimont and made Lord Dorimont bag it. What use he has for it God only knows. I have the worst forebodings, but somehow I'm strangely without passion—desperately calm. As I consider the unconscious, the well-meaning ravages of our appreciative circle I bow my head in submission to some great natural, some universal accident; I'm rendered almost indifferent, in fact quite gay (ha-ha!) by the sense of immitigable fate. Lady Augusta promises me to trace the precious object and let me have it, through the post, by the time Paraday is well enough to play his part with it. The last evidence is that her maid did give it to his lordship's valet. One would think it was some thrilling number of The Family Budget. Mrs. Wimbush, who is aware of the accident, is much less agitated by it than she would doubtless be were she not for the hour inevitably engrossed with Guy Walsingham."

Later in the day I informed my correspondent, for whom indeed I kept a sort of diary of the situation, that I had made the acquaintance of this celebrity and that she was a pretty little girl who wore her hair in what used to be called a crop. She looked so juvenile and so innocent that if, as Mr. Morrow had announced, she was resigned to the larger latitude, her superiority to prejudice must have come to her early. I spent most of the day hovering about Neil Paraday's room, but it was communicated to me from below that Guy Walsingham, at Prestidge, was a success. Towards evening I became conscious somehow that her superiority was contagious, and by the time the company separated for the night I was sure that the larger latitude had been generally accepted. I thought of Dora Forbes and felt that he had no time to lose. Before dinner I received a telegram from Lady Augusta Minch. "Lord Dorimont thinks he must have left bundle in train—inquire." How could I inquire—if I was to take the word as command? I was too worried and now too alarmed about Neil Paraday. The doctor came back, and it was an immense satisfaction to me to feel that he was wise and interested. He was proud of being called to so distinguished a patient, but he admitted to me that night that my friend was gravely ill. It was really a relapse, a recrudescence of his old malady. There could be no question of moving him: we must at any rate see first, on the spot, what turn his condition would take. Meanwhile, on the morrow, he was to have a nurse. On the morrow the dear man was easier, and my spirits rose to such cheerfulness that I could almost laugh over Lady Augusta's second telegram: "Lord Dorimont's servant been to station—nothing found. Push inquiries." I did laugh, I am sure, as I remembered this to be the mystic scroll I had scarcely allowed poor Mr. Morrow to point his umbrella at. Fool that I had been: the thirty-seven influential journals wouldn't have destroyed it, they would only have printed it. Of course I said nothing to Paraday.

When the nurse arrived she turned me out of the room, on which I went downstairs. I should premise that at breakfast the news that our brilliant friend was doing well excited universal complacency, and the Princess graciously remarked that he was only to be commiserated for missing the society of Miss Collop. Mrs. Wimbush, whose social gift never shone brighter than in the dry decorum with which she accepted this fizzle in her fireworks, mentioned to me that Guy Walsingham had made a very favourable impression on her Imperial Highness. Indeed I think everyone did so, and that, like the money-market or the national honour, her Imperial Highness was constitutionally sensitive. There was a certain gladness, a perceptible bustle in the air, however, which I thought slightly anomalous in a house where a great author lay critically ill. *"Le roy est mort—vive le roy:"* I was reminded that another great author had already stepped into his shoes. When I came down again after the nurse had taken possession I found a strange gentleman hanging about the hall and pacing to and fro by the closed door of the drawing-room. This personage was florid and bald; he had a big red moustache and wore showy knickerbockers—character-istics all that fitted into my conception of the identity of Dora Forbes. In a moment I saw what had happened: the author of "The Other Way Round" had just alighted at the portals of Prestidge, but had suffered a scruple to restrain him from penetrating further. I recognised his scruple when, pausing to listen at his gesture of caution, I heard a shrill voice lifted in a sort of rhythmic, uncanny chant. The famous reading had begun, only it was the author of "Obsessions" who now furnished the sacrifice. The new visitor whispered to me that he judged something was going on that he oughtn't to interrupt.

"Miss Collop arrived last night," I smiled, "and the Princess has a thirst for the inédit."

Dora Forbes lifted his bushy brows. "Miss Collop?"

"Guy Walsingham, your distinguished confrère—or shall I say your formidable rival?"

"Oh!" growled Dora Forbes. Then he added:"Shall I spoil it if

283

I go in?"

"I should think nothing could spoil it!" I ambiguously laughed.

Dora Forbes evidently felt the dilemma; he gave an irritated crook to his moustache. "Shall I go in?" he presently asked.

We looked at each other hard a moment; then I expressed something bitter that was in me, expressed it in an infernal "Do!" After this I got out into the air, but not so fast as not to hear, when the door of the drawing-room opened, the disconcerted drop of Miss Collop's public manner: she must have been in the midst of the larger latitude. Producing with extreme rapidity, Guy Walsingham has just published a work in which amiable people who are not initiated have been pained to see the genius of a sister-novelist held up to unmistakable ridicule; so fresh an exhibition does it seem to them of the dreadful way men have always treated women. Dora Forbes, it is true, at the present hour, is immensely pushed by Mrs. Wimbush, and has sat for his portrait to the young artists she protects, sat for it not only in oils but in monumental alabaster.

What happened at Prestidge later in the day is of course contemporary history. If the interruption I had whimsically sanctioned was almost a scandal, what is to be said of that general dispersal of the company which, under the doctor's rule, began to take place in the evening? His rule was soothing to behold, small comfort as I was to have at the end. He decreed in the interest of his patient an absolutely soundless house and a consequent break-up of the party. Little country practitioner as he was, he literally packed off the Princess. She departed as promptly as if a revolution had broken out, and Guy Walsingham emigrated with her. I was kindly permitted to remain, and this was not denied even to Mrs. Wimbush. The privilege was withheld indeed from Dora Forbes; so Mrs. Wimbush kept her latest capture temporarily concealed. This was so little, however, her usual way of dealing with her eminent friends that a couple of days of it exhausted her patience, and she went up to town with him in great publicity.

The sudden turn for the worse her afflicted guest had, after a brief improvement, taken on the third night raised an obstacle to her seeing him before her retreat; a fortunate circumstance doubtless, for she was fundamentally disappointed in him. This was not the kind of performance for which she had invited him to Prestidge, or invited the Princess. Let me hasten to add that none of the generous acts which have characterised her patronage of intellectual and other merit have done so much for her reputation as her lending Neil Paraday the most beautiful of her numerous homes to die in. He took advantage to the utmost of the singular favour. Day by day I saw him sink, and I roamed alone about the empty terraces and gardens. His wife never came near him, but I scarcely noticed it: as I paced there with rage in my heart I was too full of another wrong. In the event of his death it would fall to me perhaps to bring out in some charming form, with notes, with the tenderest editorial care, that precious heritage of his written project. But where was that precious heritage, and were both the author and the book to have been snatched from us? Lady Augusta wrote me that she had done all she could and that poor Lord Dorimont, who had really been worried to death, was extremely sorry. I couldn't have the matter out with Mrs. Wimbush, for I didn't want to be taunted by her with desiring to aggrandise myself by a public connection with Mr. Paraday's sweepings. She had signified her willingness to meet the expense of all advertising, as indeed she was always ready to do. The last night of the horrible series, the night before he died, I put my ear closer to his pillow.

"That thing I read you that morning, you know."

"In your garden that dreadful day? Yes!"

"Won't it do as it is?"

"It would have been a glorious book."

"It is a glorious book," Neil Paraday murmured. "Print it as it stands—beautifully."

"Beautifully!" I passionately promised.

It may be imagined whether, now that he is gone, the

promise seems to me less sacred. I am convinced that if such pages had appeared in his lifetime the Abbey would hold him today. I have kept the advertising in my own hands, but the manuscript has not been recovered. It's impossible, and at any rate intolerable, to suppose it can have been wantonly destroyed. Perhaps some hazard of a blind hand, some brutal ignorance has lighted kitchen-fires with it. Every stupid and hideous accident haunts my meditations. My undiscourageable search for the lost treasure would make a long chapter. Fortunately I have a devoted associate in the person of a young lady who has every day a fresh indignation and a fresh idea, and who maintains with intensity that the prize will still turn up. Sometimes I believe her, but I have quite ceased to believe myself. The only thing for us, at all events, is to go on seeking and hoping together; and we should be closely united by this firm tie even were we not at present by another.

THE TWO FACES

THE TWO FACES

I

The servant, who, in spite of his sealed stamped look, appeared to have his reasons, stood there for instruction in a manner not quite usual after announcing the name. Mrs. Grantham, however, took it up—"Lord Gwyther?"—with a quick surprise that for an instant justified him even to the small scintilla in the glance she gave her companion, which might have had exactly the sense of the butler's hesitation. This companion, a shortish fairish youngish man, clean-shaven and keen-eyed, had, with a promptitude that would have struck an observer—which the butler indeed was—sprung to his feet and moved to the chimney-piece, though his hostess herself meanwhile managed not otherwise to stir. "Well?" she said as for the visitor to advance; which she immediately followed with a sharper "He's not there?"

"Shall I show him up, ma'am?"

"But of course!" The point of his doubt made her at last rise for impatience, and Bates, before leaving the room, might still have caught the achieved irony of her appeal to the gentleman into whose communion with her he had broken. "Why in the world not—? What a way—!" she exclaimed as Sutton felt beside his cheek the passage of her eyes to the glass behind him.

"He wasn't sure you'd see anyone."

"I don't see 'anyone,' but I see individuals."

"That's just it—and sometimes you don't see them."

"Do you mean ever because of *you?*" she asked as she touched into place a tendril of hair. "That's just his impertinence, as to which I shall speak to him."

"Don't," said Shirley Sutton. "Never notice anything."

"That's nice advice from you," she laughed, "who notice everything!"

"Ah but I speak of nothing."

She looked at him a moment. "You're still more impertinent than Bates. You'll please not budge," she went on.

"Really? I must sit him out?" he continued as, after a minute, she had not again spoken—only glancing about, while she changed her place, partly for another look at the glass and partly to see if she could improve her seat. What she felt was rather more than, clever and charming though she was, she could hide. "If you're wondering how you seem I can tell you. Awfully cool and easy."

She gave him another stare. She was beautiful and conscious. "And if you're wondering how *you* seem—"

"Oh I'm not!" he laughed from before the fire. "I always perfectly know."

"How you seem," she retorted, "is as if you didn't!"

Once more for a little he watched her. "You're looking lovely for him—extraordinarily lovely, within the marked limits of your range. But that's enough. Don't be clever."

"Then who *will* be?"

"There you are!" he sighed with amusement.

"Do you know him?" she asked as, through the door left open by Bates, they heard steps on the landing.

Sutton had to think an instant, and produced a "No" just as Lord Gwyther was again announced, which gave an un-expectedness to the greeting offered him a moment later by this personage—a young man, stout and smooth and fresh, but not at all shy, who, after the happiest rapid passage with Mrs. Grantham, put out a hand with a straight free "How d' ye do?"

"Mr. Shirley Sutton," Mrs. Grantham explained.

"Oh yes," said her second visitor quite as if he knew; which, as he couldn't have known, had for her first the interest of confirming a perception that his lordship would be—no, not at all, in general, embarrassed, only was now exceptionally and especially agitated. As it is, for that matter, with Sutton's total impression that we are particularly and almost exclusively concerned, it may be further mentioned that he was not less clear as to the really handsome way in which the young man kept himself together and little by little—though with all proper aid indeed—finally found his feet. All sorts of things, for the twenty minutes, occurred to Sutton, though one of them was certainly not that it would, after all, be better he should go. One of them was that their hostess was doing it in perfection—simply, easily, kindly, yet with something the least bit queer in her wonderful eyes; another was that if he had been recognised without the least ground it was through a tension of nerves on the part of his fellow guest that produced inconsequent motions; still another was that, even had departure been indicated, he would positively have felt dissuasion in the rare promise of the scene. This was in especial after Lord Gwyther not only had announced that he was now married, but had mentioned that he wished to bring his wife to Mrs. Grantham for the benefit so certain to be derived. It was the passage immediately produced by that speech that provoked in Sutton the intensity, as it were, of his arrest. He already knew of the marriage as well as Mrs. Grantham herself, and as well also as he knew of some other things; and this gave him doubtless the better measure of what took place before him and the keener consciousness of the quick look that, at a marked moment—though it was not absolutely meant for him any more than for his companion—Mrs. Grantham let him catch.

She smiled, but it had a gravity. "I think, you know, you ought to have told me before."

"Do you mean when I first got engaged? Well, it all took place so far away, and we really told, at home, so few people."

Oh there might have been reasons; but it had not been quite right. "You were married at Stuttgart? That wasn't too far for *my* interest, at least, to reach."

"Awfully kind of you—and of course one knew you *would* be kind. But it wasn't at Stuttgart; it was over there, but quite in the country. We should have managed it in England but that her mother naturally wished to be present, yet wasn't in health to come. So it was really, you see, a sort of little hole-and-corner German affair."

This didn't in the least check Mrs. Grantham's claim, but it started a slight anxiety. "Will she be—a—then German?"

293

Sutton knew her to know perfectly what Lady Gwyther would "be," but he had by this time, while their friend explained, his independent interest. "Oh dear no! My father-in-law has never parted with the proud birthright of a Briton. But his wife, you see, holds an estate in Würtemberg from *her* mother, Countess Kremnitz, on which, with the awful condition of his English property, you know, they've found it for years a tremendous saving to live. So that though Valda was luckily born at home she has practically spent her life over there."

"Oh I see." Then, after a slight pause, "Is Valda her pretty name?" Mrs. Grantham asked.

"Well," said the young man, only wishing, in his candour, it was clear, to be drawn out—"well, she has, in the manner of her mother's people, about thirteen; but that's the one we generally use."

Mrs. Grantham waited but an instant. "Then may *I* generally use it?"

"It would be too charming of you; and nothing would give her—as I assure you nothing would give *me*—greater pleasure." Lord Gwyther quite glowed with the thought.

"Then I think that instead of coming alone you might have brought her to see me."

"It's exactly what," he instantly replied, "I came to ask your leave to do." He explained that for the moment Lady Gwyther was not in town, having as soon as she arrived gone down to Torquay to put in a few days with one of her aunts, also her godmother, to whom she was an object of great interest. She had seen no one yet, and no one—not that *that* mattered—had seen her; she knew nothing whatever of London and was awfully frightened at facing it and at what (however little) might be expected of her. "She wants someone," he said, "someone who knows the whole thing, don't you see? and who's thoroughly kind and clever, as you would be, if I may say so, to take her by the hand." It was at this point and on these words that the eyes of Lord Gwyther's two auditors inevitably and wonderfully met. But there was nothing in the way he kept it up to show he caught the encounter. "She wants, if I may tell you so, a real friend for the great labyrinth; and asking myself what I could do to make things ready for her, and who would be absolutely the best woman in London—"

"You thought naturally of *me?*" Mrs. Grantham had listened with no sign but the faint flash just noted; now, however, she gave him the full light of her expressive face—which immediately brought Shirley Sutton, looking at his watch, once more to his feet.

"She *is* the best woman in London!" He addressed himself with a laugh to the other visitor, but offered his hand in farewell to their hostess.

"You're going?"

"I must," he said without scruple.

"Then we do meet at dinner?"

"I hope so." On which, to take leave, he returned with interest to Lord Gwyther the friendly clutch he had a short time before received.

II

They did meet at dinner, and if they were not, as it happened, side by side, they made that up afterwards in the happiest angle of a drawing-room that offered both shine and shadow and that was positively much appreciated, in the circle in which they moved, for the favourable "corners" created by its shrewd mistress. Mrs. Grantham's face, charged with something produced in it by Lord Gwyther's visit, had been with him so constantly for the previous hours that, when she instantly challenged him on his "treatment" of her in the afternoon, he was on the point of naming it as his reason for not having remained with her. Something new had quickly come into her beauty; he couldn't as yet have said what, nor whether on the whole to its advantage or its loss. Till he should see this clearer, at any rate he would say nothing; so that he found with sufficient presence of mind a better excuse. If in short he had in defiance of her particular request left her alone with Lord Gwyther it was simply because the situation had suddenly turned so exciting that he had fairly feared the contagion of it—the temptation of its making him, most improperly, put in his word.

They could now talk of these things at their ease. Other couples, ensconced and scattered, enjoyed the same privilege, and Sutton had more and more the profit, such as it was, of feeling that his interest in Mrs. Grantham had become—what was the luxury of so high a social code—an acknowledged and protected relation. He knew his London well enough to know that he was on the way to be regarded as her main source of consolation for the trick Lord Gwyther had several months before publicly played her. Many persons had not held that, by the high social code in question, his lordship could have "reserved the right" to turn up that way, from one day to another, engaged to be married. For himself London took, with its short cuts and its cheap psychology, an immense deal for granted. To his own sense he was never—could in the nature of things never be—any man's "successor." Just what had constituted the predecessorship of other men was apparently that they had been able to make up their mind. He, worse luck, was at the mercy of her face, and more than ever at the mercy of it now, which meant moreover not that it made a slave of him, but that it made, disconcertingly, a sceptic. It was the absolute perfection of the handsome, but things had a way of coming into it. "I felt," he said, "that you were there together at a point at which you had a right to the ease the absence of a listener would give. I was sure that when you made me promise to stay you hadn't guessed—"

"That he could possibly have come to me on such an extraordinary errand? No, of course I hadn't guessed. Who *would?* But didn't you see how little I was upset by it?"

Sutton demurred. Then with a smile: "I think *he* saw how little."

"You yourself didn't then?"

He again held back, but not, after all, to answer. "He was wonderful, wasn't he?"

"I think he was," she returned after a moment. To which she added: "Why did he pretend that way he knew you?"

"He didn't pretend. He somehow felt on the spot that I was 'in it.'" Sutton had found this afterwards and found it to represent a reality. "It was an effusion of cheer and hope. He was so glad to see me there and to find you happy."

"Happy?"

"Happy. Aren't you?"

"Because of *you?*"

"Well—according to the impression he received as he came in."

"That was sudden then," she asked, "and unexpected?"

Her companion thought. "Prepared in some degree, but confirmed by the sight of us, there together, so awfully jolly and sociable over your fire."

Mrs. Grantham turned this round. "If he knew I was 'happy' then—which, by the way, is none of his business, nor of yours either—why in the world did he come?"

"Well, for good manners, and for his idea," said Sutton.

She took it in, appearing to have no hardness of rancour that could bar discussion. "Do you mean by his idea his proposal that I should grandmother his wife? And if you do is the proposal your reason for calling him wonderful?"

Sutton laughed. "Pray what's yours?" As this was a question, however, that she took her time to answer or not to answer— only appearing interested for a moment in a combination that had formed itself on the other side of the room—he presently went on. "What's *his?*—that would seem to be the point. His, I mean, for having decided on the extraordinary step of throwing his little wife, bound hands and feet, into your arms. Intelligent as you are, and with these three or four hours to have thought it over, I yet don't see how that can fail still to mystify you."

She continued to watch their opposite neighbours. " 'Little,' you call her. Is she so very small?"

"Tiny, tiny—she *must* be; as different as possible in every way—of necessity—from you. They always *are* the opposite pole, you know," said Shirley Sutton.

She glanced at him now. "You strike me as of an impudence—!"

"No, no. I only like to make it out with you."

She looked away again and after a little went on. "I'm sure she's charming, and only hope one isn't to gather he's already tired of her."

"Not a bit! He's tremendously in love, and he'll remain so."

"So much the better. And if it's a question," said Mrs. Grantham, "of one's doing what one can for her, he has only, as I told him when you had gone, to give me the chance."

"Good! So he *is* to commit her to you?"

"You use extraordinary expressions, but it's settled that he brings her."

"And you'll really and truly help her?"

"Really and truly?" said Mrs. Grantham with her eyes again on him. "Why not? For what do you take me?"

"Ah isn't that just what I still have the discomfort, every day I live, of asking myself?"

She had made, as she spoke, a movement to rise, which, as if she was tired of his tone, his last words appeared to determine. But, also getting up, he held her, when they were on their feet, long enough to hear the rest of what he had to say. "If you do help her, you know, you'll show him you've understood."

"Understood what?"

"Why, his idea—the deep acute train of reasoning that has led him to take, as one may say, the bull by the horns; to reflect that as you might, as you probably *would*, in any case, get at her, he plays the wise game, as well as the bold one, by treating your generosity as a real thing and placing himself publicly under an obligation to you."

Mrs. Grantham showed not only that she had listened, but that she had for an instant considered. "What is it you elegantly describe as my getting 'at' her?"

"He takes his risk, but puts you, you see, on your honour."

She thought a moment more. "What profundities indeed then over the simplest of matters! And if your idea is," she went on, "that if I do help her I shall show him I've understood them, so it will be that if I don't—"

"You'll show him"—Sutton took her up—"that you haven't? Precisely. But in spite of not wanting to appear to have understood *too* much—"

"I may still be depended on to do what I can? Quite certainly. You'll see what I may still be depended on to do." And she moved away.

III

It was not, doubtless, that there had been anything in their rather sharp separation at that moment to sustain or prolong the interruption; yet it definitely befell that, circumstances aiding, they practically failed to meet again before the great party at Burbeck. This occasion was to gather in some thirty persons from a certain Friday to the following Monday, and it was on the Friday that Sutton went down. He had known in advance that Mrs. Grantham was to be there, and this perhaps, during the interval of hindrance, had helped him a little to be patient. He had before him the certitude of a real full cup—two days brimming over with the sight of her. He found, however, on his arrival that she was not yet in the field, and presently learned that her place would be in a small contingent that was to join the party on the morrow. This knowledge he extracted from Miss Banker, who was always the first to present herself at any gathering that was to enjoy her, and whom moreover— partly on that very account—the wary not less than the speculative were apt to hold themselves well-advised to engage with at as early as possible a stage of the business. She was stout red rich mature universal—a massive much-fingered volume, alphabetical wonderful indexed, that opened of itself at the right place. She opened for Sutton instinctively at G—, which happened to be remarkably convenient. "What she's really waiting over for is to bring down Lady Gwyther."

"Ah the Gwythers are coming?"

"Yes; caught, through Mrs. Grantham, just in time. *She'll* be the feature—everyone wants to see her."

Speculation and wariness met and combined at this moment in Shirley Sutton. "Do you mean—a—Mrs. Grantham?"

"Dear no! Poor little Lady Gwyther, who, but just arrived in England, appears now literally for the first time in her life in any society whatever, and whom (don't you know the extraordinary story? you ought to—*you!*) she, of all people, has so wonderfully taken up. It will be quite—here—as if she were 'presenting' her."

Sutton of course took in more things than even appeared. "I never know what I ought to know; I only know, inveterately, what I oughtn't. So what *is* the extraordinary story?"

"You really haven't heard—?"

"Really," he replied without winking.

"It happened indeed but the other day," said Miss Banker, "yet everyone's already wondering. Gwyther has thrown his wife on her mercy—but I won't believe you if you pretend to me you don't know why he shouldn't."

Sutton asked himself then what he *could* pretend. "Do you mean because she's merciless?"

She hesitated. "If you don't know perhaps I oughtn't to tell you."

He liked Miss Banker and found just the right tone to plead. "*Do* tell me."

"Well," she sighed, "it will be your own fault—! They had been such friends that there could have been but one name for the crudity of his original *procédé*. When I was a girl we used to call it throwing over. They call it in French to *lâcher*. But I refer not so much to the act itself as to the manner of it, though you may say indeed of course that there's in such cases after all only one manner. Least said soonest mended."

Sutton seemed to wonder. "Oh he said too much?"

"He said nothing. That was it."

Sutton kept it up. "But was *what?*"

"Why, what she must, like any woman in her shoes, have felt to be his perfidy. He simply went and *did* it—took to himself this child, that is, without the preliminary of a scandal or a rupture—before she could turn round."

"I follow you. But it would appear from what you say that she *has* turned round now."

"Well," Miss Banker laughed, "we shall see for ourselves how far. It will be what everyone will try to see."

"Oh then we've work cut out!" And Sutton certainly felt that he himself had—an impression that lost nothing from a further talk with Miss Banker in the course of a short stroll in the grounds with her the next day. He spoke as one who had now considered many things.

"Did I understand from you yesterday that Lady Gwyther's a 'child'?"

"Nobody knows. It's prodigious the way she has managed."

"The way Lady Gwyther has—?"

"No, the way May Grantham has kept her till this hour in her pocket."

He was quick at his watch. "Do you mean by 'this hour' that they're due now?"

"Not till tea. All the others arrive together in time for that." Miss Banker had clearly, since the previous day, filled in gaps and become, as it were, revised and enlarged. "She'll have kept a cat from seeing her, so as to produce her entirely herself."

"Well," Sutton mused, "that will have been a very noble sort of return—"

"For Gwyther's behaviour? Very. Yet I feel creepy."

"Creepy?"

"Because so much depends for the girl—in the way of the right start or the wrong start—on the signs and omens of this first appearance. It's a great house and a great occasion, and we're assembled here, it strikes me, very much as the Roman

301

mob at the circus used to be to see the next Christian maiden brought out to the tigers."

"Oh if she *is* a Christian maiden—!" Sutton murmured. But he stopped at what his imagination called up.

It perhaps fed that faculty a little that Miss Banker had the effect of making out that Mrs. Grantham might individually be, in any case, something of a Roman matron. "She has kept her in the dark so that we may only take her from her hand. She'll have formed her for us."

"In so few days?"

"Well, she'll have prepared her—decked her for the sacrifice with ribbons and flowers."

"Ah if you only mean that she'll have taken her to her dressmaker—!" And it came to Sutton, at once as a new light and as a check, almost, to anxiety, that this was all poor Gwyther, mistrustful probably of a taste formed by Stuttgart, might have desired of their friend.

There were usually at Burbeck many things taking place at once; so that wherever else, on such occasions, tea might be served, it went forward with matchless pomp, weather permitting, on a shaded stretch of one of the terraces and in presence of one of the prospects. Shirley Sutton, moving, as the afternoon waned, more restlessly about and mingling in dispersed groups only to find they had nothing to keep him quiet, came upon it as he turned a corner of the house—saw it seated there in all its state. It might be said that at Burbeck it was, like everything else, made the most of. It constituted immediately, with multiplied tables and glittering plate, with rugs and cushions and ices and fruit and wonderful porcelain and beautiful women, a scene of splendour, almost an incident of grand opera. One of the beautiful women might quite have been expected to rise with a gold cup and a celebrated song.

One of them did rise, as happened, while Sutton drew near, and he found himself a moment later seeing nothing and nobody but Mrs. Grantham. They met on the terrace, just away from the others, and the movement in which he had the effect of arresting her might have been that of withdrawal. He quickly saw, however, that if she had been about to pass into the house it was only on some errand—to get something or to call someone—that would immediately have restored her to her public. It somehow struck him on the spot—and more than ever yet, though the impression was not wholly new to him— that she felt herself a figure for the forefront of the stage and indeed would have been recognised by anyone at a glance as the *prima donna assoluta*. She caused, in fact, during the few minutes he stood talking to her, an extraordinary series of waves to roll extraordinarily fast over his sense, not the least mark of the matter being that the appearance with which it ended was again the one with which it had begun. "The face— the face," as he kept dumbly repeating; that was at last, as at first, all he could clearly see. She had a perfection resplendent, but what in the world had it done, this perfection, to her beauty? It was her beauty doubtless that looked out at him, but it was into something else that, as their eyes met, he strangely found himself looking.

It was as if something had happened in consequence of which she had changed, and there was that in this swift perception that made him glance eagerly about for Lady Gwyther. But as he took in the recruited group—identities of the hour added to those of the previous twenty-four—he saw, among his recognitions, one of which was the husband of the person missing, that Lady Gwyther was not there. Nothing in the whole business was more singular than his consciousness that, as he came back to his interlocutress after the nods and smiles and handwaves he had launched, she knew what had been his thought. She knew for whom he had looked without success; but why should this knowledge visibly have hardened and sharpened her, and precisely at a moment when she was unprecedentedly magnificent? The indefinable apprehension that had somewhat sunk after his second talk with Miss Banker and then had perversely risen again—this nameless anxiety now produced on him, with a sudden sharper pinch, the effect of a great suspense. The action of that, in turn, was to show him that he hadn't yet fully known how much he had at stake on a final view. It was revealed to him for the first time that he "really cared" whether Mrs. Grantham were a safe nature. It was too ridiculous by what a thread it hung, but something was certainly in the air that would definitely tell him.

What was in the air descended the next moment to earth. He turned round as he caught the expression with which her eyes attached themselves to something that approached. A little person, very young and very much dressed, had come out of the house, and the expression in Mrs. Grantham's eyes was that of the artist confronted with her work and interested, even to impatience, in the judgement of others. The little person drew nearer, and though Sutton's companion, without looking at him now, gave it a name and met it, he had jumped for himself at certitude. He saw many things—too many, and they appeared to be feathers, frills, excrescences of silk and lace—massed together and conflicting, and after a moment also saw struggling out of them a small face that struck him as either scared or sick. Then, with his eyes again returning to Mrs. Grantham, he saw another.

He had no more talk with Miss Banker till late that evening—an evening during which he had felt himself too noticeably silent; but something had passed between this pair, across dinner-table and drawing-room, without speech, and when they at last found words it was in the needed ease of a quiet end of the long, lighted gallery, where she opened again at the very paragraph.

"You were right—that *was* it. She did the only thing that, at such short notice, she *could* do. She took her to her dressmaker."

Sutton, with his back to the reach of the gallery, had, as if to banish a vision, buried his eyes for a minute in his hands. "And oh the face—the face!"

"Which?" Miss Banker asked.

"Whichever one looks at."

"But May Grantham's glorious. She has turned herself out—"

"With a splendour of taste and a sense of effect, eh? Yes." Sutton showed he saw far.

"She *has* the sense of effect. The sense of effect as exhibited in Lady Gwyther's clothes—!" was something Miss Banker failed of words to express. "Everybody's overwhelmed. Here, you know, that sort of thing's grave. The poor creature's lost."

"Lost?"

"Since on the first impression, as we said, so much depends. The first impression's made—oh made! I defy her now ever to unmake it. Her husband, who's proud, won't like her the better for it. And I don't see," Miss Banker went on, "that her prettiness *was* enough—a mere little feverish frightened freshness; what *did* he see in her?—to be so blasted. It has been done with an atrocity of art—"

"That supposes the dressmaker then also a devil?"

"Oh your London women and their dressmakers!" Miss Banker laughed.

"But the face—the face!" Sutton woefully repeated.

"May's?"

"The little girl's. It's exquisite."

"Exquisite?"

"For unimaginable pathos."

"Oh!" Miss Banker dropped.

"She has at last begun to see." Sutton showed again how far *he* saw. "It glimmers upon her innocence, she makes it dimly out—what has been done with her. She's even worse this evening—the way, my eye, she looked at dinner!—than when she came. Yes"—he was confident—"it has dawned (how couldn't it, out of all of you?) and she knows."

"She ought to have known before!" Miss Banker intelligently sighed.

"No; she wouldn't in that case have been so beautiful."

"Beautiful?" cried Miss Banker; "overloaded like a monkey in a show!"

"The face, yes; which goes to the heart. It's that that makes it," said Shirley Sutton. "And it's that"—he thought it out—"that makes the other."

"I see. Conscious?"

"Horrible!"

"You take it hard," said Miss Banker.

Lord Gwyther, just before she spoke, had come in sight and now was near them. Sutton on this, appearing to wish to avoid him, reached, before answering his companion's observation, a door that opened close at hand. "So hard," he replied from that point, "that I shall be off tomorrow morning."

"And not see the rest?" she called after him.

But he had already gone, and Lord Gwyther, arriving, amiably took up her question. "The rest of what?"

Miss Banker looked him well in the eyes. "Of Mrs. Grantham's clothes."

THE BELDONALD HOLBEIN

THE BELDONALD HOLBEIN

I

Mrs. Munden had not yet been to my studio on so good a pretext as when she first intimated that it would be quite open to me—should I only care, as she called it, to throw the handkerchief—to paint her beautiful sister-in-law. I needn't go here more than is essential into the question of Mrs. Munden, who would really, by the way, be a story in herself. She has a manner of her own of putting things, and some of those she has put to me—! Her implication was that Lady Beldonald hadn't only seen and admired certain examples of my work, but had literally been prepossessed in favour of the painter's "personality." Had I been struck with this sketch I might easily have imagined her ladyship was throwing *me* the handkerchief. "She hasn't done," my visitor said, "what she ought."

"Do you mean she has done what she oughtn't?"

"Nothing horrid—oh dear no." And something in Mrs. Munden's tone, with the way she appeared to muse a moment, even suggested to me that what she "oughtn't" was perhaps what Lady Beldonald had too much neglected. "She hasn't got on."

"What's the matter with her?"

"Well, to begin with, she's American."

"But I thought that was the way of ways to get on."

"It's one of them. But it's one of the ways of being awfully out of it too. There are so many!"

"So many Americans?" I asked.

"Yes, plenty of *them*," Mrs. Munden sighed. "So many ways, I mean, of being one."

"But if your sister-in-law's way is to be beautiful—?"

"Oh there are different ways of that too."

"And she hasn't taken the right way?"

"Well," my friend returned as if it were rather difficult to express, "she hasn't done with it—"

"I see," I laughed; "what she oughtn't!"

Mrs. Munden in a manner corrected me, but it *was* difficult to express. "My brother at all events was certainly selfish. Till he died she was almost never in London; they wintered, year after year, for what he supposed to be his health—which it didn't help, since he was so much too soon to meet his end—in the south of France and in the dullest holes he could pick out, and when they came back to England he always kept her in the country. I must say for her that she always behaved beautifully. Since his death she has been more in London, but on a stupidly unsuccessful footing. I don't think she quite understands. She hasn't what *I* should call a life. It may be of course that she doesn't want one. That's just what I can't exactly find out. I can't make out how much she knows."

"I can easily make out," I returned with hilarity, "how much *you* do!"

"Well, you're very horrid. Perhaps she's too old."

"Too old for what?" I persisted.

"For anything. Of course she's no longer even a little young; only preserved—oh but preserved, like bottled fruit, in syrup! I want to help her if only because she gets on my nerves, and I really think the way of it would be just the right thing of yours at the Academy and on the line."

"But suppose," I threw out, "she should give on *my* nerves?"

"Oh she will. But isn't that all in the day's work, and don't great beauties always—?"

"*You* don't," I interrupted; but I at any rate saw Lady Beldonald later on—the day came when her kinswoman brought her, and then I saw how her life must have its centre in her own idea of her appearance. Nothing else about her mattered—one knew her all when one knew that. She's indeed in one particular, I think, sole of her kind—a person whom vanity has had the odd effect of keeping positively safe and sound. This passion is supposed surely, for the most part, to be a principle of perversion and of injury, leading astray those who listen to it and landing them sooner or later in this or that complication; but it has landed her ladyship nowhere whatever—it has kept her from the first moment of full consciousness, one feels, exactly in the same place. It has protected her from every danger, has made her absolutely proper and prim. If she's "preserved," as Mrs. Munden originally described her to me, it's her vanity that has beautifully done it—putting her years ago in a plate-glass case and closing up the receptacle against every breath of air. How shouldn't she be preserved when you might smash your knuckles on this transparency before you could crack it? And she *is*—oh amazingly! Preservation is scarce the word for the rare condition of her surface. She looks *naturally* new, as if she took out every night her large lovely varnished eyes and put them in water. The thing was to paint her, I perceived, *in* the glass case—a most tempting attaching feat; render to the full the shining interposing plate and the general show-window effect.

It was agreed, though it wasn't quite arranged, that she should sit to me. If it wasn't quite arranged this was because, as I was made to understand from an early stage, the conditions from our start must be such as should exclude all elements of disturbance, such, in a word, as she herself should judge absolutely favourable. And it seemed that these conditions were easily imperilled. Suddenly, for instance, at a moment when I was expecting her to meet an appointment—the first—that I had proposed, I received a hurried visit from Mrs. Munden, who came on her behalf to let me know that the season happened just not to be propitious and that our friend couldn't be quite sure, to the hour, when it would again become so. She felt nothing would make it so but a total absence of worry.

"Oh a 'total absence,'" I said, "is a large order! We live in a worrying world."

"Yes; and she feels exactly that—more than you'd think. It's in fact just why she mustn't have, as she has now, a particular distress on at the very moment. She wants of course to look her

313

best, and such things tell on her appearance."

I shook my head. "Nothing tells on her appearance. Nothing reaches it in any way; nothing gets *at* it. However, I can understand her anxiety. But what's her particular distress?"

"Why the illness of Miss Dadd."

"And who in the world's Miss Dadd?"

"Her most intimate friend and constant companion—the lady who was with us here that first day."

"Oh the little round black woman who gurgled with admiration?"

"None other. But she was taken ill last week, and it may very well be that she'll gurgle no more. She was very bad yesterday and is no better today, and Nina's much upset. If anything happens to Miss Dadd she'll have to get another, and, though she has had two or three before, that won't be so easy."

"Two or three Miss Dadds? Is it possible? And still wanting another!" I recalled the poor lady completely now. "No; I shouldn't indeed think it would be easy to get another. But why is a succession of them necessary to Lady Beldonald's existence?"

"Can't you guess?" Mrs. Munden looked deep, yet impatient. "They help."

"Help what? Help whom?"

"Why everyone. You and me for instance. To do what? Why to think Nina beautiful. She has them for that purpose; they serve as foils, as accents serve on syllables, as terms of comparison. They make her 'stand out.' It's an effect of contrast that must be familiar to you artists; it's what a woman does when she puts a band of black velvet under a pearl ornament that may require, as she thinks, a little showing off."

I wondered. "Do you mean she always has them black?"

"Dear no; I've seen them blue, green, yellow. They may be what they like, so long as they're always one other thing."

"Hideous?"

Mrs. Munden made a mouth for it. "Hideous is too much to say; she doesn't really require them as bad as that. But consistently, cheerfully, loyally plain. It's really a most happy relation. She loves them for it."

"And for what do they love *her?*"

"Why just for the amiability that they produce in her. Then also for their 'home.' It's a career for them."

"I see. But if that's the case," I asked, "why are they so difficult to find?"

"Oh they must be safe; it's all in that: her being able to depend on them to keep to the terms of the bargain and never have moments of rising—as even the ugliest woman will now and then (say when she's in love)—superior to themselves."

I turned it over. "Then if they can't inspire passions the poor things mayn't even at least feel them?"

"She distinctly deprecates it. That's why such a man as you may be after all a complication."

I continued to brood. "You're very sure Miss Dadd's ailment isn't an affection that, being smothered, has struck in?" My joke, however, wasn't well timed, for I afterwards learned that the unfortunate lady's state had been, even while I spoke, such as to forbid all hope. The worst symptoms had appeared; she was destined not to recover; and a week later I heard from Mrs. Munden that she would in fact "gurgle" no more.

II

All this had been for Lady Beldonald an agitation so great that access to her apartment was denied for a time even to her sister-in-law. It was much more out of the question of course that she should unveil her face to a person of my special business with it; so that the question of the portrait was by common consent left to depend on that of the installation of a successor to her late companion. Such a successor, I gathered from Mrs. Munden, widowed childless and lonely, as well as inapt for the minor offices, she had absolutely to have; a more or less humble *alter ego* to deal with the servants, keep the accounts, make the tea and watch the window-blinds. Nothing seemed more natural than that she should marry again, and obviously that might come; yet the predecessors of Miss Dadd had been contemporaneous with a first husband, so that others formed in her image might be contemporaneous with a second. I was much occupied in those months at any rate, and these questions and their ramifications losing themselves for a while to my view, I was only brought back to them by Mrs. Munden's arrival one day with the news that we were all right again—her sister-in-law was once more "suited." A certain Mrs. Brash, an American relative whom she hadn't seen for years, but with whom she had continued to communicate, was to come out to her immediately; and this person, it appeared, could be quite trusted to meet the conditions. She was ugly—ugly enough, without abuse of it, and was unlimitedly good. The position offered her by Lady Beldonald was moreover exactly what she needed; widowed also, after many troubles and reverses, with her fortune of the smallest and her various children either buried or placed about, she had never had time or means to visit England, and would really be grateful in her declining years for the new experience and the pleasant light work involved in her cousin's hospitality. They had been much together early in life and Lady Beldonald was immensely fond of her—would in fact have tried to get hold of her before hadn't Mrs. Brash been always in bondage to family duties, to the variety of her tribulations. I dare say I laughed at my friend's use of the term "position"—the position, one might call it, of a candlestick or a sign-post, and I dare say I must have asked if the special service the poor lady was to render had been made clear to her. Mrs. Munden left me in any case with the rather droll image of her faring forth across the sea quite consciously and resignedly to perform it.

The point of the communication had however been that my sitter was again looking up and would doubtless, on the arrival and due initiation of Mrs. Brash, be in form really to wait on me. The situation must further, to my knowledge, have developed happily, for I arranged with Mrs. Munden that our friend, now all ready to begin, but wanting first just to see the things I had most recently done, should come once more, as a final preliminary, to my studio. A good foreign friend of mine, a French painter, Paul Outreau, was at the moment in London, and I had proposed, as he was much interested in types, to get together for his amusement a small afternoon party. Everyone came, my big room was full, there was music and a modest spread; and I've not forgotten the light of admiration in Outreau's expressive face as at the end of half an hour he came up to me in his enthusiasm. "*Bonté divine, mon cher–que cette vieille est donc belle!*"

I had tried to collect all the beauty I could, and also all the youth, so that for a moment I was at a loss. I had talked to many people and provided for the music, and there were figures in the crowd that were still lost to me. "What old woman do you mean?"

"I don't know her name–she was over by the door a moment ago. I asked somebody and was told, I think, that she's American."

I looked about and saw one of my guests attach a pair of fine eyes to Outreau very much as if she knew he must be talking of her. "Oh Lady Beldonald! Yes, she's handsome; but the great point about her is that she has been 'put up' to keep, and that she wouldn't be flattered if she knew you spoke of her as old. A box of sardines is 'old' only after it has been opened. Lady Beldonald never has yet been–but I'm going to do it." I joked, but I was somehow disappointed. It was a type that, with his unerring sense for the *banal*, I shouldn't have expected Outreau to pick out.

"You're going to paint her? But, my dear man, she *is* painted– and as neither you nor I can do it. *Où est-elle donc?*" He had lost her, and I saw I had made a mistake. "She's the greatest of all the great Holbeins."

I was relieved. "Ah then not Lady Beldonald! But do I possess a Holbein of *any* price unawares?"

"There she is–there she is! Dear, dear, dear, what a head!"

And I saw whom he meant—and what: a small old lady in a black dress and a black bonnet, both relieved with a little white, who had evidently just changed her place to reach a corner from which more of the room and of the scene was presented to her. She appeared unnoticed and unknown, and I immediately recognised that some other guest must have brought her and, for want of opportunity, had as yet to call my attention to her. But two things, simultaneously with this and with each other, struck me with force; one of them the truth of Outreau's description of her, the other the fact that the person bringing her could only have been Lady Beldonald. She *was* a Holbein—of the first water; yet she was also Mrs. Brash, the imported "foil," the indispensable "accent," the successor to the dreary Miss Dadd! By the time I had put these things together—Outreau's "American" having helped me—I was in just such full possession of her face as I had found myself, on the other first occasion, of that of her patroness. Only with so different a consequence. I couldn't look at her enough, and I stared and stared till I became aware she might have fancied me challenging her as a person unpresented. "All the same," Outreau went on, equally held, "*c'est une tête à faire.* If I were only staying long enough for a crack at her! But I tell you what"—and he seized my arm—"bring her over!"

"Over?"

"To Paris. She'd have a *succès fou.*"

"Ah thanks, my dear fellow," I was now quite in a position to say; "she's the handsomest thing in London, and"—for what I might do with her was already before me with intensity—"I propose to keep her to myself." It was before me with intensity, in the light of Mrs. Brash's distant perfection of a little white old face, in which every wrinkle was the touch of a master; but something else, I suddenly felt, was not less so, for Lady Beldonald, in the other quarter, and though she couldn't have made out the subject of our notice, continued to fix us, and her eyes had the challenge of those of the woman of consequence who has missed something. A moment later I was close to her, apologising first for not having been more on the spot at her arrival, but saying in the next breath uncontrollably: "Why my dear lady, it's a Holbein!"

"A Holbein? What?"

"Why the wonderful sharp old face—so extraordinarily, consummately drawn—in the frame of black velvet. That of Mrs. Brash, I mean—isn't it her name?—your companion."

This was the beginning of a most odd matter—the essence of my anecdote; and I think the very first note of the oddity must have sounded for me in the tone in which her ladyship spoke after giving me a silent look. It seemed to come to me out of a distance immeasurably removed from Holbein. "Mrs. Brash isn't my 'companion' in the sense you appear to mean. She's my rather near relation and a very dear old friend. I *love* her—and you must know her."

"Know her? Rather! Why to see her is to want on the spot to 'go' for her. She also must sit for me."

"*She?* Louisa Brash?" If Lady Beldonald had the theory that her beauty directly showed it when things weren't well with her, this impression, which the fixed sweetness of her serenity had hitherto struck me by no means as justifying, gave me now my first glimpse of its grounds. It was as if I had never before seen her face invaded by anything I should have called an expression. This expression moreover was of the faintest—was like the effect produced on a surface by an agitation both deep within and as yet much confused. "Have you told her so?" she then quickly asked, as if to soften the sound of her surprise.

"Dear no, I've but just noticed her—Outreau a moment ago put me on her. But we're both so taken, and he also wants—"

"To *paint* her?" Lady Beldonald uncontrollably murmured.

"Don't be afraid we shall fight for her," I returned with a laugh for this tone. Mrs. Brash was still where I could see her without appearing to stare, and she mightn't have seen I was looking at her, though her protectress, I'm afraid, could scarce have failed of that certainty. "We must each take our turn, and

at any rate she's a wonderful thing, so that if you'll let her go to
Paris Outreau promises her there—"

"*There?*" my companion gasped.

"A career bigger still than among *us*, as he considers we
haven't half their eye. He guarantees her a *succès fou*."

She couldn't get over it. "Louisa Brash? In Paris?"

"They do see," I went on, "more than we; and they live
extraordinarily, don't you know, *in* that. But she'll do
something here too."

"And what will she do?"

If frankly now I couldn't help giving Mrs. Brash a longer
look, so after it I could as little resist sounding my converser.
"You'll see. Only give her time."

She said nothing during the moment in which she met my
eyes; but then: "Time, it seems to me, is exactly what you and
your friend want. If you haven't talked with her—"

"We haven't seen her? Oh we see bang off—with a click like a
steel spring. It's our trade, it's our life, and we should be
donkeys if we made mistakes. That's the way I saw you
yourself, my lady, if I may say so; that's the way, with a long pin
straight through your body, I've got you. And just so I've got
her!"

All this, for reasons, had brought my guest to her feet; but her
eyes had while we talked never once followed the direction of
mine. "You call her a Holbein?"

"Outreau did, and I of course immediately recognised it.
Don't *you?* She brings the old boy to life! It's just as I should call
you a Titian. You bring *him* to life."

She couldn't be said to relax, because she couldn't be said to
have hardened; but something at any rate on this took place in
her—something indeed quite disconnected from what I would
have called her. "Don't you understand that she has always
been supposed—?" It had the ring of impatience; nevertheless
it stopped short on a scruple.

I knew what it was, however, well enough to say it for her if
she preferred. "To be nothing whatever to look at? To be

unfortunately plain—or even if you like repulsively ugly? Oh yes, I understand it perfectly, just as I understand—I have to as a part of my trade—many other forms of stupidity. It's nothing new to one that ninety-nine people out of a hundred have no eyes, no sense, no taste. There are whole communities impenetrably sealed. I don't say your friend's a person to make the men turn round in Regent Street. But it adds to the joy of the few who do see that they have it so much to themselves. Where in the world can she have lived? You must tell me all about that—or rather, if she'll be so good, *she* must."

"You mean then to speak to her—?"

I wondered as she pulled up again. "Of her beauty?"

"Her beauty!" cried Lady Beldonald so loud that two or three persons looked round.

"Ah with every precaution of respect!" I declared in a much lower tone. But her back was by this time turned to me, and in the movement, as it were, one of the strangest little dramas I've ever known was well launched.

III

It was a drama of small smothered intensely private things, and I knew of but one other person in the secret; yet that person and I found it exquisitely susceptible of notation, followed it with an interest the mutual communication of which did much for our enjoyment, and were present with emotion at its touching catastrophe. The small case—for so small a case—had made a great stride even before my little party separated, and in fact within the next ten minutes.

In that space of time two things had happened; one of which was that I made the acquaintance of Mrs. Brash, and the other that Mrs. Munden reached me, cleaving the crowd, with one of her usual pieces of news. What she had to impart was that, on her having just before asked Nina if the conditions of our sitting had been arranged with me, Nina had replied, with something like perversity, that she didn't propose to arrange them, that the whole affair was "off" again and that she preferred not to be further beset for the present. The question for Mrs. Munden was naturally what had happened and whether I understood. Oh I understood perfectly, and what I at first most understood was that even when I had brought in the name of Mrs. Brash intelligence wasn't yet in Mrs. Munden. She was quite as surprised as Lady Beldonald had been on hearing of the esteem in which I held Mrs. Brash's appearance. She was stupefied at learning that I had just in my ardour proposed to its proprietress to sit to me. Only she came round promptly—which Lady Beldonald really never did. Mrs. Munden was in fact wonderful; for when I had given her quickly "Why she's a Holbein, you know, absolutely," she took it up, after a first fine vacancy, with an immediate abysmal "Oh *is* she?" that, as a piece of social gymnastics, did her the greatest honour; and she was in fact the first in London to spread the tidings. For a face-about it was magnificent. But she was also the first, I must add, to see what would really happen—though this she put before me only a week or two later. "It will kill her, my dear—that's what it will do!"

She meant neither more nor less than that it would kill Lady Beldonald if I were to paint Mrs. Brash; for at this lurid light had we arrived in so short a space of time. It was for me to decide whether my æsthetic need of giving life to my idea was such as to justify me in destroying it in a woman after all in most eyes so beautiful. The situation was indeed sufficiently queer; for it remained to be seen what I should positively gain by giving up Mrs. Brash. I appeared to have in any case lost Lady Beldonald, now too "upset"—it was always Mrs. Munden's word about her and, as I inferred, her own about herself—to meet me again on our previous footing. The only thing, I of course soon saw, was to temporise—to drop the whole question for the present and yet so far as possible keep each of the pair in view. I may as well say at once that this plan and this process gave their principal interest to the next several months. Mrs. Brash had turned up, if I remember, early in the new year, and her little wonderful career was in our particular circle one of the features of the following season. It was at all events for myself the most attaching; it's not my fault if I am so put together as often to find more life in situations obscure and subject to interpretation than in the gross rattle of the foreground. And there were all sorts of things, things touching, amusing, mystifying—and above all such an instance as I had never yet met—in this funny little fortune of the useful American cousin. Mrs. Munden was promptly at one with me as to the rarity and, to a near and human view, the beauty and interest of the position. We had neither of us ever before seen that degree and that special sort of personal success come to a woman for the first time so late in life. I found it an example of poetic, of absolutely retributive justice; so that my desire grew great to work it, as we say, on those lines. I had seen it all from the original moment at my studio; the poor lady had never known an hour's appreciation—which moreover, in perfect good faith, she had never missed. The very first thing I did after inducing so unintentionally the resentful retreat of her protectress had been to go straight over to her and say almost without preliminaries that I should hold myself immeasurably obliged for a few patient sittings. What I thus came face to face with was, on the instant, her whole unenlightened past and the full, if foreshortened, revelation of what among us all was now unfailingly in store for her. To turn the handle and start that tune came to me on the spot as a temptation. Here was a poor lady who had waited for the approach of old age to find out what she was worth. Here was a benighted being to whom it was to be disclosed in her fifty-seventh year—I was to make that out—that she had something that might pass for a face. She looked much more than her age, and was fairly frightened—as if I had been trying on her some possibly heartless London trick—when she had taken in my appeal. That showed me in what an air she had lived and—as I should have been tempted to put it had I spoken out—among what children of darkness. Later on I did them more justice; saw more that her wonderful points must have been points largely the fruit of time, and even that possibly she might never in all her life have looked so well as at this particular moment. It might have been that if her hour had struck I just happened to be present at the striking. What had occurred, all the same, was at the worst a notable comedy.

The famous "irony of fate" takes many forms, but I had never yet seen it take quite this one. She had been "had over" on an understanding, and she wasn't playing fair. She had broken the law of her ugliness and had turned beautiful on the hands of her employer. More interesting even perhaps than a view of the conscious triumph that this might prepare for her, and of which, had I doubted of my own judgement, I could still take Outreau's fine start as the full guarantee—more interesting was the question of the process by which such a history could get itself enacted. The curious thing was that all the while the reasons of her having passed for plain—the reasons for Lady Beldonald's fond calculation, which they quite justified—were written large in her face, so large that it was easy to understand them as the only ones she herself had ever read. What was it then that actually made the old stale sentence mean something so different?—into what new combinations, what extraordinary language, unknown but understood at a glance, had time and life translated it? The only thing to be said was that time and life were artists who beat us all, working with recipes and secrets we could never find out. I really ought to have, like a lecturer or a showman, a chart or a blackboard to present properly the relation, in the wonderful old tender battered blanched face, between the original elements and the exquisite final "style." I could do it with chalks, but I can scarcely do it with words. However, the thing was, for any artist who respected himself, to *feel* it—which I abundantly did; and then not to conceal from *her* I felt it— which I neglected as little. But she was really, to do her complete justice, the last to understand; and I'm not sure that, to the end—for there was an end—she quite made it all out or knew where she was. When you've been brought up for fifty years on black it must be hard to adjust your organism at a day's notice to gold-colour. Her whole nature had been pitched in the key of her supposed plainness. She had known how to be ugly—it was the only thing she had learnt save, if possible, how not to mind it. Being beautiful took in any case a new set of muscles. It was on the prior conviction, literally, that she had developed her admirable dress, instinctively felicitous, always either black or white and a matter of rather severe squareness and studied line. She was magnificently neat; everything has showed had a way of looking both old and fresh; and there was on every occasion the same picture in her draped head—draped in low-falling black—and the fine white plaits (of a painter's white, somehow) disposed on her chest. What had happened was that these arrangements, determined by certain considerations, lent themselves in effect much better to certain others. Adopted in mere shy silence they had really only deepened her accent. It was singular, moreover, that, so constituted, there was nothing in her aspect of the ascetic or the nun. She was a good hard sixteenth-century figure, not withered with innocence, bleached rather by life in the open. She was in short just what we had made of her, a Holbein for a great museum; and our position, Mrs. Munden's and mine, rapidly became that of persons having such a treasure to dispose of. The world—I speak of course mainly of the art-world—flocked to see it.

IV

"But has she any idea herself, poor thing?" was the way I had put it to Mrs. Munden on our next meeting after the incident at my studio; with the effect, however, only of leaving my friend at first to take me as alluding to Mrs. Brash's possible prevision of the chatter she might create. I had my own sense of that—this prevision had been *nil*; the question was of her consciousness of the office for which Lady Beldonald had counted on her and for which we were so promptly proceeding to spoil her altogether.

"Oh I think she arrived with a goodish notion," Mrs. Munden had replied when I had explained; "for she's clever too, you know, as well as good-looking, and I don't see how, if she ever really *knew* Nina, she could have supposed for a moment that she wasn't wanted for whatever she might have left to give up. Hasn't she moreover always been made to feel that she's ugly enough for anything?" It was even at this point already wonderful how my friend had mastered the case and what lights, alike for its past and its future, she was prepared to throw on it. "If she has seen herself as ugly enough for anything she has seen herself—and that was the only way—as ugly enough for Nina; and she has had her own manner of showing that she understands without making Nina commit herself to anything vulgar. Women are never without ways for doing such things—both for communicating and receiving knowledge—that I can't explain to you, and that you wouldn't understand if I could, since you must *be* a woman even to do that. I dare say they've expressed it all to each other simply in the language of kisses. But doesn't it at any rate make something rather beautiful of the relation between them as affected by our discovery?"

I had a laugh for her plural possessive. "The point is of course that if there was a conscious bargain, and our action on Mrs. Brash is to deprive her of the sense of keeping her side of it, various things may happen that won't be good either for her or for ourselves. She may conscientiously throw up the position."

"Yes," my companion mused—"for she *is* conscientious. Or Nina, without waiting for that, may cast her forth."

I faced it all. "Then *we* should have to keep her."

"As a regular model?" Mrs. Munden was ready for anything. "Oh that would be lovely!"

But I further worked it out. "The difficulty is that she's *not* a model, hang it—that she's too good for one, that she's the very thing herself. When Outreau and I have each had our go, that will be all; there'll be nothing left for anyone else. Therefore it behoves us quite to understand that our attitude's a responsibility. If we can't do for her positively more than Nina does—"

"We must let her alone?" My companion continued to muse. "I see!"

"Yet don't," I returned, "see too much. We *can* do more."

"Than Nina?" She was again on the spot. "It wouldn't after all be difficult. We only want the directly opposite thing—and which is the only one the poor dear can give. Unless indeed," she suggested, "we simply retract—we back out."

I turned it over. "It's too late for that. Whether Mrs. Brash's peace is gone I can't say. But Nina's is."

"Yes, and there's no way to bring it back that won't sacrifice her friend. We can't turn round and say Mrs. Brash *is* ugly, can we? But fancy Nina's not having *seen!*" Mrs. Munden exclaimed.

"She doesn't see now," I answered. "She can't, I'm certain, make out what we mean. The woman, for *her* still, is just what she always was. But she has nevertheless had her stroke, and her blindness, while she wavers and gropes in the dark, only adds to her discomfort. Her blow was to see the attention of the world deviate."

"All the same I don't think, you know," my interlocutress said, "that Nina will have made her a scene or that, whatever we do, she'll ever make her one. That isn't the way it will happen, for she's exactly as conscientious as Mrs. Brash."

"Then what *is* the way?" I asked.

"It will just happen in silence."

"And what will 'it,' as you call it, be?"

"Isn't that what we want really to see?"

"Well," I replied after a turn or two about, "whether we want it or not it's exactly what we *shall* see; which is a reason the more for fancying, between the pair there—in the quiet exquisite house, and full of superiorities and suppressions as they both are—the extraordinary situation. If I said just now that it's too late to do anything but assent it's because I've taken the full measure of what happened at my studio. It took but a few moments—but she tasted of the tree."

My companion wondered. "Nina?"

"Mrs. Brash." And to have to put it so ministered, while I took yet another turn, to a sort of agitation. Our attitude *was* a responsibility.

But I had suggested something else to my friend, who appeared for a moment detached. "Should you say she'll hate her worse if she *doesn't* see?"

"Lady Beldonald? Doesn't see what *we* see, you mean, than if she does? Ah I give *that* up!" I laughed. "But what I can tell you is why I hold that, as I said just now, we can do most. We can do this: we can give to a harmless and sensitive creature hitherto practically disinherited—and give with an un-expectedness that will immensely add to its price—the pure joy of a deep draught of the very pride of life, of an acclaimed personal triumph in our superior sophisticated world."

Mrs. Munden had a glow of response for my sudden eloquence. "Oh it will be beautiful!"

V

Well, that's what, on the whole and in spite of everything, it really was. It has dropped into my memory a rich little gallery of pictures, a regular panorama of those occasions that were to minister to the view from which I had so for a moment extracted a lyric inspiration. I see Mrs. Brash on each of these occasions practically enthroned and surrounded and more or less mobbed; see the hurrying and the nudging and the pressing and the staring; see the people "making up" and introduced, and catch the word when they have had their turn; hear it above all, the great one—"Ah yes, the famous Holbein!"—passed about with that perfection of promptitude that makes the motions of the London mind so happy a mixture of those

of the parrot and the sheep. Nothing would be easier of course
than to tell the whole little tale with an eye only for that silly
side of it. Great was the silliness, but great also as to this case of
poor Mrs. Brash, I will say for it, the good nature. Of course,
furthermore, it took in particular "our set," with its positive
child-terror of the *banal*, to be either so foolish or so wise;
though indeed I've never quite known where our set begins
and ends, and have had to content myself on this score with
the indication once given me by a lady next whom I was
placed at dinner: "Oh it's bounded on the north by Ibsen and
on the south by Sargent!" Mrs. Brash never sat to me; she
absolutely declined; and when she declared that it was quite
enough for her that I had with that fine precipitation invited
her, I quite took this as she meant it; before we had gone very
far our understanding, hers and mine, was complete. Her
attitude was as happy as her success was prodigious. The
sacrifice of the portrait was a sacrifice to the true inwardness
of Lady Beldonald, and did much, for the time, I divined,
toward muffling their domestic tension. All it was thus in her
power to say—and I heard of a few cases of her having said it—
was that she was sure I would have painted her beautifully if
she hadn't prevented me. She couldn't even tell the truth,
which was that I certainly would have done so if Lady
Beldonald hadn't; and she never could mention the subject at
all before that personage. I can only describe the affair,
naturally, from the outside, and heaven forbid indeed that I
should try too closely to reconstruct the possible strange
intercourse of these good friends at home.

My anecdote, however, would lose half the point it may have
to show were I to omit all mention of the consummate turn
her ladyship appeared gradually to have found herself able to
give her deportment. She had made it impossible I should
myself bring up our old, our original question, but there was
real distinction in her manner of now accepting certain other
possibilities. Let me do her that justice; her effort at
magnanimity must have been immense. There couldn't fail of

329

course to be ways in which poor Mrs. Brash paid for it. How much she had to pay we were in fact soon enough to see; and it's my intimate conviction that, as a climax, her life at last was the price. But while she lived at least—and it was with an intensity, for those wondrous weeks, of which she had never dreamed—Lady Beldonald herself faced the music. This is what I mean by the possibilities, by the sharp actualities indeed, that she accepted. She took our friend out, she showed her at home, never attempted to hide or to betray her, played her no trick whatever so long as the ordeal lasted. She drank deep, on *her* side too, of the cup—the cup that for her own lips could only be bitterness. There was, I think, scarce a special success of her companion's at which she wasn't personally present. Mrs. Munden's theory of the silence in which all this would be muffled for them was none the less, and in abundance, confirmed by our observations. The whole thing was to be the death of one or the other of them, but they never spoke of it at tea. I remember even that Nina went so far as to say to me once, looking me full in the eyes, quite sublimely, "I've made out what you mean—she *is* a picture." The beauty of this moreover was that, as I'm persuaded, she hadn't really made it out at all—the words were the mere hypocrisy of her reflective endeavour for virtue. She couldn't possibly have made it out; her friend was as much as ever "dreadfully plain" to her; she must have wondered to the last what on earth possessed us. Wouldn't it in fact have been after all just this failure of vision, this supreme stupidity in short, that kept the catastrophe so long at bay? There was a certain sense of greatness for her in seeing so many of us so absurdly mistaken; and I recall that on various occasions, and in particular when she uttered the words just quoted, this high serenity, as a sign of the relief of her soreness, if not of the effort of her conscience, did something quite visible to my eyes, and also quite unprecedented, for the beauty of her face. She got a real lift from it—such a momentary discernible sublimity that I recollect coming out on the spot with a queer crude amused "Do you know I believe I could paint you *now?*"

She was a fool not to have closed with me then and there; for what has happened since has altered everything—what was to happen a little later was so much more than I could swallow. This was the disappearance of the famous Holbein from one day to the other—producing a consternation among us all as great as if the Venus of Milo had suddenly vanished from the Louvre. "She has simply shipped her straight back"—the explanation was given in that form by Mrs. Munden, who added that any cord pulled tight enough would end at last by snapping. At the snap, in any case, we mightily jumped, for the masterpiece we had for three or four months been living with had made us feel its presence as a luminous lesson and a daily need. We recognised more than ever that it had been, for high finish, the gem of our collection—we found what a blank it left on the wall. Lady Beldonald might fill up the blank, but *we* couldn't. That she did soon fill it up—and, heaven help us, *how?*—was put before me after an interval of no great length, but during which I hadn't seen her. I dined on the Christmas of last year at Mrs. Munden's, and Nina, with a "scratch lot," as our hostess said, was there, so that, the preliminary wait being longish, she could approach me very sweetly. "I'll come to you tomorrow if you like," she said; and the effect of it, after a first stare at her, was to make me look all round. I took in, by these two motions, two things; one of which was that, though now again so satisfied herself of her high state, she could give me nothing comparable to what I should have got had she taken me up at the moment of my meeting her on her distinguished concession; the other that she was "suited" afresh and that Mrs. Brash's successor was fully installed. Mrs. Brash's successor was at the other side of the room, and I became conscious that Mrs. Munden was waiting to see my eyes seek her. I guessed the meaning of the wait; what *was* one, this time, to say? Oh first and foremost assuredly that it was immensely droll, for this time at least there was no mistake. The lady I looked upon, and as to whom my friend, again quite at sea, appealed to me for a formula, was as little a Holbein, or a specimen of any other school, as she was, like Lady Beldonald herself, a Titian. The formula was easy to give, for the amusement was that her prettiness—yes, literally, prodigiously, her prettiness—was distinct. Lady Beldonald had been magnificent—had been almost intelligent. Miss What's-her-name continues pretty, continues even young, and doesn't matter a straw! She matters so ideally little that Lady Beldonald is practically safer, I judge, than she has ever been. There hasn't been a symptom of chatter about this person, and I believe her protectress is much surprised that we're not more struck.

It was at any rate strictly impossible to me to make an appointment for the day as to which I have just recorded Nina's proposal; and the turn of events since then has not quickened my eagerness. Mrs. Munden remained in correspondence with Mrs. Brash—to the extent, that is, of three letters, each of which she showed me. They so told to our imagination her terrible little story that we were quite prepared—or thought we were—for her going out like a snuffed candle. She resisted, on her return to her original conditions, less than a year; the taste of the tree, as I had called it, had been fatal to her; what she had contentedly enough lived without before for half a century she couldn't now live without for a day. I know nothing of her original conditions—some minor American city—save that for her to have gone back to them was clearly to have stepped out of her frame. We performed, Mrs. Munden and I, a small funeral service for her by talking it all over and making it all out. It wasn't—the minor American city— a market for Holbeins, and what had occurred was that the poor old picture, banished from its museum and refreshed by the rise of no new movement to hang it, was capable of the miracle of a silent revolution, of itself turning, in its dire dishonour, its face to the wall. So it stood, without the intervention of the ghost of a critic, till they happened to pull it round again and find it mere dead paint. Well, it had had, if that's anything, its season of fame, its name on a thousand tongues and printed in capitals in the catalogue. *We* hadn't been at fault. I haven't, all the same, the least note of her—not a scratch. And I did her so in intention! Mrs. Munden continues to remind me, however, that this is not the sort of rendering with which, on the other side, after all, Lady Beldonald proposes to content herself. She has come back to the question of her own portrait. Let me settle it then at last. Since she *will* have the real thing—well, hang it, she shall!

THE BIRTHPLACE

THE BIRTHPLACE

I

It seemed to them at first, the offer, too good to be true, and their friend's letter, addressed to them to feel, as he said, the ground, to sound them as to inclinations and possibilities, had almost the effect of a brave joke at their expense. Their friend, Mr. Grant-Jackson, a highly preponderant pushing person, great in discussion and arrangement, abrupt in overture, unexpected, if not perverse, in attitude, and almost equally acclaimed and objected to in the wide midland region to which he had taught, as the phrase was, the size of his foot—their friend had launched his bolt quite out of the blue and had thereby so shaken them as to make them fear almost more than hope. The place had fallen vacant by the death of one of the two ladies, mother and daughter, who had discharged its duties for fifteen years; the daughter was staying on alone, to accommodate, but had found, though extremely mature, an opportunity of marriage that involved retirement, and the question of the new incumbents was not a little pressing. The want thus determined was of a united couple of some sort, of the right sort, a pair of educated and competent sisters possibly preferred, but a married pair having its advantages if other qualifications were marked. Applicants, candidates, besiegers of the door of everyone supposed to have a voice in the matter, were already beyond counting, and Mr. Grant-Jackson, who was in his way diplomatic and whose voice, though not perhaps of the loudest, possessed notes of insistence, had found his preference fixing itself on some person or brace of persons who had been decent and dumb. The Gedges appeared to have struck him as waiting in silence—though absolutely, as happened, no busybody had brought them, far away in the North, a hint either of bliss or of danger; and the happy spell, for the rest, had obviously been wrought in him by a remembrance which, though now scarcely fresh, had never before borne any such fruit.

Morris Gedge had for a few years, as a young man, carried on a small private school of the order known as preparatory, and had happened then to receive under his roof the small son of the great man, who was not at that time so great. The little boy, during an absence of his parents from England, had been dangerously ill, so dangerously that they had been recalled in haste, though with inevitable delays, from a far country—they had gone to America, with the whole continent and the great sea to cross again—and had got back to find the child saved, but saved, as couldn't help coming to light, by the extreme devotion and perfect judgement of Mrs. Gedge. Without children of her own she had particularly attached herself to this tiniest and tenderest of her husband's pupils, and they had both dreaded as a dire disaster the injury to their little enterprise that would be caused by their losing him. Nervous anxious sensitive persons, with a pride—as they were for that matter well aware—above their position, never, at the best, to be anything but dingy, they had nursed him in terror and had brought him through in exhaustion. Exhaustion, as befell, had thus overtaken them early and had for one reason and another managed to assert itself as their permanent portion. The little boy's death would, as they said, have done for them, yet his recovery hadn't saved them; with which it was doubtless also part of a shy but stiff candour in them that they didn't regard themselves as having in a more indirect manner laid up treasure. Treasure was not to be, in any form whatever, of their dreams or of their waking sense; and the years that followed had limped under their weight, had now and then rather grievously stumbled, had even barely escaped laying them in the dust. The school hadn't prospered, had but dwindled to a close. Gedge's health had failed and still more every sign in him of a capacity to publish himself as practical. He had tried several things, he had tried many, but the final appearance was of their having tried him not less. They mostly, at the time I speak of, were trying his successors, while he found himself, with an effect of dull felicity that had come in this case from the mere postponement of change, in charge of the grey town-library of Blackport-on-Dwindle, all granite, fog and female fiction. This was a situation in which his general intelligence—admittedly his strong point—was doubtless imaged, around him, as feeling less of a strain than that mastery of particulars in which he was recognised as weak.

It was at Blackport-on-Dwindle that the silver shaft reached and pierced him; it was as an alternative to dispensing dog's-eared volumes the very titles of which, on the lips of innumerable glib girls, were a challenge to his nerves, that the wardenship of so different a temple presented itself. The stipend named exceeded little the slim wage at present paid him, but even had it been less the interest and the honour would have struck him as determinant. The shrine at which he was to preside—though he had always lacked occasion to approach it—figured to him as the most sacred known to the steps of men, the early home of the supreme poet, the Mecca of the English-speaking race. The tears came into his eyes sooner still than into his wife's while he looked about with her at their actual narrow prison, so grim with enlighten-ment, so ugly with industry, so turned away from any dream, so intolerable to any taste. He felt as if a window had opened into a great green woodland, a woodland that had a name all glorious, immortal, that was peopled with vivid figures, each of them renowned, and that gave out a murmur, deep as the sound of the sea, which was the rustle in forest shade of all the poetry, the beauty, the colour of life. It would be prodigious that of this transfigured world *he* should keep the key. No—he couldn't believe it, not even when Isabel, at sight of his face, came and helpfully kissed him. He shook his head with a strange smile. "We shan't get it. Why should we? It's perfect."

"If we don't he'll simply have been cruel; which is impossible when he has waited all this time to be kind." Mrs. Gedge did believe—she *would*; since the wide doors of the world of poetry had suddenly pushed back for them it was in the form of poetic justice that they were first to know it. She had her faith in their patron; it was sudden, but now complete. "He remembers—that's all; and that's our strength."

"And what's *his*?" Gedge asked. "He may want to put us through, but that's a different thing from being able. What are our special advantages?"

"Well, that we're just the thing." Her knowledge of the needs of the case was as yet, thanks to scant information, of the vaguest, and she had never, more than her husband, stood on the sacred spot; but she saw herself waving a nicely-gloved hand over a collection of remarkable objects and saying to a compact crowd of gaping awestruck persons: "And now, please, *this* way." She even heard herself meeting with promptness and decision an occasional inquiry from a visitor in whom audacity had prevailed over awe. She had once been with a cousin, years before, to a great northern castle, and that was the way the housekeeper had taken them round. And it was not moreover, either, that she thought of herself as a housekeeper: she was well above that, and the wave of her hand wouldn't fail to be such as to show it. This and much else she summed up as she answered her mate. "Our special advantages are that you're a gentleman."

"Oh!" said Gedge as if he had never thought of it, and yet as if too it were scarce worth thinking of.

"I see it all," she went on; "they've *had* the vulgar—they find they don't do. We're poor and we're modest, but anyone can see what we are."

Gedge wondered. "Do you mean—?" More modest than she, he didn't know quite what she meant.

"We're refined. We know how to speak."

"Do we?"—he still, suddenly, wondered.

But she was from the first surer of everything than he; so that when a few weeks more had elapsed and the shade of uncertainty—though it was only a shade—had grown almost to sicken him, her triumph was to come with the news that they were fairly named. "We're on poor pay, though we manage"— she had at the present juncture contended for her point. "But we're highly cultivated, and for them to get *that*, don't you see? without getting too much with it in the way of pretensions and demands, must be precisely their dream. We've no social position, but we don't *mind* that we haven't, do we? a bit; which is because we know the difference between realities and shams. We hold to reality, and that gives us common sense, which the vulgar have less than anything and which yet must be wanted there, after all, as well as anywhere else."

Her companion followed her, but musingly, as if his horizon had within a few moments grown so great that he was almost lost in it and required a new orientation. The shining spaces surrounded him; the association alone gave a nobler arch to the sky. "Allow that we hold also a little to the romance. It seems to me that that's the beauty. We've missed it all our life, and now it's come. We shall be at headquarters for it. We shall have our fill of it."

She looked at his face, at the effect in it of these prospects, and her own lighted as if he had suddenly grown handsome. "Certainly—we shall live as in a fairy-tale. But what I mean is that we shall give, in a way—and so gladly—quite as much as we get. With all the rest of it we're for instance neat." Their letter had come to them at breakfast, and she picked a fly out of the butter-dish. "It's the way we'll *keep* the place"—with which she removed from the sofa to the top of the cottage-piano a tin of biscuits that had refused to squeeze into the cupboard. At Blackport they were in lodgings—of the lowest description, she had been known to declare with a freedom felt by Blackport to be slightly invidious. The Birthplace—and that itself, after such a life, was exaltation—wouldn't be lodgings, since a house close beside it was set apart for the warden, a house joining on to it as a sweet old parsonage is often annexed to a quaint old church. It would all together be their home, and such a home as would make a little world that they would never want to leave. She dwelt on the gain, for that matter, to their income; as obviously, though the salary was not a change for the better, the house given them would make all the difference. He assented to this, but absently, and she was almost impatient at the range of his thoughts. It was as if something for him—the very swarm of them—veiled the view; and he presently of himself showed what it was.

"What I can't get over is its being such a man—!" He almost, from inward emotion, broke down.

"Such a man—?"

"Him, *him*, HIM—!" It was too much.

"Grant-Jackson? Yes, it's a surprise, but one sees how he has been meaning, all the while, the right thing by us."

"I mean *Him*," Gedge returned more coldly; "our becoming familiar and intimate—for that's what it will come to. We shall just live with Him."

"Of course—it *is* the beauty." And she added quite gaily: "The more we do the more we shall love Him."

"No doubt—but it's rather awful. The more we *know* Him," Gedge reflected, "the more we shall love Him. We don't as yet, you see, know Him so very tremendously."

"We do so quite as well, I imagine, as the sort of people they've had. And that probably isn't—unless you care, as we do—so awfully necessary. For there are the facts."

"Yes—there are the facts."

"I mean the principal ones. They're all that the people—the people who come—want."

"Yes—they must be all *they* want."

"So that they're all that those who've been in charge have needed to know."

'Ah," he said as if it were a question of honour, "*we* must know everything."

She cheerfully acceded: she had the merit, he felt, of keeping the case within bounds. "Everything. But about him personally," she added, "there isn't, is there? so very very much."

"More, I believe, than there used to be. They've made discoveries."

It was a grand thought. "Perhaps *we* shall make some!"

"Oh I shall be content to be a little better up in what has been done." And his eyes rested on a shelf of books, half of which, little worn but much faded, were of the florid "gift" order and belonged to the house. Of those among them that were his own most were common specimens of the reference sort, not excluding an old Bradshaw and a catalogue of the town-library. "We've not even a Set of our own. Of the Works," he explained in quick repudiation of the sense, perhaps more obvious, in which she might have taken it.

As a proof of their scant range of possessions this sounded almost abject, till the painful flush with which they met on the admission melted presently into a different glow. It was just for that kind of poorness that their new situation was, by its intrinsic charm, to console them. And Mrs. Gedge had a happy thought. "Wouldn't the Library more or less have them?"

"Oh no, we've nothing of that sort: for what do you take us?" This, however, was but the play of Gedge's high spirits: the form both depression and exhilaration most frequently took with him being a bitterness on the subject of the literary taste of Blackport. No one was so deeply acquainted with it. It acted with him in fact as so lurid a sign of the future that the charm of the thought of removal was sharply enhanced by the prospect of escape from it. The institution he served didn't of course deserve the particular reproach into which his irony had flowered; and indeed if the several Sets in which the Works were present were a trifle dusty, the dust was a little his own fault. To make up for that now he had the vision of immediately giving his time to the study of them; he saw himself indeed, inflamed with a new passion, earnestly commenting and collating. Mrs. Gedge, who had suggested that, till their move should come, they ought to read Him regularly of an evening—certain as they were to do it still more when in closer quarters with Him—Mrs. Gedge felt also, in her degree, the spell; so that the very happiest time of their anxious life was perhaps to have been the series of lamplight hours, after supper, in which, alternately taking the book, they declaimed, they almost performed, their beneficent author. He became speedily more than their author—their personal friend, their universal light, their final authority and divinity. Where in the world, they were already asking themselves, would they have been without Him? By the time their appointment arrived in form their relation to Him had immensely developed. It was amusing to Morris Gedge that he had so lately blushed for his ignorance, and he made this remark to his wife during the last hour they were able to give their study before proceeding, across half the country, to the scene of their romantic future. It was as if, in deep close throbs, in cool after-waves that broke of a sudden and bathed his mind, all possession and comprehension and sympathy, all the truth and the life and the story, had come to him, and come, as the newspapers said, to stay. "It's absurd," he didn't hesitate to say, "to talk of our not 'knowing.' So far as we don't it's because we're dunces. He's *in* the thing, over His ears, and the more we get into it the more we're with Him. I seem to myself at any rate," he declared, "to *see* Him in it as if He were painted on the wall."

"Oh *doesn't* one rather, the dear thing? And don't you feel where it is?" Mrs. Gedge finely asked. "We see Him because we love Him—that's what we do. How can we not, the old darling—with what He's doing for us? There's no light"—she had a sententious turn—"like true affection."

"Yes, I suppose that's it. And yet," her husband mused, "I see, confound me, the faults."

"That's because you're so critical. You see them, but you don't mind them. You see them, but you forgive them. You mustn't mention them *there*. We shan't, you know, be there for *that*."

"Dear no!" he laughed: "we'll chuck out anyone who hints at them."

II

If the sweetness of the preliminary months had been great, great too, though almost excessive as agitation, was the wonder of fairly being housed with Him, of treading day and night in the footsteps He had worn, of touching the objects, or at all events the surfaces, the substances, over which His hands had played, which His arms, His shoulders had rubbed, of breathing the air—or something not too unlike it—in which His voice had sounded. They had had a little at first their bewilderments, their disconcertedness; the place was both humbler and grander than they had exactly prefigured, more at once of a cottage and of a museum, a little more archaically bare and yet a little more richly official. But the sense was strong with them that the point of view, for the inevitable ease of the connexion, patiently, indulgently awaited them; in addition to which, from the first evening, after closing-hour, when the last blank pilgrim had gone, the mere spell, the mystic presence—as if they had had it quite to themselves—were all they could have desired. They had received, at Grant-Jackson's behest and in addition to a table of instructions and admonitions by the number and in some particulars by the nature of which they found themselves slightly depressed, various little guides, manuals, travellers' tributes, literary memorials and other catch-penny publications; which, however, were to be for the moment swallowed up in the interesting episode of the induction or initiation appointed for them in advance at the hands of several persons whose relation to the establishment was, as superior to their own, still more official, and at those in especial of one of the ladies who had for so many years borne the brunt. About the instructions from above, about the shilling books and the well-known facts and the full-blown legend, the supervision, the subjection, the submission, the view as of a cage in which he should circulate and a groove in which he should slide, Gedge had preserved a certain play of mind; but all power of reaction appeared suddenly to desert him in the presence of his so visibly competent predecessor and as an effect of her good offices. He had not the resource, enjoyed by his wife, of seeing himself, with impatience, attired in black silk of a make characterised by just the right shade of austerity; so that this firm smooth expert and consummately respectable middle-aged person had him somehow, on the whole ground, completely at her mercy.

It was evidently something of a rueful moment when, as a lesson—she being for the day or two still in the field—he accepted Miss Putchin's suggestion of "going round" with her and with the successive squads of visitors she was there to deal with. He appreciated her method—he saw there had to *be* one; he admired her as succinct and definite; for there were the facts, as his wife had said at Blackport, and they were to be disposed of in the time; yet he felt a very little boy as he dangled, more than once, with Mrs. Gedge, at the tail of the human comet. The idea had been that they should by this attendance more fully embrace the possible accidents and incidents, so to put it, of the relation to the great public in which they were to find themselves; and the poor man's excited perception of the great public rapidly became such as to resist any diversion meaner than that of the admirable manner of their guide. It wandered from his gaping companions to that of the priestess in black silk, whom he kept asking himself if either he or Isabel could hope by any possibility ever remotely to resemble; then it bounded restlessly back to the numerous persons who revealed to him as it had never yet been revealed the happy power of the simple to hang upon the lips of the wise. The great thing seemed to be—and quite surprisingly—that the business was easy and the strain, which as a strain they had feared, moderate; so that he might have been puzzled, had he fairly caught himself in the act, by his recognising as the last effect of the impression an odd absence of the power really to rest in it, an agitation deep within him that vaguely threatened to grow. "It isn't, you see, so very complicated," the black silk lady seemed to throw off, with everything else, in her neat crisp

346

cheerful way; in spite of which he already, the very first time—that is after several parties had been in and out and up and down—went so far as to wonder if there weren't more in it than she imagined. She was, so to speak, kindness itself—was all encouragement and reassurance; but it was just her slightly coarse redolence of these very things that, on repetition, before they parted, dimmed a little, as he felt, the light of his acknowledging smile. This again she took for a symptom of some pleading weakness in him—he could never be as brave as she; so that she wound up with a few pleasant words from the very depth of her experience. "You'll get into it, never fear—it will *come*; and then you'll feel as if you had never done anything else." He was afterwards to know that, on the spot, at this moment, he must have begun to wince a little at such a menace; that he might come to feel as if he had never done anything but what Miss Putchin did loomed for him, in germ, as a penalty to pay. The support she offered, none the less, continued to strike him; she put the whole thing on so sound a basis when she said: "You see they're so nice about it—they take such an interest. And they never do a thing they shouldn't. That was always everything to mother and me." "They," Gedge had already noticed, referred constantly and hugely, in the good woman's talk, to the millions who shuffled through the house; the pronoun in question was for ever on her lips, the hordes it represented filled her consciousness, the addition of their numbers ministered to her glory. Mrs. Gedge promptly fell in. "It must be indeed delightful to see the effect on so many and to feel that one may perhaps do something to make it—well, permanent." But he was kept silent by his becoming more sharply aware that this was a new view, for him, of the reference made, that he had never thought of the quality of the place as derived from Them, but from Somebody Else, and that They, in short, seemed to have got into the way of crowding Him out. He found himself even a little resenting this for Him—which perhaps had something to do with the slightly invidious cast of his next inquiry.

"And are They always, as one might say—a—stupid?"

"Stupid!" She stared, looking as if no one *could* be such a thing in such a connexion. No one had ever been anything but neat and cheerful and fluent, except to be attentive and unobjectionable and, so far as was possible, American.

"What I mean is," he explained, "is there any perceptible proportion that take an interest in Him?"

His wife stepped on his toe; she deprecated levity. But his mistake fortunately was lost on their friend. "That's just why they come, that they take such an interest. I sometimes think they take more than about anything else in the world." With which Miss Putchin looked about at the place. "It *is* pretty, don't you think, the way they've got it now?" This, Gedge saw, was a different "They"; it applied to the powers that were—the people who had appointed him, the governing, visiting Body, in respect to which he was afterwards to remark to Mrs. Gedge that a fellow—it was the difficulty—didn't know "where to have her." His wife, at a loss, questioned at that moment the necessity of having her anywhere, and he said, good-humouredly, "Of course; it's all right." He was in fact content enough with the last touches their friend had given the picture. "There are many who know all about it when they come, and the Americans often are tremendously up. Mother and me really enjoyed"—it was her only slip—"the interest of the Americans. We've sometimes had ninety a day, and all wanting to see and hear everything. But you'll work them off; you'll see the way—it's all experience." She came back for his comfort to that. She came back also to other things: she did justice to the considerable class who arrived positive and primed. "There are those who know more about it than you do. But *that* only comes from their interest."

"Who know more about what?" Gedge inquired.

"Why about the place. I mean they have their ideas—of what everything is, and *where* it is, and what it isn't and where it *should* be. They do ask questions," she said, yet not so much in warning as in the complacency of being herself seasoned and sound; "and they're down on you when they think you go wrong. As if you ever could! You know too much," she astutely smiled; "or you *will*."

"Oh you mustn't know *too* much, must you?" And Gedge now smiled as well. He knew, he thought, what he meant.

"Well, you must know as much as anybody else. I claim at any rate that I do," Miss Putchin declared. "They never really caught me out."

"I'm very certain of *that*"—and Mrs. Gedge had an elation almost personal.

"Surely," he said, "I don't want to be caught out." She rejoined that in such a case he would have *Them* down on him, and he saw that this time she meant the powers above. It quickened his sense of all the elements that were to reckon with, yet he felt at the same time that the powers above were not what he should most fear. "I'm glad," he observed, "that they ever ask questions; but I happened to notice, you know, that no one did today."

"Then you missed several—and no loss. There were three or four put to me too silly to remember. But of course they mostly *are* silly."

"You mean the questions?"

She laughed with all her cheer. "Yes, sir; I don't mean the answers."

Whereupon, for a moment snubbed and silent, he felt like one of the crowd. Then it made him slightly vicious. "I didn't know but you meant the people in general—till I remembered that I'm to understand from you that *they're* wise, only occasionally breaking down."

It wasn't really till then, he thought, that she lost patience; and he had had, much more than he meant no doubt, a cross-questioning air. "You'll see for yourself." Of which he was sure enough. He was in fact so ready to take this that she came round to full accommodation, put it frankly that every now and then they broke out—not the silly, oh no, the intensely inquiring. "We've had quite lively discussions, don't you know, about well-known points. They want it all *their* way, and I know the sort that are going to as soon as I see them. That's one of the things you do—you get to know the sorts. And if it's what you're afraid of—their taking you up," she was further gracious enough to say, "you needn't mind a bit. What *do* they know, after all, when for us it's our life? I've never moved an inch, because, you see, I shouldn't have been here if I didn't know where I was. No more will *you* be a year hence—you know what I mean, putting it impossibly—if *you* don't. I expect you do, in spite of your fancies." And she dropped once more to bed-rock. "There are the facts. Otherwise where would any of us be? That's all you've got to go upon. A person, however cheeky, can't have them *his* way just because he takes it into his head. There can only be *one* way, and," she gaily added as she took leave of them, "I'm sure it's quite enough!"

III

Gedge not only assented eagerly—one way *was* quite enough if it were the right one—but repeated it, after this conversation, at odd moments, several times over to his wife. "There can only be one way, one way," he continued to remark—though indeed much as if it were a joke; till she asked him how many more he supposed she wanted. He failed to answer this question, but resorted to another repetition. "There are the facts, the facts," which perhaps, however, he kept a little more to himself, sounding it at intervals in different parts of the house. Mrs. Gedge was full of comment on their clever introductress, though not restrictively save in the matter of her speech, "Me and mother," and a general tone—which certainly was not their sort of thing. "I don't know," he said, "perhaps it comes with the place, since speaking in immortal verse doesn't seem to come. It must be, one seems to see, one thing or the other. I daresay that in a few months I shall also be at it—'me and the wife.'"

"Why not 'me and the missus' at once?" Mrs. Gedge

resentfully inquired. "I don't think," she observed at another time, "that I quite know what's the matter with you."

"It's only that I'm excited, awfully excited—as I don't see how one can't be. You wouldn't have a fellow drop into this berth as into an appointment at the Post Office. Here on the spot it goes to my head—how can that be helped? But we shall live into it, and perhaps," he said with an implication of the other possibility that was doubtless but part of his fine ecstasy, "we shall live through it." The place acted on his imagination—how, surely, shouldn't it? And his imagination acted on his nerves, and these things together, with the general vividness and the new and complete immersion, made rest for him almost impossible, so that he could scarce go to bed at night and even during the first week more than once rose in the small hours to move about, up and down, with his lamp—standing, sitting, listening, wondering, in the stillness, as if positively to recover some echo, to surprise some secret, of the *genius loci*. He couldn't have explained it—and didn't in fact need to explain it, at least to himself, since the impulse simply held him and shook him; but the time after closing, the time above all after the people—Them, as he felt himself on the way habitually to put it, predominant, insistent, all in the foreground—brought him, or ought to have brought him, he seemed to see, nearer to the enshrined Presence, enlarging the opportunity for communion and intensifying the sense of it. These nightly prowls, as he called them, were disquieting to his wife, who had no disposition to share in them, speaking with decision of the whole place as just the place to be forbidding after dark. She rejoiced in the distinctness, contiguous though it was, of their own little residence, where she trimmed the lamp and stirred the fire and heard the kettle sing, repairing the while the omissions of the small domestic who slept out; she foresaw herself, with some promptness, drawing rather sharply the line between her own precinct and that in which the great spirit might walk. It would be with them, the great spirit, all day— even if indeed on her making that remark, and in just that

351

form, to her husband, he replied with a queer "But will he though?" And she vaguely imaged the development of a domestic antidote after a while, precisely, in the shape of curtains more markedly drawn and everything most modern and lively, tea, "patterns," the newspapers, the female fiction itself that they had reacted against at Blackport, quite defiantly cultivated.

These possibilities, however, were all right, as her companion said it was, all the first autumn—they had arrived at summer's end; and he might have been more than content with a special set of his own that he had access to from behind, passing out of their low door for the few steps between it and the Birthplace. With his lamp ever so carefully guarded and his nursed keys that made him free of treasures, he crossed the dusky interval so often that she began to qualify it as a habit that "grew." She spoke of it almost as if he had taken to drink, and he humoured that view of it by allowing the cup to be strong. This had been in truth altogether his immediate sense of it; strange and deep for him the spell of silent sessions before familiarity and, to some small extent, disappointment had set in. The exhibitional side of the establishment had struck him, even on arrival, as qualifying too much its character; he scarce knew what he might best have looked for, but the three or four rooms bristled overmuch, in the garish light of day, with busts and relics, not even ostensibly always *His*, old prints and old editions, old objects fashioned in His likeness, furniture "of the time" and autographs of celebrated worshippers. In the quiet hours and the deep dusk, none the less, under the play of the shifted lamp and that of his own emotion, these things too recovered their advantage, ministered to the mystery, or at all events to the impression, seemed consciously to offer themselves as personal to he poet. Not one of them was really or unchallengeably so, but they had somehow, through long association, got, as Gedge always phrased it, into the secret, and it was about the secret he asked them while he restlessly wandered. It wasn't till months had elapsed that he found how little they had to tell him, and he was quite at his ease with them when he knew they were by no means where his sensibility had first placed them. They were as out of it as he; only, to do them justice, they had made him immensely feel. And still, too, it was not they who had done that most, since his sentiment had gradually cleared itself to deep, to deeper refinements.

The Holy of Holies of the Birthplace was the low, the sublime Chamber of Birth, sublime because, as the Americans usually said—unlike the natives they mostly found words—it was so pathetic; and pathetic because it was—well, really nothing else in the world that one could name, number or measure. It was as empty as a shell of which the kernel has withered, and contained neither busts nor prints nor early copies; it contained only the Fact—*the* Fact itself—which, as he stood sentient there at midnight, our friend, holding his breath, allowed to sink into him. He *had* to take it as the place where the spirit would most walk and where He would therefore be most to be met, with possibilities of recognition and reciprocity. He hadn't, most probably—*He* hadn't—much inhabited the room, as men weren't apt, as a rule, to convert to their later use and involve in their wider fortune the scene itself of their nativity. But as there were moments when, in the conflict of theories, the sole certainty surviving for the critic threatened to be that He had not—unlike other successful men—*not* been born, so Gedge, though little of a critic, clung to the square feet of space that connected themselves, however feebly, with the positive appearance. He was little of a critic—he was nothing of one; he hadn't pretended to the character before coming, nor come to pretend to it; also, luckily for him, he was seeing day by day how little use he could possibly have for it. It would be to him, the attitude of a high expert, distinctly a stumbling-block, and that he rejoiced, as the winter waned, in his ignorance, was one of the propositions he betook himself, in his odd manner, to enunciating to his wife. She denied it, for hadn't she in the first place been present, wasn't she still present, at his pious, his tireless study of everything connected with the subject?—so present that she had herself learned more about it than had ever seemed likely. Then in the second place he wasn't to proclaim on the house-tops any point at which he might be weak, for who knew, if it should get abroad that they were ignorant, what effect might be produced—?

"On the attraction"—he took her up—"of the Show?"

He had fallen into the harmless habit of speaking of the place as the "Show"; but she didn't mind this so much as to be diverted by it. "No; on the attitude of the Body. You know they're pleased with us, and I don't see why you should want to spoil it. We got in by a tight squeeze—you know we've had evidence of that, and that it was about as much as our backers could manage. But we're proving a comfort to them, and it's absurd of you to question your suitability to people who were content with the Putchins."

"I don't, my dear," he returned, "question anything; but if I should do so it would be precisely because of the greater advantage constituted for the Putchins by the simplicity of their spirit. They were kept straight by the quality of their ignorance—which was denser even than mine. It was a mistake in us from the first to have attempted to correct or to disguise ours. We should have waited simply to become good parrots, to learn our lesson—all on the spot here, so little of it is wanted—and squawk it off."

"Ah 'squawk,' love—what a word to use about Him!"

"It isn't about Him—nothing's about Him. None of Them care tuppence about Him. The only thing They care about is this empty shell—or rather, for it isn't empty, the extraneous preposterous stuffing of it."

"Preposterous?"—he made her stare with this as he hadn't yet done.

At sight of her look, however—the gleam, as it might have been, of a queer suspicion—he bent to her kindly and tapped her cheek. "Oh it's all right. We *must* fall back on the Putchins. Do you remember what she said?—'They've made it so pretty now.' They *have* made it pretty, and it's a first-rate show. It's a first-rate show and a first-rate billet, and He was a first-rate poet, and you're a first-rate woman—to put up so sweetly, I mean, with my nonsense."

She appreciated his domestic charm and she justified that part of his tribute which concerned herself. "I don't care how much of your nonsense you talk to me, so long as you *keep* it all for me and don't treat *Them* to it."

"The pilgrims? No," he conceded—"it isn't fair to Them. They mean well."

"What complaint have we after all to make of Them so long as They don't break off bits—as They used, Miss Putchin told us, so awfully—in order to conceal them about Their Persons? She broke Them at least of that."

"Yes," Gedge mused again; "I wish awfully she hadn't!"

"You'd like the relics destroyed, removed? That's all that's wanted!"

"There *are* no relics."

"There won't be any *soon*—unless you take care." But he was already laughing, and the talk wasn't dropped without his having patted her once more. An impression or two nevertheless remained with her from it, as he saw from a question she asked him on the morrow. "What did you mean yesterday about Miss Putchin's simplicity—its keeping her 'straight'? Do you mean mentally?"

Her "mentally" was rather portentous, but he practically confessed. "Well, it kept her up. I mean," he amended, laughing, "it kept her down."

It was really as if she had been a little uneasy. "You consider there's a danger of your being affected? You know what I mean—of its going to your head. You do know," she insisted as he said nothing. "Through your caring for him so. You'd certainly be right in that case about its having been a mistake for you to plunge so deep." And then as his listening without reply, though with his look a little sad for her, might have denoted that, allowing for extravagance of statement, he saw there was something in it: "Give up your prowls. Keep it for daylight. Keep it for *Them*."

"Ah," he smiled, "if one could! My prowls," he added, "are what I most enjoy. They're the only time, as I've told you before, that I'm really with *Him*. Then I don't see the place. He isn't the place."

"I don't care for what you 'don't see,'" she returned with vivacity; "the question is of what you do see."

Well, if it was, he waited before meeting it. "Do you know what I sometimes do?" And then as she waited too: "In the Birthroom there, when I look in late, I often put out my light. That makes it better."

"Makes what—?"

"Everything."

"What is it then you see in the dark?"

"Nothing!" said Morris Gedge.

"And what's the pleasure of that?"

"Well, what the American ladies say. It's so fascinating!"

IV

The autumn was brisk, as Miss Putchin had told them it would be, but business naturally fell off with the winter months and the short days. There was rarely an hour indeed without a call of some sort, and they were never allowed to forget that they kept the shop in all the world, as they might say, where custom was least fluctuating. The seasons told on it, as they tell on travel, but no other influence, consideration or convulsion to which the population of the globe is exposed. This population, never exactly in simultaneous hordes, but in a full swift and steady stream, passed through the smoothly-working mill and went, in its variety of degrees duly impressed and edified, on its artless way. Gedge gave himself up, with much ingenuity of spirit, to trying to keep in relation with it; having even at moments, in the early time, glimpses of the chance that the impressions gathered from so rare an opportunity for contact with the general mind might prove as interesting as anything else in the connexion. Types, classes, nationalities, manners, diversities of behaviour, modes of seeing, feeling, of expression, would pass before him and become for him, after a fashion, the experience of an untravelled man. His journeys had been short and saving, but poetic justice again seemed inclined to work for him in placing him just at the point in all Europe perhaps where the confluence of races was thickest. The theory at any rate carried him on, operating helpfully for the term of his anxious beginnings and gilding in a manner—it was the way he characterised the case to his wife—the somewhat stodgy gingerbread of their daily routine. They hadn't known many people and their visiting-list was small— which made it again poetic justice that they should be visited on such a scale. They dressed and were at home, they were under arms and received, and except for the offer of refreshment—and Gedge had his view that there would eventually be a *buffet* farmed out to a great firm—their hospitality would have made them princely if mere hospitality ever did. Thus they were launched, and it was interesting; so that from having been ready to drop, originally, with fatigue they emerged as even-winded and strong in the legs as if they had had an Alpine holiday. This experience, Gedge opined, also represented, as a gain, a like seasoning of the spirit—by which he meant a certain command of impenetrable patience.

The patience was needed for the particular feature of the ordeal that, by the time the lively season was with them again, had disengaged itself as the sharpest—the immense assumption of veracities and sanctities, of the general soundness of the legend, with which everyone arrived. He was well provided certainly for meeting it, and he gave all he had, yet he had sometimes the sense of a vague resentment on the part of his pilgrims at his not ladling out their fare with a bigger spoon. An irritation had begun to grumble in him during the comparatively idle months of winter when a pilgrim would turn up singly. The pious individual, entertained for the half-hour, had occasionally seemed to offer him the promise of beguilement or the semblance of a personal relation; it came back again to the few pleasant calls he had received in the course of a life almost void of social amenity. Sometimes he liked the person, the face, the speech: an educated man, a gentleman, not one of the herd; a graceful woman, vague, accidental, unconscious of him, but making him wonder, while he hovered, who she was. These chances represented for him light yearnings and faint flutters; they acted indeed within him to a special, an extraordinary tune. He would have liked to talk with such stray companions, to talk with them *really*, to talk with them as he might have talked had he met them where he couldn't meet them—at dinner, in the "world," on a visit at a country-house. Then he could have said—and about the shrine and the idol always—things he couldn't say now. The form in which his irritation first came to him was that of his feeling obliged to say to them—to the single visitor, even when sympathetic, quite as to the gaping group—the particular things, a dreadful dozen or so, that they expected. If he had thus arrived at characterising these things as dreadful the reason touched the very point that, for a while turning everything over, he kept dodging, not facing, trying to ignore. The point was that he was on his way to become two quite different persons, the public and the private—as to which it would somehow have to be managed that these persons should live together. He was splitting into halves, unmistakably—he who, whatever else he had been, had at least always been so entire and in his way so solid. One of the halves, or perhaps even, since the split promised to be rather unequal, one of the quarters, was the keeper, the showman, the priest of the idol; the other piece was the poor unsuccessful honest man he had always been.

There were moments when he recognised this primary character as he had never done before; when he in fact quite shook in his shoes at the idea that it perhaps had in reserve some supreme assertion of its identity. It was honest, verily, just by reason of the possibility. It was poor and unsuccessful because here it was just on the verge of quarrelling with its bread and butter. Salvation would be of course—the salvation of the showman—rigidly to *keep* it on the verge; not to let it, in other words, overpass by an inch. He might count on this, he said to himself, if there weren't any public—if there weren't thousands of people demanding of him what he was paid for. He saw the approach of the stage at which they would affect him, the thousands of people—and perhaps even more the earnest individual—as coming really to see if he were earning his wage. Wouldn't he soon begin to fancy them in league with the Body, practically deputed by it—given, no doubt, a kindled suspicion—to look in and report observations? It was the way he broke down with the lonely pilgrim that led to his first heart-searchings—broke down as to the courage required for damping an uncritical faith. What they all most wanted was to feel that everything was "just as it was"; only the shock of having to part with that vision was greater than any individual could bear unsupported. The bad moments were upstairs in the Birthroom, for here the forces pressing on the very edge assumed a dire intensity. The mere expression of eye, all-credulous, omnivorous and fairly moistening in the act, with which many persons gazed about, might eventually make it difficult for him to remain fairly civil. Often they came in pairs—sometimes one had come before—and then they explained to each other. He in that case never corrected; he listened, for the lesson of listening: after which he would remark to his wife that there was no end to what he was learning. He saw that if he should really ever break down it would be with her he would begin. He had given her hints and digs enough, but she was so inflamed with appreciation that she either didn't feel them or pretended not to understand.

This was the greater complication that, with the return of the spring and the increase of the public, her services were more required. She took the field with him from an early hour; she was present with the party above while he kept an eye, and still more an ear, on the party below; and how could he know, he asked himself, what she might say to them and what she might suffer *Them* to say—or in other words, poor wretches, to believe—while removed from his control? Some day or other, and before too long, he couldn't but think, he must have the matter out with her—the matter, namely, of the *morality* of their position. The morality of women was special—he was getting lights on that. Isabel's conception of her office was to cherish and enrich the legend. It was already, the legend, very taking, but what was she there for but to make it more so? She certainly wasn't there to chill any natural piety. If it was all in the air—all in their "eye," as the vulgar might say—that He *had* been born in the Birthroom, where was the value of the sixpences they took? where the equivalent they had engaged to supply? "Oh dear, yes—just about *here*"; and she must tap the place with her foot. "Altered? Oh dear, no—save in a few trifling particulars; you see the place—and isn't that just the charm of it?—quite as *He* saw it. Very poor and homely, no doubt; but that's just what's so wonderful." He didn't want to hear her, and yet he didn't want to give her her head; he didn't want to make difficulties or to snatch the bread from her mouth. But he must none the less give her a warning before they had gone *too* far. That was the way, one evening in June, he put it to her; the affluence, with the finest weather, having lately been of the largest and the crowd all day fairly gorged with the story. "We mustn't, you know, go *too* far."

The odd thing was that she had now ceased even to be conscious of what troubled him—she was so launched in her own career. "Too far for what?"

"To save our immortal souls. We mustn't, love, tell too many lies."

She looked at him with dire reproach. "Ah now are you going to begin again?"

"I never *have* begun; I haven't wanted to worry you. But, you know, we don't know anything about it." And then as she stared, flushing: "About His having been born up there. About anything really. Not the least little scrap that would weigh in any other connexion as evidence. So don't rub it in so."

"Rub it in how?"

"That He *was* born—" But at sight of her face he only sighed. "Oh dear, oh dear!"

"Don't you think," she replied cuttingly, "that He was born anywhere?"

He hesitated—it was such an edifice to shake. "Well, we don't know. There's very little *to* know. He covered His tracks as no other human being has ever done."

She was still in her public costume and hadn't taken off the gloves she made a point of wearing as a part of that uniform; she remembered how the rustling housekeeper in the Border castle, on whom she had begun by modelling herself, had worn them. She seemed official and slightly distant. "To cover His tracks He must have had to exist. Have we got to give *that* up?"

"No, I don't ask you to give it up *yet*. But there's very little to go upon."

"And is that what I'm to tell Them in return for everything?"

Gedge waited—he walked about. The place was doubly still after the bustle of the day, and the summer evening rested on it as a blessing, making it, in its small state and ancientry, mellow and sweet. It was good to be there and it would be good to stay. At the same time there was something incalculable in the effect on one's nerves of the great gregarious density. This was an attitude that had nothing to do with degrees and shades, the attitude of wanting all or nothing. And you couldn't talk things over with it. You could only do that with friends, and then but in cases where you were sure the friends wouldn't betray you. "Couldn't you adopt," he replied at last, "a slightly more discreet method? What we can say is that things have been *said*; that's all *we* have to do with. 'And is this really'—when they jam their umbrellas into the floor—'the very *spot* where He was born?' 'So it has, from a long time back, been described as being.' Couldn't one meet Them, to be decent a little, in some such way as that?"

She looked at him very hard. "Is that the way *you* meet them?"

"No; I've kept on lying—without scruple, without shame."

"Then why do you haul me up?"

"Because it has seemed to me we might, like true companions, work it out a little together."

This was not strong, he felt, as, pausing with his hands in his pockets, he stood before her; and he knew it as weaker still after she had looked at him a minute. "Morris Gedge, I propose to be *your* true companion, and I've come here to stay. That's all I've got to say." It was not, however, for "You had better try yourself and see," she presently added. "Give the place, give the story away, by so much as a look, and—well, I'd allow you about nine days. Then you'd see."

He feigned, to gain time, an innocence. "They'd take it so ill?" And then as she said nothing: "They'd turn and rend me? They'd tear me to pieces?"

But she wouldn't make a joke of it. "They wouldn't *have* it, simply."

"No—They wouldn't. That's what I say. They won't."

"You had better," she went on, "begin with Grant-Jackson. But even that isn't necessary. It would get to him, it would get to the Body, like wildfire."

"I see," said poor Gedge. And indeed for the moment he did see, while his companion followed up what she believed her advantage.

"Do you consider it's *all* a fraud?"

"Well, I grant you there was somebody. But the details are naught. The links are missing. The evidence—in particular about that room upstairs, in itself our Casa Santa—is *nil*. It was so awfully long ago." Which he knew again sounded weak.

"Of course it was awfully long ago—that's just the beauty and the interest. Tell Them, *tell* Them," she continued, "that the evidence is *nil*, and I'll tell Them something else." She spoke it with such meaning that his face seemed to show a question, to

which she was on the spot of replying, "I'll tell Them you're a—"
She stopped, however, changing it. "I'll tell Them exactly the
opposite. And I'll find out what you say—it won't take long—to do
it. If we tell different stories *that* possibly may save us."

"I see what you mean. It would perhaps, as an oddity, have a
success of curiosity. It might become a draw. Still, They but
want broad masses." And he looked at her sadly. "You're no
more than one of Them."

"If it's being no more than one of Them to love it," she
answered, "then I certainly am. And I'm not ashamed of my
company."

"To love *what?*" said Morris Gedge.

"To love to think He was born there."

"You think too much. It's bad for you." He turned away with
his chronic moan. But it was without losing what she called
after him.

"I decline to let the place down." And what was there indeed
to say? They *were* there to keep it up.

V

He kept it up through the summer, but with the queerest
consciousness, at times, of the want of proportion between his
secret rage and the spirit of those from whom the friction came.
He said to himself—so sore his sensibility had grown—that They
were gregariously ferocious at the very time he was seeing
Them as individually mild. He said to himself that They were
mild only because *he* was—he flattered himself that he was
divinely so, considering what he might be; and that he should,
as his wife had warned him, soon enough have news of it were
he to deflect by a hair's breadth from the line traced for him.
That was the collective fatuity—that it was capable of turning on
the instant both to a general and to a particular resentment.
Since the least breath of discrimination would get him the sack
without mercy, it was absurd, he reflected, to speak of his
discomfort as light. He was gagged, he was goaded, as in

omnivorous companies he doubtless sometimes showed by a strange silent glare. They'd get him the sack for that as well, if he didn't look out; therefore wasn't it in effect ferocity when you mightn't even hold your tongue? They wouldn't let you off with silence—They insisted on your committing yourself. It was the pound of flesh—They *would* have it; so under his coat he bled. But a wondrous peace, by exception, dropped on him one afternoon at the end of August. The pressure had, as usual, been high, but it had diminished with the fall of day, and the place was empty before the hour for closing. Then it was that, within a few minutes of this hour, there presented themselves a pair of pilgrims to whom in the ordinary course he would have remarked that they were, to his regret, too late. He was to wonder afterwards why the course had at sight of the visitors— a gentleman and a lady, appealing and fairly young—shown for him as other than ordinary; the consequence sprang doubtless from something rather fine and unnameable, something for example in the tone of the young man or in the light of his eye, after hearing the statement on the subject of the hour. "Yes, we know it's late; but it's just, I'm afraid, *because* of that. We've had rather a notion of escaping the crowd—as I suppose you mostly have one now; and it was really on the chance of finding you alone—!"

These things the young man said before being quite admitted, and they were words anyone might have spoken who hadn't taken the trouble to be punctual or who desired, a little ingratiatingly, to force the door. Gedge even guessed at the sense that might lurk in them, the hint of a special tip if the point were stretched. There were no tips, he had often thanked his stars, at the Birthplace; there was the charged fee and nothing more; everything else was out of order, to the relief of a palm not formed by nature as a scoop. Yet in spite of everything, in spite especially of the almost audible chink of the gentleman's sovereigns, which might in another case exactly have put him out, he presently found himself, in the Birthroom, access to which he had gracefully enough granted, almost treating the visit as personal and private. The reason—well, the reason would have been, if anywhere, in something naturally persuasive on the part of the couple; unless it had been rather again, in the way the young man, once he was in the place, met the caretaker's expression of face, held it a moment and seemed to wish to sound it. That they were Americans was promptly clear, and Gedge could very nearly have told what kind; he had arrived at the point of distinguishing kinds, though the difficulty might have been with him now that the case before him was rare. He saw it suddenly in the light of the golden midland evening which reached them through low old windows, saw it with a rush of feeling, unexpected and smothered, that made him a moment wish to keep it before him as a case of inordinate happiness. It made him feel old shabby poor, but he watched it no less intensely for its doing so. They were children of fortune, of the greatest, as it might seem to Morris Gedge, and they were of course lately married; the husband, smooth-faced and soft, but resolute and fine, several years older than the wife, and the wife vaguely, delicately, irregularly, but mercilessly pretty. Somehow the world was theirs; they gave the person who took the sixpences at the Birthplace such a sense of the high luxury of freedom as he had never had. The thing was that the world was theirs not simply because they had money—he had seen rich people enough—but because they could in a supreme degree think and feel and say what they liked. They had a nature and a culture, a tradition, a facility of some sort—and all producing in them an effect of positive beauty—that gave a light to their liberty and an ease to their tone. These things moreover suffered nothing from the fact that they happened to be in mourning; this was probably worn for some lately-deceased opulent father—if not some delicate mother who would be sure to have been a part of the source of the beauty; and it affected Gedge, in the gathered twilight and at his odd crisis, as the very uniform of their distinction.

He couldn't quite have said afterwards by what steps the point had been reached, but it had become at the end of five minutes a part of their presence in the Birthroom, a part of the young man's look, a part of the charm of the moment, and a part above all of a strange sense within him of "Now or never!" that Gedge had suddenly, thrillingly, let himself go. He hadn't been definitely conscious of drifting to it; he had been, for that, too conscious merely of thinking how different, in all their range, were such a united couple from another united couple known to him. They were everything he and his wife weren't; this was more than anything else the first lesson of their talk. Thousands of couples of whom the same was true certainly had passed before him, but none of whom it was true with just that engaging intensity. And just *because* of their transcendent freedom; that was what, at the end of five minutes, he saw it all come back to. The husband, who had been there at some earlier time, had his impression, which he wished now to make his wife share. But he already, Gedge could see, hadn't concealed it from her. A pleasant irony in fine our friend seemed to taste in the air—he who hadn't yet felt free to taste his own.

"I think you weren't here four years ago"—that was what the young man had almost begun by remarking. Gedge liked his remembering it, liked his frankly speaking to him; all the more that he had offered, as it were, no opening. He had let them look about below and then had taken them up, but without words, without the usual showman's song, of which he would have been afraid. The visitors didn't ask for it; the young man had taken the matter out of his hands by himself dropping for the benefit of the young woman a few detached remarks. What Gedge oddly felt was that these remarks were not inconsiderate of him; he had heard others, both of the priggish order and the crude, that might have been called so. And as the young man hadn't been aided to this cognition of him as new, it already began to make for them a certain common ground. The ground became immense when the visitor presently added with a smile: "There was a good lady, I recollect, who had a great deal to say."

It was the gentleman's smile that had done it; the irony *was* there. "Ah there has been a great deal said." And Gedge's look at his interlocutor doubtless showed his sense of being sounded. It was extraordinary of course that a perfect stranger should have guessed the travail of his spirit, should have caught the gleam of his inner commentary. That probably leaked in spite of him out of his poor old eyes. "Much of it, in such places as this," he heard himself adding, "is of course said very irresponsibly." *Such places as this!*—he winced at the words as soon as he had uttered them.

There was no wincing, however, on the part of his pleasant companions. "Exactly so; the whole thing becomes a sort of stiff smug convention—like a dressed-up sacred doll in a Spanish church—which you're a monster if you touch."

"A monster," Gedge assented, meeting his eyes.

The young man smiled, but he thought looking at him a little harder. "A blasphemer."

"A blasphemer."

It seemed to do his visitor good—he certainly *was* looking at him harder. Detached as he was he was interested—he was at least amused. "Then you don't claim or at any rate don't insist—? I mean you personally."

He had an identity for him, Gedge felt, that he couldn't have had for a Briton, and the impulse was quick in our friend to testify to this perception. "I don't insist to *you*."

The young man laughed. "It really—I assure you if I may—wouldn't do any good. I'm too awfully interested."

"Do you mean," his wife lightly inquired, "in—a—pulling it down? That's rather in what you've said to me."

"Has he said to you," Gedge intervened, though quaking a little, "that he would like to pull it down?"

She met, in her free sweetness, this appeal with such a charm! "Oh perhaps not quite the *house*—!"

"Good. You see we live on it—I mean *we* people."

The husband had laughed, but had now so completely ceased to look about him that there seemed nothing left for him but to talk avowedly with the caretaker. "I'm interested," he explained, "in what I think *the* interesting thing—or at all events the eternally tormenting one. The fact of the abysmally little that, in proportion, we know."

"In proportion to what?" his companion asked.

"Well, to what there must have been—to what in fact there *is*— to wonder about. That's the interest; it's immense. He escapes us like a thief at night, carrying off—well, carrying off everything. And people pretend to catch Him like a flown canary, over whom you can close your hand, and put Him back in the cage. He won't *go* back; he won't *come* back. He's not"— the young man laughed—"such a fool! It makes Him the happiest of all great men."

He had begun by speaking to his wife, but had ended, with his friendly, his easy, his indescribable competence, for Gedge—poor Gedge who quite held his breath and who felt, in the most unexpected way, that he had somehow never been in such good society. The young wife, who for herself meanwhile had continued to look about, sighed out, smiled out—Gedge couldn't have told which—her little answer to these remarks. "It's rather a pity, you know, that He *isn't* here. I mean as Goethe's at Weimar. For Goethe *is* at Weimar."

"Yes, my dear; that's Goethe's bad luck. There he sticks. *This* man isn't anywhere. I defy you to catch him."

"Why not say, beautifully," the young woman laughed, "that, like the wind, He's everywhere?"

It wasn't of course the tone of discussion, it was the tone of pleasantry, though of better pleasantry, Gedge seemed to feel, and more within his own appreciation, than he had ever listened to; and this was precisely why the young man could go on without the effect of irritation, answering his wife but still with eyes for their companion. "I'll be hanged if He's *here*!"

It was almost as if he were taken—that is, struck and rather held—by their companion's unruffled state, which they hadn't meant to ruffle, but which suddenly presented its interest, perhaps even projected its light. The gentleman didn't know,

Gedge was afterwards to say to himself, how that hypocrite was inwardly all of a tremble, how it seemed to him his fate was being literally pulled down on his head. He was trembling for the moment certainly too much to speak; abject he might be, but he didn't want his voice to have the absurdity of a quaver. And the young woman–charming creature!–still had another word. It was for the guardian of the spot, and she made it in her way delightful. They had remained in the Holy of Holies, where she had been looking for a minute, with a ruefulness just marked enough to be pretty, at the queer old floor. "Then if you say it *wasn't* in this room He was born–well, what's the use?"

"What's the use of what?" her husband asked. "The use, you mean, of our coming here? Why the place is charming in itself. And it's also interesting," he added to Gedge, "to know how you get on."

Gedge looked at him a moment in silence, but answering the young woman first. If poor Isabel, he was thinking, could only have been like that!–not as to youth, beauty, arrangement of hair or picturesque grace of hat–these things he didn't mind; but as to sympathy, facility, light perceptive, and yet not cheap, detachment! "I don't say it wasn't–but I don't say it *was*."

"Ah but doesn't that," she returned, "come very much to the same thing? And don't They want also to see where He had His dinner and where He had His tea?"

"They want everything," said Morris Gedge. "They want to see where He hung up His hat and where He kept His boots and where His mother boiled her pot."

"But if you don't show them–?"

"They show *me*. It's in all their little books."

"You mean," the husband asked, "that you've only to hold your tongue?"

"I try to," said Gedge.

"Well," his visitor smiled, "I see you *can*."

Gedge hesitated. "I can't."

"Oh well," said his friend, "what does it matter?"

"I do speak," he continued. "I can't sometimes not."

"Then how do you get on?"

Gedge looked at him more abjectly, to his own sense, than ever at anyone—even at Isabel when she frightened him. "I don't get on. I speak," he said—"since I've spoken to *you*."

"Oh *we* shan't hurt you!" the young man reassuringly laughed.

The twilight meanwhile had sensibly thickened, the end of the visit was indicated. They turned together out of the upper room and came down the narrow stair. The words just exchanged might have been felt as producing an awkwardness which the young woman gracefully felt the impulse to dissipate. "You must rather wonder why we've come." And it was the first note for Gedge of a further awkwardness—as if he had definitely heard it make the husband's hand, in a full pocket, begin to fumble.

It was even a little awkwardly that the husband still held off. "Oh we like it as it is. There's always *something*." With which they had approached the door of egress.

"What is there, please?" asked Morris Gedge, not yet opening the door, since he would fain have kept the pair on, and conscious only for a moment after he had spoken that his question was just having for the young man too dreadfully wrong a sound. This personage wondered yet feared, and had evidently for some minutes been putting himself a question; so that, with his preoccupation, the caretaker's words had represented to him inevitably: "What is there, please, for *me*?" Gedge already knew with it moreover that he wasn't stopping him in time. He had uttered that challenge to show he himself wasn't afraid, and he must have had in consequence, he was subsequently to reflect, a lamentable air of waiting.

The visitor's hand came out. "I hope I may take the liberty—?" What afterwards happened our friend scarcely knew, for it fell into a slight confusion, the confusion of a queer gleam of gold—a sovereign fairly thrust at him; of a quick, almost violent motion on his own part, which, to make the matter worse, might well have sent the money rolling on the floor; and then of marked blushes all round and a sensible embarrassment; producing indeed in turn rather oddly and ever so quickly an increase of communion. It was as if the young man had offered him money to make up to him for having, as it were, led him on, and then, perceiving the mistake, but liking him the better for his refusal, had wanted to obliterate this aggravation of his original wrong. He had done so, presently, while Gedge got the door open, by saying the best thing he could, and by saying it frankly and gaily. "Luckily it doesn't at all affect the *work*!"

The small town-street, quiet and empty in the summer eventide, stretched to right and left, with a gabled and timbered house or two, and fairly seemed to have cleared itself to congruity with the historic void over which our friends, lingering an instant to converse, looked at each other. The young wife, rather, looked about a moment at all there wasn't to be seen, and then, before Gedge had found a reply to her husband's remark, uttered, evidently in the interest of conciliation, a little question of her own that she tried to make earnest. "It's our unfortunate ignorance, you mean, that doesn't?"

"Unfortunate or fortunate. I like it so," said the husband. "'The play's the thing.' Let the author alone."

Gedge, with his key on his forefinger, leaned against the door-post, took in the stupid little street and was sorry to see them go—they seemed so to abandon him. "That's just what They won't do—nor let *me* do. It's all I want—to let the author alone. Practically"—he felt himself getting the last of his chance—"there *is* no author; that is for us to deal with. There are all the immortal people—*in* the work; but there's nobody else."

"Yes," said the young man—"that's what it comes to. There should really, to clear the matter up, be no such Person."

"As you say," Gedge returned, "it's what it comes to. There *is* no such Person."

The evening air listened, in the warm thick midland stillness, while the wife's little cry rang out. "But *wasn't* there—?"

"There was somebody," said Gedge against the door-post. "But They've killed Him. And, dead as He is, They keep it up, They do it over again, They kill Him every day."

He was aware of saying this so grimly—more than he wished—that his companions exchanged a glance and even perhaps looked as if they felt him extravagant. That was really the way Isabel had warned him all the others would be looking if he should talk to Them as he talked to *her*. He liked, however, for that matter, to hear how he should sound when pronounced incapable through deterioration of the brain. "Then if there's no author, if there's nothing to be said but that there isn't anybody," the young woman smilingly asked, "why in the world should there be a house?"

"There shouldn't," said Morris Gedge.

Decidedly, yes, he affected the young man. "Oh, I don't say, mind you, that you should pull it down!"

"Then where would you *go*?" their companion sweetly inquired.

"That's what my wife asks," Gedge returned.

"Then keep it up, keep it up!" And the husband held out his hand.

"That's what my wife says," Gedge went on as he shook it.

The young woman, charming creature, emulated the other visitor; she offered their remarkable friend her handshake. "Then mind your wife."

The poor man faced her gravely. "I would if she were such a wife as you!"

VI

It had made for him, all the same, an immense difference; it had given him an extraordinary lift, so that a certain sweet aftertaste of his freedom might a couple of months later have been suspected of aiding to produce for him another and really a more considerable adventure. It was an absurd way to reason, but he had been, to his imagination, for twenty minutes in good society—that being the term that best described for him the company of people to whom he hadn't to talk, as he phrased it, rot. It was his title to good society that he had, in his doubtless awkward way, affirmed; and the difficulty was just that, having affirmed it, he couldn't take back the affirmation. Few things had happened to him in life, that is few that were agreeable, but at least *this* had, and he wasn't so constructed that he could go on as if it hadn't. It was going on as if it had, however, that landed him, alas! in the situation unmistakably marked by a visit from Grant-Jackson late one afternoon toward the end of October. This had been the hour of the call of the young Americans. Every day that hour had come round something of the deep throb of it, the successful secret, woke up; but the two occasions were, of a truth, related only by being so intensely opposed. The secret had been successful in that he had said nothing of it to Isabel, who, occupied in their own quarter while the incident lasted, had neither heard the visitors arrive nor seen them depart. It was on the other hand scarcely successful in guarding itself from indirect betrayals. There were two persons in the world at least who felt as he did; they were persons also who had treated him, benignly, as feeling after *their* style; who had been ready in fact to overflow in gifts as a sign of it, and though they were now off in space they were still with him sufficiently in spirit to make him play, as it were, with the sense of their sympathy. This in turn made him, as he was perfectly aware, more than a shade or two reckless, so that, in his reaction from that gluttony of the public for false facts which had from the first tormented him, he fell into the habit of sailing, as he would have said, too near the wind, or in other words—all in presence of the people—of washing his hands of the legend. He had crossed the line—he knew it; he had struck wild—They drove him to it; he had substituted, by a succession of uncontrollable profanities, an attitude that couldn't be understood for an attitude that but too evidently *had* been.

This was of course the franker line, only he hadn't taken it, alas! for frankness—hadn't in the least really adopted it at all, but had been simply himself caught up and disposed of by it, hurled by his fate against the bedizened walls of the temple, quite in the way of a priest possessed to excess of the god, or, more vulgarly, that of a blind bull in a china-shop—an animal to which he often compared himself. He had let himself fatally go, in fine, just for irritation, for rage, having, in his predicament, nothing whatever to do with frankness—a luxury reserved for quite other situations. It had always been his view that one lived to learn; he had learned something every hour of his life, though people mostly never knew what, in spite of its having generally been—hadn't it?—at somebody's expense. What he was at present continually learning was the sense of a form of words heretofore so vain—the famous "false position" that had so often helped out a phrase. One used names in that way without knowing what they were worth; then of a sudden, one fine day, their meaning grew bitter in the mouth. This was a truth with the relish of which his fireside hours were occupied, and he was aware of how much it exposed a man to look so perpetually as if something had disagreed with him. The look to be worn at the Birthplace was properly the beatific, and when once it had fairly been missed by those who took it for granted, who indeed paid sixpence for it—like the table-wine in provincial France it was *compris*—one would be sure to have news of the remark.

News accordingly was what Gedge had been expecting—and what he knew, above all, had been expected by his wife, who had a way of sitting at present as with an ear for a certain knock. She didn't watch him, didn't follow him about the house, at the public hours, to spy upon his treachery; and that could touch him even though her averted eyes went through him more than her fixed. Her mistrust was so perfectly expressed by her manner of showing she trusted that he never felt so nervous, never tried so to keep straight, as when she most let him alone. When the crowd thickened and they had of necessity to receive together he tried himself to get off by allowing her as much as possible the word. When people appealed to him he turned to her—and with more of ceremony than their relation warranted: he couldn't help *this* either, if it seemed ironic—as to the person most concerned or most competent. He flattered himself at these moments that no one would have guessed her being his wife; especially as, to do her justice, she met his manner with a wonderful grim bravado— grim, so to say, for himself, grim by its outrageous cheerfulness for the simple-minded. The lore she *did* produce for them, the associations of the sacred spot she developed, multiplied, embroidered; the things in short she said and the stupendous way she said them! She wasn't a bit ashamed, since why need virtue be ever ashamed? It *was* virtue, for it put bread into his mouth—he meanwhile on his side taking it out of hers. He had seen Grant-Jackson on the October day in the Birthplace itself—the right setting of course for such an interview; and what had occurred was that, precisely, when the scene had ended and he had come back to their own sitting-room, the question she put to him for information was: "Have you settled it that I'm to starve?"

She had for a long time said nothing to him so straight— which was but a proof of her real anxiety; the straightness of Grant-Jackson's visit, following on the very slight sinuosity of a note shortly before received from him, made tension show for what it was. By this time, really, however, his decision had been taken; the minutes elapsing between his reappearance at the domestic fireside and his having, from the other threshold, seen Grant-Jackson's broad well-fitted back, the back of a banker and a patriot, move away, had, though few, presented themselves to him as supremely critical. They formed, as it were, the hinge of his door, that door actually ajar so as to show him a possible fate beyond it, but which, with his hand, in a spasm, thus tightening on the knob, he might either open wide or close partly or altogether. He stood at autumn dusk in the little museum that constituted the vestibule of the temple, and there, as with a concentrated push at the crank of a windlass, he brought himself round. The portraits on the walls seemed vaguely to watch for it; it was in their august presence—kept dimly august for the moment by Grant-Jackson's impressive check of his application of a match to the vulgar gas—that the great man had uttered, as if it said all, his "You know, my dear fellow, really—!" He had managed it with the special tact of a fat man, always, when there *was* any, very fine; he had got the most out of the time, the place, the setting, all the little massed admonitions and symbols; confronted there with his victim on the spot that he took occasion to name afresh as, to *his* piety and patriotism, the most sacred on earth, he had given it to be understood that in the first place he was lost in amazement and that in the second he expected a single warning now to suffice. Not to insist too much moreover on the question of gratitude, he would let his remonstrance rest, if need be, solely on the question of taste. *As* a matter of taste alone—! But he was surely not to be obliged to follow that up. Poor Gedge indeed would have been sorry to oblige him, for he saw it was exactly to the atrocious taste of unthankfulness the allusion was made. When he said he wouldn't dwell on what the fortunate occupant of the post owed him for the stout battle originally fought on his behalf, he simply meant he *would*. That was his tact—which, with everything else that has been mentioned, in the scene, to help, really had the ground to itself. The day *had* been when Gedge couldn't have thanked him enough—though he had thanked him, he considered, almost fulsomely—and nothing, nothing that he could coherently or reputably name, had happened since then. From the moment he was pulled up, in short, he had no case, and if he exhibited, instead of one, only hot tears in his eyes, the mystic gloom of the temple either prevented his friend from seeing them or rendered it possible that they stood for remorse. He had dried them, with the pads formed by the base of his bony thumbs, before he went in to Isabel. This was the more fortunate as, in spite of her inquiry, prompt and pointed, he but moved about the room looking at her hard. Then he stood before the fire a little with his hands behind him and his coat-tails divided, quite as the person in permanent possession. It was an indication his wife appeared to take in; but she put nevertheless presently another question. "You object to telling me what he said?"

"He said 'You know, my dear fellow, really—!'"

"And is that all?"

"Practically. Except that I'm a thankless beast."

"Well!" she responded, not with dissent.

"You mean that I *am*?"

"Are those the words he used?" she asked with a scruple.

Gedge continued to think. "The words he used were that I give away the Show and that, from several sources, it has come round to Them."

"As of course a baby would have known!" And then as her husband said nothing: "Were *those* the words he used?"

"Absolutely. He couldn't have used better ones."

"Did he call it," Mrs. Gedge inquired, "the 'Show'?"

"Of course he did. The Biggest on Earth."

She winced, looking at him hard—she wondered, but only for a moment. "Well, it *is*."

"Then it's something," Gedge went on, "to have given *that* away. But," he added, "I've taken it back."

"You mean you've been convinced?"

"I mean I've been scared."

"At last, at last!" she gratefully breathed.

"Oh it was easily done. It was only two words. But here I am." Her face was now less hard for him. "And what two words?"

"'You know, Mr. Gedge, that it simply won't do.' That was all. But it was the way such a man says them."

"I'm glad then," Mrs. Gedge frankly averred, "that he *is* such a man. How did you ever think it *could* do?"

"Well, it was my critical sense. I didn't ever know I had one—till They came and (by putting me here) waked it up in me. Then I had somehow, don't you see? to live with it; and I seemed to feel that, with one thing and another, giving it time and in the long run, it might, it *ought* to, come out on top of the heap. Now that's where, he says, it simply won't 'do.' So I must put it—I *have* put it—at the bottom."

"A very good place then for a critical sense!" And Isabel, more placidly now, folded her work. "*If*, that is, you can only keep it there. If it doesn't struggle up again."

"It can't struggle." He was still before the fire, looking round at the warm low room, peaceful in the lamplight, with the hum of the kettle for the ear, with the curtain drawn over the leaded casement, a short moreen curtain artfully chosen by Isabel for the effect of the olden time, its virtue of letting the light within show ruddy to the street. "It's dead," he went on; "I killed it just now."

He really spoke so that she wondered. "Just now?"

"There in the other place—I strangled it, poor thing, in the dark. If you'll go out and see, there must be blood. Which, indeed," he added, "on an altar of sacrifice, is all right. But the place is for ever spattered."

"I don't want to go out and see." She locked her hands over the needlework folded on her knee, and he knew, with her eyes on him, that a look he had seen before was in her face. "You're off your head, you know, my dear, in a way." Then, however, more cheeringly: "It's a good job it hasn't been too late."

"Too late to get it under?"

"Too late for Them to give you the second chance that I thank God you accept."

"Yes, if it *had* been—!" And he looked away as through the ruddy curtain and into the chill street. Then he faced her again. "I've scarcely got over my fright yet. I mean," he went on, "for you."

"And I mean for *you*. Suppose what you had come to announce to me now were that we had *got* the sack. How should I enjoy, do you think, seeing you turn out? Yes, out *there*!" she added as his eyes again moved from their little warm circle to the night of early winter on the other side of the pane, to the rare quick footsteps, to the closed doors, to the curtains drawn like their own, behind which the small flat town, intrinsically dull, was sitting down to supper.

He stiffened himself as he warmed his back; he held up his head, shaking himself a little as if to shake the stoop out of his shoulders, but he had to allow she was right. "What would have become of us?"

"What indeed? We should have begged our bread—or I should be taking in washing."

He was silent a little. "I'm too old. I should have begun sooner."

"Oh God forbid!" she cried.

"The pinch," he pursued, "is that I can do nothing else."

"Nothing whatever!" she agreed with elation.

"Whereas here—if I cultivate it—I perhaps *can* still lie. But I must cultivate it."

"Oh you old dear!" And she got up to kiss him.

"I'll do my best," he said.

VII

"Do you remember us?" the gentleman asked and smiled—with the lady beside him smiling too; speaking so much less as an earnest pilgrim or as a tiresome tourist than as an old acquaintance. It was history repeating itself as Gedge had somehow never expected, with almost everything the same except that the evening was now a mild April-end, except that the visitors had put off mourning and showed all their bravery—besides showing, as he doubtless did himself, though so differently, for a little older; except, above all, that—oh seeing them again suddenly affected him not a bit as the thing he'd have supposed it. "We're in England again and we were near; I've a brother at Oxford with whom we've been spending a day, so that we thought we'd come over." This the young man pleasantly said while our friend took in the queer fact that he must himself seem to them rather coldly to gape. They had come in the same way at the quiet close; another August had passed, and this was the second spring; the Birthplace, given the hour, was about to suspend operations till the morrow; the last lingerer had gone and the fancy of the visitors was once more for a look round by themselves. This represented surely no greater presumption than the terms on which they had last parted with him seemed to warrant; so that if he did inconsequently stare it was just in fact because he was so supremely far from having forgotten them. But the sight of the pair luckily had a double effect, and the first precipitated the second—the second being really his sudden vision that everything perhaps depended for him on his recognising no complication. He must go straight on, since it was what had for more than a year now so handsomely answered; he must brazen it out consistently, since that only was what his dignity was at last reduced to. He mustn't be afraid in one way any more than he had been in another; besides which it came over him to the point of his flushing for it that their visit, in its essence, must have been for himself. It was good society again, and *they* were the same. It wasn't for him therefore to behave as if he couldn't meet them.

These deep vibrations, on Gedge's part, were as quick as they were deep; they came in fact all at once, so that his response, his declaration that it was all right—"Oh *rather*; the hour doesn't matter for *you!*"—had hung fire but an instant; and when they were well across the threshold and the door closed behind them, housed in the twilight of the temple, where, as before, the votive offerings glimmered on the walls, he drew the long breath of one who might by a self-betrayal have done something too dreadful. For what had brought them back was indubitably not the glamour of the shrine itself—since he had had a glimpse of their analysis of that quantity; but their critical (not to say their sentimental) interest in the queer case of the priest. Their call was the tribute of curiosity, of sympathy, of a compassion really, as such things went, exquisite—a tribute *to* that queerness which entitled them to the frankest welcome. They had wanted, for the generous wonder of it, to judge how he was getting on, how such a man in such a place *could*; and they had doubtless more than half-expected to see the door opened by somebody who had succeeded him. Well, somebody *had*—only with a strange equivocation; as they would have, poor things, to make out themselves, an embarrassment for which he pitied them. Nothing could have been more odd, but verily it was this troubled vision of their possible bewilderment, and this compunctious view of such a return for their amenity, that practically determined in him his tone. The lapse of the months had but made their name familiar to him; they had on the other occasion inscribed it, among the thousand names, in the current public register, and he had since then, for reasons of his own, reasons of feeling, again and again turned back to it. It was nothing in itself; it told him nothing—"Mr. and Mrs. B. D. Hayes, New York"—one of those American labels that were just like every other American label and that were precisely the most remarkable thing about people reduced to achieving an identity in such other ways. They could be Mr. and Mrs. B. D. Hayes and yet could be, with all presumptions missing—well, what these callers were. It had quickly enough indeed cleared the situation a little further that his friends had absolutely, the other time, as it came back to him, warned him of his original danger, their anxiety about which had been the last note sounded among them. What he was afraid of, with this reminiscence, was that, finding him still safe, they would, the next thing, definitely congratulate him and perhaps even, no less candidly, ask him how he had managed. It was with the sense of nipping some such inquiry in the bud that, losing no time and holding himself with a firm grip, he began on the spot, downstairs, to make plain to them how he had managed. He routed the possibility of the question in short by the assurance of his answer. "Yes, yes, I'm still here; I suppose it *is* in a manner to one's profit that one does, such as it is, one's best." He did his best on the present occasion, did it with the gravest face he had ever worn and a soft serenity that was like a large damp sponge passed over their previous meeting—over everything in it, that is, but the fact of its pleasantness.

"We stand here, you see, in the old living-room, happily still to be reconstructed in the mind's eye, in spite of the havoc of time, which we have fortunately of late years been able to arrest. It was of course rude and humble, but it must have been snug and quaint, and we have at least the pleasure of knowing that the tradition in respect to the features that do remain is delightfully uninterrupted. Across that threshold He habitually passed; through those low windows, in childhood, He peered out into the world that He was to make so much happier by the gift to it of His genius; over the boards of this floor—that is over *some* of them, for we mustn't be carried away!—his little feet often pattered; and the beams of this ceiling (we must really in some places take care of *our* heads!) he endeavoured, in boyish strife, to jump up and touch. It's not often that in the early home of genius and renown the whole tenor of existence is laid so bare, not often that we are able to retrace, from point to point and from step to step, its connexion with objects, with influences—to build it round again with the little solid facts out of which it sprang. This therefore, I need scarcely remind you, is what makes the small space between these walls—so modest to measurement, so insignificant of aspect—unique on all the earth. *There's nothing like it*," Morris Gedge went on, insisting as solemnly and softly, for his bewildered hearers, as over a pulpit-edge; "there's nothing at all like it anywhere in the world. There's nothing, only reflect, for the combination of greatness and, as we venture to say, of intimacy. You may find elsewhere perhaps absolutely fewer changes, but where shall you find a *Presence* equally diffused, uncontested and undisturbed? Where in particular shall you find, on the part of the abiding spirit, an equally towering eminence? You may find elsewhere eminence of a considerable order, but where shall you find *with* it, don't you see, changes after all so few and the contemporary element caught so, as it were, in the very fact?" His visitors, at first confounded but gradually spellbound, were still gaping with the universal gape—wondering, he judged, into what strange pleasantry he had been suddenly moved to explode, and yet beginning to see in him an intention beyond a joke, so that they started, at this point, they almost jumped, when, by as rapid a transition, he made, toward the old fireplace, a dash that seemed to illustrate precisely the act of eager catching. "It is in this old chimney-corner, the quaint inglenook of our ancestors—just there in the far angle, where His little stool was placed, and where, I daresay, if we could look close enough, we should find the hearthstone scraped with His little feet—that we see the inconceivable child gazing into the blaze of the old oaken logs and making out there pictures and stories, see Him conning, with curly bent head, His well-worn hornbook, or poring over some scrap of an ancient ballad, some page of some such rudely-bound volume of chronicles as lay, we may be sure, in His father's window-seat."

It was, he even himself felt at this moment, wonderfully done; no auditors, for all his thousands, had ever yet so inspired him. The odd slightly alarmed shyness in the two faces, as if in a drawing-room, in their "good society" exactly, some act incongruous, something grazing the indecent, had abruptly been perpetrated, the painful reality of which stayed itself before coming home—the visible effect on his friends in fine wound him up as to the sense that *they* were worth the trick. It came of itself now—he had got it so by heart; but perhaps really it had never come so well, with the staleness so disguised, the interest so renewed and the clerical unction demanded by the priestly character so successfully distilled. Mr. Hayes of New York had more than once looked at his wife, and Mrs. Hayes of New York had more than once looked at her husband—only, up to now, with a stolen glance, with eyes it hadn't been easy to detach from the remarkable countenance by the aid of which their entertainer held them. At present, however, after an exchange less furtive, they ventured on a sign that they hadn't been appealed to in vain. "Charming,

charming, Mr. Gedge!" Mr. Hayes broke out. "We feel that we've caught you in the mood."

His wife hastened to assent—it eased the tension. "It *would* be quite the way; except," she smiled, "that you'd be too dangerous. You've really a genius!"

Gedge looked at her hard, but yielding no inch, even though she touched him there at a point of consciousness that quivered. This was the prodigy for him, and had been, the year through—that he did it all, he found, easily, did it better than he had done anything else in life; with so high and broad an effect, in truth, an inspiration so rich and free, that his poor wife now, literally, had been moved more than once to fresh fear. She had had her bad moments, he knew, after taking the measure of his new direction—moments of readjusted suspicion in which she wondered if he hadn't simply adopted another, a different perversity. There would be more than one fashion of giving away the Show, and wasn't *this* perhaps a question of giving it away by excess? He could dish them by too much romance as well as by too little; she hadn't hitherto fairly grasped that there might *be* too much. It was a way like another, at any rate, of reducing the place to the absurd; which reduction, if he didn't look out, would reduce *them* again to the prospect of the streets, and this time surely without appeal. It all depended indeed—he knew she knew that—on how much Grant-Jackson and the others, how much the Body, in a word, would take. He knew she knew what he himself held it would take—that he considered no limit could be imputed to the quantity. They simply wanted it piled up, and so did everyone else; wherefore if no one reported him as before why were They to be uneasy? It was in consequence of idiots tempted to reason that he had been dealt with before; but as there was now no form of idiocy that he didn't systematically flatter, goading it on really to its *own* private doom, who was ever to pull the string of the guillotine? The axe was in the air—yes; in a world gorged to satiety there were no revolutions. And it had been vain for Isabel to ask if the other thunder-growl also hadn't come out of the blue. There was actually proof positive that the winds were now at rest. How could they be more so?—he appealed to the receipts. These were golden days—the Show had never so flourished. So he had argued, so he was arguing still—and, it had to be owned, with every appearance in his favour. Yet if he inwardly winced at the tribute to his plausibility rendered by his flushed friends, this was because he felt in it the real ground of his optimism. The charming woman before him acknowledged his "genius" as he himself had had to do. He had been surprised at his facility until he had grown used to it. Whether or no he had, as a fresh menace to his future, found a new perversity, he had found a vocation much older, evidently, than he had at first been prepared to recognise. He had done himself injustice. He liked to be brave because it came so easy; he could measure it off by the yard. It was in the Birthroom, above all, that he continued to do this, having ushered up his companions without, as he was still more elated to feel, the turn of a hair. She might take it as she liked, but he had had the lucidity—all, that is, for his own safety—to meet without the grace of an answer the homage of her beautiful smile. She took it apparently, and her husband took it, but as a part of his odd humour, and they followed him aloft with faces now a little more responsive to the manner in which on *that* spot he would naturally come out. He came out, according to the word of his assured private receipt, "strong." He missed a little, in truth, the usual round-eyed question from them—the inveterate artless cue with which, from moment to moment, clustered troops had for a year obliged him. Mr. and Mrs. Hayes were from New York, but it was a little like singing, as he had heard one of his Americans once say about something, to a Boston audience. He did none the less what he could, and it was ever his practice to stop still at a certain spot in the room and, after having secured attention by look and gesture, suddenly shoot off: "Here!"

They always understood, the good people—he could fairly love them now for it; they always said breathlessly and unanimously "There?" and stared down at the designated point quite as if some trace of the grand event were still to be made out. This movement produced he again looked round. "Consider it well: *the* spot of earth—!" "Oh but it isn't *earth*!" the boldest spirit—there was always a boldest—would generally pipe out. Then the guardian of the Birthplace would be truly superior—as if the unfortunate had figured the Immortal coming up, like a potato, through the soil. "I'm not suggesting that He was born on the bare ground. He was born *here*!"—with an uncompromising dig of his heel. "There ought to be a brass, with an inscription, let in." "Into the floor?"—it always came. "Birth and burial: seedtime, summer, autumn!"—that always, with its special right cadence, thanks to his unfailing spring, came too. "Why not as well as into the pavement of the church?—you've *seen* our grand old church?" The former of which questions nobody ever answered—abounding, on the other hand, to make up, in relation to the latter. Mr. and Mrs. Hayes even were at first left dumb by it—not indeed, to do them justice, having uttered the word that called for it. They had uttered no word while he kept the game up, and (though that made it a little more difficult) he could yet stand triumphant before them after he had finished with his flourish. Only then it was that Mr. Hayes of New York broke silence.

"Well, if we wanted to see I think I may say we're quite satisfied. As my wife says, it *would* seem your line." He spoke now, visibly, with more ease, as if a light had come: though he made no joke of it, for a reason that presently appeared. They were coming down the little stair, and it was on the descent that his companion added her word.

"Do you know what we half *did* think—?" And then to her husband: "Is it dreadful to tell him?" They were in the room below, and the young woman, also relieved, expressed the feeling with gaiety. She smiled as before at Morris Gedge, treating him as a person with whom relations were possible, yet remaining just uncertain enough to invoke Mr. Hayes's opinion. "We *have* awfully wanted—from what we had heard."

But she met her husband's graver face; he was not quite out of the wood. At this she was slightly flurried—but she cut it short. "You must know—don't you?—that, with the crowds who listen to you, we'd have heard."

He looked from one to the other, and once more again, with force, something came over him. They had kept him in mind, they were neither ashamed nor afraid to show it, and it was positively an interest on the part of this charming creature and this keen cautious gentleman, an interest resisting oblivion and surviving separation, that had governed their return. Their other visit had been the brightest thing that had ever happened to him, but this was the gravest; so that at the end of a minute something broke in him and his mask dropped of itself. He chucked, as he would have said, consistency; which, in its extinction, left the tears in his eyes. His smile was therefore queer. "Heard how I'm going it?"

The young man, though still looking at him hard, felt sure, with this, of his own ground. "Of course you're tremendously talked about. You've gone round the world."

"You've heard of me in America?"

"Why almost of nothing else!"

"That was what made us feel—!" Mrs. Hayes contributed.

"That you must see for yourselves?" Again he compared, poor Gedge, their faces. "Do you mean I excite—a—scandal?"

"Dear no! Admiration. You renew so," the young man observed, "the interest."

"Ah there it is!" said Gedge with eyes of adventure that seemed to rest beyond the Atlantic.

"They listen, month after month, when they're out here, as you must have seen; then they go home and talk. But they sing your praise."

Our friend could scarce take it in. "Over *there!*"

"Over there. I think you must be even in the papers."

"Without abuse?"

"Oh we don't abuse everyone."

Mrs. Hayes, in her beauty, it was clear, stretched the point.

"They rave about you."

"Then they *don't* know?"

"Nobody knows," the young man declared; "it wasn't any-one's knowledge, at any rate, that made us uneasy."

"It was your own? I mean your own sense?"

"Well, call it that. We remembered, and we wondered what had happened. So," Mr. Hayes now frankly laughed, "we came to see."

Gedge stared through his film of tears. "Came from America to see *me?*"

"Oh a part of the way. But we wouldn't, in England, have missed you."

"And now we *haven't!*" the young woman soothingly added.

Gedge still could only gape at the candour of the tribute. But he tried to meet them—it was what was least poor for him—in their own key. "Well, how do you like it?"

Mrs. Hayes, he thought—if their answer were important— laughed a little nervously. "Oh you see."

Once more he looked from one to the other. "It's too beastly easy, you know."

Her husband raised his eyebrows. "You conceal your art. The emotion—yes; that must be easy; the general tone must flow. But about your facts—you've so many: how do you get *them* through?"

Gedge wondered. "You think I get too many—?"

At this they were amused together. "That's just what we came to see!"

"Well, you know, I've felt my way; I've gone step by step; you wouldn't believe how I've tried it on. *This*—where you see me— is where I've come out." After which, as they said nothing: "You hadn't thought I *could* come out?"

Again they just waited, but the husband spoke: "Are you so awfully sure you *are* out?"

Gedge drew himself up in the manner of his moments of emotion, almost conscious even that, with his sloping shoulders, his long lean neck and his nose so prominent in proportion to other matters, he resembled the more a giraffe. It was now at last he really caught on. "I *may* be in danger again—and the danger is what has moved you? Oh!" the poor man fairly moaned. His appreciation of it quite weakened him, yet he pulled himself together. "You've your view of my danger?"

It was wondrous how, with that note definitely sounded, the air was cleared. Lucid Mr. Hayes, at the end of a minute, had put the thing in a nutshell. "I don't know what you'll think of us—for being so beastly curious."

"I think," poor Gedge grimaced, "you're only too beastly kind."

"It's all your own fault," his friend returned, "for presenting us (who are not idiots, say) with so striking a picture of a crisis. At our other visit, you remember," he smiled, "you created an anxiety for the opposite reason. Therefore if *this* should again be a crisis for you, you'd really give us the case with an ideal completeness."

"You make me wish," said Morris Gedge, "that it might be one."

"Well, don't try—for our amusement—to bring one on. I don't see, you know, how you can have much margin. Take care—take care."

Gedge did it pensive justice. "Yes, that was what you said a year ago. You did me the honour to be uneasy—as my wife was."

Which determined on the young woman's part an immediate question. "May I ask then if Mrs. Gedge is now at rest?"

"No—since you do ask. *She* fears at least that I go too far; she doesn't believe in my margin. You see we *had* our scare after your visit. They came down."

His friends were all interest. "Ah! They came down?"

"Heavy. They brought *me* down. That's *why*—"

"Why you *are* down?" Mrs. Hayes sweetly demanded.

"Ah but my dear man," her husband interposed, "you're not

down; you're *up*! You're only up a different tree, but you're up at the tip-top."

"You mean I take it too high?"

"That's exactly the question," the young man answered; "and the possibility, as matching your first danger, is just what we felt we couldn't, if you didn't mind, miss the measure of."

Gedge gazed at him. "I feel that I know what you at bottom *hoped*."

"We at bottom 'hope,' surely, that you're all right?"

"In spite of the fool it makes of everyone?"

Mr. Hayes of New York smiled. "Say *because* of that. We only ask to believe everyone *is* a fool!"

"Only you haven't been, without reassurance, able to imagine fools of the size that my case demands?" And Gedge had a pause while, as if on the chance of some proof, his companion waited. "Well, I won't pretend to you that your anxiety hasn't made me, doesn't threaten to make me, a bit nervous; though I don't quite understand it if, as you say, people but rave about me."

"Oh *that* report was from the other side; people in our country so very easily rave. You've seen small children laugh to shrieks when tickled in a new place. So there are amiable millions with us who are but small shrieking children. They perpetually present new places for the tickler. What we've seen in further lights," Mr. Hayes good-humouredly pursued, "is your people *here*—the Committee, the Board, or whatever the powers to whom you're responsible."

"Call them my friend Grant-Jackson then—my original backer, though I admit for that reason perhaps my most formidable critic. It's with him practically I deal; or rather it's by him I'm dealt with—*was* dealt with before. I stand or fall by him. But he has given me my head."

"Mayn't he then want you," Mrs. Hayes inquired, "just to show as flagrantly running away?"

"Of course—I see what you mean. I'm riding, blindly, for a fall, and They're watching (to be tender of me!) for the smash that may come of itself. It's Machiavellic—but everything's possible. And what did you just now mean," Gedge asked—"especially if you've only heard of my prosperity—by your 'further lights'?"

His friends for an instant looked embarrassed, but Mr. Hayes came to the point. "We've heard of your prosperity, but we've also, remember, within a few minutes, heard *you*."

"I was determined you *should*," said Gedge. "I'm good then—but I overdo?" His strained grin was still sceptical.

Thus challenged, at any rate, his visitor pronounced. "Well, if you don't; if at the end of six months more it's clear that you haven't overdone; then, *then*—"

"Then what?"

"Then it's great."

"But it *is* great—greater than anything of the sort ever was. I overdo, thank goodness, yes; or I would if it were a thing you *could*."

"Oh well, if there's *proof* that you can't—!" With which and an expressive gesture Mr. Hayes threw up his fears.

His wife, however, for a moment seemed unable to let them go. "Don't They want then *any* truth?—none even for the mere look of it?"

"The look of it," said Morris Gedge, "is what I give!"

It made them, the others, exchange a look of their own. Then she smiled. "Oh, well, if they think so—!"

"You at least don't? You're like my wife—which indeed, I remember," Gedge added, "is a similarity I expressed a year ago the wish for! At any rate I frighten *her*."

The young husband, with an "Ah wives are terrible!" smoothed it over, and their visit would have failed of further excuse had not at this instant a movement at the other end of the room suddenly engaged them. The evening had so nearly closed in, though Gedge, in the course of their talk, had lighted the lamp nearest them, that they had not distinguished, in connexion with the opening of the door of communication to the warden's lodge, the appearance of another person, an eager woman who in her impatience had barely paused before advancing. Mrs. Gedge—her identity took but a few seconds to become vivid—was upon them, and she had not been too late for Mr. Hayes's last remark. Gedge saw at once that she had come with news; no need even, for that certitude, of her quick retort to the words in the air—"You may say as well, sir, that they're often, poor wives, terrified!" She knew nothing of the friends whom, at so unnatural an hour, he was showing about; but there was no livelier sign for him that this didn't matter than the possibility with which she intensely charged her "Grant-Jackson, to see you at once!"—letting it, so to speak, fly in his face.

"He has been with you?"

"Only a minute—he's there. But it's you he wants to see."

He looked at the others. "And what does he want, dear?"

"God knows! There it is. It's his horrid hour—it *was* that other time."

She had nervously turned to the others, overflowing to them, in her dismay, for all their strangeness—quite, as he said to himself, like a woman of the people. She was the bareheaded goodwife talking in the street about the row in the house, and it was in this character that he instantly introduced her: "My dear doubting wife, who will do her best to entertain you while I wait upon our friend." And he explained to her as he could his now protesting companions—"Mr. and Mrs. Hayes of New York, who have been here before." He knew, without knowing why, that her announcement chilled him; he failed at least to see why it should chill him so much. His good friends had themselves been visibly affected by it, and heaven knew that the depths of brooding fancy in him were easily stirred by contact. If they had wanted a crisis they accordingly had found one, albeit they had already asked leave to retire before it. This he wouldn't have. "Ah no, you must really see!"

"But we shan't be able to bear it, you know," said the young woman, "if it *is* to turn you out."

Her crudity attested her sincerity, and it was the latter, doubtless, that instantly held Mrs. Gedge. "It *is* to turn us out."

"Has he told you that, madam?" Mr. Hayes inquired of her—it being wondrous how the breath of doom had drawn them together.

"No, not told me; but there's something in him there—I mean in his awful manner—that matches too well with other things. We've seen," said the poor pale lady, "other things enough."

The young woman almost clutched her. "Is his manner very awful?"

"It's simply the manner," Gedge interposed, "of a very great man."

"Well, very great men," said his wife, "are very awful things."

"It's exactly," he laughed, "what we're finding out! But I mustn't keep him waiting. Our friends here," he went on, "are directly interested. You mustn't, mind you, let them go until we know."

Mr. Hayes, however, held him; he found himself stayed. "We're so directly interested that I want you to understand this. If anything happens—"

"Yes?" said Gedge, all gentle as he faltered.

"Well, *we* must set you up."

Mrs. Hayes quickly abounded. "Oh *do* come to us!"

Again he could but take them in. They were really wonderful folk. And with it all but Mr. and Mrs. Hayes! It affected even Isabel through her alarm; though the balm, in a manner, seemed to foretell the wound. He had reached the threshold of his own quarters; he stood there as at the door of the chamber of judgement. But he laughed; at least he could be gallant in going up for sentence. "Very good then—I'll come to you!"

This was very well, but it didn't prevent his heart, a minute later, at the end of the passage, from thumping with beats he could count. He had paused again before going in; on the other side of this second door his poor future was to be let loose at him. It was broken, at best, and spiritless, but wasn't Grant-Jackson there like a beast-tamer in a cage, all tights and spangles and circus attitudes, to give it a cut with the smart official whip and make it spring at him? It was during this moment that he fully measured the effect for his nerves of the impression made on his so oddly earnest friends—whose earnestness he verily, in the spasm of this last effort, came within an ace of resenting. They had upset him by contact; he was afraid literally of meeting his doom on his knees; it wouldn't have taken much more, he absolutely felt, to make him approach with his forehead in the dust the great man whose wrath was to be averted. Mr. and Mrs. Hayes of New York had brought tears to his eyes, but was it to be reserved for Grant-Jackson to make him cry like a baby? He wished, yes, while he palpitated, that Mr. and Mrs. Hayes of New York hadn't had such an eccentricity of interest, for it seemed somehow to come from *them* that he was going so fast to pieces. Before he turned the knob of the door, however, he had another queer instant; making out that it had been, strictly, his case that was interesting, his funny power, however accidental, to show as in a picture the attitude of others—not his poor pale personality. It was this latter quantity, none the less, that was marching to execution. It is to our friend's credit that he *believed*, as he prepared to turn the knob, that he was going to be hanged; and it's certainly not less to his credit that his wife, on the chance, had his supreme thought. Here it was that—possibly with his last articulate breath—he thanked his stars, such as they were, for Mr. and Mrs. Hayes of New York. At least they would take care of her.

They were doing that certainly with some success when he returned to them ten minutes later. She sat between them in the beautified Birthplace, and he couldn't have been sure afterwards that each wasn't holding her hand. The three together had at any rate the effect of recalling to him—it was too whimsical—some picture, a sentimental print, seen and admired in his youth, a "Waiting for the Verdict," a "Counting the Hours," or something of that sort; humble respectability in suspense about humble innocence. He didn't know how he himself looked, and he didn't care; the great thing was that he wasn't crying—though he might have been; the glitter in his eyes was assuredly dry, though that there *was* a glitter, or something slightly to bewilder, the faces of the others as they rose to meet him sufficiently proved. His wife's eyes pierced his own, but it was Mrs. Hayes of New York who spoke. "*Was* it then for that—?"

He only looked at them at first—he felt he might now enjoy it. "Yes, it was for 'that'. I mean it was about the way I've been going on. He came to speak of it."

"And he's gone?" Mr. Hayes permitted himself to inquire.

"He's gone."

"It's over?" Isabel hoarsely asked.

"It's over."

"Then we go?"

This it was that he enjoyed. "No, my dear; we stay."

There was fairly a triple gasp; relief took time to operate. "Then why did he come?"

"In the fulness of his kind heart and of *Their* discussed and decreed satisfaction. To express Their sense—!"

Mr. Hayes broke into a laugh, but his wife wanted to know. "Of the grand work you're doing?"

"Of the way I polish it off. They're most handsome about it. The receipts, it appears, speak—"

He was nursing his effect; Isabel intently watched him and the others hung on his lips. "Yes, speak—?"

"Well, volumes. They tell the truth."

At this Mr. Hayes laughed again. "Oh *they* at least do?"

Near him thus once more Gedge knew their intelligence as one—which was so good a consciousness to get back that his tension now relaxed as by the snap of a spring and he felt his old face at ease. "So you can't say," he continued, "that we don't want it."

"I bow to it," the young man smiled. "It's what I said then. It's *great*."

"It's great," said Morris Gedge. "It couldn't be greater."

His wife still watched him; her irony hung behind. "Then we're just as we were?"

"No, not as we were."

She jumped at it. "Better?"

"Better. They give us a rise."

"Of income?"

"Of our sweet little stipend—by a vote of the Committee. That's what, as Chairman, he came to announce."

The very echoes of the Birthplace were themselves, for the instant, hushed; the warden's three companions showed in the conscious air a struggle for their own breath. But Isabel, almost with a shriek, was the first to recover hers. "They double us?"

"Well—call it that. 'In recognition.' There you are." Isabel uttered another sound—but this time inarticulate; partly because Mrs. Hayes of New York had already jumped at her to kiss her. Mr. Hayes meanwhile, as with too much to say, but put out his hand, which our friend took in silence. So Gedge had the last word. "And there *you* are!"

NOTES

"To 'do something about art,'" wrote Henry James in the New York Preface to his novel *The Tragic Muse*, "–art, that is, as a human complication and a social stumbling block – must have been for me early a good deal of a nursed intention, the conflict between art and 'the world' striking me thus betimes as one of the half-dozen great primary motives." James's shorter fiction bears eloquent testimony to the author's fascination with this primary motif. James wrote over thirty stories either narrated by, or focusing on writers, painters and sculptors and on their treatment at the hands of a world which, whether in its vacuous veneration or benighted neglect, fails utterly to understand them. That James considered himself a victim of such misunderstanding goes some way towards explaining the venom which the theme of the artist in society could draw from his pen – and the venom runs thick and fast in the stories collected in this volume, some of which represent James at his cruellest.

Among the repeated preoccupations of these stories is the sting in the tail of artistic fame and fortune. Obsessive devotion to the (fictitious) American poet Jeffrey Aspern in 'The Aspern Papers' poisons not only the story's critic-narrator, but also reduces the poet's now decrepit *belle* and her niece to acts of unexpectedly cool calculation. If the narrator will do anything to lay his hands on the poet's papers, Juliana Bordereau is quite happy to have the "publishing scoundrel" pay through his nose for less than a whiff of their possible presence, while Miss Tina (or Miss Tita, as she was in the first published version of the story) is finally more than willing to trade the precious papers for a proposal of marriage. 'The Aspern Papers' is based on a true story James overheard in Florence in January 1887 about a certain Captain Silsbee who took lodgings in Florence in the house of the octogenarian Claire Claremont, onetime mistress of Lord Byron. Silsbee knew that this lady, who lived with her middle-aged niece, possessed a valuable collection of letters by Byron and Shelley and hoped, on the death of the elder Miss Claremont, to procure them from the younger. Like Miss Tina, however, the surviving Miss Claremont stipulates marriage as a condition of exchange.

'The Birthplace' draws more openly on identifiable literary history to make its point about the antinomies of artistic immortality. In an unsuppressed scoff at the sanctity of Stratford-on-Avon, the cult of the national bard culminates in the absurd (and transatlantic) celebration of an entirely cynical performance of unctuous rites at his shrine. And literary laurels have still more sinister consequences in 'The Death of the Lion', where the public acclamation of novelist Neil Paraday – by folk who can't manage more than twenty pages of his novels – ultimately drives the sickly celebrity to his grave. Another novelist, Henry St. George in 'The Lesson of the Master', knows only too well that his reputation is absurdly inflated, but doesn't shrink from enjoying its social benefits in the form of the attractive Miss Fancourt (the name is as inspired as that of Lyon in 'The Liar'), while disposing of his rival, Paul Overt, by preaching the lesson of his own artistic failure to instill in the aspiring young writer a horror of domestic involvement. In a sense this is the darkest of all James's stories about art and artists. On the one hand, the master's invocation of "the great thing" to which the true artist aspires might reasonably be taken as James's own aesthetic credo: "The sense of having done the best – the sense which is the real life of the artist and the absence of which is his death, of having drawn from his intellectual instrument the finest music that nature had hidden in it, of having played it as it should be played." The master's own duplicity in the story, on the other hand, cannot but cast a shadow of cynicism over his brilliant doctrine. Where, one is left asking, is the lesson of the master to be read: in his credo or in his conduct?

The one story in this collection not ostensibly concerned with a professional artist figure is 'The Two Faces', but James had good reasons for publishing it alongside 'The Aspern

Papers' and 'The Liar' in Volume XII of the New York edition (1907-9). When May Grantham presents to the world the monstrosity of "feathers, frills, excrescences of silk and lace" she has created out of poor young Lady Gwyther, her triumphant expression is described as "that of the artist confronted with her work". As in 'The Liar', the execution of a work of art is little more than a jilted lover's attempt at revenge that ultimately backfires. If we never get to see either May Grantham's handiwork or Oliver Lyon's portrait of Colonel Capdose - not to mention a single line of Aspern, Paraday or Henry St. George - the art of the real master is abundantly evident throughout all these stories. Not least in 'The Two Faces', as Henry James himself felt bold enough to affirm in his Preface to the New York edition: "It may conceal rather than exhale its intense little principle of calculation; but the neat evolution, as I call it, the example of the turn of the *whole* coach and pair in the contracted court, without the 'spill' of a single passenger or the derangement of a single parcel, is only in three or four cases (where the coach is fuller still) more appreciable."   *Ed.*

THE ASPERN PAPERS

First appeared in *Atlantic Monthly*, March-May 1888. The present text is that of the New York edition (1907-9), Volume XII.

p. 9   *the Gordian Knot*: an intricate knot tied by Gordius, king of ancient Phrygia. According to the oracle, whoever should loosen it would rule Asia. Instead of untying it, Alexander the Great cut it with his sword.

p. 11 *Mrs. Siddons...Queen Caroline...Lady Hamilton*: Sarah Siddons (1755-1831), celebrated English tragic actress; Queen Caroline (1768-1821), estranged wife of George IV who refused to renounce the title of Queen; Emma

Hamilton (1765–1815), beautiful wife of Sir William Hamilton, British ambassador in Naples, who became the mistress of Admiral Lord Nelson.

p. 12 *Orpheus and the Mænads*: Orpheus, the legendary poet who with his song persuaded the lord of the underworld to release his wife Euridice from the dead, but lost her by failing to obey the condition that he must not look back at her until they reached the land of the living. He was punished for this failure, according to one version of the legend, by being torn to pieces by the Mænads, the wild Thracian priestesses of Bacchus.

p. 14 *quartier perdu*: a formerly fashionable, but subsequently deserted district.

p. 15 *felze*: a cabin at the back of a gondola.

p. 17 *nom de guerre*: assumed (or campaign) name.

p. 17 *padrona*: lady of the house.

p. 17 *scagliola*: imitation of ornamental marble used in floors and columns.

p. 22 *C'est la moindre des choses*: that's the least I can do.

p. 23 *louche*: suspicious.

p. 25 *comme il faut*: seemly, proper.

p. 26 *terra firma:* dry land, i.e. somewhere other than Venice.

p. 30 *forestieri:* foreigners.

p. 30 *quartiere:* quarters, apartment.

p. 32 *locus standi:* standing, position of authority.

p. 34 *serva:* maid.

p. 42 *contadina and pifferaro:* peasant woman and piper.

p. 49 *passeggio:* stroll.

p. 50 *avvocato:* lawyer.

p. 50 *capo d'anno:* New Year's Day.

p. 55 *Santo Dio!:* Good God!

p. 56 *Sardanapalus:* last king of Assyria, died 626 BC.

p. 62 *giro:* roundabout walk.

p. 71 *combinare:* arrange.

p. 73 *parti:* a good match.

p. 73 *padrona di casa:* landlady.

p. 78 *donna*: here, woman-servant.

p. 93 *poste restante:* department in a post office where letters are kept until called for.

p. 94 *quella vecchia:* that old woman.

p. 94 *roba da niente–un piccolo passagio brutto ... Poveretta!*: a contemptible affair – an ugly little procession ... Poor thing!

p. 105 *Dove commanda?*: Where to?

p. 105 *tenda:* awning.

p. 107 *Bartolommeo Colleoni, the terrible condottiere:* Bartolommeo Colleoni (1400–75), famous captain of one of the feared mercenary armies – *condottiere* – who left most of his wealth to the Venetian Republic, stipulating that an equestrian staute be erected in his memory in St. Mark's Square. The statue was not finally put in place until 1496, eight years after the death of its creator, the Florentine sculptor Andrea del Verrochio (1435–88).

p. 109 *strategems and spoils:* echoing the words of Lorenzo in Shakespeare's *The Merchant of Venice* , who claims that a man who is not moved by music is only fit for "treasons stategems and spoils" (V, i).

THE LIAR

First appeared in the *Century Magazine*, May-June 1888. The present text is from the New York edition (1907–9), Volume XII.

p. 115 *Mr. Le Fanu:* Joseph Sheridan Le Fanu (1814–73), Irish novelist and writer of short stories, best known for his ghost stories.

p. 120 *carte blanche:* a free hand.

p. 122 *Trasteverina:* inhabitant of the Trastevere, a district in Rome. The Trasteverians have a reputation for courage, strength and defiance.

p. 123 *Werther's Charlotte:* in *The Sorrows of Young Werther* (1774) by Johann Wolfgang von Goethe (1749–1832), the sensitive artist Werther is hopelessly in love with Charlotte, who is engaged to someone else.

p. 123 *Thackeray's Ethel Newcome:* in *The Newcomes* (1852–3) by William Makepeace Thackeray (1811–63), Ethel Newcome's brother and grandmother try, unsuccessfully, to steer Ethel towards a grand marriage.

p. 126 *Bacchante:* a reveller, a priest or worshipper of Bacchus, the god of wine.

p. 151 *Moroni:* Giovanni Battista Moroni (1525–78), Italian Renaissance painter famous for his portraits. 'The Tailor', in the National Gallery, London, is one of his best-known works.

p. 155 *Jamais de la vie!:* never in your life!

p. 169 *n'en parlons plus!:* let's say no more about it!

p. 169 *cher grand maître:* literally: "dear great master", a deferential way of addressing an artist. James himself in his later years welcomed and encouraged younger writers to address him thus.

THE LESSON OF THE MASTER

First appeared in the *Universal Review*, July-August 1888. The present text is that of the New York edition (1907–9), Volume XV.

p. 181 *Il s'attache à ses pas:* he follows her every step.

p. 190 *à fleur de peau:* skin-deep, superficial.

p. 194 *mot:* remark.

p. 202 *Cela c'est passé comme ça?:* It happened just like that?

p. 204 *jamais de la vie!:* never in your life!

p. 206 *père de famille:* father.

p. 206 *mornes:* glum.

p. 208 *mœurs:* morals.

p. 211 *C'est d'un trouvé:* He's a wonder.

p. 212 *duenna:* a chaperon.

p. 213 *Comment donc?:* how so?

p. 218 *il ne manquerait plus que ça!:* that's all we need!

p. 222 *carton-pièrre:* papier mâché.

p. 222 *Lincrusta-Walton:* thick embossed and patterned wall-paper designed by Frederick Walton, the original patentee of linoleum.

p. 222 *brummagem:* counterfeit. Deriving from a variation of the town name, Birmingham, where counterfeit coins were made in the 1670s.

p. 224 *n'en parlons plus!:* let's say no more about it.

THE DEATH OF THE LION

First appeared in the *Yellow Book*, April 1894. The present text is that of the New York edition (1907–9), Volume XV.

p. 254 *passe encore:* that is yet to (come to) pass; with a possible play on "pas encore": not yet.

p. 277 *Gustave Flaubert's doleful refrain about the hatred of literature:* James is probably thinking of a famous comment the French novelist Gustave Flaubert (1821–80) made in a letter to Louise Colet (14 June 1853): "You can calculate the worth of a man by the number of his enemies, and the importance of a work of art by the harm that is spoken of it."

p. 277 *valet de place:* porter.

p. 277 *Valhalla:* in Norse mythology, the hall of slain warriors who live there in bliss under the god Odin.

p. 281 *ces dames:* these women.

p. 283 *Le roy est mort–vive le roy:* the king is dead, long live the king.

p. 283 *inédit:* unpublished.

p. 283 *confrère:* colleague.

THE TWO FACES

First appeared under the title 'The Faces' in *Harper's Bazaar*, 15 December 1900. The present text is that of the New York edition (1907–9), Volume XII.

p. 300 *procédé*: conduct.
p. 300 *lâcher*: to throw over, abandon.
p. 300 *prima donna assoluta*: the absolute prima donna.

THE BELDONALD HOLBEIN

First appeared in *Harper's Monthly Magazine*, October 1901. The present text is that of the New York edition (1907–9), Volume XVIII.

p. 317 *Bonté divine, mon cher–que cette vieille est donc belle!*: Good heavens, my dear fellow–how beautiful the old woman is!
p. 317 *Où est-elle donc*: Where is she?
p. 318 *c'est une tête à faire*: it's a face worth doing.
p. 318 *succès fou*: a huge success.
p. 329 *bounded on the north by Ibsen and on the south by Sargent*: Henrik Ibsen (1828–1906), the Norwegian dramatist referred to affectionately by James as "the northern Henry", and John Singer Sargent (1856–1965), American painter, who painted James's portrait in 1913. Of the portrait, which hangs in the National Portrait Gallery, London, James wrote that it showed "Sargent at his very best and poor old H.J. not at his worst; in short a living breathing likeness and a masterpiece of painting."

THE BIRTHPLACE

First appeared in James's collection of tales, *The Better Sort* (1903). The present text is that of the New York edition (1907–9), Volume XVII.

p. 343 *an old Bradshaw*: Bradshaw's Railway Guide, a time-table of passenger trains in Britain, issued until 1961.

p. 351 *genius loci*: the spirit of the place.

p. 362 *Casa Santa*: Holy House.

p. 371 *The play's the thing*: an echo of Shakespeare's *Hamlet* (end of II, ii): "The play's the thing/Wherein I'll catch the conscience of the king."

p. 374 *compris*: included in the price.